POVEGLIA ISLAND

CRAIG GODFREY

Black Rose Writing | Texas

ISBN: 978-1-68513-186-9
PUBLISHED BY BLACK ROSE WRITING
www.blackrosewriting.com

Printed in the United States of America
Suggested Retail Price (SRP) $25.95

Poveglia Island is printed in Calluna

*As a planet-friendly publisher, Black Rose Writing does its best to eliminate unnecessary waste to reduce paper usage and energy costs, while never compromising the reading experience. As a result, the final word count vs. page count may not meet common expectations.

Cover design by Sebastian Godfrey

For Libby ...
My island rock in life's wild ocean.
Inspired by our Adventures in Italy

POVEGLIA ISLAND

POVEGLIA ISLAND

PROLOGUE

Town of Vataea, south of Vesuvius, 23rd August 79AD

Aulis Cethegus the soldier jerked awake into the land of the living. Back from the dead. Back from nightmares dark and worrisome. The trauma of warfare was forever with him. Splitting open enemy skulls with a single swipe of the gladius or watching women, heavy with child, thrown screaming from the fortified walls of Jerusalem, weighed like an anvil about the neck of any man to witness such carnage. But Aulis Cethegus had seen it all and more. More than any man should.

Aulis struggled to vanquish the memories. But dark visions of the 'Great Revolt', as the recent Jewish-Roman War was named, were forever present.

Life in the Judea garrison had been tough but disciplined under leadership of the Roman Governor Gessius Florus. Aulis was aware the man had a lust for gold. Florus favoured the Greek citizens over the Jews in Jerusalem, whom he taxed relentlessly in the name of Emperor Nero.

The Jews became ever more restless under the Roman occupiers. Taxes increased even more. The Jews revolted. In an attempt to restore law and order Gessius Florus plundered the Jewish Temple on the hill in Jerusalem. The treasures within, the Roman Governor claimed, belonged to the Emperor. Many Jews of nobility were arrested, which only caused further unrest, prompting a larger-scale rebellion. The Roman garrison of Judea was eventually overrun by the rebels and many Roman soldiers were killed. Evacuation was ordered and Aulis's garrison was charged with the protection of Judea's King Agrippa II, a Roman supporter and the greedy governor Gessius Florus.

Although it had been thirteen years since that violent upheaval, Aulis Cethegus remembered the moment clearly when he had been singled out by the Roman Governor as they camped in Syria.

The powerful man sat at a campaign trestle in his marquee scratching orders onto wax slates with a stylus. The six centurions, personal guards to Florus, stood at attention eyeing Aulis with discreet inquisitiveness. The open tent flap through which Aulis had entered, and the one behind the governor were tied open. But little breeze was to be had in the stifling heat of the Syrian desert.

Gessius Florus finally looked up at Aulis through hooded, sly eyes. He was clearly fatigued with travel and the tent stank of unwashed fatness, there being nowhere to wash these past weeks. A dish of frankincense smouldered on a bronze stand, but its spicy lemon fragrance was no challenge for the cloying malodour surrounding them.

Florus dared not smile at Aulis for fear of portraying familiarity or favouritism to the soldier's colleagues. He waved a hand dismissively and the guards filed out through the main entrance one at a time, retaking positions on the periphery.

'Aulis Cethegus,' the governor grunted. Cethegus stood firmly erect and to attention, but now that his name was called he looked into the eyes of this man he knew was acquainted personally with Emperor Nero. 'You come to me as a brave soldier and an honest man.' Gessius Florus shooed sand flies hovering over a terracotta salver of dried dates. He popped one in his mouth and chewed it slowly with sore gums. 'A man of discretion,' the governor mulched. 'Capable of keeping a secret. Not a man with loose lips. Am I correct Cethegus?'

Aulis felt beads of sweat trickle down his cheeks and prayed they did not appear as signs of fear.

'Yes governor. You have been informed correctly.' Aulis watched the fat jowls salivate, the tight mouth opened and a second date vanished behind the large man's gluttonous red lips. Florus studied Aulis carefully. He knew this centurion, Aulis Cethegus, to be as loyal as any soldier in the Roman army. 'You have four years remaining before you retire from the imperial army, am I right?'

'Yes governor.'

'And as I am certain you have been informed, I am here to muster another legion and then to return to Jerusalem and retake the city from those filthy Jews.' Aulis nodded. Every soldier in the camp expected no less. 'Then I am sending you with the Legio XII Fulminata to guard the Euphrates border. You will camp at Melitene until your return to Rome.' Aulis's pleasure at this news did not go unnoticed. 'But there is a price you must pay for this post,' Florus said. 'A price you should pay for this position of relative safety that should exempt you from battle.'

'Governor?'

The large man stood awkwardly and Aulis caught a glimpse of pain on the man's face as he arched his back pushing out his considerable belly. Florus stepped to the marquee entrance and checked they were not being spied upon. When he was satisfied, he moved with a quicker step to a travelling trunk that Aulis could only assume were the governor's private possessions. Florus scavenged through the wardrobe before fishing out what he was searching for; a tightly rolled bundle wrapped with goatskin and tied with leather laces. He returned to the comfort of his fold up chair and placed the parcel, with extreme reverence, on the trestle.

'You must swear to me now,' the governor continued. 'Against the wrath of Jupiter, that you will keep our secret on your person at all times. You must swear not to tell a soul of its contents; not even your dear wife, Herminia, as she sleeps in your arms.' Aulis flinched at the sound of his beloved's name. 'Oh yes Aulis Cethegus,' the fat man said. 'I know all about you. I know about your wife Herminia and your humble dwelling in Vataea; the perfect place for you to hide this object until I send for it, if the gods be willing, in the next few years.'

'Governor. May I enquire as to its contents.'

Gessius Florus looked up at Aulis and paused. The item wrapped in the goatskin could start wars. And wars for what? Not land and fortune. It could cause a spiritual war attracting the anger of his own emperor towards him.

'Lean forward Aulis Cethegus, for what I am about to show you controls immense power, particularly over the damned Jews.'

• • • • •

Another tremor, stronger than the one that had awakened Aulis, shook the earth beneath Vataea once more. Instantly Aulis' head ached. *Oh, how it ached. The wine ... yes, the wine.* His tired battle scarred body could not handle it like in the days of his youth. Tremors were common living in the shadows of Vesuvio. But these, now, seemed more persistent. Aulis's thoughts went to Herminia, his wife the past nineteen years, who lay at his side. At first he had thought she had awakened him with a subtle nudge? A nudge fuelled by passion? Aulis's thoughts returned to the night before when he and Herminia were certain their five-year-old daughter Sybilia slept. He smiled at the memory. Aulis looked to his wife, but Herminia slept soundly, undisturbed by the ground's tremor. For Aulis was a light sleeper, something ingrained in all retired centurions – veterans of one battle or another for the gargantuan Roman Empire. The empire that Aulis had served so faithfully for twenty-five years.

Aulis looked to the bedside lamp. It had been a gift from their widow neighbour Augustina for mending her roof. She had had it specially made by an apprentice potter, Remus, with the name Aulis Cethegus embossed into the small terracotta oil lamp along with the name of their town, Vataea. The small lamp had burnt out hours earlier and Aulis reprimanded himself for not extinguishing it before he slept. Olive oil was cheap but should not be wasted. This waste could attract the wrath of the gods and misfortune. But the wine and lovemaking had sent him to the land of dreams without warning.

Land of dreams he tutted. *More so the land of nightmares.*

Immediately the acrid stink of smouldering sulphur offended his nostrils. It was a subtle reminder of Vesuvio. The mountain had been smoking increasingly for more than three days as the earth tremors increased in frequency. Aulis listened a moment, assuring himself Herminia was indeed asleep and not pretending in one of her playful moods. But she lay on her side with her back to him, snoring softly, her perfectly formed lips pouting ever so quietly. He slipped from under the single woollen cover, his naked body slick with sweat for the morning was still and hot. Damn it he thought, will this heat never leave us? Immediately the ground at his feet trembled again, but faintly. *Ah Vesuvio, you devil's mistress, you'll wake the dead with your shaking and rumbles of late.*

The centurion made his way to the window facing south and tossed back the sacking drape. Fine ash filtered through. Vesuvio was half a day's walk from his town of Vataea, but still she shook the ground beneath him. In the distance the conical mountain smoked ever more ominously and Aulis knew the Commander of the Roman Navy, Pliny the Elder, would be expecting his report. This would mean half a day's walk to the port town of Herculaneum. Aulis sighed. He was beginning to wish he had never allowed himself to be talked into such a responsible duty by his friend Blandinus Hispallus, a retired colleague. He sensed his past relationship with Governor Gessius Florus was also behind the promotion.

Although Aulis's old legs were still strong, his bones ached these days and it would mean a two-day round trip. But the extra money was generous and allowed him such luxuries as scented oils from Egypt for Herminia or the Germanic Rhine wines he so much enjoyed, for their pleasant sweetness.

Aulis hefted the heavy pottery water jug to splash water into a washbowl for his toilet, but it was empty. He would have to fill it from a reserve trough outside on the public plaza. Another stronger tremor brought his thoughts back to Pliny the Elder. Aulis had of course never met the great admiral himself, and why should he? Pliny the Elder – proper name Gaius Plinius Secundi – was a close friend of the recently deceased Emperor Vespasian; so why should he wish to meet with any of the minions who did his bidding – the gathering of information, statistics and natural phenomena; to be recorded in Pliny's manuscripts; the most famous being *Naturalis Historia*. Aulis smiled at the thought of an audience with the Admiral. *Maybe Pliny the Elder spoke of my efforts with the great emperor.*

More likely not!

His efforts?

Pliny the Elder was a noted author, naturalist and philosopher. His prolific body of work was stored in libraries all over the Empire. Even in Alexandria, Aulis had heard. Pliny the Elder had scouts all over the countryside recording all kinds of anomalies and now, Aulis was certain, the great man would be watching the very same smoking volcano from his cliff side Villa at Misenum on the bay coast, thirteen leagues from the volcano. Besides, Aulis had completed a census for the commander. A census for his town of Vataea. This manuscript listed the citizens of Vataea; from Aulus Fuferus the green-grocer to the banker Lucius Caecilius Jucundus. Yes, Pliny the Elder would be expecting to hear from him. And especially now; to report on the volcanic activity from this position.

A fresh plume of black smoke rose from the mountain's pinnacle. To Aulis it looked like an umbrella pine with an especially long trunk, before splitting off in branches. It was white in places, otherwise black with ash. Now the plume was drifting over the town of Pompeii five leagues further south, and between Vataea and the volcano.

Aulis shuddered and his thoughts drifted to Herminia's brother Caecilius. Caecilius was a potter in Pompeii. The man worked tirelessly firing pots and amphora for the wine merchants of Pompeii whose wine was the finest in the region; made from the fat green grapes that grew prolifically in the rich volcanic soil. Caecilius had almost lost his life when Vesuvio stirred the last time, sixteen years earlier. Pompeii was badly damaged and Caecilius foot was crushed when a wall fell, crushing his leg. Now, as a cripple, he was fortunate to make a reasonable living as a master potter, a trade he could manage well with the aid of a crutch or the support of a bench. And, had Aulis known, that the disaster sixteen years previous, represented an abortive attempt by the volcano to blast out a vent. The monster had remained apparently dormant while the pressure inside the mountain grew and grew.

Aulis said a quiet prayer to Jupiter. That was sixteen years ago he consoled himself, and minor tremors were common.

But the renewed tremors and smoke? What *was it* with the smoke?

Aulis Cethegus stepped out into his yard, his own small peristyle where his chained guard dog Brutus greeted him with a drooling tongue and wagging tail. This was their own tiny private space and where Sybilia could play and Herminia could hang their washed clothes to dry. A tethered goat supplied fresh milk and four mangy, noisy chickens provided eggs.

Yes, life was good.

Aulis returned Brutus's affection and stretched his weary bones with a thought to some of the wealthier residents of Vataea. Some had magnificent and large peristyles with gardens, fountains and fruit trees at the centre of their massive villas. Aulis had been invited into one, the Villa of Cato Livianus, the fish sauce merchant near the east gate. Aulis had stood in awe before frescoes of exotic gardens and mosaics at his feet; of cornucopia, fish and exotic African animals. The merchant even had erotic frescoes in his private quarters. Although, this was only hearsay from one of the Cato's loose tongued servants whom Aulis had spoken to.

But Aulis Cethegus was not an envious man. Envy was for fools. He was more than content with his lot. His payout from the army had been generous. He had the love and devotion of a beautiful woman – and good cook – He had a healthy daughter, although Sybilia had been something of a surprise at his age; he was in his forty-sixth year. And except for the aches and pains of a few battle scars he was in good health. *Yes*, Aulis thought, life was good. His only regret was that he had not seen his twenty-six-year-old son Atquitus for four years now. Not since he was posted to Britannia to help secure the Empire's outpost of Londinium; almost lost to the barbarian Queen Boudicea eighteen years earlier.

Aulis skimmed ash from the surface and splashed water over his head from a near empty trough. Herminia would need more water, as today was washday. Aulis wondered about the smoke and ash. Maybe she would abandon the idea today. Nevertheless he would have to fill the trough from a fountain in the common square.

Refreshed somewhat, he pulled on sandals and skirt. He wrapped a toga about his shoulders – proud to do so as a citizen of the Roman Empire – and fastened it with a bronze fibula shaped like a lion, a gift from Herminia. Swinging a leather bucket, he stepped out through his gate and onto the street. Here, on the corner outside Atticus the Fuller, he relieved himself into one of the jars especially placed on the street to receive urine, the fuller's most precious laundry solvent. Aulis looked over his shoulder; the streets were filling earlier than usual with anxious pedestrians.

'Ah Cethegus,' a toothless woman of low standing caught the centurion's attention. She held the arm of her nineteen-year-old daughter Floriana, a spinster of unfortunate appearance although her body was supple. Floriana was the hag's only asset. She was desperate to marry off for the dowry. The toothless woman sneered and with an arm about her red-faced daughter's shoulder she exposed Floriana's firm white breast and squeezed it firmly. 'When will that soldier boy of yours return to Vataea? Floriana cannot wait for ever you know.'

Aulis felt embarrassment for the poor girl. With marriageable considered to be thirteen, Floriana was now past her prime. He returned his standard answer in passing. 'Now old woman, I have told you in the past, Atquitus has not the dowry for such a fine specimen as Floriana.'

Floriana smiled shyly.

'Bah!' the hag spat, and shoved her daughter ahead of her along a cobbled street now an inch under ash.

Aulis approached the neighbourhood fountain at the Plaza of the Leopard Fountain, and was immediately accosted by Philo Vestalis the baker from the bakery to the south of the fountain. 'This is a bad omen Aulis,' he muttered, 'a bad omen indeed. The springs have dried up. There is no water. I cannot even find enough to make bread.'

Aulis looked at the bronze faucet adorning the fountain. The head of a leopard normally spewed water without respite into a stone trough of abundance. Now it was dry. Vesuvio had severed the town's water supply.

'A bad omen I say ... '

Aulis had no time to answer his friend. The ground shook afresh. This time more violently. A low growling rumble followed the shake and together with two dozen others Aulis and the baker vied for the best positions to view Vesuvio.

'Mighty Jupiter have mercy!' A voice cried out. 'It is the wrath of Vulcan.'

'What sin have we committed to deserve this?' Another cried out.

The fearful blast of black cloud burst towards the heavens forcing ahead of it molten rock and tongues of fire. Fissures appeared at their feet. Somewhere close by screams warned of a column crashing into the street.

'Herminia! Sybilia!' Aulis cried out and rushed to his home.

'Aulis!' Herminia met her husband on the street. 'Where were you? I woke and ...

'Sybilia?' Aulis asked of his daughter.

'She's inside.'

Immediately the ash thickened. The plume of smoke had already reached the town of Pompeii ...

And now it drifted high above Vataea where fine black ash was being replaced by finger-sized pumice raining about them and growing larger and heavier by the second. Within moments the streets were covered in volcanic detritus.

'Get inside,' Aulis yelled. 'Quickly!'

Aulis slammed the shutters against the choking ash. 'We must leave,' he shouted. The falling pumice on the tiled roof was deafening.

Herminia's face stiffened with worry. 'Leave. Where to?'

'Herculaneum.'

Instantly a distressed woman – a neighbour – tripped over their threshold. 'Augustina,' Herminia cried out.

'Have you heard?' The neighbour sobbed.

'Heard what?'

'Pompeii is buried under ash. Thousands have fled. Many more are dead.'

'Who told you this?'

'Livianus, my brother, he said many refugees are headed this way. But he fears Vataea is doomed as well ... oh gods protect us ...'

'And it's happening here,' Aulis yelled. 'Hurry.'

The room darkened. The thick black plume of ash, dirt and smoke was descending. Blocking out the sun. Sybilia appeared in the doorway, blackened tears pouring down the child's cheeks from crying and smoke. Aulis lifted his daughter into his arms. He turned to their neighbour. 'Augustina come with us.'

'But Aulis,' Herminia shouted. 'Surely we are safe inside ... safe here.'

'I fear not. Besides I must get to Herculaneum.' Aulis kissed his daughter and put her down. 'Fetch your favourite doll. We're going on an adventure. Alright?'

'I'm scared papa,' the five-year-old bawled.

'Everything will be fine.' He spun her about and slapped her on the backside. 'Quickly now. Who's your favourite doll? Decima or Flavia?'

'Flavia.' The little girl cried out and ran to her bedside. Aulis took up his precious scrolls, his month's work at the census for Vataea, and other important notes. 'I must get these to the commander.' He rolled them into a leather satchel and hooked it over his shoulder. He strapped his prized gladius in its wood and leather sheath to his hip and pulled his bronze helmet, with its plume of feathers, over his head. 'Tie pillows on your heads.' Aulis ordered. He took his purse. It was light but he had two gold aureus, four silver denarius and at least ten bronze coins. Enough for emergencies.

But Aulis Cethegus had one final responsibility. He had been charged with the safety of something he knew was of immense spiritual importance. An item the Jews would die for. For thirteen years he had kept the bronze spearhead that had pierced the body of the prophet known as Jesus of Nazareth. The holy relic stolen by Governor Florus when he sacked the Jewish Temple in Jerusalem. For reasons Aulis never knew the governor had never sent for it and it remained hidden behind the wall of Aulis's peristyle. Secretly safe.

But now?

Aulis took care that he was alone and knelt in ash and falling pumice before the north wall. He felt the red clay bricks that concealed the parcel. They were firmly in place. All was as it should be. He had made a secret map of the precious item's location and now thought it wise that he took that information too, to Herculaneum along with the census.

Outside on the streets Vataea was being pummelled. Buildings were being systematically buried under a constant rain of pumice – an aerated volcanic rock spat from the volcano and solidified in the atmosphere. The sun became a red orb framed in black. The black devoured the orb. It was morning but the streets were dark as night. Some ten leagues distant great tongues of fire leapt from Mount Vesuvio, made even more frightening by the blackness of doomsday. The untamed forests about the pinnacle, now blazing red.

Screams grew closer and Aulis heard the collapse of the first roofs from the weight of volcanic ash. Tremors chased more thunder, but this thunder came from the earth beneath them. From the underworld of Hades itself.

Pandemonium smothered Vataea, as readily as the accumulating hot pumice and the metres of ash that would follow. Poor man rich man, all were now in the hands of the gods. There was no time to collect up the family treasures.

Aulis, his wife and daughter and Augustina spilt onto the street and into the flow of panic. It was now hailing stones. Most people fled for the south gate – the furthest exit from the volcano. There was no time to feel foolish with pillows strapped to their heads, for all about them citizens of Vataea were falling, many dying from head wounds. Aulis the centurion held his daughter Sybilia tight to his chest. He felt useless. These people, many friends and neighbours he would normally risk his own life to protect, were now beyond rescue.

Family first.

Pushing Herminia ahead of him Aulis struggled to shove a path through the panicked crowd. Augustina followed, tugging at his toga with one hand and holding a cloth over her mouth with the other. All about them devastation continued. Abandoned drinks sat on open tavern benches while loaves and loose change was deserted on the baker's counter.

They passed the Villa of Remus the importer at the moment his front wall collapsed back into the peristyle and garden. Aulis noticed Remus's slave Buca tipping a sack of silverware down the well for safekeeping from looters. Fool he thought. Escape while you can.

Some took sanctuary in cellars or ground floor rooms. These people would perish from suffocation, trapped where they thought they were most safe. On the opposite side of the street half a dozen slaves and their master huddled beneath stairs. They too would soon die when masonry crashed down upon the structure fatally trapping them.

The streets were littered with abandoned possessions – some even roped into carts – where the beasts of burden had been freed to help their owners escape. Beyond the south gate anarchy ruled; many looters and robbers taking advantage of the horror stalking them.

Aulis shoved people aside. There was no time to be a hero to anyone but his own. He was still a strong man, stronger than many his own age, but now he was being put to the test. 'Papa,' Sybilia cried out. Aulis held her tight. Too tight. 'Papa, Flavia!'

'What?'

'Flavia!' the child screamed. Aulis twisted about. Sybilia's favourite doll was being trampled where it fell. Aulis leant down but was instantly caught up in the stampede. He caught a gnarly hand darting out for his purse, tied to his belt. He felt a tug. The purse came free. Aulis did not hesitate. He drew his sword, a blade not used in anger for years. The first move was swift. Lethal ... and the gnarly hand swung by tendons. The thief shrieked in agony.

Finish what you started.

The second move was an undercut. The short-bladed gladius plunged deep into the robber's gut. The man screamed afresh and fell to the ground clutching at his spilling intestines with his remaining hand. Aulis savings clattered along the paved road. But so did the grasping fortune seekers. Desperately poor men and women, young and old, scooped up the spoils and continued their flight. Aulis could only watch on as bodies beat past him and he now held Sybilia tighter than ever.

'Come,' Herminia beckoned her man in a calmer tone than she expected. 'There's naught we can do.'

Two leagues beyond the south gate and the refugees had dispersed in all directions. But as night fell most headed west to the bay where they hoped an escape by sea would be safer. Rumours of the commander of the Roman Navy, Pliny the Elder, launching ships to rescue citizens from the shores, had merit. As now sails could be seen as ships battled the increasingly violent seas created by gales blowing towards the port towns of Stabiae, Herculaneum, Surrentum and Oplontis.

The eerie darkness cleared as the deadly plume was falling more to their east and to the south, now presenting a drifting column of smoke. It seemed they were beyond the worst of the smoke. But the ash was less forgiving.

The night was eerily dark and no guard manned the gates of Herculaneum. Beyond the walls the streets were alarmingly deserted except for the odd scream or the scurry of a disturbed looter. Aulis, Herminia, Sybilia and Augustina hurried by the deserted buildings.

'Aulis!' A voice cried out from the darkness. 'Aulis. Is that really you?' It was then the refugees realised they looked more like ghosts; caked in ash, their eyes red and cheeks streaked with tears and sweat.

'Blandinus! Blandinus Hispallus!' Aulis called back.

'Yes.' Blandinus hurried to them swinging a lantern. 'Thank Jupiter you are alive. How is it at Vataea?'

'I fear it is lost my friend. And Pompeii also.'

'Yes. I heard this.'

'This is my wife Herminia and daughter Sybilia. And this is Augustina, our neighbour,' Aulis lifted his daughter off his shoulders placing her on the street. 'Herminia, this is my colleague with whom I have been assisting the great commander ... '

Blandinus interrupted with a forced friendly nod. 'We must hurry Aulis. I fear Herculaneum will answer to Vulcan within the hour.'

'But the smoke, the ash. It appears to blow in the opposite direction.'

'Yes my friend, but something more sinister approaches.'

'Sinister?'

'Yes Aulis. Boiling mud. We must hurry.'

Herminia. 'Where is everyone?'

'Down at the waterfront. We await the ships. My family too. They should be there by now. You have the scrolls I see. Good. Come quickly.'

Blandinus led the troupe down the main street of Herculaneum, treading with experience between the darkened buildings. He turned into an alley and found steps that led to the waters of the bay. Aulis froze a moment as cries and wails floated up to them on a stiff breeze from the waterfront.

'Quickly, stay together. Follow me.' Blandinus rushed through the alley where they crossed another wide street. Here they were greeted by a tall stone building with stone steps leading up between ionic columns. The massive wooden doors were bolted shut. Blandinus took a huge iron key from his toga. Aulis noticed it had curled wards of differing sizes at one end of the shank stem with threads at the end of the shaft for extra security. Blandinus fumbled in the dark taking the lock, greased with animal fat, in his left hand and easily opened the lock that held the doors firmly secured.

'The library,' Aulis told his wife. 'Where we must deposit these records for safe keeping.' Blandinus shoved one door open and ushered them in. He closed the door behind them and bolted it against looters. The grand entrance was lit by a handful of lamps. 'Thank Jupiter,' Blandinus panted. 'Cassius the librarian has left us some light. Come, come.'

They hurried down gently inclining stone stairs to the underground library passing a marble fountain still spilling water into its shallow rectangular basin. More columns, coloured with bright reds and yellows, supported the vaulted ceiling. Ahead lay pitch darkness. Blandinus led the way with his lantern while Aulis took a lamp also, and, with Sybilia dragging her favourite doll behind her, they followed Blandinus through to the main library.

'Here,' Blandinus reached for Aulis's leather satchel. 'The scrolls my friend. I shall store them here and pray to the gods they are saved along with us.'

Aulis watched Blandinus store the precious information, including the map for the hidden holy relic, into triangular shelves, amongst thousands of other documents.

'Now we must leave for the shore. I hear our great admiral, Pliny, is approaching with ships to save us.'

The waterfront was in chaos. Earlier the sea had retreated due to the earthquake; a phenomenon that terrified witnesses. Now Strong winds had whipped up waves, taller than men, which crashed upon the shore. Many had lit large bonfires to signal the ships but it soon became apparent the ships had been forced to turn back. Rumours were whispered that Admiral Pliny himself had been taken by the volcano; suffocated they said, by the bitch's fine ash.

On the beach, several arched stone boathouses were filling with desperate families, cowering from the gale force winds blowing ash and smoke back in from the bay. Blandinus bade farewell to Aulis and his family and went looking for his own family while Aulis made room for Herminia, his daughter and Augustina in the further most boathouse. Suddenly Aulis heard a blood-curdling scream. He turned about sharply as smoke lifted some paces distant to reveal a soldier threatening a woman with his gladius. Aulis rushed forward. 'He stole my purse,' the woman shouted to Aulis. 'Help me, please.' The soldier saw Aulis approach.

'Back hero, or I'll cut your balls off and tie them about your ugly neck.'

Aulis ignored the threat and drew his sword. He crouched into a defensive position and took careful steps forward but the swirl of thick smoke returned to shroud the attacker. Aulis heard a slash and the dreadful scream of the woman as her throat was cut. Through the toxic smoke Aulis saw the woman fall face into the sand. Dead.

'Bastard!' Aulis cried out lunging at the soldier now keen to escape with the woman's money pouch. The first slash caught the assassin in the back of the calf, severing tendons. The soldier called out in pain, fell to the beach and rolled onto his back to defend himself.

'Mercy,' the man bawled. 'She was but a rich merchant's wife with plenty more hidden gold. Mercy, I beseech you.' But Aulis' anger was unforgiving. He threw himself onto the wounded killer holding his short sword with two hands, plunging it through the squealing man's heart with so much force he severed ribs as the blade made its exit through his body and buried itself in the beach.

Behind him scores of witnesses looked on in fearful awe, amongst them his own family. Aulis Cethegus was once again the centurion; one of the empires professional trained killers. He withdrew his blade, his anger spent, and looked into the terrified eyes of his daughter Sybilia. Her eyes were red raw with smoke and tears. Sybilia was trembling feverishly. Aulis felt a needle had been thrust through his own heart. What was happening in this cruel world? What had he become? Replacing his bloodied sword back in its sheath he made steps towards her. Steps of impossible reconciliation ...

When the most frightening thunderous sound of damnation approached like an army of demons from the underworld. Aulis had not a moment to blink. With his eyes locked on Sybilia he – and the entire surviving population – were blasted with a pyroclastic cloud that struck with such speed and intensity that all were instantly killed. The heat was so intense brains boiled, exploding craniums while hair, skin and clothing ignited, vaporising flesh and guts. Following this annihilating blast was a flow of boiling mud.

The days and weeks that followed cooled and solidified the mud, burying the town of Herculaneum for generations to come ...

Along with Pompeii and Vataea, Surrentum and Oplontis buried under volcanic rock, Herculaneum would remain a folk story for nearly two millennia.

PART ONE
HOBART TO ROME

CHAPTER ONE

Iron Pot Lighthouse. River Derwent Estuary.
Winter's morning 2019.

Chef's day off, Tuesday.

The blue sky above was faultless. The hue of an ancient turquoise gemstone with a copper phosphate shroud from horizon to horizon where not a single cloud blemished the heavens.

Spring was in the air.

Jameson regulated his breathing and checked his depth gauge; the digital screen read sixteen metres. Visibility was good – fifty metres easily. His dive buddy Stu gave him the thumbs up. Together they had already bagged seven large crayfish squirrelled away in rocky gullies that dipped into the seabed at twenty metres or less.

The Iron Pot, a flat 1.7-hectare sandstone island at the mouth of the River Derwent, and home to silver gulls, pied oystercatchers and black faced cormorants was also a Mecca for crayfish; always had been, Jameson was told by old hands who had a lifetime fishing this estuary.

And Jameson respected the island's history. Home to a lighthouse since 1830 after the nearby wreck of the *Hope* in 1827. And even stranger than fiction a gothic inspired lighthouse keeper's residence was built on the rock in 1884. Complete with iron laced balcony, dormer windows and a suburban front door it looked completely out of place surrounded by the sea and perched on its desolate foundation only twenty feet above sea level. Not a stranger sight anywhere in the colonies greeted visiting ships. The tapered rectangular lighthouse stood guard at its shoulder along with weatherboard outhouses arrogantly defying the inevitable wrath of mother nature. But even stranger was the sight of seaweed dangling from the balcony and lighthouse after a huge storm in 1895, when thirty-metre waves exploded over the structure. The foundations shifted and its life was doomed.

Jameson allowed his body to drift with the relentless swell, like a pendulum swinging towards the rock face only metres away. He floated amongst the forest of kelp with its fronds reaching for the skies through shafts of brilliant sunlight. He felt at peace with nature. Jameson twisted onto his back and looked towards the surface where their dive-boat, the twelve metre forty-year-old *Shanty* was anchored fifty metres from the island. A day off from the toiling heat of a restaurant kitchen doesn't get much better than this. Jameson's eyes followed the anchor chain to the anchor on the seabed, where it had clawed amongst rocks; when another crayfish caught his attention. Jameson kicked off with his flippers but the wryly crustacean noted the intruder and pushed back into the crevice. Jameson hovered over the fissure. It was wedged deeply but with a little effort Jameson was determined to extract his trophy. A three-kilo prize at least. The armour-plated delicacy put up a fight but was no match for the determined predator.

Stu, watching from the forest, was immediately at his side and bagged the crayfish with the others. Suddenly something grabbed Jameson's eye. An anomaly revealed by the disturbed sand resting in the crevice. Jameson reached in. The shape was familiar, imperfectly round yet covered with encrustation. Stu watched on. Their eyes met, peering at each other through goggles while Stu shrugged his shoulders inquisitively ...

When an ominous shadow passed over them.

Jameson snapped his head towards the surface. His eyes bulged. Stu wheeled about and together they watched the great white shark swim overhead. It swam purposefully, less than a metre below the surface, with majestic grace. As awesome as it was to witness such a sight in the wild, now was not the time ...

Or place.

Stu let out an audible gulp. Jameson grabbed his arm. *Settle. Stay on the bottom. Sharks don't attack divers on the seabed. Right?*

Maybe.

Jameson knew these creatures well. He'd watched David Attenborough. Great whites are nomads of the deep. They can swim 3000 kilometres a month. They cruise at the speed of an Olympic swimmer. All day, every day. New Zealand to Tasmania ... three weeks. When attacking they hit at sixty kilometres an hour. The two watched in awe and as the giant fish circled close to the island. But then it turned back, and started to swim towards them.

On the surface the *Shanty* skipper Barrie Duggan saw the dorsal fin. It sliced through the water at nearly a metre in height. His heart sank. He felt as if a giant hand had slapped his face.

'Jesus! No!'

The fifty-year-old rushed to the port side in time to watch the monster dive. His eyes scanned across the surface looking for diver's bubbles. He spotted them thirty metres further away; a collective assembly of bubbles that told him his two mates were together. He snapped his head to where he last saw the fin and followed its wake ...

Towards the bubbles.

Jameson's grip on Stu's arm was like a clamp. But Stu was too fixated on the great white to notice. The shark was clearly hungry. A one tonne ravenous torpedo of muscle and might – a torpedo wrapped in a tight-sandpapered skin of morbid shades of grey with an unmistakable under belly of poison lead white – a white that spilled about its mouth, accentuating the red gums of death and crowning at the point of its nose.

Jameson directed Stu to back with him into the kelp forest. They were now over a sandstone ledge at ten metres depth. To the south the ledge dropped away dramatically, a no-man's land in the great white's favour. Jameson was certain the shark had not seen them. But its ampullae of Lorenzini as the Nature Channel called them – receptor pores under its nose that detect the tiniest of electric fields surrounding all living creatures – *did* sense them.

Great Whites are prowling ambushing predators that attack at sixty kilometres an hour. Jameson could hear Attenborough's voice over and over ... they attack at sixty kilometres an hour.

Jameson checked his air pressure gauge. He estimated five minutes, tops. He signalled Stu who would have much the same reserve of air. Maybe less, Jameson thought, he was breathing heavily with fear. The shark cruised over the kelp forest; its fronds seemingly tickling the belly of the monster. It circled, came about, and then negotiated the forest towards them.

Skipper Duggan felt useless. No. More than useless. Utterly helpless. He snatched up a boat hook. *At least he was armed.* Then leant over the gunwale and searched the clear waters for some sign ...

And prayed for good luck.

The great white tightened its circles. It sensed terror. And close by. With a powerful stroke of its great tail it narrowed the gap between it and its prey – prey frozen in fear amongst the roots of kelp – when unexpectedly Jameson noticed a cave. It was ten to fifteen metres away tunnelling under the foundation of the tiny island, like decay might burrow into the base of a molar. Jameson punched a finger towards the hollow. He called out to Stu; his voice a muffled holler with a mouth full of regulator.

They kicked off.

Powerful direct strokes.

Now the great white *saw* its prey. The creature changed direction like a surface to air missile. The distance between them shortened with alarming speed. The shark dived to the seafloor swimming over the discarded dive bag. Crayfish scattered, clattering over the sandstone. Back to safety. Jameson was first into the tight opening almost ripping his tank from its harness. Stu was right behind him. For the briefest of moments, the cave filled with darkness as the huge fish passed the opening. The two men watched wide-eyed. As the shark swam on ...

But to where?

In the short term they were safe but now had only four minutes of air. Jameson paddled his arms and looked about them. They were crammed into a grotto of only about two square metres. It led nowhere. With their frantic movements, they had disturbed silt which clouded about them, when something caught Jameson's eye. A pottery shard. It was old stoneware and looked familiar. He shoved it under the rubber cuff of his wetsuit, along with the disc anomaly found earlier and shuffled forward once more to peer out from the cavern. Behind him Stu's bubbles sounded heavier and more prevalent. There was no sign of the shark. Jameson swam about to face Stu. Stu was on the verge of panic. He was hyperventilating. Jameson made hand signs for his mate to slow his breathing. He took Stu by both wrists and drew his facemask close to Stu's. When he was certain Stu had settled his heart rate he pointed to his air pressure gauge. They had barely two minutes remaining. Jameson gave Stu the thumbs up.

We have to surface.

Stu nodded nervously. His eyes blood red behind the glass. His face taught with fright. Jameson swam back into the open. He looked about. The once inviting kelp with its comforting sanctuary, now waved back with menace. The hull of the twenty metre *Shanty* overhead was teasingly close yet so far away. Shafts of clear spring sunlight lanced through the forest of kelp. It was picture perfect. 'A Kodak moment' as Jameson's mum loved to say. Sky blues, sea greens, vegetation yellows and gold's.

Indeed a Kodak moment.

Jameson felt a surge of hope.

Then in the not too distant. A silvery flash reflected from the sun above. A silvery flash reflected off the battleship grey and the shiny white of the persistent predator. Jameson backed slowly into the cave. Slowly for the fear of attracting attention. Stu feared the worst and his breathing picked up. Jameson looked at his mate's pressure gauge. There was less than a minute.

Christ!

Okay, Jameson managed in sign language. He jerked his thumb towards the surface. *It's now or never mate.* He kicked off with his flippers and swam away from the grotto and into the open motioning for Stu to follow.

Come on mate.

Stu was paralysed. Jameson reached back in and clamped Stu's arm, wrenching him into the open. He jerked his thumb towards the *Shanty*, tugged at Stu's arm and kicked hard for the surface. Stu's head snapped left and right.

No shark.

With renewed courage Stu launched himself off the seabed and joined Jameson. Both men raced for the surface; hands by their side and beating flippers like seals feeding on a school of fish.

Overhead Barrie Duggan scoured the water. He saw the shark at twelve o'clock between the *Shanty* and the Iron Pot. Air bubbles exploded on the surface at two o'clock, ten metres from the boat. Barrie knew the boys were surfacing. And fast. *That means they know the shark's there.* Barrie snapped his head back twelve o'clock. The dorsal fin rose, turned ...

Then dived.

Christ no!

Barrie speared the boat hook into a sack on the stern deck. He knew it was saturated with fish blood and guts from their morning's fishing. It was wet and heavy. Ensuring the bag was entangled in the hook he hefted the mess overboard and, gripping the other end firmly, he slapped the surface frantically striking the water repeatedly.

Come on ya bastard ... come on ...

Stu surfaced first. He discarded his weight belt and tank on the move and struck out for the *Shanty* thrashing the water like a poor swimmer in a rip. Jameson was right behind him. Barrie watched the great white glide under the stern. He slapped the water in a frenzy of deliberate moves to bait the monster. Amidships Stu hit the hull. He heaved up onto a tire fender ...

But slipped and dropped back into the water. Below him Jameson took a kick to the head. Stu surfaced. Took a second hold on the slippery tire. Jameson came up beneath him ...

Heave ...

Stu took hold. Clambered up the side, spun about and stabbed a hand towards Jameson. The shark surfaced two metres away charging for the bloodied sack. It turned to its side. Jaws wide ...

Eyes rolled back ...

Sixty kilometres an hour.

Barrie Duggan reeled back in horror. The massive tooth-filled head launched up out of the water towards him. Razor teeth. Red gums. The burley bag draped about its nose. The coal black eyes shot open and targeted Barrie before the brute crashed back into the sea under a huge plume of water ...

And continued towards Jameson.

Stu locked his hand around Jameson's wrist. Grinding his teeth. He tugged. He wrenched hard. Jameson rose out of the water. He tucked his legs up in a foetal position. The great white sliced through the water barely millimetres away when ...

Stu lost his grip.

Jameson slipped. Plunging back into the sea. He fell hard, landing on his back against the four-metre shark.

For a brief moment Jameson saw his life flash before him. It was like slamming against a giant electric sander. The shark's skin hard and abrasive. Jameson somersaulted along the tail ...

And sank.

Jameson couldn't remember how deep he descended before he kicked off back for the surface. But now he jettisoned his own tank and weights. He struck out for the *Shanty*. The shark turned.

Hurry! Christ hurry.

The cries seemed distant. In another world. Barrie was now at Stu's side. He reached over with the boat hook. Jameson took it with both hands. The shark closed in. Jaws wide. Eyes rolled back.

Sixty kilometres an hour.

Heave...

Jameson lifted half way out. His legs thrashing in the water in a wild attempt to climb the hull.

One metre.

Jaws yawning. Shredders set.

Half a metre.

There was a loud scream. An adrenalin fuelled shriek from Stu. With one leg hooked over the gunwale and the other on the buffer tire he clamped a fist full of Jameson's wetsuit and yanked hard. He yanked so hard he almost dislocated Jameson's shoulder. Barrie stabbed his hands under Jameson's armpits.

Heave ...

Jameson was hauled skywards like a hooked Blue Fin.

Ya!

Never was a cheer so heartfelt. Together Barrie and Stu threw Jameson unceremoniously onto the deck. Barrie rushed back to the gunwale.

'Bugger me!' he screamed out. 'That bastard's half the length of me boat!'

Jameson hurried after his mates to the bow where they watched the fin weave slowly into deeper water and away. To the east of the island lay 'the bricks' as the seafarers referred to the reef between the Iron Pot, Cape Direction and South Arm. A hundred metres further on the shark dived amongst the rocks. Jameson calmed himself the best way he knew, with his usual rhetoric. 'Well. That was fun,' he muttered in a sort of nervous groan.

'Fun! Fun!' Stu had another opinion. 'I thought I was a goner.' He looked Jameson in the eye; then lowered his eyes to the deck in embarrassment. He knew he had lost his nerve earlier. But hell, that was as close to death as I ever want to get, he thought quietly.

Jameson slapped Stu on the back. 'Yeh,' Jameson said. 'That *was* close. Thanks mate. Hey Baz,' Jameson called back to their skipper preparing to raise the anchor. 'How about some of that cheap rum you normally stick in our morning coffee?'

'You're on.' Barrie's jocular smile returned. The nuggetty fifty-year-old builder and Jameson had been mates nearly six years now, since Jameson hired him to help with extensions to his beach house, Melanoma Cottage at Storm Bay.

'Why the hell ya call it Melanoma Cottage?' Barrie had asked when he first saw the waterfront shanty perched on a small cliff overlooking the River Derwent.

'Well everyone that came here and looked out across the water used to say, what a great spot – hence Melanoma Cottage.'

Jameson watched Barrie ferret about in his wheelhouse. He was like good wine he joked with mates – got better with age; a handsome man in a rugged way whose favourite comment was 'Women like old rugged men but men aren't too keen on old rugged women!'

Something lying on the deck caught Barrie's eye. He picked up the encrusted disc studying it carefully and rubbed at it with forefinger and thumb. 'What's this then?'

'What's what?'

'This?' Barrie held the curiosity up for all to see.

'Ah!' In all the excitement Jameson had forgotten his finds. 'If I'm correct that's a coin.'

'Coin huh? Ya could fool me, where'd ya find it?'

'Hiding in a cray nest.'

'Speaking of crays, we lost the lot,' Stu grumbled. 'Jesus, we had some big ones too.'

'You can dive back in and fetch 'em if you want. They might still be in the bag.'

'Yeh right. I'd rather jump from a plane without a parachute.'

'How do ya know it's a coin?' Barrie persisted, still rubbing at the crumbling encrustation.

Jameson took the artefact. 'It's a coin alright. Dutch I reckon.' Jameson rubbed harder at the granulated surface coming away freely. 'Yes Dutch. It's a guilder, 17th century!' Suddenly the realisation hit. 'What the hell?' Jameson held the coin into the sunlight for verification. The three gathered about.

'So what's a 17th century Dutch coin doing in the Derwent,' Stu asked.

'Wait a minute.' Jameson remembered the pottery shard tucked under his wetsuit cuff. He pulled it free and smiled like the fox in the henhouse.

Barrie. 'Now what?'

'This, lads,' Jameson said with a theatrical flourish. 'Is also 17th century and Dutch. Well it's probably made in Germany but they were common on all merchant ships plying the Spice Islands in the 17th and 18th century.'

'What was?'

'This is a piece of a wine bottle.'

'And how the hell can you tell that?'

Jameson knew the Bellamine style bottle well. The stoneware with the face of a bearded man on the shoulder was popular for nearly three centuries he explained to Barrie and Stu. This was indeed only a shard, but the face of the bearded man, as little as it was to go on, was unmistakable.

'Okay smart arse,' Barrie reached into the wheelhouse and grabbed rum and mugs. 'How do ya know it's 17th century?'

'Well by the width of the neck for one thing. There's not much of it here I know, but enough to tell. The older the bottle the wider the neck. And,' Jameson rolled his bottom lip and took on the demeanour of an antique's expert. I would say early 1650s.'

'Okay,' Barrie held chipped mugs by three handles and freely poured the rum. 'I'll buy. Early 1650s huh. How's that?'

Jameson held the half-exposed coin for all to see. 'Check the date. You can see it clearly.'

'1652.'

'Jesus your right.'

'So, I'm surmising the coin and this shard were on the same ship, since they are both Dutch and the same period. Reasonable deduction?'

'Okay.'

'And the coin was probably only minted a few years earlier, so early 1650s sounds likely to me.'

'You're a clever bastard,' Barrie passed the mugs around. 'Cheers.'

Stu. 'Are you trying to say there's a wreck down there? A 17th century Dutchie. That's a bit before English settlement here, isn't it?'

'Hundred and fifty years before, but hey, stranger things have happened.' Jameson looked at the Iron Pot. A swell was picking up and clouds had appeared, turning the turquoise blue sea into greys and dark blues. He turned back to his work colleague long enough for Stu to register his thoughts.

Jameson. 'I've an idea ... '

Stu. 'Stuff that. I'm not going back in there. Not today. Probably never.'

'What about our gear. We lost tanks and weights.'

'We can buy new ones. As a matter of fact, I may never need them again.'

Jameson took another long look across at the rocks towards shore. The monster could be anywhere. 'You're right. Let's sleep on it.'

'Well on that note I'll head back to Hobart.' Barrie twisted the ignition on the twin 903 Cummins diesel and 295 horses roared into life. The *Shanty* farted smoke and bubbles. Barrie hauled in the anchor, securing it before reversing away from the rocky island, which had somehow taken on a sinister appearance all of a sudden. He steered the *Shanty* into a stiffening southerly. Fifty metres out Barrie engaged forward gear and spun the wheel to starboard, careful to avoid the rocks between the Cape Direction reefs and the Iron Pot Island. He was ten metres into a wide circle when the blurred vision started. Barrie felt his knees give way. Without warning consciousness deserted him and he collapsed to the deck, half in half out of the wheelhouse.

'Barrie!' Stu was the first at his side. 'Christ!'

'He's had a fit.'

'A what?'

'An epileptic fit.'

'Jesus Christ!'

The *Shanty's* bow rose on a swell. They were closer to the Iron Pot than they realised and ocean swell was now rolling onto the cliff face exploding into salty foam.

'Grab the wheel.' Jameson yelled. Stu jumped over Barrie's stiffened body diving onto the wheel. He turned hard to starboard. The boats bow dipped into a trough and rose once more. Stu saw the channel between the Iron Pot and shore ... and turned to port and towards a reef just below the surface ...

A reef he knew nothing about.

Barrie's body jerked and twitched. He frothed at the mouth. Jameson dropped to his knees. He dragged Barrie out of the wheelhouse and onto the deck and rolled him onto his side stuffing an oilskin under his head for support.

'Shit!' Stu stood at the helm – his face deathly white. He could steer ... but that was about it. 'Is he dying?'

'No. He's had a fit. He'll be all right in a minute ... I hope.'

'How do you stop this thing?'

'You don't. Just steer us out into deep water.'

Seconds passed. Barrie stirred. He opened his eyes, watery and bloodshot. 'What the ... wha ... what happened?'

'You had a fit mate, Jameson said with a tone of relief.

Stu. 'Thank Christ Baz. You scared the shit out of us.'

Immediately Barrie sensed they were motoring. 'Where are we?'

'It's all good mate,' Jameson said. 'You've only been out a couple of minutes. Stu's at the wheel.'

Barrie positioned his head to face up at Stu at the helm of his fishing boat. Stu beamed back like Popeye. 'Argh. All's good cap'n. I'll have us through the channel and out to sea in no time.'

'Channel!' Barrie cried out. 'Help me up ... '

Barrie struggled but he was groggy and in danger of collapsing again.

Jameson. 'Easy Baz ... '

'Help me up fa Christ's sake,' Barrie shouted. With Jameson's help he pulled himself up against the wheelhouse. 'Oh shit!' The skipper's eyes were instantly alert. He shoved Stu aside and took the wheel. They were moving fast, too damned fast. Eight knots. Close by to port *and* starboard waves smashed over submerged rocks.

'Oh shit!' Stu swallowed hard. Is that what I think it is?'

'Yes you idiot! We're over a reef.' Barrie reduced speed to a crawl. His first thought was to reverse out but he could not control his course if he did. The swell here could easily launch them onto the jagged rocks.

'What's the plan?'

No answer. Barrie punched the switch on his Chart Plotter. He chewed his bottom lip and gripped the wheel. A second later the GPS came to life. The only sounds registering were the low rhythmic chug of the 295-horsepower diesel and waves crushing over the nearby rocks. The monitor screen displayed black background – deep water – against a green graph – the rocks. 'Read the sonar depths out ... loud!' Barrie said with nervous calm. Jameson watched the screen while Barrie's eyes stayed glued ahead out through the wheelhouse window.

Jameson. 'Fourteen ... is that metres?'

'No. Feet.'

Deep breaths all around. The *Shanty* forged ahead. There was no going back now.

'Twelve ... ten ... eight ... '

Stu's face tightened. He swallowed hard and prayed he hadn't stuffed up.

'Six ... four ... ' the green on the chart plotter screen flickered. Jameson could feel his heart beating fast once more. If they holed the boat here there was a good chance they would have to swim for it. Either side was close, a hundred metres tops –but that white pointer!

That great white shark ... was still in the area.

'Two ... one ... '

Instantly they felt a shudder. The keel was dragging over submerged rocks. 'Oh Christ no!' Barrie snapped his head to the plotter screen. All three braced themselves for the worst.

'Four!' Jameson almost screamed. 'Six ... we're over it ...'

'Maybe sonny Jim ... don't hold ya breath yet.'

Jameson's mouth dropped open. 'Shit no! Four ... no ... four ... two ... four .... six ... Jesus!'

Stu joined Jameson in the chant. 'Eight ... ten ... twelve ... '

Barrie was familiar enough with the reef. 'We're through!' Those words from the skipper were magic.

'You sure?'

A pause ... then. 'Yeh. I'm sure.'

The three yahooed.

'Jesus Christ!' Stu huffed in a huge sigh of relief. 'I don't wanna do that again in a hurry.'

'Don't worry mate,' Barrie said. 'Ya won't be doin' it on this boat.'

'You alright Baz?' Jameson finally asked.

'Yeh, all good.'

'You gave us a scare there mate.'

'So,' Barrie completely changed the subject. 'More artefacts for your collection.' The skipper nodded to the coin and pottery shard abandoned on the wheelhouse dashboard in the emergency.

Jameson grinned back. His beach house home at Storm Bay forty minutes drive south of Hobart was crammed with collectibles; mostly artefacts from historic shipwrecks, relics from Tasmania's colonial past or old bottles dating back hundreds of years. His bed, overlooking the Derwent, resided amongst shelves weighted down with books – mostly reference and non-fiction – over two thousand at last count. And Jameson now couldn't wait to be amongst them researching a possible lost Dutch ship in this area.

'He's got collectin' bad Baz,' Stu said, relieved that moods had changed. 'And you know what? There's no known cure.'

Jameson raised his mug of rum. 'Here's to that.' The three saluted, drank, winced.

'Hey Baz,' Jameson said through clenched teeth. 'There's a house auction at North Hobart this Wednesday. An old Italian bloke's estate and there's lots of old building materials apparently. Interested?'

Barrie looked keen. As a builder, he specialised in restoring old properties. Old windows, doors and fittings were becoming scarce. And Jameson was no stranger to the auctioneers with his interest in antiques. 'Wednesday ya say.'

'Yeh. Noon.'

'Why don't I pick you up in me truck, say eleven,' the builder offered.

'Sweet. As long as ya don't do a wobbly behind the wheel.'

'Get stuffed!'

CHAPTER TWO

Three hours later. Melanoma Cottage. Storm Bay. Tasmania.

'Shark! What shark?' Jameson's partner, twenty-eight-year-old Elspeth looked more gorgeous than ever when she was fired up. It sent a shiver down Stu's spine. She leapt from the couch where she had been curled up with a novel. The two men, their unruly hair sticky from the salt air, prepared themselves for the broadside.

'Stu!' Elspeth now raised her voice. 'What shark Stu?' Over her shoulder the muted flat screen television on the wall, surrounded by prints of old maps and sailing ships, broadcast the evening news.

'Nice one Stu.' Jameson was less than happy. 'Tell her what a great dive we had,' he had said' as they drove to Storm Bay. 'Tell her about the coin. Tell her about the Dutch pottery shard, tell her we accidentally lost the crays ... but don't mention Baz or the shark. Right?'

Right.

'It was nothin' El,' Stu lied. And he looked the lie. Elspeth glared at Jameson for the truth, hands on hips, her head slightly angled with her arresting shiny coal black hair cascading down her back while she ran a tongue over her bottom lip in determination. Jameson knew there was no escape from his fiery Lebanese girlfriend.

'It was a bully,' Jameson stretched the truth. 'One and a half metre. Nothing ... '

Stu huffed.

'Bullshit.'

'Okay. So it was bigger.'

'And?'

Argh! What the hell? 'It was huge,' Jameson threw his arms wide. 'A white pointer. Five metres I reckon. Could have swallowed Barrie's boat.'

Elspeth gasped.

'No seriously. It wasn't *that* big and we were never in danger. It just swam by when we were on the bottom ... eh Stu?'

'Right. Exactly. No danger El. None at all.'

Elspeth shook her head. She loved Jameson. She felt he *was* the one and the feeling was reciprocated. They had been together going on two years now, meeting at the restaurant, The Hook, Line and Sinker, where Jameson was the chef, and Stu his sous chef. She worked in the dining room while completing her masters in Ancient and Modern History at the University of Tasmania and was now assistant curator at the Tasmanian Museum. If anything happened to Jameson, well ...

'Christ!' Jameson's attention was immediately drawn to the news on the television. 'Is that what I think it is?' He dived for the remote and scrolled up the volume.

'This is the first time in seventy-two years that Vesuvius has shown any sign of life,' the newsreaders narration was mechanical. News these days was one catastrophe after another. A wide shot of the mountain showed wisps of smoke spiral lazily from the pinnacle, then cut to drone footage over the ancient crater. Hundreds of metres below the threatening glow of molten lava could be seen against the black of night, bubbling beneath a brittle crust of rock. Beneath this live footage the words 'breaking news' scrolled horizontally across the screen with other news information; suicide bomber detonates in a market place in Islamabad followed by nineteen dead and then the latest cricket scores. The three watched a moment. The lava spill was minimal but mesmerising; an erupting volcano in such a highly-populated area was a rare sight. A rare sight indeed.

And fatally beautiful.

The newsreader continued. 'Whilst experts say this activity is overdue, they say a minor eruption is imminent ...'

'She last erupted in 1944,' Jameson said. 'During the American occupation of Italy. You know they say she goes off every seventy years. Remember Pompeii?' Who hadn't heard of Pompeii? 'Well forty-four and seventy makes ... ah ... '

Stu. 'Hundred and fourteen right?'

'2014!'

'Right. It's now 2017, she's three years overdue.'

Stu. 'Pompeii was totally trashed, wasn't it?'

'Yes, in 79AD.'

'There ya go again! 79AD huh? Not 81 or 75?'

'No. 79.'

'He's a wealth of knowledge El. You ought'a register him for Millionaire Hot Seat.'

'I just happen to be interested in history,' Jameson said to Stu in his own defence. 'Dates stay with me like the names of Warnie's girlfriends stay with you.'

Touché.

Jameson moved to the open kitchen. He paused a moment looking through the floor to ceiling windows to watch Pacific gulls squawking noisily as they swooped on a lone fisherman, old Bluey Baker the neighbour, gutting a haul of flatties at the base of the ten-metre cliff outside. Beyond the bay the water was chopping up. The afternoon sea breeze was kicking in.

'Coffee?'

Jameson took nodding heads watching the television as an affirmative. He filled the electric kettle with his tank water and flicked the switch. 'Of course, 1944 was nothing like 79AD,' he said re-joining the others.

'No?' Stu asked, still glued to the screen. 'How bad was it then?'

'The lava spewed over the western slopes wiping out two villages.'

'Christ what a way to die!'

'Oh I don't think anyone died. It was like slow motion. Like a fifteen-metre wave of molten lava but moving at a walking pace. It just crushed and bulldozed everything in its path until it stopped short in the foothills.'

'Christ.'

'And I'll tell you something else for nothing,' Jameson had a thought. 'I'll bet you didn't know the English dropped a bomb on Pompeii.'

Elspeth. 'No!'

'Sure did. When the allied forces landed in Naples they believed the Nazis were hiding ammunition there. One bomb landed on the House of the Faun. You can see parts of the bomb exposed today. Sitting all rusty amongst ancient columns.'

'How awful,' Elspeth moaned. 'I didn't know that.'

'True.'

The screen cut to an advertisement for a local nursery. A painfully annoying advertisement where the owner has insisted on recording his own ad. He can't act. He can't speak coherently and yet he's allowed himself to be filmed for television. It's called vanity advertising Elspeth had been told. She snatched the remote and hit mute. 'So, no crayfish for dinner?' She pretended to be disappointed.

'Sorry El,' Stu apologised. 'I dropped them and the bag split and the buggers took off and ... '

'When you saw the shark no doubt?'

'Ah ... '

Jameson poured coffees. 'Never fear, there's plenty more fish in the sea.'

'Stu. 'There is?'

Jameson passed Elspeth her mug. 'Then I'll go iron my clothes for work tomorrow,' she said.

The two watched Elspeth take to the stairs; a spiral stair built around the trunk of an old ghost gum. 'Come on Stu,' Jameson said loud for Elspeth's benefit. 'You bring the coffees and I'll grab the rods. If old Bluey Baker can catch a feed of flatties so can we.'

CHAPTER THREE

2AM local time. Tuesday.

Feliciano Vineyards. Eleven kilometres South East of Mount Vesuvius. Italy.

Fulvia Conte leant his shovel against the pit wall. The short man had dug over his own height of a hundred and fifty centimetres – but the earth here in the vineyard was pleasantly easy to dig, being rich volcanic soil. He stood in his trench, a hundred and seventy centimetres deep, a metre wide and not quite two metres long. Now he felt he had earned a cigarette. In the soft light of a pencil torch lying at his feet in the bottom of the pit, Fulvia tapped a smoke from the packet; a packet of ESSE Black he had helped himself to from his wife's side of the bed when he crawled out at midnight. Sure, they were woman's cigarettes but he liked menthol and besides, *she smoked his.* He speared the cigarette between expectant lips and, with a dirty calloused hand, he flicked a flame alive from his Zippo. Holding the Zippo bought a smile. He had stolen it from an American tourist who thought he was smarter than him. The tobacco sparkled immediately and the antiquity looter allowed the toxic vapour to gather into a tight cloud before drawing it into his lungs in one greedy breath. The pleasure was instantaneous as the smoke absorbed into his bloodstream.

Ah. It felt good.

'Are you crazy!' A hand far more powerful than his snatched the cigarette. It was instantly crushed into the ground in a scattering of sparks. Fulvia's overseer followed the reprimand with a slap across the top of his head. Forty-eight-year-old Silvano Marchetti was not a man to cross. What he lacked in height he made up for in strength. Blinded in his left eye – not from combat but from the clawing of a jilted lover – had made his sense of hearing and smell more acute than most. His clandestine operations had made him a wealthy man and he didn't need fools like Fulvia to spoil his plans. He knelt on all fours leaning into Fulvia's pit.

'What the hell are you doing, Stupido. I have warned you before.' He jerked an open hand as if to deliver a backhander. Fulvia cowered. Marchetti reached in and snatched the cigarettes from the man's shirt pocket. 'That's right *figlio di puttana.* You get down in that hole and dig like I pay you to dig.'

Marchetti crushed the packet in his fist and stood carefully to peer out from the vines that concealed their night's operation. All about them were homes of honest hard working Campanians. The closest home was only two hundred metres away and built unknowingly on these two-thousand-year-old ruins that Marchetti was certain was the lost town of Vataea. He stood silently, still a moment. A chameleon of the dark in his black slacks and black sports sweater. Fulvia's light, he hoped, had not attracted unwanted attention. Now, as stealthfully as he had approached, he slipped away to visit the other three diggers nearby.

Fulvia continued digging. The money was good, five hundred Euros a night to dig holes and keep his mouth shut. But Fulvia had ambitions of going solo. *Maybe I will find this lost city Vai ... Vee ... Vataea or whatever it's called.* Fulvia had lived and worked in this part of Campania for more than twenty of his thirty-four years. There had always been talk by the farming folk about here that another city buried by Vesuvio was somewhere in this region, and that there was treasure to be found.

'Pezzo di merda,' Fulvia muttered under his breath. 'Yes, you piece of shit Marchetti. One day.'

Marchetti stole through the vines, a thief on a moonless night. All about him the grapes were close to harvesting and he knew they would have to speed up the operation. He found his way to an older model black Lancia van with signwriting on the sides, *Resina Explosivo*. It was parked hard against a grape-pressing outbuilding. On the other side of the building the road Via Mariconda led from the Bay of Naples inland and through the village of Mariconda. Well it was once a village, Marchetti thought, now it was all one big metropolis flowing all the way to Napoli. A lone truck rolled noisily along the road passing the vineyards, its lose manifold making enough racket to wake the dead.

The night was still. The air warm.

Marchetti waited until the truck dissolved into the night and knocked on the side of the parked van once, followed immediately by four sharper taps. The rear door opened and Marchetti stepped up into the dark interior. Silence was maintained until the soundproof doors closed behind him and a soft light illuminated computer equipment, GPS, ground penetrating radar and other technology required by professional antiquity thieves. Strapped securely on its own bench was their latest technical achievement, a Matrice 600 DJI drone with its gimballed Panasonic GH4 camera, the operation of which, partner in crime, Ricco Ricci, had proudly mastered.

Marchetti's colleague Ricco Ricci was a square-jawed, rock-faced ex Italian commando. At thirty-eight he had retired from Italy's elite Special Forces Frogmen six years earlier. Ricco had the shoulders of a silver-back gorilla, indeed some of his colleagues joked he was built like a wardrobe with fists to match; like rock crushers they said. Even his large ears appeared squarish. Inherently distrustful of fellow men, naturally technical and instinctively inquisitive Ricci immediately knew something was up.

'What is it?' His voice baritone and raw.

'That idiot Fulvia. He lights a cigarette for Christ's sake. He knows as well as you and I that the carabinieri are watching out for us, he may as well have lit a bonfire.'

'Fool.'

'I swear I will fill the hole back with him in it one day.'

A sudden but slight tremor shook the van. Ricco Ricci's eyes widened as he watched a ripple flutter across the surface of his thermos coffee. 'Merda! Vesuvio ... she awaken again my friend. Maybe *she* will bury your stupido digger.'

Fulvia sucked in a sharp breath. He knew Vesuvio's temperament well, but when the damned volcano threatened to fill in his trench he had a renewed respect. And the thought of being buried alive frightened the life out of the god-fearing man. A second clump of soft earth and vine root fell across his boots. *Merda*! More work.

He brushed aside the thought of another cave-in and filled his mind with dreams of what luxuries his illicit income would bring him. Fulvia dug with renewed energy. It was becoming more and more difficult to lift the loose dirt above his head. He would have to consider widening the hole and carving some steps. Fulvia entertained these thoughts but he knew he would have to consult Marchetti first – when his enthusiasm was rewarded. His shovel jarred in his hands. He tapped his shovel blade again and again. Yes, he had struck something solid. He dropped to his knees the best he could in the confined space and floated his torch beam over the anomaly. Fulvia's immediate impression was that he had uncovered a human skull. He shuddered. But then he realised it was rock hard.

Impossibile.

Fulvia brushed the surface dirt free with his hand.

No ... it can't be!

Now with more care ... with as much respect as a looter could muster ... the man dug with his fingers ... slowly exposing his prize.

Some minutes after 8AM.
Little Arthur Street. North Hobart. Wednesday.

The narrow one-way street, Little Arthur, started as a horse and cart lane back in the 1850s. Now it was part and parcel of a trendy suburb with many restaurants, cafes, bars, pubs and bakeries. There is even a private art cinema. 'A little Brunswick Street in Melbourne,' Hobartians like to agree, over their latte and hummingbird cake.

Barrie parked his V8 pickup in the council car park off Little Arthur, already nearly full with shoppers and probably more than a few auction punters. The house auction in the green weatherboard cottage was half way up Little Arthur Street on the right-hand side. Jameson fed the parking meter; grateful it boasted a three-hour limit.

The cottage was small with a dilapidated picket fence in need of repair and paint, but the backyard proved deceivingly large.

'Typical wog house,' Barrie muttered to Jameson, pointing out colourful gnomes in the garden and concrete lions inside the front gate, all damaged.

'Yes, very Italian,' Jameson smiled at his older mates endearing term for any migrant arriving in Australia in the 1950s and 60s. 'Apparently the owner was a furniture restorer as well as a builder. These guys throw nothing away so you should find a bargain or two Baz.'

'Italian builder huh? What was his name?'

'Don't know. But he was in his eighties and died suddenly of a stroke.'

The driveway hugging the side of the building was overgrown with weeds and Scotch thistles. Jameson and Barrie filed after the dozens of other punters, all trampling the weeds and thistles and heading to the outbuildings searching for that illusive bargain.

Bordering the perimeter of the property were neglected grape vines and the obligatory lemon tree. There were three sheds. One original and in dire need of support. One a Bunnings self-erect job not ten years old and the other, the original cottage lavatory, was crammed with gardening tools, rusting tins of insecticides and cobwebs. Jameson cast an eye over the junk, for most was just that, junk, looking for that discarded antique stone jar or rare Hobart Town bottle. Nothing. 'I'm going inside.'

'See ya in there.' Barrie already saw potential in a pile of window frames. One, a lead light, had particularly caught his eye; leaning against an old carpenter's lathe. And in the older shed he was certain he recognised Huon pine boards, dozens of them, which he would have to inspect without drawing unwanted attention from the competition.

Inside the cottage was depressingly dark. For a builder, the old man had let his talents lapse. The smell of dampness suggested a leaking roof and the mouldy carpet hinted of stale urine. In a nutshell, it was depressing. Jameson saw nothing of immediate interest. The only advantage was that the rooms were so dim and dank most punters made a hasty retreat. Their numbers decreased steadily.

Good sign.

Even the auctioneer and his two assistants stood out on the front porch in the fresh air. But Jameson was firstly a collector.

And there was no known cure.

The deceased's son, a middle aged Italian wearing overalls, stood with the auctioneers. He lit a cigarette and watched prospective buyers coming and going. Mostly going. Jameson guessed the man had taken up his father's profession. He had a chiselled unshaven face, small dark eyes constantly darting about and large calloused hands. He also appeared to have back problems as he stood stooped and drew on his cigarette with addictive pleasure. None of the men on the front porch appeared overly positive about the outcome of this auction. The auctioneer stifled a yawn. It would be routine. A quick sale, get rid of all this crap, secure a fair price on the cottage, and back to the office for a wash.

Jameson moved through the kitchen; a 1980s time warp. From here, typically, a central passageway ran to the front door with two rooms off either side. Each room was lit with a forty-watt globe; bare. No shades. Two of these were bedrooms, one the deceased's bedroom. The bed was a four-poster, blackwood, circa 1910. 'That's worth buying,' Jameson thought but it needs a lot of restoration. Not Jameson's interest. Compared to the other rooms this bedroom was relatively tidy. Clearly the old boy spent most of his last years in this room. An old analogue television sat where it had the past twenty years, on top of a chest of draws – also blackwood – with a small late model flat screen television propped against it. A gift from the son, Jameson wondered. Both televisions were marked as one lot. Lot 48. Jameson moved to the wardrobe; white laminate, gold coloured alloy railing and doorknobs. 1970s? Totally out of character. Lot 93. This old boy was clearly frugal, Jameson sighed to himself. Other punters had left the wardrobe doors open. Inside hung the man's clothes, a Vinnie's collection that stank of mothballs. Who uses mothballs these days? Jameson lifted shoeboxes from the top shelf. Personal papers, even his old driving licenses. Gold plate cuff links, two men's wrist watches with expanding bands and one ladies watch. Leather band and a tarnished brass buckle – the dead wife's? None appeared in working order. The old man threw nothing away, it seemed. Jameson opened an old and worn leather wallet. It smelt of second hand shoes. It had been rifled. All that remained were a senior's card, a frequent shopper card, an Italian Club membership and a driver's licence. Void. It appeared the deceased had surrendered his licence five years earlier. Jameson read a name in Italian on another document. Signor Peppe Ricardo Drago. Jameson brushed aside a collection of neckties. The wardrobe was drab. No goodies here. An old coal scuttle, late Victorian, sat on the fireplace hearth where it was used for firewood. It was still full of kindling. Lot 105. But again, not Jameson's interest.

Deflated Jameson inspected a wooden framed clock on the mantelpiece. He looked behind it when the winding key fell to the floor. Bending to pick it up boxes under the bed caught his eye and he immediately thought of the box of Great War memorabilia he had bought at Gowan's Auctions a year earlier. That box of treasures was discovered under similar circumstances.

Shadows passed down the hall. Jameson waited. He was alone. He dropped to his knees and slid the closest box towards him. Lot 128. He now noted two boxes; both marked lot 128. Personal photo albums. Jameson flicked pages. The random album he had chosen showed black and white photos of a young Italian man in his twenties. He was handsome and fit. Then Jameson saw a likeness to the deceased man's son on the porch. There were photos at the beach, family shots, playing ball, dogs playing. Pretty much personal and uninteresting. Jameson caught a date in fading ink inside the front cover. 1953. He tossed the album back into the box and took another. He quickly flicked a few pages. Ruins! Photos of ruins. They were clearly in Italy before the old man migrated. Now Jameson's interest was piqued. Jameson counted five photo albums. Some shots showed allied forces after the war. Tanks in the streets. Citizens cheering and one photo of a sunken ship in what Jameson guessed was Naples Harbour. He shoved the box well back out of sight and dragged the second, heavier cardboard box towards him. Jameson tucked back the flaps of the lid and took a sharp short breath. This box was far more intriguing.

'There you are,' Barrie's familiar voice sought out Jameson kneeling in the dim light behind the bed. 'Anything interestin'?'

Without warning two punters pushed past Barrie and into the bedroom. Jameson recognised the first as Bill Patmore, an antiques dealer with the morals of a suicide bomber. Jameson jumped to his feet kicking the box under the bed and acted out dusting himself down.

'Interesting?' Jameson answered loudly. 'Nar. A load of crap really.'

Barrie looked like a schoolboy on Guy Fawkes night making silent faces and thumbs up behind the intruder's backs. Jameson ignored him and sat on the bed pretending to retie his runner. Patmore, who knew Jameson from his shop, chose to ignore him. The dealer picked up the clock. Inspected it briefly. 'French mantle clock. Eight-day chime. Art Deco 1950s. Shit condition. Value fifty bucks if ya lucky.'

'Here's the key,' Jameson said, and handed the bronze alloy winder to the sour faced dealer. Patmore pretended to have only just recognised Jameson. He nodded a grunt, tossed the key onto the mantle and walked around the bed inspecting its carpentry. Finally, he scratched something onto his A4 catalogue print out and left the room.

'What are ya up to?' Barrie grinned when the two were out of earshot. 'Ya look as sneaky as a shithouse rat.'

Another couple invaded their space. Jameson stood, pulling the bedspread down as far as he dared. 'Tell you later,' he said and led Barrie back to the yard. Barrie took the lead and with a hand dragging Jameson by his arm they entered the older shed where they were alone, for the moment.

Barrie nodded to the far wall. 'Check that out.'

Jameson squinted into the dark and saw a dozen empty glass flagons. The old Italian once made home brew; the dead vines were testament to that. 'Flagons Baz?'

'No. Not the friggin' flagons. Look what's behind 'em.'

Jameson stepped into the shed to be welcomed by cobwebs, grime and dust. Suddenly he saw what had made Barrie so animated. In the shadows, behind a false wall, breached while Barrie inspected the Huon Pine planks, was an urn; some three hundred centimetres tall and decorated with what any fool could see was a scene from ancient Greece.

'Christ Baz,' Jameson clumsily climbed over the planks; skittling flagons and ignoring spiders only to catch his sweater on a nail ...

New from Gazmans. $49.99. Great.

He reached in behind the pine, sliding the loose panel aside. Copy Greek urns were common, made for tourists by the thousands. But this was good, the pottery fine and the artistry well executed, not clumsy or stencilled. But it couldn't possibly be the real thing. *Could it?* Jameson felt *the* rush. That rush of adrenalin whenever he made a discovery, whether at an auction site or a 19th Century rubbish dump. He switched his mobile to torch and threw light into the secret space – and his heart sank. Crammed in next to the urn was a dismantled potter's wheel. This meant one thing. The urn was a fake and the old Italian had a covert interest.

'Hey Jam!' Barrie hissed. 'Jam ... someone's coming.'

By the time the auctioneer, his assistants and the owner's son entered the shed Jameson had perched himself on the Huon pine pile. The false panel was back in place and Jameson looked as dodgy as Barrie leaning one handed against the doorframe whistling some obscure tune.

'I'll have to ask you to move sir,' the auctioneer said bluntly to Jameson. 'The auction's about to start and you're sitting on lot 1.

'Thirty metres of architrave, a tonne of pine, four dormer window frames – with sashes – one lead light and three antique doors, one cedar with six coats of paint by the look of it, five hundred and eighty bucks. I'm a happy man Jam.'

'Good Baz, I'm happy for you. But now it's my turn. Quick. Inside.'

With the yards and sheds auctioned the few remaining punters moved inside. Jameson waited patiently in the passageway for lot 128. Eventually the dwindling punters squeezed into the tiny bedroom.

'Clock, twenty-nine dollars, wardrobe and contents ninety dollars and Patmore won the bed against another dealer, one hundred and forty dollars.' The auction was less than a success for the vendor. The beneficiary moved to the porch in disgust, and to smoke a cigarette. Patmore left to drive his ute up from the car park for collection. Only five punters remained, one was Barrie and one Jameson.

'Lot 128,' the auctioneer said lamely. 'Lot 128.'

The assistant searched about. Shrugged.

'Try under the bed,' Jameson offered casually.

'Ah.' The assistant slid the closest box out from under the four-poster.

'Boxes of personal sundries,' the auctioneer droned. 'Do I have an offer of fifty? Fifty dollars ... no ... thirty. Thirty dollars ... ' It was hard to imagine a more tedious face than that of the auctioneer at that moment. He would be lucky to cover costs with his commission in Little Arthur Street today. 'Twenty dollars ... ' Only the shuffling of impatient feet and a muffled cough answered. 'Ten then. Surely someone will offer me ten ... '

'Five,' Jameson said quietly.

'Sold!' The auctioneer's gavel couldn't slap his folder quick enough.

Barrie's favourite buntline hitch knots never failed. He tied off the last knot and looked at his handy work. He and Jameson had loaded the pickup with his bargains. Jameson returned from the cottage carrying his boxes and a hessian potato sack. He lifted the potato sack carefully onto the front seat and revealed its contents. The tall two-handled urn bore all the signs of an ancient Greek urn with its iconic black and orange designs.

'Ya didn't!' Barrie looked shocked.

'Didn't what?'

'Ya nicked that vase.'

'Firstly Baz it's not a vase. It's an urn, or proper name Krater.'

'Crater?'

'Krater with a K. And, secondly, I didn't nick it. I convinced the owner it was an old pot plant and gave him twenty bucks for it.'

'So in other words ya nicked it. Nice.'

'So what's with the boxes ya sneaky bastard?'

Jameson pulled back the flaps on the second box. Barrie peered inside none the wiser.

'Shards of pottery I recognised as ancient *and* Roman,' Jameson said. He pulled a scrunched newspaper free. The date 1951 did not go unnoticed by the builder and the fact it was printed in Italian. But what the paper protected was of far more interest.

Barrie. 'What is it?'

Jameson carefully lifted the pottery dish free. It was the size of a small ashtray, just as shallow. Jameson had recognised the satin glazed terracotta coloured pottery instantly as terra sigilatta and most likely first century AD Roman, but in style only. 'But there is something not quite right about this dish Baz.' Jameson had studied Roman pottery after purchasing his first piece from an antiquities dealer in London on eBay a year earlier. He had read quite a lot about the pottery ...

'And I am certain this is a fake.'

'So why are ya so excited if it's a fake?'

'Well that's what I hope to find out amongst all these family albums. This old Italian bloke was knocking out forgeries, probably back in the 50s and as late as the ... Jesus I don't know ... the 1990s. And these are bloody good fakes. Look at this, will you?'

Barrie accepted everything at face value. 'It looks old to me Jam.'

'And hey,' Jameson looked at the urn. 'For twenty bucks I'm going to have fun finding out exactly what the bloke was up to.'

'I'm happy for ya mate,' Barrie twisted the key in the ignition and the V8 juddered sending shudders through the cabin. 'So,' Barrie grinned. 'Down to Knoppies? It's your shout I reckon.'

Four hours earlier. Narrow alleyway near Piazza Capuana. Naples East. Italy. Early Wednesday morning.

Vice Sovrintendente Renato Di Stefano smelt the garbage truck before he saw it. It climbed the steep and narrow via Rasolli like a bloated hippopotamus, devouring restaurant garbage from the alleyway skips with insatiable greed. With a silent nod to his colleague, officer Dino Abandonato on the opposite side of the alleyway, Di Stefano pressed back into a fire exit and vanished. Black outfit, black exit, dark of night.

He felt a surge of excitement; a chameleon of the darkness. The truck passed leaving in its wake a lingering stink that competed with the blanketing smoke of Vesuvio. It was summer and with the nights clinging to twenty degrees Celsius – and the air still – the reek of spoilt fish and rotten meat clung about the alleyways with nowhere to go, like demons in purgatory.

Overhead in the dark of night Di Stefano could just make out the myriad of old iron balconies. Hazardous hundred-and-fifty-year-old landings wide enough for a few pot plants and to hang the washing. That was about it. These balconies adorned the five-storey stucco covered facades. The less fortunate occupied the attic apartments above. The luckier ones had a view of Naples Bay. Some managed to install air-condition units. Most seemed to support satellite dishes. Some were screened with wooden shutters layered with multiple coats of paint and others were simply draped in washing.

Di Stefano located his colleague in the darkness of the exit opposite. He motioned for him to join him.

'4.20 sir,' Officer Abandonato said quietly, rolling back his black skivvy cuff over his watch face. 'They're twenty minutes late. You don't suppose ... '

'They'll be here. My snitch has been reliable in the past and he knows I'm good for the other two hundred Euros when he delivers.'

The vice superintendent of the Culture Commandos – as the antiquities police were known – pushed back into the tight space of the shop exit.

'Here, squeeze in, don't be shy, I won't bite,' Di Stefano smiled showing off his white teeth.

Abandonato enjoyed working with his boss. The man had a sense of humour. He also had a sense of patriotic pride for Italy and her ancient heritage. Like his super, Abandonato had joined the carabinieri to combat art theft. He knew the looting of tombs and monuments by the tombaroli – tomb raiders – was a growing multi-billion Euro business. It was a scourge, a cancer against what was widely accepted as mankind's inheritance, and had to be protected at all costs. But at 26 Abandonato's super was fifteen years his elder. Abandonato knew the handsome charismatic Di Stefano had done the hard yards, old school. He worked his way up to chief assistant in the Polizia dei Giochi e delle Scommesse; the gaming and betting police and he knew he had seen some serious crime in his time. He felt safe with his super, although tonight he wondered why the man had not ordered backup. Corruption within the force came to mind.

Suddenly Di Stefano squeezed Abandonato's arm like a vice. But Abandonato saw the attic light at the same moment.

'Time for action.' Di Stefano checked his double barrel semi-automatic handgun tucked neatly into the belt at the back of his black leather slacks. He knew it was packed and ready with two eight-slug clips. 'Check your weapon.'

Abandonato's smile evaporated. He wanted to say *Jesus Christ I hope we don't have to use them* but said instead. 'Checked sir,' and crossed himself.

From this moment everything moved quickly.

As a distant clock chimed the half hour, a red van sped up the alleyway towards them. Headlights off. *Clack clack.* Two van doors opened and slammed shut. With one hand flat against Abandonato's chest Di Stefano pushed his colleague back against the wall and peered carefully around the brickwork. The van was ten metres away, down the steep lane. Two figures huddled outside the *target* door. A soft light spilt from a mobile screen as one man made a call … clearly to the man in the attic above. From where he stood Di Stefano's trained eye suspected the two men looked Sicilian.

Hard to say. But they were big devils.

A face appeared at the attic window. Now Di Stefano realised the window was ajar. The face made a preliminary recon. The man with the mobile stepped backwards into the middle of the alleyway to make a hurried wave with one hand as he ended the call.

'Ready?' Di Stefano whispered to Abandonato. Abandonato took a deep breath. And nodded.

About the same time.
Melanoma Cottage. Tasmania. Wednesday.

Jameson took his second beer from the fridge the moment Elspeth walked in the back door unstrapping her bike helmet. Jameson grinned. No. It was more a laugh.

'What do you think you're laughing at chef,' Elspeth screwed up her nose in that cute way Jameson found irresistible. She knew very well what he was laughing at. *That* helmet.

'You look like Ant Man under that helmet … seriously Beth. Ant Man on steroids.'

Elspeth crossed the room and shoved the helmet playfully on Jameson's head. He allowed her, her moment. She stepped back with head on a tilt stroking her chin.

'And?' Jameson pondered her verdict.

'Your right about the helmet of course,' she smirked.

'Oh?'

'You look like a dickhead.'

'Thanks.'

'Where's *my* beer?' she asked.

'In the fridge. You can help yourself after that comment.'

Elspeth stripped off the bike leathers, loaned to her by the owner of the Vespa she had ridden home on from work – Claire, her best friend. Claire, an archivist at the Tasmanian Library, had flown to London for a holiday – and to see her brother, a graphic designer in Battersea.

'When does Claire get back anyway?' Jameson asked, capitulating and fetching Elspeth a beer.

'She's got another two weeks I think. I don't know how she drives that thing twenty-four-seven. Feel my cheeks. They're freezing.' Jameson answered by rolling the chilled bottle along her cheek. 'Can't feel a thing,' Elspeth said. 'My cheeks are colder than the beer.'

'When's your beetle ready anyway,' Jameson asked of Elspeth precious VW sedan that she normally relied on; now at the mechanics with a dodgy gearbox.

'Maybe Friday.'

'Well we better try to co-ordinate so you drive to work with me.'

'All a bit hard with your hours.' Elspeth backed up to the wood heater to thaw.

'Maybe.'

Elspeth attention was drawn to the dining room table. It was strewn with open albums of old photos, loose snapshots and a dozen pieces of rather unusual pottery half wrapped in yellowing newspaper. 'So how was the auction?'

'Very interesting.'

'What's this lot then?'

'I'm not really sure yet. But I think I'm onto something.'

'Oh?'

'Well it was a house auction ...'

'Yes, you said, in North Hobart.'

'Yeh. Some old Italian guy who had a stroke. In his eighties, I believe. Well the house, a cute cottage really but it needs a lot of work, was crammed with stuff – junk mostly. Baz got some bargains though, builder's stuff in the sheds and I bought two boxes of personal stuff I found under the old guy's bed ... photos.' Jameson necked his beer and tipped his head towards the table. 'He was a furniture restorer apparently, and a builder in his younger days. Had a restoration business out the back, his son told me. But when I looked in the boxes there's these pottery shards and two complete pieces. It's all Roman but here's the rub. The two complete pieces are fake.'

'Fake?' Elspeth stepped up to the table picking up the Terra Sigilatta dish. 'How can you tell?'

'It's too solid for one thing. Too heavy. Here.' He picked up a shard of similar material. 'Feel the difference. This shard is genuine. I reckon he has used this for comparison.'

'Who? The old man?'

'Yes. There's photos of him as a young guy in the 50s back in Italy visiting ruins.'

'Really? That's pretty cool.'

'Yes. Clearly he souvenired stuff back then.'

'Hmm. You wouldn't get away with that today.'

'Exactly.'

Suddenly Elspeth spotted the Greek Krater 'pot plant' that Jameson had paid the son twenty dollars for. It sat in the centre of the top shelf of books. 'Oh god! Did you buy that as well.'

'Yep. Pretty neat isn't it?'

'That's a fake of course ... isn't it?'

'I'm fairly certain. I mean if it was the genuine article it would fetch twenty grand at Sotheby's ... '

'*Fairly* certain!'

'Well here's the thing El. I found that pot along with a dismantled potter's wheel and other potter's tools. Hidden it was, like the old guy was trying to hide something and I'm guessing he was making fakes.'

'Faked antiquities?'

'Yes.'

'Who for?'

'Well I don't know. He was a forger. Probably selling to art dealers or collectors. I'm hoping for answers in this lot.' Jameson pointed with his stubby at the photos.

'Say,' Elspeth had a thought, 'how come you aren't at work?'

'We're quiet tonight so I took the night off.'

'Great,' Elspeth smiled. 'What's for dinner? Don't tell me, chilli con carne leftovers.' Jameson nodded approvingly. 'So, you'd like me to fix a salad I'm guessing while you pore over that lot,' she said.

'I do declare El, you're psychic.'

Nothing tastes better than a pot of stew, soup or chilli con carne left overnight. It was an easy meal. The salad was crisp and fresh, even if it was a chilly winter's night outside, and Jameson was soon sorting through his potpourri of a lonely stranger's memories.

'Five albums, in excess of six hundred photos; many of them taken at one ancient site or another. And this.' Jameson held the dog-eared Christies Auction catalogue up for Elspeth to see. *Christies 1962.* He flicked through the yellowing pages with photos of rare antiquities to go under the hammer. Jameson recognised kraters like his recent purchase, lidded pyxides, two handled shallow bowl kylixs and amphora all decorated in the traditional ancient terracotta and black glazes with geometric designs, scenes from Olympia or scenes of war favouring the Greeks as conquerors. The auctioneer's estimates were printed below each item.

'Look at the estimates will you; five hundred pounds, eight hundred pounds ... Jesus! Here's a painted amphora for four hundred. Imagine that. That alone would fetch ten grand today.'

'Yes well,' Elspeth poured more Lubiano Stefano pinot noir into their glasses. 'They all belong in a museum,' she said. Jameson of course was well aware of her opinion of collectors and hoarders. 'In a museum where everyone can enjoy them.'

'That's one woman's opinion. I tend to disagree.'

'Of course you do.' Elspeth picked up the Terra Sigilatta dish. 'So you think this is a fake.'

'It just doesn't feel right.'

'How would you like to find out for certain?'

'How?'

'My old professor at Uni, Gilbert Pitt, as well as lecturer in ancient and modern histories is the curator of the University's moderate collection of antiquities.'

'The university has a museum?'

'Yes. Its only small. Locked away in the Arts Faculty but it's kept as a reference museum. It was bequeathed by Lady Marjorie Petri. Her husband was an ambassador somewhere in the Middle East before the war – in the 1930s – and put together a private collection. Anyway, before she died in the early seventies she donated the collection to the university. I've spent hours in there, I'm sure I talked about it.'

'Bit before my time.'

'I'll email him now, can't be too difficult to find his address.' Elspeth fetched her laptop when she had a thought. 'Hey!'

'What?'

'I'm certain I remember seeing auction house catalogues in the collection's library. Sotheby's, Bonham's, Christies ... all the big players. They might be worth checking as well. If you think your man was selling ... you never know. Worth a try.'

'Well if he was selling it would be through the big players, as you say. When was Sotheby's established in Australia, do you know?'

Elspeth snapped open her computer and hit Google. 'Here it is, 1983.'

'Well that's a pretty good time frame, I mean that could be prime time for our Italian mate.'

'What's his name anyhow.'

'Well here's the thing. I read his name on an old driver's licence at the house sale. It was Vince Renzo ... apparently. But the name on the inside cover of three of these album covers is Peppe Ricardo Drago.'

'So, it's a different guy.'

'No way. Look at this.' Jameson pointed to a young man, twenty maybe, on a beach posing with a dog and a ball. It appeared to be early 1950s. 'See?' Jameson pointed to the man's left hand between thumb and forefinger. 'That's a tattoo or a birth mark ... more likely a tattoo though,' he said of the dark smudge. Jameson passed Elspeth a magnifying glass to float over the image. 'And see this photo.' It was clearly the same man thirty years later. There's the same mark.'

'I wonder if he changed his name when he migrated to Australia?'

'Possibly.'

'More like probably.'

'So why?'

'Something to hide.'

'But we'll call him Peppe huh?'

'Peppe it is then. Try Googling him?'

'Good idea.' Jameson searched *Peppe Ricardo Drago* while Elspeth found Professor Gilbert Pitt's email address on the University of Tasmania web site. She typed a quick 'Hello, remember me?' Followed by an introduction to Jameson and their request. Elspeth hit send. Jameson had no luck with Google search. He typed in Vince Renzo instead and immediately scored an Italian named Renzo of Hobart, Tasmania. But he was born in 1961 and his Christian name turned out to be Victor. 'That's the son,' Jameson mused. 'Sour faced bastard he was. Look at the photo. Same guy.' It was neither a web page nor Facebook. 'It's a Mercury article for 2011. He was arrested on a drug charge. Selling am-phebs. Stupid bastard.'

Elspeth checked the photo taken outside the Supreme Court in Salamanca Place. The small black eyes looked left of camera; he was clearly trying to avoid the press photographer. 'Victor you say?' Elspeth said. Doesn't look like a Victor to me, more a loser.'

Immediately Elspeth's laptop pinged. 'Way to go professor!' Elspeth cried out. 'It's ... ' she looked at the wall clock. 'It's after 9.30 and the old professor's still up and online.' She speed-read the email. 'That's what I always liked about Professor Pitt. He was always a doer; prompt and reliable.'

'What's he say?'

'Said he will look forward to seeing me again and meeting you. He has a free lecture between nine and ten in the morning. But you'll have to go alone,' Elspeth said. 'Some of us work nine to five.'

After 10PM

'Want to take hot chocolate to bed?' Elspeth stood and stretched. The open fire was dwindling; it was a choice of tossing a fresh log on the fire or bed. She yawned. Outside the waves collided with the rock ledge in eternal rhythmic harmony. Elspeth found them hypnotic, comforting and the thought of hot chocolate in a warm bed made her yawn once more.

'Thanks,' Jameson said without really listening. He was too engrossed in his cache. He sat on the floor with legs spread, finally sorting through the bottom of the second box. Both boxes, he had noted, were made for the Chinese export market from sturdy cardboard once packaging glass jars of hoisin sauce from an address in Shanghai. The recipient had been Wing & Co. Hobart. Jameson noticed a packaging date, 1986. Thirty years old and strong as the day they were made.

So far Jameson had five photo albums, well-loved and tatty. He had several hundred loose photos, mostly small black and white snaps, and an assortment of ancient shards, which he would take to the professor tomorrow for show and tell.

Jameson. 'What's this?'

'What?'

Jameson lifted the cardboard flaps at the bottom of the second box and pulled what appeared to be an old exercise book free. Dirt from the ancient shards, dead moths and other long deceased insects fell from the cover. Jameson leant over the fireplace and blew the detritus free. 'It's all in Italian.'

'What did you expect?' Elspeth answered watching the beetle wings flare and crackle in the flames.

'Hmm.' Jameson flicked through the pages. The writing was neat, the layout tidy and paragraphs were headed with dates.

'Lunedì, Martedì, Mercoledì ... ' he read aloud. 'Similar to French,' he declared. 'Lundi, Mardi, Mercredi ... Monday, Tuesday, Wednesday ...'

Elspeth stepped over the piles of memories, stacked in Jameson's orderly groups on the floor rug. 'I'll make the chocolate,' she said. 'Jaffa or peppermint?'

'This is a diary,' Jameson said, distracted.

'No shit Sherlock,' Elspeth teased.

'Jameson threw the book on the album pile and jumped to his feet taking Elspeth in his arms. 'I'll take the diary to Romilda tomorrow,' Jameson said, speaking of his Italian kitchen lady. 'She can translate it for me.'

'Great,' Elspeth tried to wriggle free but Jameson held her tight. 'Jaffa or Peppermint?' she asked a second time.

'Neither,' he grinned. 'I've a better idea.'

Italy. Narrow alleyway near Piazza Capuana. Naples East. Early morning.

Vice Sovrintendente Renato Di Stefano stood silently with officer Dino Abandonato in the blackness of the fire exit. His thoughts went to his wife Angelina snug in bed where he left her. She was not unlike the movie star Angelina Jolie; a real-life Venus, still beautiful at forty-three, inside and out.

Stay focused Di Stefano told himself. This operation was big. Bigger than Ben Hur as he had heard his American counterparts say. He hated the tombaroli as the tomb raiders were called. Stealing Italy's heritage. Stealing *his* heritage and for what, short term riches just to feed the greedy gloating private collectors around the world; rich men with a penchant to decorate their homes with ancient marbles or priceless Etruscan urns.

Priceless. That was a laugh. These treasures weren't priceless. Everything has a price. *This* was the problem.

Immediately the man from the attic window opened the door onto the street where the two men and the red van waited. Di Stefano stole one eye around the brickwork. This man Di Stefano guessed was also Sicilian. He noted the only exchange was a nod. Attic man rattled a key ring, searching in the dark for one key in particular. A moment later he unlocked another door, a larger arched door, leading to a storage facility under his mid-nineteenth century apartment. The van's rear doors were thrown open while Attic man and one of the van men struggled with a heavy blanket-wrapped bundle. A figure. Di Stefano smiled at the irony. Carried horizontally it looked human in form ... as if the men were disposing of a dead body with rigor mortis. But Di Stefano knew this had to be an ancient statue. He waited while three other smaller, yet not insignificant, items were carried to the van. All were wrapped in what appeared to be blankets.

The Sovrintendente turned to his subordinate and whispered. 'Check your weapon.' Abandonato presented his Af2011-A1 double barrel semi-automatic handgun loaded with two clips of .45s, eight in each. With the pistol at chest level, nozzle aimed skyward, Abandonato tried to swallow but his mouth was as dry as Vesuvio's crater.

'Checked,' he finally managed softly.

'Check it again.'

Abandonato re-checked his weapon. Loaded. Safety catch off.

Di Stefano. 'On my signal you cross to the fire exit opposite and cover me.'

Silent nod ... Abandonato had a second attempt at swallowing cottonwool.

Immediately Di Stefano leapt from the cover of darkness. He was totally exposed, legs spread wide, both hands in control of his semi-automatic. 'Non si muovono!' he yelled out. Abandonato leapt for the cover of the opposite wall.

'Adesso!'

The Sicilians twisted about ...

Totally surprised ...

And looking at ten year's prison.

Attic man pulled a side arm. Di Stefano fired. The slug was wide slamming into the van door. The van driver slipped behind the wheel. The motor sparked to life the moment the second van man dived on top of the contraband. Attic man lowered his pistol. He had Di Stefano in his sights but another shot thundered in the alleyway. Abandonato's bullet smacked into Attic man's right shoulder and his body twisted violently from the hit.

Lights above filled windows.

Faces pushed against glass.

Suddenly the slightest of a tremor unnerved the men. The shake was short and brief but enough to loosen pot plants from a balcony high above. The heavy terracotta vessels filled with damp dirt and plants pounded the alleyway exploding in shards of pottery. An iron balcony rail slammed onto the van roof. The men ducked for shelter as car alarms and fire bells answered the call of Vesuvio. The alleyway was in a state of pandemonium. Di Stefano snapped his head skywards. The sound of falling rubble and pots ceased. He heard the van engage a gear. He swung his semi-automatic towards the van and squeezed off three shots. The windscreen shattered but the van sped past in a fishtail of squealing tires.

They had escaped.

Now both the Carabinieri stepped back into the open. Guns levelled. Attic man scowled at the retreating van. There was nowhere to run. Crying in pain he threw his hands into the air and surrendered.

CHAPTER FOUR

Other side of the world. 8.20AM. Little Arthur Street

Against Jameson's better judgement a clandestine visit to Vince Renzo's old cottage seemed a clever idea. Jameson was convinced there was more to the secret hiding space with the false panel, and more clues to Vince's nefarious activities. And 8.20 in the morning seemed a reasonable hour to pay a visit rather than snooping about at night. Besides the cottages in this street were close knit and a torch in the dark would definitely look suspicious.

The front gate in the picket fence was locked. A *SOLD* sticker had been plastered diagonally across the real estate agency's sign and the driveway gate was pulled shut. A Good sign that the house was deserted. Jameson lifted the latch on the driveway gate, forcing it inwards against the weeds. It protested on corroded hinges when Jameson had a sudden thought. The son may just have stayed here the night.

Nar, I doubt it. But what if he did?

Jameson knocked on the door.

Christ! What will I say if he is here?

No answer. All clear.

Jameson hurried along the overgrown driveway and moved directly to the old shed. It was remarkably vacant since the sale and the rotting timbers looked ready to collapse any moment. The hidey-hole was now an open void. The false panel lay abandoned in the dirt and several vertical planks had been removed. The dismantled potter's wheel remained discarded. In dozens of pieces. Unloved ... *but what secrets could you tell?*

Jameson dropped to his knees and forced more planks free. The grey palings were soft with rot and some even crumbled in his hands when he exposed a cache of rusted tins – baked-bean tins in size – and he recognised the labels immediately; they were metal oxides like sodium, potassium and calcium. A tin of Alumina was familiar. These products, Jameson knew, from art lessons in grade ten. They were all ingredients for glazing pottery and porcelain. Other tins carried the dyes for the glazes, mostly shades of rust orange, black and yellows. *Popular colours in ancient Attica ...*

A shoe scuffed behind him.

Jameson swung about. His jaw dropped open. Sprung by the son Victor Renzo. The man looked cranky and stood over Jameson with his huge calloused hands swinging free at his side.

'What do you think you're up to then?' The black beady eyes held his gaze. 'Well?'

'I ... ah ... I came back to see if I could find a lid for that pot plant I bought off you yesterday,' Jameson lied looking as guilty as a novice shoplifter.

The man stood so close Jameson caught his rancid onion breath. 'Pot plants don't have lids.' Renzo spat.

'I know,' Jameson answered without pause. 'I showed it to a mate and he said the same thing. He reckons it's a pickle jar.' This lie came a little easier. 'And he said it should have a lid.'

'I think you should leave.' There was no friendship lost here.

Jameson stood in the cramped space but Renato didn't budge, intimidating Jameson.

'Your dad was a potter eh?' Jameson tried to make casual conversation while brushing himself down. No answer. 'It's just that I noticed all this old potter's stuff,' Jameson persisted. 'And I wondered if he made the pot plant ... pickle jar or whatever it is.'

'I wouldn't know,' Renzo glowered. 'Now I asked you to leave,' he said coldly, stepping back.

Thursday Morning. University of Tasmania. Arts Faculty.
Just after 9AM.

Professor Gilbert Pitt was Father Christmas in comparison to the secretive Victor Renzo. Jameson was immediately at ease with the man wearing suit trousers with a tartan waistcoat over a yellow shirt with an old fashioned mauve bow tie. Early seventy something, Gilbert Pitt. Old school. Heart of gold. He was one of those academics who wore his reading glasses at half-mast, perched on his nose like a pair of pince-nez where – when focus was required – he would tip back his head, raise the chin and narrow the eyes. If dialogue was required, the head dipped and the subject was scrutinised over the top of the spectacles.

Jameson watched his luxuriant shaggy black eyebrows rise and fall as he spoke, almost like a conductor delivering direction. 'But where's Elspeth?' he said, his head dodging about expectantly. Jameson explained she had to be at work at nine. 'Pity, I was so looking forward to seeing Elspeth. Clever girl that one. You two are an item I take it.'

'Yes professor. Nearly two years now.'

'You're a lucky fellow. But I trust you know that. Oh, listen to me, what would I know. *Of course* you know you're a lucky man. Now, this is the artefact in question eh?' The professor alluded to the parcel Jameson had tucked under his arm. He led Jameson through to the museum, an area the size of a lecture room yet all the windows were darkened with blinds. He switched on the fluorescents. There were, maybe, twenty glass cabinets of varying sizes and ages. Whilst most were wood framed and old, some were aluminium and modern.

'A miss-mash of cases, but we rely on donations here Jameson. There is no budget for a museum and we rely on volunteers to do what is required to keep this place ship-shape.'

Jameson was lost for words. The collection covered the most famous civilisations – Egypt, Greece, Rome – whilst Jameson also recognised antiquities from Mesopotamia, the Phoenicians, the Etruscans and other ancient civilisations of the Levant and South America.

'Incredible,' Jameson finally sighed. 'I had no idea this was here.'

'Have a look around. In the meantime let me see this find of yours. Bought at a local auction Elspeth said.'

'Yes.'

The professor unwrapped the urn carefully onto a small padded worktop. His analysis was instant. 'Oh yes. Fake. There's no two ways about it.'

'I was afraid you'd say that.'

'But I must tell you,' the professor's head tipped back and the eyes narrowed onto a patch of geometric design in black and orange glaze. 'It's a gooden.'

'That's what I thought.'

'It's not a Greek copy by the way.'

'Oh.'

'No. It's Etruscan. You see this tall figure hear with the hooked nose and carrying that large mallet ... well that's the Etruscan demon Charun. He escorts the deceased to the underworld. This Krater, if it was the real thing, would have been made as a funerary urn and left in a tomb.'

'Etruscan, north Italy. That all fits with the story then.'

'The original would be about 300BC I would say.'

'I wonder where the original is?' Jameson asked. 'I mean this has been copied from an original hasn't it.'

'Almost certainly.'

'How do you know for certain this is a fake? How can you tell?'

'I have handled too many of these in the past and it's hard to explain, but you know straight away, it just doesn't feel right. For one thing this pottery is more highly fired than the ancient kilns. If you give it a gentle flick it has a higher resonance.' And the man

demonstrated with a flick of the finger resulting in a subtle 'ping.'
'And the pottery is heavier...'

'Yes. I thought that.'

'Then you will know what I am talking about when I say the surface is soapy if I can use that word.'

Jameson was impressed. 'I think I do, yes.'

'And the tone of the painted glaze is darker and more uniform than ancient pottery. There is no variation in the firing temperatures like the ancients would have experienced. Yes, it's definitely a fake. But, as I said, it's a gooden.'

'What of the style?'

'Oh the style is good, well copied, and I'm thinking if you were to scour thousands of photographs of genuine museum pieces I wouldn't be surprised if the original showed up. This was probably copied from a photograph ... hey, I tell you what. We have hundreds of auction catalogues going back to the 60s ... the 50s even in the museum library ...'

'El told me that.'

'Yes, well you are welcome to go through them, I could even lend you a dozen at a time if you wish to peruse at your leisure.'

'That's very kind professor.'

'I discovered a Sicilian amphora once where the spears the soldiers were carrying were held in the wrong fashion. Totally out of style. It was a very clever fake, very clever indeed, but for the fact the spears position was totally out of character.'

Jameson rewrapped his *prize* when he felt the weight of the two shard samples he had brought along in his pocket. 'Oh, I nearly forgot these.' Jameson handed the terracotta glazed shards to the professor.

'Hmm. Terra Sigilatta. Roman. Probably first century AD, or CE for Christian era as the politically correct insist on saying these days instead of AD for Anno Domini, the Latin phrase that has been around since the 6th century.'

'But are those shards genuine?'

'Oh god yes, absolutely.' The professor nodded to the wrapped krater. 'So what will you do with it now,' he asked, imagining the vessel turning up in a top end auction somewhere. 'You'll not try and sell it will you?'

'I ... ah.' That is exactly what had gone through Jameson's mind. 'I ... I guess I'll turn it into a pot plant professor.'

'Atta boy. That's about all it is good for.

Hook, Line and Sinker Seafood Restaurant.
Hobart Waterfront. 9.35AM

Italian born Romilda Amarosa met Jameson's request for a translation of the Italian diary with circumspection and one of her priceless scrunched faces, like she had been asked to eat something she didn't like ... Greek food for example.

'Why you ask?' the fifty-three-year-old Italian women asked in her usual brash and bossy tone. The cooks in the kitchen were 'her boys,' she was their mamma and pity help anyone who crossed her path. 'What this? Thees Italiano.'

'Yes Romilda,' Jameson was prepared for this. 'That's why I'm asking you to translate it.'

'All!'

'No, no. Just enough for me to know what it is. I think it's a diary.'

'Diary?' The woman's face scrunched anew. 'What this diary? What diary?'

'I think this is a day by day account of an Italian man back in 1950s and 60s.'

'Ah Diary!'

'Yes diary.'

'Why not you tell me thees before?' Romilda turned pages with feigned interest.

'Who this Peppe Ricardo Drago?'

'That's what I hoped you'd tell me.'

'Drago mean ... ah ... ' Romilda frowned afresh searching her brain for the translation. 'Ah ... what you say ... big lizard with fire mouth.'

'Dragon.'

'Si, si. Dragon.'

Jameson turned pages for her. 'Lunedi is Monday, Martedi is Tuesday, correct?'

'Si.' Romilda finally showed some interest. It seemed she was now convinced that she wasn't being involved in anything traitorous. 'Drago say here he like history. He write about San Sebastiano al Vesuvio ... ah Vesuvio ... volcano si. I know thees things.'

The Italian spelling *vulcano* now stood out to Jameson. Romilda read on. 'Villages Massa di Somma and Ottaviano. Drago, he was there. 1944. See Marzo ... march, si? 18 to 23. Much fire. Much red rock.' Romilda thought of the translation. 'Si. Lava ... you know thees word. Me think same in English. Lava.'

Tasmanian Museum. Thursday. 10.45AM

The landline shrilled in Elspeth's office the moment she stood to leave for an appointment with her boss, the museum director Charles Bean. She was about to walk out the door, ignore the phone; but something warned her it was important.

'Jameson! Everything alright?'

'Alright! Alright! ... Wait 'till you hear this.'

'Look I have an appointment with Charles, I'll call you back ...

But Jameson wouldn't hear of it. '... Romilda told me our man Drago wrote of Pompeii, Herculaneum as well as ... wait for it ... Vataea.'

'Jam, Charles Bean ... my boss, is waiting.'

'*Vataea* for Christ's sake! The word is written clear as a bell. I don't know why I didn't spot it last night.'

'I'll call you back in ten minutes ... '

'Jesus Beth. Vataea.'

Elspeth sighed heavily. This enthusiasm of Jameson's was contagious. 'Please excuse my ignorance. But what is Vataea?'

'Vataea,' Jameson almost yelled into the receiver. 'Is the lost Vesuvius town. Unlike Pompeii and Herculaneum rediscovered in the 18th century, Vataea has never been found.'

'Oh.'

'And our Peppe Ricardo Drago, a name I'm beginning to warm to I might add, speaks of it in his diary ... '

'So it is a diary?'

'Yes. I pressured Romilda but she really couldn't quite work it out so I'm going to see Angelo and get a more precise translation.'

'Angelo at Saint Michaels?'

'Yes. I called him. He'll see me this afternoon.'

'Good luck.' Elspeth knew that Jameson's last meeting with the thirty-eight-year-old priest was quite animated. The debate on life after death and Jameson's insistence that what follows death is *lights out* did not sit well with the passionate theologian.

Tasmanian Museum. Curator's Office. Thursday 11.15AM

Tasmanian Museum Director Charles Bean was pleasantly old fashioned. In his early sixties, he had an insatiable taste for fine wine, gourmet food, suede suits and all the finer pleasures in life. He also exercised etiquette; manners taught by his hard-working English parents who would be so proud of their only child Charles; should they still be alive.

Elspeth knocked and entered the director's office. 'Elspeth.' The man rose behind his desk in greeting and offered her his hand. 'You look absolutely radiant this morning,' he added smartly. Elspeth noted his belly seemed larger since the last time they met.

'Thankyou.' Elspeth had had the position of assistant curator for over a year now and knew Charles Bean for what he was, a gentleman. Certainly, he was possessed with an appreciative eye for anything in a skirt, but he happened to be a harmless voyeur. *Men are from Mars*, right? Elspeth took the seat offered.

'Yes my dear, simply radiant. It must be that sea air now you have moved in with your own personal chef.'

'Sea air and all his good cooking,' Elspeth answered. And she wanted to say, *and all the great sex* too, but said instead. 'I have to watch my weight.'

'Which reminds me,' Bean said as he sat and shuffled through papers on his untidy desk. 'I must get that recipe for abalone Jameson promised to email me.'

'Done. I'll remind him tonight. You wanted to see me.'

'Yes.' He sorted amongst the notes he was looking for and tapped them vertically on his desk into a neat group before stapling them together at a corner. 'How would you like a trip to Rome?'

'Ro ... Rome sir?'

'Yes Rome.'

'Rome Italy?'

'Where else?'

'Ah ... of course. But why? I mean what's happening?'

'Remember I wrote in a museum memo a few months back that there was a possibility of the Tacito marbles, the marbles found by Signor Tacito in the Bay of Naples back in the 1920s, being loaned to the Tasmanian Museum?'

'From the sunken city of Baiae?'

'The very same, yes. Well the collection is finally ready to tour down under and we have been chosen to exhibit them after Fremantle and Canberra.'

'Cool. I mean that's fantastic.'

'And, Elspeth, I have chosen you to represent us ... the Tasmanian Museum.'

'Well that's great ... but ... ah ... how do you mean?'

'Well Signore Aberto Ferraro of the Museo Nazionale Romano in Rome has requested a representative from each museum to be at a briefing regarding the safe transportation of the collection and also to be instructed, personally, on how each exhibit is to be presented. There is quite a protocol to adhere to, which is fair enough. He already has specifications of our own gallery areas but he is adamant about meeting representatives in person. So ... Voila.'

'What about Cassandra? I mean don't get me wrong sir, I'm crazy about going. But won't she be put out. I mean Cassandra is the exhibitions manager.'

'She's ill with tonsillitis I'm afraid and we are talking leaving Saturday for a Monday deadline in Rome.'

'Wow!' Elspeth couldn't believe her luck. 'I mean ... wow!'

'Why don't you see if your personal chef can ride along. He will have to pay his own way of course but we are paying accommodation for you and it will be no problem extending the budget a little to reserve doubles instead of singles.' Charles Bean's real motivation was the fact he would prefer Jameson to accompany Elspeth; especially after the life-threatening debacle in Jamaica recently when Elspeth was sent to learn conservation skills at the sunken city of Port Royal only to be pursued by a corrupt official with connections to a drug cartel.

'I ... ah ... wow again. I know he'll go if he can get off work and I know August is slow in the restaurant biz, so maybe.'

'Then here.' The museum director handed Elspeth the stapled documents. 'All you need to know is in this broad sheet. You better call Jameson, we need to book airfares ASAP.'

'ASAP,' Elspeth repeated, looking at the documents like a stunned mullet. It was all so sudden. She took a deep breath. 'Yes, I understand.'

'Elspeth. I am talking like this afternoon. There are seats being held by Etihad Air for Saturday at noon. Flying out of Melbourne. Flight Centre said the seats will only be held until 4PM today.'

.....

'Rome!' Jameson yelled. He was on speakerphone. He plated up Harissa Salmon Hot Rock and a Mediterranean Bar-b-qued Octopus. First two diners. The restaurant was filling early for lunch and a call from El had to be important for her to call during service. 'Are you kidding me?'

'No.'

Jameson wedged his mobile between ear and shoulder and pinged the service bell. A waiter appeared.

Jameson to Elspeth. 'Spill.'

Jameson to waiter. 'Table fourteen, salmon ... harissa on the side.'

Back to Elspeth. 'Tell me quickly. Twenty-five words or less.' He didn't mean to sound arrogant. El would understand.

Elspeth. 'Sorry. I know you're busy.' She poured out the deal – *twenty-five words or less.*

Jameson threw a handful of fresh Tasmanian scallops into a smoking pan with butter and olive oil. Extra virgin. The firm sweet molluscs hissed and sizzled. Tarragon and lemon followed. He cooked and listened. 'That's crazy El.' Silence.

'Are you in or not,' Elspeth pressured. 'Charles Bean has to know ... like now Jam'.'

'Jesus ... I can't believe this opportunity has come along at this very moment ... Crazy.'

'In or out?'

'Are you mad? I'm in ... I think ... '

'What do you mean, you think?'

'I mean I hope.'

'Hope?'

'I hope I can get the week off.' Jameson's mind was racing. 'I know it's crazy but this is not to be missed.' The chef's mind was on the lost city of Vataea, hardly Rome. *Naples was close to Rome, wasn't it?* But now was not the time to discuss this. Two new orders appeared on the kitchen monitor screen. 'Let me talk to my boss, I'll call you after lunch.'

Elspeth felt good. Anything was possible. Jameson finished the scallop dish with a deglazing splash of sauvignon blanc, a dollop of sour cream, a smart reduction, cracked black pepper and served the scallops over steamed rice ...

$24.95. Lunch special.

2.10PM.

The last lunch order. A bouillabaisse to die for – so critics agreed – left the kitchen leaving behind the aroma of Marseille; market fresh shellfish, garlic, fennel, Pernod.

Gastronomic brilliance with simplicity.

Jameson watched his favourite meal of all time head out the door to a paying guest and tore the crusty end from a spare baguette. He soaked up the sauce left in the pan. *Heaven forbid. Can food ever taste better than this?* Jameson rushed three mouthfuls. Then went to see the boss.

As crazy as it all seemed chef's leave *could* be arranged. It was short notice but it could be managed.

'Are you certain?' Jameson stood in the boss's office doorway wiping his hands vigorously for the umpteenth time on a wet tea towel. Cleo Sackville, the Swiss trained restaurant manager, a no-nonsense operator who looked more like a woman's magazine editor than a restaurateur, was comfortable making hasty decisions.

'Look Jameson, the kitchen's overstaffed for August. Do me a favour and take some leave.' She scanned her executive chef's file on her twenty-inch Apple Mac. screen. 'You're owed two weeks already and I'd rather you take it now than in summer.'

'Are you sure?'

'Sure I'm sure. I'd follow Elspeth around the world too if I were in your shoes. Go. Just sort all the kitchen rosters.'

'Done.'

'Really?' Elspeth was ecstatic. 'I mean *Really?*'

Jameson was crammed into his own tiny office, annexed between the restaurant kitchen and fire exit. 'Yes really,' he answered. Elspeth wanted to scream with excitement. 'I've got to go ... I have to call Charles Bean.'

Jameson was still trying to come to terms with his hasty decision. Stu would run the kitchen but the rosters needed work and there were specialist menus to complete and he wanted to supervise the orders for the coming week. Before him, on his desk, a box of over ripe avocadoes had been dumped for his attention. He had suppliers to sort out. *Stu would be fine* he told himself. He looked at his reflection on the computer screen and said with confidence, *no one is indispensible ...*

Yeh right.

Saint Mary's Cathedral. Harrington Street. Hobart. 4.20PM

Jameson walked the one and a half kilometres from the restaurant to Saint Mary's – mostly a gentle incline towards the foothills of Mount Wellington. He needed time to think. Everything was moving fast. He stopped to catch his breath at the Harrington Street entrance where stone steps cut through the grassy embankment – and he gazed up at one of Hobart's finer constructions; Saint Mary's Cathedral. Jameson knew its history. Colonial Hobart Town was one of his main passions and he knew a small wooden chapel was first consecrated on this site for the Roman Catholic Church in 1822. That humble structure made way for this Gothic styled sandstone and slate erection of mighty proportions aspiring towards the heavens as a testament to man's love of God ... *well*, Jameson thought, *at least that is what the faithful would have you believe.* The afternoon sun arched towards the cathedral's western wing, the sunlight now accentuating the scenes from the gospels in the 14th century styled stained glass windows. Jameson looked at his watch. He was late.

Father Angelo greeted Jameson in the vestry. The priest sorted books on religious studies and at first seemed preoccupied. 'Jameson, come in, take a seat, I won't be a moment.' He stacked books in three separate piles. 'I can't stand clutter,' he said; and then took Jameson's offered hand in both of his. 'Nice to see you again ... sit, sit.'

Jameson smelt stale cigarettes. Even priests have vices. They both sat. The thirty-eight-year-old priest had a kindly, intelligent face and the red rosy cheeks of a man out in the cold. 'Thanks for seeing me ... father.' Jameson hated the title. It sounded ... *well contrived*, coming from an atheist like himself.

Father Angelo read his mind. 'Angelo.'

'Angelo. Yes. Thanks for sparing the time.'

'So, we meet again. The Lord certainly acts in many a strange way,' the priest alluded to their last conversation six months earlier, discussing the afterlife, or lack thereof.

'Well I ... '

'It's all right Jameson. We are all entitled to our own opinion. So, you want some translation done eh? Italian to English.'

'Yes.' Jameson went on to explain the diary and its mysteries. He finally took Vince Renzo's diary from his leatherwork satchel and opened it at page one. 'There are also hundreds of photos that came with this.'

Father Angelo said nothing. He leant forward and concentrated on the diary like it was a rare tome from the Vatican. He read excerpts from random pages then looked at an assortment of black and white photos Jameson had selected. Finally, he leant back in his desk chair, an old artificial leather-covered swivel with a broken arm.

'I knew this man, Signor Renzo,' the priest said. 'Quite well in fact.'

'Oh,' Jameson said. 'Did you know his real name was Peppe Ricardo Drago?'

'The Dragon,' Father Angelo huffed an involuntary laugh. 'Yes I did actually. But we never discussed it and I figured he had something to hide. Many Italian immigrants had shady pasts from the war years. But he was a law-abiding citizen here, so who was I to stir the pot? He was a good catholic and attended mass here regularly. He lived in Little Arthur Street not a kilometre from here … but you knew that. That's where you purchased the diary is it not?'

'Yes.' Jameson cut to the chase. 'I know he talks of Pompeii in the diary and I know he was in the area in 1944 when the allied forces liberated Naples from the Nazis.' Father Angelo looked questioningly at Jameson. 'Romilda,' Jameson explained. 'One of my kitchen ladies, translated little bits here and there.'

'Romilda Amorosa and her husband Mario.'

'This is their church too huh?' Jameson said.

'Indeed, most of the Italian community worship here.' The priest was about to suggest Jameson try it some time, but thought better of it. 'Signor Renato mentioned once that he was a soldier stationed in Naples during the war. He told me he met Mussolini once, with a security contingent. He spoke freely about those years as a twenty-three-year-old soldier. And yes, he was also there in 1944 when the allied forces took Naples in the four days liberation war as he called it. This time without a uniform.'

Jameson thought hard then decided *if you can't trust a priest who can you trust?* 'Father … ah Angelo.'

The priest leant forward like he was in the confessional booth. 'Yes Jameson.'

'Have you heard of the lost city of Vataea?'

'That was the name of one of the towns when Vesuvius buried Pompeii was it not?' The man of god had studied ancient and modern histories.

'Yes, that's the one. Turn to the back of the diary. You'll see where I have marked the page with a yellow sticker.

'Oh yes … Vataea. The word jumps out when you bring it to mind.'

'Could you translate that page please?'

Father Angelo scrolled down the page. He was a second-generation Italian- Australian of parents born in Pisa and was raised speaking Italian at home.

'Yes,' Father Angelo smiled. 'It is all very familiar to me and what I read here is totally believable. Vince Renzo was ... what can I say? A colourful character who lead a colourful, albeit ... shall I say unpredictable life.'

'Meaning?'

Father Angelo looked at Jameson carefully. He was not comfortable talking ill of the dead but ... *well, now he was gone ... And after all, everyone knew Vince Renzo twisted the rules, at times he was downright dishonest.*

'Signor Renzo ... Vince Renzo told me he learnt furniture restoration in Italy,' the priest started. 'He specialised in rococo and baroque to start with, restoring damaged pieces from the palaces and mansions of the rich, that had been looted by the Germans. He told me he even worked on war-damaged furniture in the Royal Palace. Then he became an accomplished wood carver and did much restoration in churches like San Paulo Maggiore. Ironically it was this underpaid and unappreciated restoration work for the church that got him in trouble.'

'How's that?'

'He acquired a taste for art treasures, many of which were on open display in churches and chapels. After the war, he travelled through the hill top villages of Tuscany and remote areas, visiting five and six-hundred-year-old chapels. Here he would visit a church, select an old painting or rare icon hanging high up on the church walls, mostly ill lit and in need of restoration. He would then meet with the local church authority and offer to restore the artwork for a mere pittance. Back in his makeshift workshops he would copy the painting, age it suitably and return the copy to the church where it would be re-hung and forgotten. Now he *owned* the originals, many were the works of such notables as Stefano Di Giovanni, Bellini or Botticelli ...'

'No!'

'Oh yes. He told me he even managed a small Leonardo da Vinci once. A Mother Mary and baby Jesus on a wood panel, which he sold to a private collector for five thousand US dollars. Of course, this all happened back in the 50s.'

'When did he tell you this, was it a confession?'

'Jameson. A priest must never divulge sins confessed to the Lord.'

'So? ... ah how them?'

'I knew Renato from the church here, ten years, until his recent death. I just think as he got older he wanted people to know the truth. In a way it *was* like a confession, and although he told me in confidence I know he told others in his lifetime. Some aspects were discussed openly.' Father Angelo thought a moment. 'He was a masterful potter as well.'

'Yes, I knew that.'

'Look.' The priest presented a small pottery dish from behind a pile of books on the desk. 'He gave me this.'

Jameson recognised the low shallow two-handled dish as a kylix from Attica, maybe 200 to 400 BC. The bread and butter plate sized bowl was decorated with Grecian soldiers complete with spears, swords and shields with their captives about to be beheaded. It was expertly executed but had the hallmarks of the fake he had purchased at the auction. Jameson held the kylix. He felt its weight and structure. It had clearly been fired at a higher temperature than the ancients could have managed and the heat had been too uniform in the kiln. The glaze also had the soapy feel about it that professor Gilbert Pitt had pointed out to him. And it stank of stale cigarettes.

Father Angelo noted Jameson's reaction. 'I use it as an ashtray ... with Vince's blessing of course.'

Jameson returned the dish and looked back to the diary. 'Vataea father ... Angelo. What has he written about Vataea?'

Father Angelo inspected the diary again. 'He has written here of Vataea because he discovered where it is buried.'

'Where?' Jameson asked a little too enthusiastically.

'He doesn't say where specifically. Well actually he hasn't discovered it. He says here that he was dealing with a man only known at Dita.' Father Angelo rechecked the translation. 'Yes Dita ... that's strange.'

'Why?'

'Well Dita means fingers in Italian.' The priest thought a moment. 'It's not an Italian name, it must be a ... well a nickname or a coded name.'

'Dita? D-i-t-a?'

'Yes. Fingers. I have a feeling this Dita person is not Italian.'

'Why?'

'Because it is not a typical nickname, if that's what it is, that would be bestowed on an Italian by Italians. It seems more English.'

'Hmm. Or Australian. What else of Vataea?' Jameson followed this blunt request with a latent 'please.'

'Well Victor has only mentioned the name Vataea once. He then writes here of his being shown genuine artefacts from the ancient town and then being asked to reproduce them. The originals were sold to wealthy collectors with the expertise to know what was genuine and what was not. The copies were mostly sold to occupying allies and later the many unwitting tourists who came to the west coast of Italy after the war. Mostly American and English ... oh and he rather smugly writes here that it was a pleasure to know they wasted their money on what they thought was Italy's ancient heritage.'

'He didn't sell direct then.'

'No. Clearly he was the faker. He must have sold them to a middleman. I doubt he would have worked for anyone, not in a business such as this.' Father Angelo noted the torn butt of several pages, clearly torn from the back of the diary. 'What's this?'

'Yes, I was hoping you could throw some light on that. Missing pages huh?'

The priest ran an eye over the last page. The writing had gotten lackadaisical, untidy. But the name of a village caught his eye, and then the name of a chapel. 'Cappella di san Vito Patiro and then San Sebastiano Al Vesuvio. I know of this place,' Angelo said. I had a colleague, Brother Ferdinando who helped raise funds for the restoration of neglected churches and chapels in Campania. It became an obsession with him. I remember him showing me photos of this chapel ... and others. Before and after photos, you know. This chapel, the Patiro, was one of his favourites, damaged in the 1944 eruption and restored in 2012. The chapel was built in the middle 18th century if I remember correctly.

'San Sebastiano huh?'

'Yes. San Sebastiano is on the western slopes of Vesuvius. It was buried under ash. But has been rebuilt since.'

'Could you please explain what is written at the bottom of the page here?' Jameson pointed to the last page before the missing sheets. 'There appears to be more names.'

'That is Bernardo Brunelleschi. But it doesn't say who he is.'

'Oh, and that? Jameson tapped the page with a finger. 'Riposare in pace?'

'Rest in peace.'

'Rest in peace?'

'Yes. Once again it is not exactly an Italian term but we all know what that means.'

'Hmm. Brother Fernando, Angelo. Where is he these days? I mean could we ask him about this chapel.'

'Brother Fernando is still studying for his priesthood. He is only twenty-five you see. He now studies theology at Italy's Pontifical Gregorian University.'

'In Rome?'

'Yes. His Eminence from the Seminary of the Good Shepherd in Sydney, where Brother Fernando lives, believes it is important for enthusiastic young seminarians to study in Rome in order to fully understand the church.' Father Angelo could read Jameson like a book. 'Would you like me to email him?'

'Could you? That'd be great.'

'I'll do better than that, I'll put you both in touch, Brother Fernando loves a good historic mystery.' Jameson waited while Angelo typed his details into his Mac. 'If you want more help,' the priest said. 'I'll need more time to read the whole diary.'

'Thanks. But I'm off to Italy Saturday so I'll need to hang onto it, sorry.'

'My! Italy! Is that a coincidence or did you just make a sudden decision?'

'A stroke of luck more like it. Elspeth has to go for work so I managed time off and will go with her.'

'Work in Italy? Didn't I see on the news where Vesuvius is stirring?'

'Only a little smoke. Anyhow we're flying into Rome; well up to the north.' Jameson explained the whole museum deal, then added. 'But I'll be shooting down to Naples for sure. I have to follow this up. I'd never forgive myself if I didn't. And if you could hook me up with Fernando that'd be great.'

'I'm sure you two will get on. I'll let him know you'll be in Rome and maybe you could meet him for a coffee?'

Jameson tucked the diary back in his satchel and made to leave.

'Jameson.'

'Yes Father?'

'I'd be very interested to hear how you go with all this, very interested indeed.

'I'll keep you posted.'

CHAPTER FIVE

The moment Jameson walked through Melanoma Cottage's door Elspeth pounced. A passionate wet kiss. Arms locked about his neck. One leg kicked back. 'There's no going back now,' she squealed with the exuberant grin of a lotto winner. Jameson returned the love. Elspeth pulled away and waved airline tickets in his face like hundred dollar bills.

'How far is Naples from Rome?' Jameson said out of nowhere.

'Naples? Why?'

'Well I thought … ah … we could train down, or hire a car. You know … sightsee.'

Elspeth stepped back, slightly incredulous.

'There's a smoking volcano there at the moment. Does the word Vesuvius ring any bells.'

'Yes and there is an ancient lost town of Vataea to discover. I'll be famous. We'll be famous.'

Elspeth remained calm. 'Jameson. I'm going to Rome on important museum business.'

'Yes. And I'm really proud of you. But … well … you know … the photos and the diary. Not *all* roads lead to Rome you know.'

'Huh, think you're funny don't you?'

'That was clever actually.' Jameson pressed his mobile conjuring up Siri, *his personal intelligent assistant,* as the mobile screen read. *How can I help you* Siri's robotic voice asked. 'Siri,' Jameson spoke into his mobile. 'How far is Naples from Rome?'

Siri answered. 'Rome, Italy is about 228 kilometres from Naples, Italy, by car. Or about 188 kilometres as the crow flies.'

Jameson pocketed his phone. 'Cool.'

'So is that the only reason you wanted to go? To skulk off down to Naples?'

'I saw Angelo this afternoon.'

'Father Angelo?'

'Yes. I told you …'

'And?'

Jameson told Elspeth all he had learnt from his meeting with the priest.

'But Naples!' The enthusiasm drained from Elspeth's eyes. 'Really?'

'Don't be like that,' Jameson noted the spark fade. 'This is the chance of a lifetime. I can train down for the night on my own while you hob-nob with the museum boys in Rome if you don't want to join me. I mean you only need two days in Rome, and it's not as if you haven't been before.'

'Fine.' Elspeth was remarkably composed. 'I'll just have to hob-nob, as you so eloquently put it, with Claire.'

'Claire?'

'Yes. We've been texting. She's going to fly over from London to join us … well me, anyhow.'

'Really?' Now it was Jameson's turn to be less than enthused. Hyperactive twenty-two-year-old Claire could be a handful, especially as a travel buddy; with her vivacious, flirtatious nature constantly attracting trouble. And with her long chestnut hair she was hardly unattractive. It was not as if Jameson disliked Elspeth's university friend, it was just that she was so scatty she could be annoying at times. And besides two was company and three … well.

'I thought you liked Claire,' Elspeth said.

'I do. It's just that every time she opens her mouth her brain falls out.'

'That's a bit harsh.'

'Hey, remember that time she drank too much champagne and scooped up a hand full of fish oil tablets and threw them into her mouth thinking they were liquorice bullets?'

'Yes,' Elspeth smiled at the memory. 'We were lucky she made it to the balcony to throw up.'

Jameson resigned himself to the thought of Claire's company. At least Elspeth would have a friend if she decided not to travel down to Naples with him. 'So,' he said, 'what time's our flight?'

Melanoma Cottage. Friday Morning. 7AM

Jameson sat at his kitchen table, two hands snug about a mug of hot coffee. He had been too excited to sleep. Out the window Storm Bay's waves were evident, frothy headed and chilly. Piled untidily about him on the table were a dozen antiquity auction catalogues loaned to him by professor Gilbert Pitt from the Tasmanian University. The dates ranged from the early sixties to the late nineties. He studied the photo on top of the pile and smiled. His perseverance had been rewarded. In a Christie's of London catalogue dated 1986 he was certain he had made a positive ID. The photo was black and white but the artwork was so similar to the fake Krater sitting on the table it had to be it. He read the caption below the photo:

Lot 127. Etruscan Krater with the figure of Charun holding his mallet. Circa 300BC. Estimate: 350 pounds.

Upstairs he heard Elspeth awaken. The TV sparked to life with an overbearing Harvey Norman commercial. 'Jameson,' Elspeth shouted down from the bedroom. 'News is on.'

'What.'

'News is about to start. I just saw a newsflash for Naples.' Jameson took to the spiral staircase three steps at a time. 'Naples has been put on full alert.' As they both stared at the screen the CNN reporter stood near the Bay of Naples with the smoking volcano in the background:

'With today's sophisticated technology scientists have identified three hazardous zones,' the reporter said. 'These immediate areas around Vesuvius have been allocated colours; red, yellow and blue and an evacuation plan is in place should the emergency arise. Also, the National Institute of Geophysics and Vulcanology, which monitors Vesuvius twenty-four-seven sends updates and warnings to the army and police to be on alert.'

The screen cut to the anchor-man in the CNN Rome studio. 'And what do we know about these colour zones?'

'The red zone is the area immediately surrounding the volcano.' The reporter's image was replaced by a map of Italy, suitably colour coded in the Campania area surrounding the volcano and encompassing Naples. This red zone is in greater danger of pyroclastic flows, or mixtures of gases and solids at high temperature which, at high speed can destroy in a short time everything in its path. But these pyroclastic flows will more than likely follow old routes of eruptions in the past making it possible to predict what areas will be affected by the flow. The red zone, where six-hundred-thousand people are at risk, would be evacuated by trains and busses. There are eighteen towns situated in this area, around Vesuvius. But the three million souls at risk in Naples would be a more difficult operation. The yellow zone you see here on the chart corresponds to the area affected by the pyroclastic particles like ash and lapilli, should there be an eruption, which would create a burden on roofs of buildings and cause collapse,' the reporter said with suitable drama. 'These particles, I have been told, may also cause problems to air traffic, although at this stage the northerly wind is sending the volcanic ash south and away from cities like Rome or the northern cities of Florence or Venice.'

'This doesn't look good,' Elspeth sat up in bed with her arms hugging her knees to her chest. 'God I hope our flight's not cancelled.'

'Nar,' Jameson tried to remain positive. 'Look at Etna a couple of years ago, and then that volcano disruption in Iceland. It'll blow over, if you'll excuse the pun ...'

Elspeth waved a hand to silence him ...

The reporter continued 'The blue zone that you see here falls within the yellow zone, but is subject to other problems like fallout of ash and lapilli or mud flows. The residents of the red zone would be moved before the eruption.' The reporter moved from the path of emergency workers conducting a fire drill. This also made for a more dramatic backdrop for his report. 'I should mention here,' the reporter went on. 'That each of the eighteen municipalities in the evacuation zones have already been assigned a neighbouring municipality where the residents would be safe to continue daily life, and, where activities like school could continue. I have here an expert, Roberto Guadagna from the Vesuvio Emergency Plan.' The camera panned to a rather conservative-looking man, with contrasting wild hair teasing in the breeze blowing in off the Mediterranean.

'Signor Guadagna, please explain to our viewers the procedure should there be an emergency.'

'It is expected that, as in the worst eruption in recent centuries, like the one in 1631, only 10% of the yellow zone would actually suffer damage. But of course volcanos are notoriously unpredictable and the effect can only be more accurately forecast when the height of the eruption column and the direction of the wind is determined. This yellow zone effects the provinces of Avellino, Benevento, Salerno and Naples.'

'Hear that,' Elspeth frowned. 'Naples.'

The expert continued. 'In 1631, the eruption was totally unexpected. At around 7am darkness fell over the entire area with continuous earthquakes every few minutes. At about 2am a heavy rainfall created mudslides of volcanic ash mixed with debris and melted snow – it was December you understand. Buildings in its path toppled. At about 11:00AM on the second day, after continuous earthquakes, a large mass of ash, gas and stones shot out of the crater and spilled down on all sides of the erupting cone, covering it almost completely. Reports at the time speak of the apparent disintegration, or liquefaction, of the mountain. The flowing pyroclastics sped downward along the main valleys, destroying all vegetation and buildings in its path and killing all living peoples in its way. Some 10 minutes later, a five-metre tsunami caused by earthquakes hit the shores. When the eruption was over, at least 3000 and maybe up to 6000 people were dead.

Reporter. 'It last erupted in 1944 did it not?'

'Yes, that is correct. That eruption caused minor damage really, in comparison to other eruptions, but still twenty-six people died. The village of San Sebastiano took the brunt of it as a slow-moving wall of volcanic rock, lava and debris crushed and burned everything in its path. It was well documented by US newsreels at the time, by crews here to film the allied landings.'

The Rome studio was quick to locate footage and the famous 1944 newsreel played, showing the ten-metre wall of molten lava devouring the village and toppling its church spire.

'There have been more than thirty eruptions since the one that buried Pompeii,' the reporter said. 'What are your predictions today?'

'That's put him on the spot,' Jameson was tiring of the journalistic sensationalism.

'It wouldn't be a pretty picture,' the expert looked forlorn. 'Given its past potential Vesuvio could wipe out the city of Naples, three million people. But of course the other scenario would be a repeat of 1944, where the lava flow settled down the slopes of the mountain before doing too much damage.'

CNN. 'So it is not all gloom and doom?'

'I sincerely hope not. But the mountain is not to be taken lightly.'

'Well you heard it here first on CNN. Naples could quite easily be Vesuvius's next victim. Thankyou Signor Guadagna,' the reporter looked more than pleased with his report. 'That was Signor Guadagna of the Vesuvio Emergency Plan here in Naples.'

Elspeth swung her legs off the bed and stood, naked, stretching her muscles. Her long silky black hair settled half way down her olive skinned back. Elspeth chose to ignore Jameson's dancing eyes and snatched a discreet look in the mirror. 'So are you still keen to go to Naples?'

Jameson caught her mood. 'Sensationalism.' He scooped up the remote and hit mute. He shook his head in disgust. 'Bloody journalists always hamming it up and trying to cause panic.'

Elspeth's eyes scrolled down the full-length mirror. 'I'll just have fruit for breakfast thanks.'

Palazzo della Questura. Via Medina. Naples. 8AM

Police Headquarters was buzzing. The austere, square and sobering grey eight-storey building of concrete and iron was on high alert. Vesuvio was smouldering and an eruption, albeit minor, seemed imminent and Rome was sending troops to help with emergencies and guard the city. The good citizens of Naples were nervous. And the bad ... well they prayed for anarchy.

Vice Sovrintendente Renato Di Stefano gulped his espresso double shot. He had spent too long arguing with his superior, the sovrintendente capo Bruno Esposito. Now his coffee was cold. He winced, smacking his lips and headed directly for the lifts and to the holding cells. His prisoner, the wounded Sicilian tombaroli known to be Pasquale Guagliardi, had been transferred to an interview room, three metres by four, steel panelled walls and a bulletproof two-way mirror.

Di Stefano stepped into the antechamber behind the mirror where his subordinate, Dino Abandonato, watched a police medico apply finishing touches to what was only a superficial bullet wound. Secretly Abandonato was thankful he had not actually killed the man. Di Stefano watched the tombaroli through the mirror. 'Anything?'

Abandonato. 'Nothing signor.'

Di Stefano caught Abandonato glancing at his watch. 'I've been with the capo della polizia,' he told his colleague of the chief of police. The fool is not concerned with this scum stealing our treasures and selling to the highest bidder. He fears Vesuvio more than the mafia.' Abandonato said nothing. These were strong words and provocative and he wanted nothing to do with it. Di Stefano waited for the medico to leave, leaving the prisoner alone with one wrist handcuffed to the leg of the interview table. 'Don't let anyone enter this viewing room, got it?'

'Si signor.'

Di Stefano entered the interview cell. He threw a phone book on the table and spun the chair, back to front, and sat with his with legs spread wide and his arms resting on the back of the chair facing the prisoner. He pressed record on the mandatory recorder. Intro complete he asked immediately. 'Who were the other two men?'

'Silence.'

'I said ... '

'I don't know. Never seen them before.'

'Maybe. Maybe not. But I still think you know who they were. Or at least who sent them.'

Silence.

'Who are you taking orders from?' Nothing. 'I said ... '

'You got a cigarette?'

'Cigarettes kill. Don't you know that.'

Silence.

'Who's the boss? Give *me* something and I'll toss *you* something ... like tell the judge you co-operated. You'll get a reduced sentence.'

'Reduced sentence for what. So, I met some people at 4AM. So what. I've done nothing illegal.'

'Oh? You pulled a gun on an officer of the law.'

Silence.

'I saw you loading heavy items into the van. What were they?'

No answer.

'You just don't get it do you. I know you're down the bottom of the ladder. Small fry supplier. So why protect those arseholes who are making the millions. Huh?'

Silence.

Di Stefano's eyelid twitched. He could feel his impatience weakening. 'I'll ask you one more time. What did you load into the van?'

The prisoner grew more arrogant. 'Garden ornaments.'

Di Stefano's reaction was swift. He jumped to his feet, stabbed a finger onto the recorder 'off' button, snatched the phone book and belted the prisoner about the head. Abandonato behind the mirror stiffened. He rushed to the door and checked the corridor. All was clear. He twisted back to the two-way mirror.

'What did you load into the van?' Di Stefano now hovered over the prisoner who jerked at his cuffed wrist while cowering, ready for the next blow. 'Nothing … j-just some old garden statues … copies made of concrete … eighty years old no more …'

'Figlio di puttanta! You lie you son of a whore. They were statues from Baiae weren't they. A statue of Venus stolen from the Bay five years ago. What were the other bundles. Tell me or so help me I'll see you spend years behind bars. Well?' Di Stefano leant over the man like a starved predator. 'Answer me.'

'Ma' va te ne a fanculo!'

Slam!

The phone directory crashed into the side of the man's face. The prisoner cried out in pain. 'No. *You* go fuck yourself, tombaroli!' Di Stefano swung the book high, ready for a relaunch.

'Wait!' Pasquale Guagliardi threw his free hand up to protect his head. 'Please … no more.'

'Well?'

'You'll put in a good word for me.'

'If you tell me the truth.'

'And no one will know I talked, right?'

'Si.' Di Stefano dropped the book back onto the table and pressed 'record.'

Museo Di Anatomia Umana.
5 Via Luciano Armanni. Naples. 8AM

The Museum of Human Anatomy, housed in the old Monastery of Saint Patricia, closed every August. For the small investment of three thousand Euros to the janitor – the museum was the perfect temporary centre of operations for Cambino Salvi Cardinale and his antiquity 'business.'

And now Vesuvio erupts! Who would have guessed.

Moving shop was a constant necessity when 'in the field,' as Cambino liked to call his operations in Campania, Sicily and Tuscany.

Cambino Salvi Cardinale was known to a rare few. And known by even fewer still by the name his Sicilian parents bestowed upon him. In the trade he was known only as Uomo di Specchi; or Man of Mirrors. Whether his love of antique mirrors blossomed through vanity, or simply the passion for mirrored glass that had groomed souls throughout history, no one knew. Certainly no one was going to ask. The fiercely private self-made multi-millionaire had risen from the rubble of poverty in Palermo. Now he was king of the pile, amassing his fortunes from beneath the ruins left behind by his ancient ancestors.

Fifty-eight-year-old Cambino had cut his teeth looting as a youth, digging at night at the ancient city of Morgantina, an archaeological site in central east Sicily. With the closest modern village of Aidone two kilometres away it was a looters paradise. Cambino stole through the night breaking into tombs to claim pots and grave goods. And one summer's night he hit the jackpot finding a 4th century BC beaten gold phiale, or libation bowl, decorated with acorns, beechnuts and bees. He sold it to a black marketeer in Palermo for six hundred US dollars. Seventeen-year-old Cambino discovered later that the dealer had sold it for twenty thousand US dollars to an overseas collector. This information had a profound effect on the young tomb robber and he vowed and declared that in the future he would deal and not dig. *Let some other fool do the dirty work* he told himself. *I will be the best in the business.*

That was forty-one years earlier.

He moved up the ladder of snakes swiftly. Cambino owned his first Mercedes at twenty-one; brand new from the showrooms of Frascati in Rome. He paid cash. However, success had come at a price well above gold. The Man of Mirrors – with the attractive dark features, legacy of a Moroccan ancestor, and the salt and pepper hair of an elderly gentleman – was wheelchair bound. He lost the use of both legs in a car accident on highway SS163 on Italy's Amalfi Coast in 2006. Besides his handicap life had been good. He continued to amass wealth with the ease of a ruthless businessman unafraid of taking risks.

And then came the blow no one wants to hear about.

The news of the tumour eating away at his bowel came like a blow from Vulcans hammer. The chemotherapy along with radiation therapy had sent the cancer into remission. But of late, the past few months, niggling symptoms had returned. Abdominal pains, bloating and loss of appetite had all run up the red flag.

'Ciao.' Cambino completed the call with a middleman in Houston he only knew as Ron and slipped his hundred thousand Euro GoldVish luxury mobile, by Emmanuel Gueit, into the coat pocket of his coal black William Fioravanti suit; thirty thousand dollars. The suit hugged perfectly his silk Giorgio Armani shirt. Mauve. Eight hundred dollars. He inspected his Salvatore Ferragamo Python Loafers. Black; two thousand six hundred dollars. They didn't need laces; the shoes had platinum shackle style buckles. He adjusted his cuff links. These grotesque little items were made of gold taken from the teeth of holocaust victims and re-moulded into the shape of molars; thousand dollars the pair on the black market.

There was no mirror on hand in the Museo Di Anatomia Umana so Cambino manoeuvred his wheelchair amongst the museum displays, stopping in front of a tall specimen jar displaying baby Siamese twins. He read the label. They died in 1887. Their stillborn corpses pickled in formalin were in remarkable condition. They gazed back in some kind of macabre embrace. He caught a distorted reflection of himself in the glass and adjusted his white silk Ralph Lauren tie; three hundred and fifty dollars.

Cambino did not hear the door to the fire exit open and close behind him. But the scent of the woman heralded his companion. Her fresh sweat misted with a stairwell draught and drifted lazily before him. He turned to greet his protector.

'Drishya.'

'Cambino. Here you are,' she said in her husky soft voice. 'I should have known. In here with all the ghoulish displays that so fascinate you.'

Man of Mirrors gazed long and hard at this most beautiful of creatures. Drishya was Indian. But Caucasian interference somewhere in her background lightened her skin to a milk chocolate; in comparison to the dark chocolate skin of the peasants in the Northern Indian village where she grew up. Today, as per usual, she looked stunning. Her body an hourglass of toned muscle. She wore a purple toga, one shoulder exposed and a gold leaf embroidered orange silk scarf over her raven black hair. Cambino knew she was twenty-six, but she looked much younger. Her skin was smooth as stainless steel; her crystal clear eyes a rich dark brown and she could deliver a smile to crush the mettle of any man. But to Cambino – thirty-two years her senior and wheelchair bound – Drishya was more a daughter. The daughter he never had. And on Drishya's part, she had grown fond of the man over the seven years they had been together and Cambino was the father she never really knew.

In return Drishya offered protection. She was trained from the age of nine in martial arts and had been indoctrinated by masters in eastern Asia with Triad connections. Drishya had been at Cambino's side since she was eighteen when he financed her studies for a master's degree in ancient civilisations. He had made her a wealthy woman who returned boundless respect and protection.

Cambino's sharp ear heard the reversing beeps of a vehicle in the laneway two storeys below. He wheeled to the museum gallery window craning his neck to peer out discreetly, watching the red van back up the alley. Close by emergency sirens blared. They had been constant since the earth tremors.

'These tremors,' he said over his shoulder as he stared out the window. 'They are unsettling. Have you seen Vesuvio this morning? The ash appears to be getting worse.'

Drishya nodded. 'We will be free to return to Venice soon. More importantly, look at this.' Drishya unwrapped a parcel she had placed next to a display case, waiting for this moment. It was a bronze head of Bacchus with the giveaway green patina of excavation. 'Bacchus,' she explained. 'Bronze. Well cast, handsome features, typical of the first century ... '

Cambino. 'Part of an oil lamp is it not?'

'Exactly.'

Cambino knew it had great importance, as Drishya would not normally waste his time with anything trivial. 'Well?'

'It came from a vineyard eleven kilometres south-east of Vesuvio. Dug at three metres.' Drishya noted her boss's eye twitch with recognition. 'Found amongst the remains of a private dwelling.' she added.

'Could it be a random villa?'

'No. I am told the site is widespread.'

'So are you suggesting it is possibly Vataea?' They had recently spoken of Vataea and rumours were about that the ancient town had been discovered. But they *were* only rumours. Drishya's smile answered his question. Man of Mirrors eyes softened in a daydream.

Vataea.

The lost city had eluded scholars for centuries. It was buried somewhere in the Campania foothills or plains. But under several metres of ash and two thousand years of modern civilisation, finding its whereabouts seemed an impossibility.

'Vataea,' he repeated in a whisper. 'Just think of its riches. A time capsule of ancient Rome. Bronze statues worth hundreds of thousands each, frescos worth millions, trinkets like this lamp worth tens of thousands ... each! Do the math.'

Drishya smiled knowingly. But she knew there was a far greater attraction to Vataea for the Man of Mirrors.

'And the *Lance of Destiny*,' Drishya almost whispered as if each pickled deformity in the museum was listening. 'Do you really think you can find it?'

'Undoubtedly my dear.'

Both Cambino and Drishya had read the transcripts made from the papyrus scrolls incinerated by Vesuvio's pyroclastic blast in 79AD. These scrolls were stored away as unreadable carbonised artefacts until recently, when a scientific breakthrough enabled conservators to X-ray and read them.

'You see,' Cambino had explained to Drishya. 'Conservators realised that the ink the scribes had used over 2000 years ago contained large traces of metals, including lead. And by using an X-ray microscope they could see what was written on these scrolls. Many were destined for Pliny the Elder's private villa but as you know he died that black day as well.'

'Fascinating. And the map?'

'Yes ... the map.' Cambino had explained to Drishya that of particular interest to scholars was one scroll that spoke of a retired centurion called Aulis Cethegus who was entrusted with a holy relic by the Roman governor of Judea Province, Gessius Florus, during the first Jewish-Roman War. 'A war which we now know was started in the year 66,' Cambino said. 'The great revolt as it was also called was fanned by Roman and Jewish ethnic tensions. Gessius Florus demanded extra taxes from the Jews and he plundered the Jewish Temple claiming all moneys for the emperor Nero.'

'That's when the lance was looted, yes?'

'Yes. But the results were devastating with Gessius having to flee Judea and return with the Syrian army to help quell the riots. Six thousand Romans were massacred before Cethegus was sent home to Vataea. Amongst the loot from the Jewish Temple was that Holy relic spearhead which, as I told you, Cethegus was charged with safekeeping.' Cambino rolled the bronze head of Bacchus in his hand. He savoured its weight and wondered at its history. 'For thirteen years,' he continued explaining to Drishya. 'This Holy relic remained hidden in a wall cavity in the humble house of loyal Cethegus. He had awaited instruction all this time. None came. Then in 79AD, as you well know, Vesuvio entered the story. The incinerated scrolls tell of Aulis Cethegus' flight with his family from the volcano to Herculaneum ... and, more importantly, the map tells of the location of the holy relic. Hidden in the cavity on the north side of his peristyle. We can only assume Cethegus was killed in Herculaneum. However his map, drawn and signed by Cethegus himself, confirms the lance head was used to pierce the chest of the crucified Jesus of Nazareth, a holy relic revered even then by the Jews of Jerusalem until, it was looted by the Roman Governor Gessius Florus ...'

'And,' Drishya said aloud, remembering the transcript. '*We know it was hidden by me, Aulis Cethegus, in the house of Cethegus opposite Atticus the Fuller ...* '

'Yes. Near the Plaza of the Leopard Fountain south of Philo Vestalis the Baker. Find Vataea and X marks the spot.'

'It won't be that easy Cambino,' Drishya voice purred softly.

'No it won't. But we must look Drishya. We must persevere.'

'Do you really believe it has healing powers?' Drishya asked.

'To the true believer, yes,' Cambino wheeled to the next window and watched the red van waiting at the roller doors below. 'The lance was written about in the Gospel of John; 19:31-37,' he went on. '*One of the soldiers pierced Jesus side with a lance and immediately there came out blood and water.* The scriptures even recorded the name of this soldier, Longinus.'

Drishya nodded warmly. She had heard it all before.

Cambino lifted Bacchus from where the jolly wine drinking god listened silently on his knee, and inspected the ancient craftsmanship once more. 'Who's dig is this?' Cambino asked of the dozens of tombaroli who were in his pocket.

'Marchetti and Ricco Ricci.'

'They're good operators. Keep an eye on them.'

Two floors down the roller door squealed on its rusted chain. Cambino wheeled to his temporary work desk where he watched the red van enter the garage on his split screen monitor. 'This van, this is Pasquale Guagliardi is it not?'

'Yes.'

'With the marble Venus from Baiae.'

'Yes. And two other marbles from the same area.' Drishya headed back to the fire stair with the ease of a model on the cat-walk; pausing at the last moment to declare over her shoulder. 'They're late. Keep an eye on your monitor, let me know if you are unsatisfied with what you see.'

Loading Bay. Two floors down.

'You're four hours late. Why?'

The first Sicilian, the driver of the red van had had dealings with Drishya before. He fidgeted. 'We had trouble.'

'Trouble! What trouble?'

'Carabinieri.'

'Carabinieri. Where?'

'At the pickup. Guagliardi was shot ... '

'Shot! Killed?'

'No, I don't think so, but surely he's been arrested. We made the pickup after 4AM but were ambushed. The police were waiting. We lay low before coming here, in case we were followed. That's why we are late.'

The other Sicilian deliveryman – a stocky and rather ugly man with a large nose and wide nostrils – had opened the back of the van and stood waiting. He glared at Drishya, taken by her beauty but not impressed with his partner's kowtow response to this arrogant woman. 'Enough of the talk,' he said sourly. 'Piero. Give me a hand with this.'

Drishya ignored the man's presence. 'How many police?' she asked Piero.

'Only two I think,' the driver said. 'We managed to escape. They shot at us for Christ's sake.'

'Hey Piero!' the other man persisted.

Drishya. 'Only two you say. That sounds like the culture police.'

'That's what *I* thought.'

'Which means … '

'Piero, for Christ's sake …'

'Who is this man?' Drishya said coldly, without facing the other man.

'Guido,' Piero said.

'Guido who?'

'Guido the stud,' Guido said with impertinence. 'So unless you want a real man stop the small talk and … '

Two floors up in the gallery Man of Mirrors grinned at the monitor. Fool, he laughed to himself.

Drishya's answer was swift and calculated. Her gloved hand darted out at the speed of a toad's tongue. Her fingers of steel encompassed Guido's neck and squeezed. The man choked a cough. Pinioned at arms-length he threw a futile punch. Drishya's other hand shot forward, stabbing a taloned finger up each nostril. She lifted and tore backwards ripping the man's nose. He screamed in pain as blood spouted from the wound.

'Get unloaded and get out.' Drishya looked to her own crew. Three men in the shadows of the loading bay who waited her orders. 'Help them and see this place is locked down fast. Ten minutes.'

Galley of Human Anatomy. Second floor.

Drishya glided between the cabinets of the macabre to Cambino watching the monitor. He looked suitably proud. 'You heard all that?' she said.

'Heard it,' he answered softly, his voice breaking with emotion. 'I felt the man's pain.'

'Not that. Did you hear the Carabinieri have possibly arrested Pasquale Guagliardi.'

'Yes. I heard that too.'

'The man owes us nothing. He will talk, certainly. We need to move on.'

'Pity.' Cambino picked up a calcified foetus on its wooden stand resting on his desk. The time faded label read that the specimen had remained in the body of a woman for twenty-eight years and was only discovered in her womb when she died. 'I was just starting to enjoy the ambience here,' he said in a tone he knew humoured Drishya.

Drishya looked out the window and watched the gate close. The van had departed.

'Venezia?' she asked.

'Si. Venezia. But I need you to follow up this Vataea lead. I was beginning to believe the place was a myth. Now this.' His hand stroked the Bacchus lamp. 'A two-metre by two-metre mosaic from Pompeii bought 1.2 million on the black market last month. Vataea would be hiding hundreds of them.'

'Do the math,' Drishya smiled.

'Yes goddess, do the math.'

Palazzo della Questura. Via Medina. Naples. 8.45PM

'Uomo di Specchi! Man of Mirrors.' Vice Sovrintendente Renato Di Stefano rubbed the stubble on his chin. He hadn't slept for fifteen hours and was growing fatigued and impatient. He snapped at his prisoner Pasquale Guagliardi. 'What kind of bullshit name is that?'

'That's all I know. Honest.'

Di Stefano put a hand back on his torture weapon of choice, the Naples phone book.

'That is the truth,' the prisoner pleaded, his head throbbing from the last clout. 'I have asked around, and the man is a ghost. You must believe me. No one has ever seen him.'

'Well how do you do your dealings with him.'

'A woman. I don't know her name either and rarely see her. She is beautiful, like a model, tall and slim. Graceful. And dark skinned. Indian I think.'

'Hmm. So how do you contact *her*?'

'Through a series of phone numbers. Sometimes as many as three.'

'Give them to me.'

'I only have the one number.' Pasquale Guagliardi tapped a finger to his head. 'Up here. I call and it gets passed on.'

Di Stefano looked into the two-way mirror and nodded to his own reflection. He knew his colleague Dino Abandonato was listening on the other side of the glass. Abandonato entered the interview room a moment later and passed his supervisor the prisoner's mobile.

Di Stefano inspected the mobile, and then passed it to his prisoner. 'Call the number.'

'But I ... '

'Call the number. Now.'

'What will I say?'

'Say you have a marble bust. That is of an important man, maybe a senator, dug from an unknown villa in ... ' Di Stefano thought a moment. 'Found near Sorrento.' The carabinieri leant in close to his quarry. His eyes narrowed and Guagliardi caught his hot angry breath on his face. 'And no funny business.'

The prisoner called the number. It was answered immediately. 'Ciao.'

'This is Pasquale ... ' pause ... 'Pasquale ... yes. I need to contact Uomo di Specchi ...' pause. 'I have a fine piece, from a previously unexcavated villa near Sorrento ... a marble bust. The best I've ever seen dug. It is possibly a senator.' Pause. 'Ciao.'

Di Stefano snatched the phone the moment the call was disconnected. 'Well.'

'We have to wait. They'll call back.'

'How long?'

'I don't know. Sometimes it takes hours.'

Di Stefano sighed heavily. He studied his prisoner a moment, with his wrist handcuffed to the table leg.

'Sometimes they call back quickly. A marble bust is a big prize so maybe sooner than later.'

Di Stefano said nothing. Leaving his prisoner, he went to fetch coffee and a cigarette from one of the smokers in the building. He returned with a lit cigarette and passed it to his prisoner and joined his colleague behind the mirror.

On the wall in the interview room antechamber a small television flashed 'breaking news.' The two men watched in silence for a moment as footage of boiling lava broached fissures in Vesuvio's crater wall and slowly, menacingly, rolled down the north-west slope. Di Stefano looked to the looter's mobile in his hand and sipped his espresso.

'What are your plans sir?' Dino Abandonato asked him.

'We wait.'

Museo Di Anatomia Umana. 5 Via Luciano Armanni. Naples. 9.15AM

In the loading bay of the museum the Man of Mirror's beautiful protector, Drishya supervised the recent acquisitions of the marble Venus and two other pieces from the sunken city of Baiae in the Bay of Naples. One, the torso of the goddess Diana, Drishya thought, should fetch a handsome price; quarter of a million at least. But the other of a naked child, a boy, that was once a fountain ornament, would bring much less. Twenty thousand maybe, she guessed.

The pieces were wrapped in plastic sheets and surrounded by liquid foam before being placed in custom made crates for transport to a waterfront storage warehouse; an old disused tobacco factory in an industrial area of Venice. The crates were marked garden ornaments or exterior furniture. Neither the warehouse storemen nor the carpenter – all ex-prisoners – knew of the next destination. They were paid well to keep their mouths shut and knew the consequences for a loose tongue was certain death. They had all heard stories of human remains discovered weighted down with concrete boots at the bottom of the bay.

Yes, Drishya smiled. The enterprise was a well-oiled and secretive endeavour and the alluring Indian was fiercely proud to be a part of it. Her mobile played Wagner's *Ride of the Valkyries*. She swiped the screen.

'Yes.' Drishya recognised the dealer's voice immediately. She relaxed. The contact spoke of a marble bust of a man, dug at a previously unrecorded site. He explained that his contact thought the fine regal bust was that of a senator.'

'Have you seen it?'

'No, of course not. And the man says it is too ... shall we say fresh ... to send a photo in case it is intercepted. But the source is reliable, a man who buys only quality. He is based in Naples.'

'Name?'

'Guagliardi ... Pasquale Guagliardi ... '

Drishya's hairs bristled. 'I'll call you back.'

Drishya swept into the gallery on the second floor, her toga sweeping behind her like a silk sheet drying in a sea breeze. Cambino turned at her approach, catching a glimpse of her long slender leg before urgency demanded his full attention.

'We must leave immediately!' She explained the call. 'It's a set up. Guagliardi is in custody. The police have put him up to this.'

'What of the source caller.'

'My guess is that he is an innocent pawn. We can't take the risk. We need to evac ... now!'

'Alright. Notify Lagoste. What will you do about the contact?'

'I'll set up a false rendezvous.'

'Excellent. Two weeks away has been enough. I miss Poveglia already.'

Palazzo della Questura. Via Medina. Naples. 9.40AM

The obnoxious stink of sulphur permeated the streets of Naples as Vesuvio's fine ash dusted the streets like powdered-sugar on cannoli. Housewives brought in their washing, freeing up balconies. They closed windows and shutters. Shopkeepers kept their wares indoors while vehicles slowed, their windscreen wipers barely clearing. The mood on the streets, Di Stefano was aware, was one of sombre excitement. All about the city television sets broadcast news updates on the temperamental mountain:

'The conditions are very similar to the eruption of 1944,' the newsreader commented. 'Authorities insist there is no need for panic. However an explosion within the crater this morning at 7.06AM ruptured an inner crust with lapilli and scoria thrown 150 metres into the air ... '

Immediately *Breaking News* scrolled across television screens..

'We now have footage from a news helicopter over the volcano that lava is exposed deep within the crater. We will cross live shortly to cameras on the ground where it's reported the army are already evacuating residents there.' The newsreader was briefly interrupted by information on his desktop screen. 'I have also been informed it appears this eruption is to be a repeat of 1944, and all eruptions since 1631, including the 1906 eruption. In other words Naples is in no immediate danger. I repeat Naples is in no immediate danger.'

Di Stefano changed channels. Similar footage aired of a smoking volcano, but from a different direction. Different helicopter. 'We have here in the studio Signor Navali from the Vesuvio Observatory,' the reporter announced. 'Whose responsibility it is to inform the Civil Commission Department who in turn consult the experts in the National Commission for the prediction and prevention of major risks created in an emergency.'

'For the record,' Signor Navali stated. 'I would like to say Vesuvio's behaviour at this stage, however, is not necessarily indicative of an imminent eruption. All could easily turn to normal and not affect the population.'

'Sounds positive.' Di Stefano said optimistically. Suddenly the looter's mobile shrilled in Di Stefano's hand; a god-awful electronic alien attack phone ring.

No caller I.D.

He rushed into the interview room. 'Answer it. Arrange to meet at one of your usual rendezvous locations in two hours time ... '

'But I ... '

'Shut it! Tell them another buyer is interested and two hours from now is all you've got.'

The carabinieri slammed the mobile hard into Gaugliardi's chest. 'Ciao,' the prisoner said. The police listened. Clearly the person on the other mobile was doing the talking. Di Stefano held up two fingers, he shook them angrily in his prisoner's face. *Two hours*, he mouthed silently tapping his watch.

'Si si ... Etna.' The prisoner looked at Di Stefano's watch. 'Midday. Si.' He disconnected.

'Etna!' Di Stefano scowled.

'Etna Pizzeria,' the prisoner said. 'It's at Via Filangieri Piazza. It's busy there. We meet at the back of the restaurant.'

Museo Di Anatomia Umana. 5 Via Luciano Armanni.
Naples. 11.30AM

With only eight pieces of ancient statuary remaining to worry about, Drishya's supervision saw the crated artefacts off the premises within the hour. They were packed into a freight container amongst assorted vintage garden furniture on the flat tray of a truck and now headed for the train station in Naples. Here they were destined for Venice where the city of islands and endless waterfrontage made distribution easier. In Venice they would await collection in a few days.

Now only the Etruscan ossuary needed attention. This magnificent and extremely rare and desirable piece had been sold to a private collector in Houston for 1.3 million US dollars. The clay fired sarcophagus originally made for a wealthy woman two-and-a-half thousand years earlier – with a life sized figure of the recipient reclining on the full length of the lid – had been cut into three sections, to be freighted separately. At its final destination an expert antiquities restorer would re-attach the pieces. This was a common practise to fool the authorities.

Usually the pieces were hidden amongst furniture to be exported by sea to Dubai where they were then airfreighted to the United States via India. From the United States a provenance could be forged. Many items ended up in private collections in the United Kingdom, Middle East or Europe with legitimate documentation that recorded their past history. A provenance. Maybe in a private American collection since 1950 or even earlier. Once this provenance was established Man of Mirrors could export from the United States without attracting too much attention. It was complicated, took time but the enterprise was most lucrative.

The ossuary, stolen from a previously undiscovered tomb in Tuscany, had been stored the past five years at The Geneva Freeport, a Swiss warehouse complex where goods of all descriptions could be stored in confidence without incurring taxes or duties or any questions asked. Cambino had used this facility for eighteen years now and had in storage thousands of ancient artefacts, all of which should be in museums. But now they languished in obscurity until the appropriate buyers could be found or until the stolen treasures had 'cooled off.'

Drishya watched the flat tray truck, with their crates hidden in a container of garden furniture, leave the premises for the train station. The driver Matteo and his brother-in-law Marco were simple folk. Local Neapolitan peasants whom Drishya knew she could trust. The safety of their families depended on it. She gave them a thousand Euros each with the guarantee of another five thousand to be transferred into their accounts once the items arrived safely in Venice. They were happy men. This was easy money.

Drishya punched the button to the loading bay door and the rusting roll of steel and peeling paint squealed and scraped as it closed behind the truck. She turned quickly and as she suspected the third man Christofano watched her with his unashamed lascivious leer. Christofano she did not trust. He had no family to threaten and there was no love lost between the pair.

'Well don't stand there,' Drishya's eyes narrowed. 'Get on with it.'

Christofano lifted the headphones from around his neck placing them defiantly over his ears. He cranked up the tunes and sat at the wheel of the forklift. Drishya watched patiently as he placed the three ossuary crates onto the tray of a Nissan pickup. The rear suspension lowered considerably and the front reared up noticeably. Drishya signalled to the man she was not happy with the positioning of the crates and jerked her head for him to get out of the forklift. Christofano jumped free, lighting a cigarette, as Drishya slipped onto the operator's seat. Christofano cranked up the music even further on his headphones and turned his back walking away to hide his irritation. Drishya saw her chance. She slammed the gear to forward and turned the forklift in a tight circle ...

Full throttle.

Christofano sensed the danger. But too late. He twisted about as the raised fork blade caught him in the throat. With Drishya's forward momentum he was thrown backwards against a brick wall where any chance to scream was severed as quickly as his head. The forklift jarred hard against the bricks and Christofano's head rolled along the lifting blade where it fell with a sickening thud to the concrete floor. Drishya reversed away and as the headless body crumbled down the wall she looked up into the security camera smiling to Cambino, who she knew was watching her handiwork.

Two floors above Cambino watched in awed admiration. Although the security monitor was in black and white he knew the black specks across Drishya's beautiful face were splashes of blood. He watched her stare into the monitor in silence, eventually sliding her tongue to where she could reach the closest drips.

Etna Pizzeria. Via Filangieri Piazza 12.40PM

Di Stefano turned to his colleague officer Abandonato. 'We've been stood up,' he sighed, then nodded to their prisoner Pasquale Guagliardi. 'Cuff him and return him to the prison van, but maintain vigilance and be certain you aren't seen. The bastard is probably out there somewhere. He either got spooked or saw us.'

'Will I wait for you sir,' Abandonato asked knowing his superior liked to walk –police headquarters was only ten blocks away.

'Yes, wait.' Di Stefano looked to the pizza cook busy at the wood fired oven. The man was skilfully wheeling a pizza blade, portioning a huge Margarita. 'How long Augusto?'

'Five minutes signor.'

Abandonato. 'You ordered pizza?'

'Why not? It's lunch time.' Di Stefano fished into his pocket for loose change that rattled somewhere deep.

Watching the police through the window from across the piazza was a nondescript Neapolitan in a grubby singlet, shorts and sandals as he chewed his bottom lip.

'Don't worry Dino,' Di Stefano said to his subordinate. 'I've ordered a large pizza so you can share.'

12.50PM. The pizzeria land line shrilled. The cook wiped floury hands down his apron and snatched up the receiver. 'Etna Pizzeria, ciao.'

'What did the polizia want?'

'Thank god you stayed away.'

'I'm just across the piazza idiot. How much do they know?'

The cook strained to peer out the front window. The area had cleared of passers-by and Vesuvio ash seemed to be thicker on the ground. But there was no sign of his colleague on the other end of the call. 'They know you didn't show up.'

'Don't get smart,' the colleague spat. 'That Pasquale's led them to your pizzeria. Now what?'

Palazzo della Questura. Via Medina. Naples. 1.30PM

'They must have been watching,' prisoner Pasquale Guagliardi told Di Stefano.

'Or you tipped them off,' Di Stefano scowled. 'Tipped them off somehow when you called. A coded word maybe. Do you know what the sentence is for selling Italy's treasures? It's up there with treason, pezzo di merda ... '

'I have one more address,' Pasquale said unexpectedly.

'Where?'

'I have heard talk of the Museo Di Anatomia Umana. It is closed during August but I hear it served as a temporary exchange point the past week or so.'

Dino Abandonato needed no orders. 'I'll organise a car signor.'

With Napoli's military and police resources stretched to the maximum because of the eruption there was to be no backup, no assistance from the police headquarters. Di Stefano however, did not care. He would have his day and catch these bastards sooner than later and he would have the last laugh up on that podium in front of thousands of fellow officers, as the president pinned a medal onto his chest.

The streets around the Museo Di Anatomia Umana at 5 Via Luciano Armanni, were deserted. The sky overhead was black and the sun a blood orange. Locals kept indoors. Army trucks were the only vehicles as they bulldozed the ash to the sides of the main thoroughfares for emergency access.

'There it is,' Di Stefano pointed to the handsome stone building, built in the late nineteenth century he guessed. The museum was on the first and second floors. Other floors were for administration. A loading bay and separate warehouse had been built on the ground floor. This access was around the back via a side lane. The gate was closed. 'Park there.' Abandonato parked across the lane entrance.

Di Stefano leant forward, close to the windscreen craning his neck to peer up at the façade through a windscreen-wiper cleared fan shape in the ash. . The building looked deserted. 'How in heaven's name does a museum get used as an antiquities thieve's den?'

'They close every August signor.'

'I know that but ... oh forget it.' Di Stefano climbed from the car and tried the gate. It was fastened with chain and padlock. He took bolt cutters from the boot of his unmarked police vehicle and was about to snip the gate when an armoured car rolled by and stopped. Di Stefano flashed his badge. No words were exchanged and the armoured vehicle moved on.

Di Stefano waited until the armoured vehicle turned a corner. 'You armed?' he asked his colleague.

'Of course.'

'Let's do this then.' They slipped through a narrow opening in the gate and, with semi-automatic double-barrel handguns drawn, they approached the roller door to the loading bay at the rear of the building. Di Stefano noted the recent tire tracks in the ash. 'They lead back to the gate and they're fresh over older layers of ash. I have a feeling we're too late.' The roller door was secured.

'Your bolt cutters won't work on that sir.'

'Your right. Try the side door.'

'Locked.'

'Keep an eye out.' Di Stefano attacked the door with the heel of his boot. The third kick was accompanied with a loud cracking sound of the wooden doorframe splintering. The door crashed open on the fourth attack.

'That was a bit too easy sir. You'd think a museum would have better security.'

'A museum of human anatomy! Why?'

With guns raised they took to the stairwell. 'We'll start at the second floor,' Di Stefano whispered. 'Then work our way to the loading bay.' With pistol in his right hand he reached for the door handle with his left.

Abandonato covered him, off to one side. 'Museum of Human Anatomy, what kind of museum *is* that exactly?' Abandonato said softly.

'Deformed foetuses for starters,' Di Stefano said with a forced smile. 'I remember coming here with a class when I was about ten.' The fire exit door swung open into the main exhibit room.

The younger policeman reeled back. He stood, gun poised, gaping down an ill lit hallway at showcase after showcase of human skeletons. The one closest was of a dissected corpse displaying all visceral workings.

'That's a plaster cast,' Di Stefano said of the exhibit. 'An antique one at that.' The two men stepped into the gallery, quietly closing the fire door behind them. Abandonato was unsettled by the displays. His head jarring left and right nervous for villains whilst his attention was disturbed by this amazing collection. He passed an entire wall of shelves crammed with glass jars containing deformed foetuses, whole or partial. Some were full term babies, hunched into glass containers of formalin for the entire world to see. Other jars contained severed heads; adult male, female or babies and all pickled – some with their brains removed for scientific study. All were a hundred years old or more.

The main exhibit hall was, maybe fifty metres long. White stucco pillars, in a nineteenth century baroque style supported an arched ceiling. The walls were white. The cabinets golden mahogany. And the exhibits decaying orange, yellows and browns. Some natural light filtered in through tinted windows while outside the sun struggled to penetrate the volcanic plume, offering a bushfire glow that amplified the macabre setting.

Abandonato felt the hairs on the back of his neck bristle. He was keen to move on. But one thing seemed certain. They were alone with the ghosts of scientific experiments. Di Stefano passed the wall of skulls; a thousand at least. All neat in rows and each with a number etched onto the forehead. He stopped to inspect a shelf of tiny skeletal figures; like the skeletons of meerkats. But this was the Museo Di Anatomia Umana – human anatomy. The tiny figures, like horror movie action figures, were foetus skeletons; all flesh removed and standing on their wooden stands like experimental trophies on a mantelpiece. All were from centuries past. All were human.

'Sir,' Abandonato hissed for his superior's attention. 'Sir.'

'Yes. What is it?'

Abandonato pointed to a desk under a window. It was a curator's desk complete with security monitor. Although the building was closed up some ash dust had settled on the desk and in the right light a faint outline of items recently removed could be seen. 'There's been a laptop here.'

'I agree.' The shape was unmistakable and the ghost trails of the power lead and monitor cords were evident. 'And that's an internal circuit security monitor.' Di Stefano powered up the monitor. Immediately six split screen images appeared. 'Fire exit, main entrance, rear lane, loading bay one, loading bay two, street.'

'What's that?' the younger carabinieri's eye was a little sharper than Di Stefano. 'Loading bay.'

They both studied the black and white image. The high angled camera offered a wide shot of the museum loading bay where little else but a forklift was parked in the garage and …

'Is that what I think it is sir?'

Di Stefano was already at the internal stair. He was certain they were alone but he was not taking any chances. He pushed the stairwell door open and threw himself against the inner wall of the loading bay. Abandonato followed. The air was stale and humid … and they both smelt the familiar redolence of blood.

And lots of it.

Di Stefano's eyes searched the shadows. A long narrow rectangular window over the roller door allowed a shaft of light to unfurl across the austere space, but the object poorly lit on the monitor was out of sight. Behind the forklift.

Assured the museum had been abandoned Di Stefano holstered his pistol and hurried around the forklift. He stopped three metres from the headless corpse, careful not to disturb a crime scene. The victim's severed head lay where it had landed, the face with mouth and eyes wide open in terror. The stench was horrendous; a nauseous cocktail of blood, stale sweat and faeces. Di Stefano heard a splash onto the concrete directly behind him. Abandonato had lost his lunch.

'God man, haven't you seen a dead body before?'

'Not like that sir.' The carabiniere wiped his mouth with his handkerchief. 'Sorry.'

'What a waste of pizza,' The superintendent said dryly. 'You better call in forensics.'

PART TWO
ROMA AND THE TOMBAROLI
TOMB ROBBERS

CHAPTER SIX

Rome. Hotel Tunisi. On the perimeter of Vatican City on Via Tunisi. Sunday morning.

Etihad's Boeing 777-300ER touched down three minutes early at Rome's Leonardo da Vinci airport. Not bad service considering it is a twenty-five-hour journey over the equator to the northern hemisphere and on to the other side of the planet. And it went with the ease Jameson and Elspeth expected of twenty first century travel. The taxi ride across Rome to the hotel however, was another story entirely.

With the speedo twitching over 100k, the fifty something insalubrious, pale, jaundiced-eyed cab driver managed to steer with one elbow while combing his hair, chatting on his mobile and smoking a cigarette.

'Multi-talented,' Elspeth giggled in Jameson ear as they were tossed about in the back seat. The driver even found time for outbursts of road rage that included swerving, fist shaking and screamed profanities – clearly vulgar – even to English speaking visitors. Suited men carrying briefcases on pedestrian crossings were nothing but targets. Yet a pretty young Italian lady illegally jaywalking had the driver plant his foot on the brake without a care in the world for the unsuspecting vehicle following.

'When in Rome,' Jameson laughed back. Both were excited, in awe. The adventure had begun. Like millions of others, Rome had to be one of their most favourite cities in the world.

'I think he expected a tip,' Elspeth noted, hefting her backpack from the footpath onto her back, with one eye on their taxi weaving between cars off into the distance.

'Tip!' The idiot had a death wish.'

A sudden commotion commanded their attention. A familiar voice. Loud and excited. 'Yay ... Dudes you're early.' Claire crashed through the glass turnstile doors of the Hotel Tunisi like an amphitheatre thespian at the opening of a play.

'Claire!'

'Wow,' Claire bowled past a porter who was trying to take Elspeth's pack. 'How's this for a turnout guys? I never thought we'd catch up in Rome.' The girls hugged. 'Roma ... bellissimo Roma.' Claire shouted turning to Jameson. 'Dude! What are ya gawking at?' Jameson was taken aback. Claire had cut her hair short and dyed it orange red. She reminded him of Beaker out of the Muppet Show.

'Jesus,' Jameson grinned. 'You've been in London too long.'

'Well thanks. I'm pleased to see you too ... pal.'

Elspeth had seen photos on Facebook. Her best friend's hair was of no surprise. Nor were the ripped jeans and short faux leather jacket with worldly destination stickers embroidered into the fabric. 'When did *you* arrive?' Elspeth asked, dodging impatient pedestrians while Jameson gave Claire a welcome embrace.

'Last night, late.' Bodies pushed by in both directions. Everyone was in hurry; tourists *and* Romans.

Elspeth. 'What's everybody's hurry?'

'The Vatican's right there Beth,' Claire nodded to their hotel suggesting Vatican City was right behind it. 'And Saint Peter's opens at ten.' Claire's jaw dropped open. 'Christ guys, hurry and check in, breakfast goes off at ten thirty. I'm starved and its quarter past already.'

'This is breakfast?' Claire eyed the table laid out with prosciutto, cold meats, cheeses – including Gorgonzola – muesli, tinned fruit, yoghurt tubs and some fresh fruits, mainly rock hard kiwi and oranges. At least the breadbasket was full of crusty bread and a toaster waited nearby. Self-serve.

Claire stood before the spread, open mouthed, and unafraid of an audience. 'Where's the menu, the eggs and bacon?'

Jameson looked about the tiny breakfast room. The three occupied tables were watching on. 'It's called a Continental breakfast Claire,' he said out the corner of his mouth.

'U-huh!' Claire said, unimpressed. 'I've just come from London dude, and every morning it's been a hot English breakfast of sausages, eggs, black pudding, crunchy bacon and toast for this girlie.'

'What about baked beans?'

'Oh yeh, forgot ... and baked beans.'

Elspeth listened with a smile as she filled a bowl with muesli and grabbed a cherry yoghurt. 'Have you picked up an English accent?'

Now Claire hammed it up. 'Ya think so, does ya?' she said in her best rendition of a Cockney taxi driver.

'You've only been away two weeks,' Jameson mocked.

'Yeh, but the boys back home love an English accent.'

'You reckon?'

Claire stood and threw her serviette onto the table. 'What's the day's plan then?'

'I'm free today,' Elspeth said. 'But tomorrow's going to be museum time, all of it. I have a meeting at ten with Signor Aberto Ferraro.' Elspeth said the name with theatrical importance emphasising an Italian accent. 'At the Museo Nazionale Romano.'

Claire looked at Jameson. 'That leaves you and me babe?' she winked.

'I've my own appointment with Father Angelo's mate, a Brother Ferdinando, near here somewhere ... ' Jameson took a piece of paper from his pocket where he had written the address from the brother's latest email. 'Wherever Caffe Santo Giolitti is.'

Claire frowned. 'Jesus! Ya not getting religious on us are you?'

Jameson went on to explain his own mission in Rome.

'Mate,' Claire's mouth was wide open once more. 'That's incredible. But you know that volcano ... what's it called?'

'Vesuvius.'

'Yeh, that's the one ... well ya know it's erupting or something don't you? I saw it on the news.'

Jameson looked at Claire, avoiding eye contact with Elspeth. 'There's a bit of an ash plume happening that's all. Nothing serious.'

'Nothing serious ... it's a volcano dude.'

Elspeth rubbed her forehead. 'Indiana Jones here thinks he's onto Vataea, a lost ancient town ... like Pompeii.'

Claire. 'Vat ... what?'

'Vataea. Pompeii's lost sister city,' Jameson answered. 'It was found in the 1940s apparently ... and then lost again. I'm training down to Naples, probably Tuesday. It's only a few hours away. I've come this far, I've got to check it out.'

'Ya wrong though ...' Claire declared.

'What?'

'Ya wrong about that volcano. I saw it on the news on the plane from London last night. It's spewing out lava now dude.' Jameson wanted to kick Claire in the shins under the table but she stood out of range. He pulled a 'keep quiet' face instead. 'Naples huh,' Claire went on. 'I didn't know it was so close to Rome anyways.'

Elspeth stood, looked at Jameson. 'It's after eleven so you better go find your Brother Ferdinando ... '

'And us girlies will go shopping,' Claire said, returning to her *proper* English accent.

'Shopping!'

'We're in Rome Beth. Rome! I can hardly believe it.' Suddenly Claire's face tightened and the smile vanished. 'Jesus! I'll be right back.' Claire hurried through the dining room and disappeared into the foyer. Jameson looked at Elspeth. 'Was that what I think it was?'

'Yep.' Elspeth had seen her friend panic like that before.

'I.B.S.'

'Irritable bowel syndrome,' Elspeth acknowledged. 'She should take Imodium pills. I don't know how she travels like that.'

'She can put the food away I noticed,' Jameson said, watching the dining room doors swing shut. 'And she's put on weight.'

'Well keep that to yourself,' Elspeth elbowed Jameson with a cheeky grin. *Dude.'*

●   ●   ●

Baby-faced Brother Ferdinando was watching out for Jameson. He stood in his black wool cassock, trimmed with black silk, at the entrance to the Caffe Santo Giolitti. Stooped and with his hands clutched behind his back he looked much older than his twenty-nine years. And with Saint Peter's dome towering over the surrounding buildings of Vatican City, the man looked quite at home.

Jameson's first impression was that the man was shy, until his hand shot forward almost comically in introduction. 'You have to be Jameson.'

'Yes ...' Jameson drew a sudden blank at what he should call the man. *Brother?*

'Ferdinando ... please.'

'Ferdinando,' Jameson acknowledged. 'Nice to put a face to emails. Thanks for seeing me. I appreciate this.'

'It's always good to see another Aussie,' the priest said with a flourish of one hand towards the café door. 'I reckon you'd be a coffee lover.' Immediately the aroma of espresso invaded Jameson's senses. 'The Italians like their coffee fast, strong and burning hot.'

Twenty or more people stood along a narrow bar supping their espressos. One would leave and another immediately take their position. 'See. Fast. But we will take a seat and take our time. Maybe have two or three coffees.' Ferdinando noticed Jameson eyeing the class cabinet of cakes; panforte, lemon polenta, ricotta filled cannoli, biscotti and pastries. 'Awesome huh?' Ferdinando said in a most unpriestly tone.

Jameson smiled. He was thinking of Claire and not himself. A table became vacant and the priest hurried to claim it before someone else should beat him. Jameson joined Ferdinando at the cramped table near the street window. 'We'll pay extra for this table, but it's worth it.' Ferdinando smiled.

The café was noisy and crammed with locals. But the ambience was vibrant. Everyone pinging with caffeine and sugary pastries. Outside on the streets, Rome passed by. Young men, old men, tourists, beautiful women, toothless beggars, cardinals and choirboys. Everyone had their own agenda and no one, it seemed, ever tired of Rome.

The waiter, who looked Moroccan, slid between the tightly packed tables with skill. He was slim. And he needed to be Jameson thought.

'Espresso.' The waiter said, floating the tiny cups to their table top. Two waters appeared in the other hand.

'Grazie.'

'So have you learnt Italian yet?' Jameson asked Ferdinando.

'Some. But not nearly enough. But I get by. My Latin's good though.' The priest put a heaped spoon of raw brown sugar in his cup. Stirred. Sipped. 'So, you go first,' the priest said. 'Father Angelo gave me some info, but tell me your story.'

Jameson brought Brother Ferdinando up to speed.

'So,' the priest said, after a moment's thought, 'you think this old Italian migrant, Vince you said, knew where Vataea was and left clues in this diary of yours.' Jameson nodded. For the first time in Rome he was recognising the accent of another Aussie. 'Can you imagine just how important a find like that would be?'

'As incredible as it sounds. And yes, I do.'

'Well ... ' Brother Ferdinando lowered his voice, dragging his chair closer to Jameson. 'I have something to tell you that you may find interesting.'

'Shoot.'

'Father Angelo told you I'm a second-generation Italian.'

'Ah ... yes.'

'So you know my parents came from Pozzuoli, on the coast south of Naples.'

'No I didn't, but go on.'

'Well I came back for six months when I finished Uni, and I got tied up with fund raising ... finding money to restore chapels and other religious sites damaged by Vesuvius back in 1944.'

'Yes I knew that bit.'

'Well since your first email I've been making enquiries.' Brother Ferdinando looked about the cramped room, almost conspiratorially. 'I made a lot of friends in the villages on the slopes of Vesuvius in 2012, villages like San Sebastiano Al Vesuvio.' Jameson sat erect. 'Thought that'd grab you ... '

'And?'

'Well I heard something interesting about the Capella di San Vito Patiro, the chapel mentioned in your diary. Rosa Brunetti, that's Mrs Brunetti who is now in her sixties, told me her mother Rosa spoke of a man called Drago who was caught defacing a crypt in the chapel.'

'Drago!'

'Yes. It means ... '

'Dragon,' Jameson said without hesitation. 'I know.'

'You have heard the name before?'

'Yes,' Jameson said. 'That was Vince Renzo's name before he migrated to Australia. He changed it for some reason.'

'Interesting.'

Jameson. 'Which crypt was he defacing?'

'Well the chapel is tiny, you've seen photos, haven't you?'

Jameson nodded.

'Well only a few have been allowed to have their cremated remains kept in the chapel,' Ferdinando said. 'The one that was damaged belonged to Bernardo Brunelleschi, a popular mayor of San Sebastiano during the early war years.'

'Bernardo Brunelleschi?' Jameson eyes widened at the name.

'Yes.'

'Riposte in pace,' Jameson whispered quoting the diary. His voice barely audible.

'Rest in peace,' Brother Ferdinando translated. 'Amen to that.'

'No,' Jameson looked the priest in the eye. 'You see 'Riposte in pace' is quoted in Vince's diary, under the name ... Bernardo Brunelleschi!'

'Oh.'

'So what happened to Drago?' Jameson asked. 'Do you know?'

'Mrs Brunetti told me the man had been under suspicion for stealing icons. Apparently on the pretext of restoring them. You see he would take the originals away to his workshop where he would copy them, making fakes to return to the church as the restored works, and keeping the originals. Then a small painting by artist Botticelli, of Christ suffering on the cross, was seen for what it was, a copy. Apparently an expert who trained at Sotheby's before the war, then an officer with the British occupying forces in the late 40s, was assisting in rebuilding San Sebastiano and surrounding villages. He was with a group of artisans rescuing religious treasures from churches and chapels.

Jameson. 'So where was the Botticelli?'

'In the chapel ...'

'Capella di San Vito Patiro?'

'Yes.'

'So there is no doubt about it. Vince Renzo, known as Drago, hid the missing pages from his diary in the chapel. And now I realise where.'

'What?' Brother Ferdinando was now caught up in the excitement. 'How ... I mean where?'

'You said he was caught defacing a crypt,' Jameson confirmed.

'Yes. Brunelleschi the Mayor's crypt.'

'Well that's where he's hidden the missing pages from the diary.'

'In the mayor's crypt ... of course,' Ferdinando said excitedly.

Jameson had *that* feverish look in his eye. 'I have to get to Naples.'

'Ah … Jameson.'

'What?'

'Haven't you been watching the news?' Brother Ferdinando jerked his chin to a flat screen high on the wall playing silently to a boisterous crowd of caffeine addicts. Jameson watched a drone shot taken in the crater. The camera widened the shot from the thick plume of acrid smoke belching from the crater, while in the background molten lava and rock could be seen spewing over the edge. 'And it looks like its following the 1944 flow path down the north-west slopes towards San Sebastiano.'

Feliciano Vineyard.
Eleven kilometres south-east of Mount Vesuvius. Sunday

With his vineyard covered in a fine powdery ash, seventy-nine-year-old Signor Bianchi was happy to move away and stay with his sister Maria at Positana on the west coast of Italy, one hour's drive south. The sea air would do him good and he would tell Maria the authorities told him to evacuate until Vesuvio settled. As the small four-carriage train rattled south he smiled at his good fortune. Five thousand Euros to let these men hire his vineyard for one month. Easy money. And, god and Vesuvio willing, he would return in time to harvest his grapes.

The train clattered over the narrow ravine bridge. Either side fell away sixty metres or more but this didn't bother Signor Bianchi; he had made the trip several times before. But what did bother him was the thought of the culture police discovering he had allowed looters on his property.

Bah! He thought. I've lived there thirty years and never found any sign of any ruins. *Let them dig.* And Signor Bianchi smiled afresh at the thought of the five thousand Euros.

Antiquities looter Fulvia Conte forked at his mozzarella, tomato and prosciutto lunch trying to avoid eating the volcanic ash all about them in the vineyard. It was futile. Even his bread was spoilt. He was hungry from all the digging and tried to ignore the unwelcome ash. He looked to his two accomplices whom he only knew by their first names; Santo and Eulalia. They were of similar age, strong, hard workers and discreet; although they towered over Fulvia's 150 centimetres.

Fulvia brushed ash from his eyes where a sudden breeze shook the tarpaulin covers erected overhead, and the fine volcanic ash fell like snow. The tarpaulins were a brilliant idea Fulvia knew. His boss Silvano Marchetti had put information about the district; a rumour that several rusty and temperamental unexploded bombs – dropped by allied forces during the landing in 1943 – had been found in the vineyard. The ruse was genius. Locals stayed away and any culture police that may be flying overhead would be notified, on enquiry, of the danger.

Brilliant.

Marchetti had even told them the chief of the Carabinieri bomb squad had been paid off. They had four weeks here to dig at their leisure.

Pure genius.

The tombaroli Silvano Marchetti and Ricco Ricci, who employed Santo, Eulalia and Fulvia, had used these workers several times over the years. They were trusted. But now, Fulvia considered, the stakes were higher. He knew they had rediscovered the lost city of Vataea, Pompeii's sister, thought to have been discovered in the 1940s and lost once more. Artefacts had appeared on the tourist market sixty years ago, Fulvia had been told. But then all leads went cold. Marchetti and Ricci, of course, denied the site was that of Vataea.

Now, only days before, Fulvia had discovered a rare and valuable marble statue of a man; a wealthy toga clad roman citizen. The statue was in remarkable condition. And at four metres down into the ground it was easy to understand how the simple old farmer who owned this vineyard had never found ruins in the past.

Then, around the same time, Fulvia found an oil lamp. It was partly covered with ash; concreted ash from Vesuvio. And under the concretion he could just read the name Aulis Cethegus and the letters 'v a t' ... this had to be Vataea. And besides Fulvia dug the lamp from a humble dwelling. This was no villa. He knew instinctively he was digging a common residential site.

Fulvia looked to Santo struggling with his own lunch. The three men were covered in fine ash. Santo avoided eye contact and Fulvia had reservations about the man. Santo had been with him when he found the lamp. The bastard was always prying Fulvia scowled. Always looking over his shoulder. *Did he know I kept the lamp? Did he know I had sold it with other artefacts a week earlier?*

Fulvia said nothing to his colleagues and closed his plastic lunch box shoving it into his backpack when Marchetti appeared through the vines. He poured bottle water over a bunch of grapes and plucked at them as he spoke. 'Twenty minutes is up. Let's get back into it.'

'Fulvia says this is the lost city of Vataea,' Santo told Marchetti, clearly stirring trouble. He shook ash from his hair and pulled a straw hat over his head.

'No. It's a villa,' Marchetti lied. 'We know by the statue Fulvia found. A villa belonging to some small-time merchant we think.'

A slight tremor rolled under foot.

Everyone looked across to Vesuvio. Its plume now reaching to the clouds. 'Come on, let's move it,' Marchetti said again. He turned to Fulvia. 'Fulvia, come with me.'

'Signor?'

'I said come with me. I want a word. And bring your pack.'

Fulvia was thrown so violently, so mercilessly against the barrel room wall his eyes bled. His short seventy-kilo body was no challenge against the one hundred and twenty kilo thug Ricco Ricci. Fulvia tasted blood in his mouth. He tried to stand but another crushing punch into his gut was delivered like a hammer blow from Vulcan.

'Please … I meant no … '

'How much have you taken already?' Marchetti up-ended Fulvia's backpack onto a bench and sorted through it. 'A silver ladle … Mamma Mia, silver for Christ's sake.' He picked up a bronze box with intricate and well preserved millefiori enamel, porca miseria. 'This is rare … and two bronze coins, one silver denarius, a white clay statuette of a mother-goddess holding a child … ' Marchetti's eyes narrowed and his face turned angry. 'Where's the lamp?'

'Lamp signor?' Fulvia's voice was weak and high pitched.

'The lamp Santo said had writing on it. You found it a week ago. It's at your house yes?' Marchetti was dribbling with anger.

Ricco Ricci arms hung at his side like blacksmith hammers. 'How long have you been stealing?'

'I … I … '

'I asked you a question,' Ricco Ricci lifted the small man off the floor by the neck. Fulvia choked, spluttering blood. 'I said I … '

'This is the first time … I swear.'

'Liar!' Another anvil like fist crushed Fulvia's jaw. The tomb looters heard bones snap. Ricco Ricci dragged the small-time crook to the wine press. The antique press was built into the packed earth floor with vertical wooden staves protruding a metre above ground level. At two metres in diameter and with cast iron braces and screw-press it was a formidable piece of apparatus designed to crush a tonne of grapes at a time. Ricco Ricci heaved the semi-conscious looter into the vat where he crashed head and shoulders first, folding into a pathetic bundle at the bottom. 'Liar,' the torturer screamed down at the man. 'How long have you been stealing from us?'

The irony! Stealing from the thieves.

Ricco Ricci unhinged the press and lowered it into position ready to crush grapes. Now Fulvia was trapped … pinioned even if he were able to crawl out himself. Fulvia screamed for mercy. The screw press turned. Fulvia felt the lid compressing him. 'Twice,' he screamed out. 'Twice only.'

'The lamp. What was the word written on it?' The screw turned another cycle.

'Vataea!' Fulvia squealed. 'I read v a t – and I guessed the full word was Vataea.'

Marchetti looked at Ricci. They were incredulous that something should turn up with the name of the lost city embossed onto it. It was rare beyond belief. Artefacts with markings of *Pompeii* were almost unheard of. Now the two men knew, if this lamp fell into the wrong hands, namely the government, the search would be relentless. Not to mention them all being arrested.

'Please signor,' Fulvia pleaded miserably. 'I will say nothing.'

'Where is the lamp now?'

'I sold it ...'

'Sold it!'

'Yes. With other pieces ...'

'Who did you sell it to?'

'To Bernardo Ramazzotti. Nothing really valuable. I swear in god's name. Please ... dear god ... please let me out.'

'Who is this Ramazzotti?'

'Small time dealer ... he ...'

'Where?'

'He has a small antique shop in via Genarro Serra ... near the Piazza del Plibicito.'

Ricco Ricci looked at Marchetti. Marchetti nodded slightly ...

And the press descended. Fulvia's shoulders squashed together. His rib cage shattered. The only saving grace for the small-time looter was that the pain was so severe he blacked out seconds before his skull crushed, burst open and his brains spilt through the juice grate.

Via Genarro Serra ... near the Piazza del Plibicito. Naples.

Bernardo Ramazzotti soon realised the giant of a man with a square jaw and fists like mallets was not a customer when Ricco Ricci pushed into the pathetically narrow space behind the counter pinning the antique dealer against the wall.

'Fulvia Conte,' the muscle man said. 'Name ring any bells?'

'No,' he answered defiantly. But knew otherwise.

'Doesn't matter none.' The intruder said. 'It's the artefacts he sold you. Where are they?' Ricco Ricci looked about the small and narrow shop. It was dark, smelt of musty books, was ill lit; the conditions outside not helping.

'Who are you?' Ramazzotti dared ask.

'Carabinieri, culture polizia. You've been buying illegal excavated artefacts.'

'You're not carabinieri. Where's your I.D.?'

Ricco Ricci took the man by the groin and squeezed. He squeezed hard. Ramazzotti eyes watered and he let out a painful gasp. 'I ... sold ... them,' he wheezed.

'To whom?'

'I sold them as a job lot to another dealer. They'd be on their way to Rome by now.

CHAPTER SEVEN

Museo Nazionale Romano. Palazzo Massimo. Rome.

With a dozen shoe shops and the same amount of specialty boutiques viewed, the girls were shopped out ... for the moment. Besides the thermometer read 37 Celsius in the busy streets.

'What's next?'

'Fancy going to the museum?'

'Which museum Beth. The whole city's a museum.'

'Nazionale.'

'Oh ... *your* museum.'

'Yes. I'm keen to familiarise myself with it before my meeting tomorrow. Now's a good time.' Elspeth lifted her shopping bag. I've got my shoes, you got a scarf, the museum's air-conditioned.'

'Air-conditioned. You've got me.'

Elspeth and Claire stood before a carved marble sarcophagus. The intricate and detailed carving made it one of the most treasured artefacts in Rome's most famous museum. It was breathtaking, gobsmackingly beautiful.

'That's freaking awesome. Will you look at that carving? Jesus.' Claire tried to read the label on the wall. 'What's it say Beth? Shit it's all in Italian.'

A voice came from behind. 'It ees the famous sarcophagus of Portonaccio, 180 years into Christian era, Magnifico, si?'

Both girls turned.

The handsome Italian grinned back, his bright dark eyes darting from Elspeth and then to Claire and back again; finally settling on Claire who was clearly enchanted by the curly dark haired man with a hair bun on the top of his head. He looked a bit of a nerd, but Claire liked nerds. He was in his late twenties and slim with a fresh face and a friendly smile displaying milk white teeth.

'These carving, eet represent a battle scene on several planes and ees focused on the ... how you said ... haughty Roman knight depicted in the capacity of universal victor.'

'Come again?' Claire stood open mouthed. Confused.

'These scenes are of combat, barbarians and captives,' he said of the magnificently sculptured figures. 'See the Romans soldiers here cross river in long boats to catch chieftains on other side. Ah ... does I make sense to you?'

'Not really,' Elspeth turned side on to the man, hissing at Claire out of the corner of her mouth 'Close your mouth girl, you'll catch a fly.'

'Me Vincenzo,' the Italian made a slight bow to Claire.

'Me Claire,' Claire shot back. 'I mean, I'm Claire ... my name's Claire.'

'I am guide. I speak English, si.'

'We don't need a guide, thank you,' Elspeth said bluntly. She had been warned about the Italian men and well ... here he was.

'No, no. I no want to guide you. I hear you ask question so I ... '

'Museum guide huh?' Claire asked.

'Si. But no here. I from Napoli.' He thought a moment. 'Actually I born in Venice but I live in Napoli and sometime, I guide in Rome. In Napoli I guide at Pompeii and Herculaneum. But Vesuvio, she smoke,' and Vincenzo made a *poof* sound as if describing an explosion. 'Pompeii, Herculaneum, she close while volcano ... *poof.*' Vincenzo laughed at himself.

'Pompeii and Herculaneum closed?' Elspeth showed sudden interest.

'Si. Two day now. So Vincenzo come to Rome. Museum good. You like, aren't you?'

Claire. 'Si ... I mean yes.'

'I give you guide tour through museum yes? Free, no moneys.'

Elspeth. 'No.'

Claire. 'Yes.'

'I meant no, thank you,' Elspeth corrected. Vincenzo answered with a pretend sad face. Claire took Elspeth by the arm, taking her aside.

Claire to Vincenzo. 'Un momento.'

'Si.'

'You've gotta loosen up babe,' Claire whispered to her friend out of the guide's earshot.

'I've got this thing about Italian men Claire.'

'So have I.'

'I don't mean that. I mean they're only after one thing.'

'So!'

Both girls giggled. Vincenzo standing four metres away looked complacent, almost as if he had lost interest.

'He *is* kind of cute,' Elspeth capitulated.

'Cute!' Claire said louder than intended. 'He's a hunk ... well ... a nerdy hunk.'

'One hour. Okay.'

'Yessss.' Claire pumped the air.

'And if he gets touchy feely we're out of here, right?'

'Maybe.'

'Claire!'

'Alright already.'

'So, tell me Vincenzo, Elspeth asked as they headed towards the Imperial Rome exhibits. 'How long does it take to get to Naples? Did you train or car maybe.'

'No train, no car. I have Vespa si.'

'Get outa here!' Claire put both hands to her face. 'I've got a Vespa.'

'Really. Where you from, England?'

'No, Australia.'

'Ah Australia. Si, si. Kangaroo yes? Melbourne … Sydney?'

'Hobart Vin,' Claire skipped backwards facing Vincenzo and Elspeth as they followed.

''obart?'

'Yes. That little island at the bottom of Australia. Tasmania.'

'Ah si. Tasmanian devil.'

'That's the one. What kind of Vespa have *you* got?' Claire asked excitedly.

Immediately Vincenzo's face brightened. 'I have Vespa scooter … 1965 … '

'1965! Holy crap.'

'Si. But I … ah … how you say … res, rest …'

'Restore.'

'Si. Restore. Me and my brother Antonio. We restore it. Fix motor with electric start. Since I come from Naples I put eight hundred kilometres on clock.'

'Wow. What colour?'

'Blue. 150cc, three speed manual.' And as an after-thought he added. 'She have box for passenger … '

'Sidecar!'

'Si.'

'Get outta here. Sidecar. Jesus Beth. A Vespa with a side car.'

'Si. Like treasures in thees museum. Rare … huh? You say you have Vespa.'

'Yes Vin. 2013 Vespa GTS 250cc belt-driven auto with 35 litre Givi top box … '

'250cc,' Vincenzo whistled. 'And colour?'

'Bronze.'

'Bronze not so good.'

'Yeh, ya right. But it was bronze when I bought it, second hand like.'

'You *really* like Vespa,' Vincenzo asked warily.

'Yeh dude, love 'em.'

'Because I have cousin in Naples who has Vespa Museum.'

'Get outa here!'

'Si, really. He is mechanic who always love the Vespa. He has ... what you say? Private museum. More than twenty Vespa I'm thinking. Near Erclona in East Naples.'

'Cousin huh?'

'Si. I put him in book I make. A Book for Agenzia Nazionale del Turismo.'

'Tourist Bureau?'

'Si. We make book for tourist called 'Secret Naples'. Is good. Very informative. We sell many books.'

Elspeth had had enough of scooter talk. 'Okay then,' she nodded to a museum sign. 'Roma Imperiale,' this way.'

'Claire doesn't mess about.' Jameson said of Vincenzo watching Claire leaning over an ATM. Standing with his arms crossed and his back to Claire, keeping a watchful eye on passers-by, was Vincenzo. 'Tour guide you say?'

'Yes, he's really cool. I think Claire's smitten.'

'But they've only just met.'

'Three hours ago.'

'Three hours ... and she's smitten!'

'We're in Rome remember. Besides, they discovered they both have a Vespa and pop, it was love at first sight.'

'Hmm.' Jameson watched the animated guide. He looked harmless enough and if he was a tour guide *he would have to know his stuff, right?* 'The man-bun's kinda over the top,' Jameson said quietly, never a fan of the latest trend.

'I think it's cute. It's all the rage now, you should grow one.'

'Yeh right.'

'How did your meeting with the priest go?

'Ah! We need to talk. I ...'

'Jamo!' Claire interrupted, dragging Vincenzo towards them by the hand. Both giggled. 'This is Vincenzo, our very own tour guide. Vin, this is the Jameson I told you all about him.'

Jameson was impressed with the Italian's handshake. Strong and firm and he held Jameson's eye. 'How are ya mate?' Vincenzo said in a fun Aussie accent.

'Good mate,' Jameson returned the Aussie greeting.

'Vin's taking us to a bar,' Claire said. 'Where the locals go and not some touristy joint.'

'Si.'

'Sounds good to me Vincenzo. I hope the Italian beer is cold and wet.'

Climbing the Spanish steps was hot work but worth the effort. Claire passed Elspeth her mobile. 'Beth, take a shot of me and Vin.' Spilling down the steps were thousands of tourists vying for best positions for a sunset photo although sunset was still hours away.

Vincenzo led then them through Plaza de Espagna by the Fontana della Barcaccia and along Via Gregoriana.

'Dude. How much further,' Claire panted. The humidity in the still air of the late afternoon was stifling.

'Near. Very near.' Vincenzo was lean and fit and Claire's extra kilos were slowing down her speed but not her enthusiasm. Besides it was *hot*.

'Man that beer's going to taste good,' Claire said catching up with their guide and snatching his shirt tail to slow him. 'Don't get me wrong Vin, I love walking ... but what's with all these steps?'

'Must be mid-thirties,' Jameson said stopping to snatch a breath, hands resting on knees.

Vincenzo checked the weather on his mobile. 'Thirty eight ... nearly there, one hundred metres.'

L'Oasi was a local bar for young Romans along a narrow lane amongst a maze of streets that left the visitors lost in minutes. The bar, wedged between a trattoria and a small supermarket, was housed in a nineteenth century four-storey stone building covered in crumbling stucco splashed with peeling Pastels from the 1960s. The few tables outside were fully occupied and the litre mugs of beer dripping condensation were only minutes away.

Inside was standing room only. No air-conditioning but half a dozen electric ceiling fans took up the challenge.

They found a position at the mahogany bar with its brass rail running its full length.

'Vincenzo!' A voice cried out over the noisy chatter.

'Aberto. Ciao.'

The barman shook hands over the bar with Vincenzo. Vincenzo introduced the others.

'You like Rome?' the barman switched to English.

'Very much,' Elspeth spoke for the other two.

'You're a regular here then,' Jameson asked Vincenzo.

'You could say that, si.' Vincenzo ordered drinks without asking the others, four stubbies of Birra Moretti, straight from a chiller with crushed ice sliding down the outside of the bottles. He insisted on buying the first round. Jameson was impressed. Their beers vanished in a few mouthfuls. Jameson bought another round and as a group vacated their table they pounced. Chilled beer *and* a seat under a fan *and* they were in Rome ...

'Life doesn't get much better than this,' Claire chuckled. 'Up your bum!'

After explaining to Vincenzo the Australian answer to 'salute', they slowed on the third beer.

'Elspeth told me you drove up from Naples,' Jameson said. 'On a Vespa no less.'

'Si. Yes.'

'How long did that take?'

'Five hours. But I stop for break ... for espresso, yes.'

'What's the best way for me to get to Naples?' Jameson asked.

'Train I am thinking. Why? You want to go Naples?'

'Yes.' Jameson paused looking at Elspeth. 'I must get to San Sebastiano.'

Vincenzo. 'San Sebastiano al Vesuvio?'

Elspeth rolled her eyes.

'Yes,' Jameson answered the Italian avoiding Elspeth's stare.

'Mamma Mia,' Vincenzo was shocked. 'San Sebastiano. But why?'

Jameson explained he wanted to visit the chapel.

'But you see news do you not?'

'Thankyou Vincenzo,' Elspeth said.

'San Sebastiano ... she in path of the lava flow ... how you say ... déjà vu. The lava follow same 1944 eruption path.'

'Maybe.'

'Si.'

'Nothing's happened yet. The lava flow might stop,' Jameson now looked hopefully at Elspeth. 'It could stop any minute ... I mean that's what they say on the news ... couldn't it?'

'Jameson,' Vincenzo looked suddenly serious. 'No one ... no Italiano he would go there now. Just army and polizia. The village, she empty.'

'You mean evacuated?' Claire offered.

'Si'

'Tell him the truth,' Elspeth said, annoyed that Jameson was being so persistent.

'Yeh dude,' Claire drained her beer and looked about to grab the waiter's attention. 'Tell Vin the whole story.'

Vincenzo looked at Jameson eagerly. His head tipped to one side waiting for an explanation.

'Ah what the hell.' Jameson told Vincenzo everything. From the Hobart auction to his meeting with Brother Ferdinando earlier in the day near the Vatican. The Italian historian listened in silence. Finally ...

'Vataea Jameson. Do you realise the importance of such a find?'

'Of course.'

'Vataea,' Vincenzo whistled. 'Then I am in my friend.'

Jameson sat upright. 'In? In what?'

'We find thees Vataea together.'

'Wait ... ah ... no. Vincenzo! '

'Why no?'

'Well ... ah ... I know nothing about you for one thing.'

'I am Vincenzo. Tour guide.' And the cheerful Italian showed two rows of those milk white teeth. 'What more do you want to know.'

'You should be reporting this to the authorities,' Elspeth said to Jameson.

'Authority!' Vincenzo gasped. 'No! Non a una buona idea ... ah ... not good idea. Not yet.'

Elspeth. 'And why not?'

'Many bad peoples in Italia authority. Jameson is right, si ... *we* need to investigate first.'

Elspeth slumped back in her chair defeated.

'We?' Jameson screwed up his face.

'Si. You need Italiano for speaking.'

Claire. 'What about the volcano dude?'

'Bah! Ees nothing. Vesuvio, like Jameson say, she settle soon.'

'But you said yourself San Sebastiano has been evacuated,' Elspeth insisted.

'Si. But the army ... the polizia ... they must do thees things for peoples soundness, yes?'

'Then I'm in too boys.' Claire called out over the bar din. The fresh beers arrived. Claire snatched up the tab and took a ten and a five from the bum bag belted about her waist when Elspeth noticed a small glass jar of cayenne pepper.

'What's the cayenne for?'

'Terrorists.'

'You serious.'

'Dam right I'm serious. It's against the law to buy capsicum spray so I decided to carry cayenne.'

'For terrorists?'

'Yeh ... you just never know these days when some right wing fanatic cockhead is going to try and take you hostage. This is Europe dude!"

'Fair enough.'

'Vincenzo!' Another familiar face pushed between the tables towards them.

'Luciana,' Vincenzo stood and gave the stunning twenty-three-year-old red head waitress a hug. She returned the affection by locking her hands around his neck. Claire's heart sank.

Luciana's eyes bubbled. 'When did you arrive?'

'Yesterday. Pompeii, she close. Vesuvio si. Big smoke.' Vincenzo insisted on speaking English in front of his new Australian friends.

'How bad is this Vesuvio,' Luciana asked with concerned interest. Vincenzo described the latest news. Elspeth looked at Claire who was clearly disappointed. They exchanged shrugs ... *oh well* ...

'How is mamma,' Luciana asked. 'Is she worried?'

'Mamma's good ... '

'Mamma!' Claire repeated rather loudly.

'Oh sorry,' Vincenzo was all smiles. 'These my friends, from Australia. Thees ees my sister Luciana.'

'Sister!' Claire jumped to her feet and took Luciana's hand. 'Nice to meet you ... sister. I'm Claire.'

'And you work here?' Elspeth asked the waitress.'

'Si. I live here as well.' She jerked her chin to the upper floors of the bar.

'And I live here with Luciana,' Vincenzo said. 'When I am in Rome.'

The Spaghetti Carbonara was not what Jameson expected. The pasta too al dente, the pancetta too fatty and not enough egg yolk sauce. But Spaghetti Carbonara was a Roman institution and Jameson was determined to try a plate the Roman way.

When in Rome ... right.

'I hear this pasta ... she named after the Carbonari – coal men what come to Rome from Umbria,' Vincenzo's eyes sparkled from the Tuscan wine at the Trattoria next to the bar, where hunger had eventually led them.

'I heard it was inspired by the American GI's,' Jameson said. 'Who were making use of their egg and bacon rations during the war.'

'Interesting.'

'So, what have we finally decided,' Elspeth asked forking clams and fettuccine hungrily from her plate of Marinara. With the others bent on travelling down to Naples she had persuaded them to wait until after her meeting at the museum, until Tuesday. The trains were still running – one every two hours – so an early afternoon train would see them in Naples terminal before 5PM.

Just quietly Elspeth hoped the volcano would sabotage their plans. Outwardly Elspeth could only smile. *That's nearly two days away*, she thought to herself. *My meeting at the museum is at 10AM tomorrow. The brief will be all afternoon followed by the official cocktail party that evening.*

'So what will we do tomorrow while Els at the museum?' Jameson looked to their new friend for guidance.

'Tomorrow,' Vincenzo squeezed Claire's hand under the table. 'Tomorrow I will show you *my* Rome, si?'

CHAPTER EIGHT

Lost in the Romance of Ancient Rome. Monday

Claire stood in awe amongst the ruins of the Forum where they sat in the shade on the steps of the Temple of Jupiter. 'Lord Byron, Mark Twain, Shelley, Charles Dickens,' she said in a reverent whisper. 'They all came here you know.'

'You could never tire of this place,' Jameson craned his neck to the top of the Corinthian pillars where swifts nested, lazy in the heat. 'So much history.'

'It's just one giant museum dude,' Claire sighed.

Vincenzo sat, leaning back against a giant column with one knee tucked up and his chin resting on his fist, reminding Claire of Rodin's bronze statue *The Thinker*. He smiled cheekily at Claire. Jameson noted the two had a chemistry. They were of matching intellect with Claire's archivist background and Vincenzo's experience as a historian and guide. Conversations had been inspirational and Jameson had learnt a great deal about the ancient Roman way of life.

'You like antiques I hear you say?' Vincenzo finally asked Jameson.

'Yes mate.'

'What antiques you like?'

'You oughta see his house Vin,' Claire said with pride. 'I mean it's full of history, all sorts of interesting stuff.'

'You have house?' The Italian asked incredulous.

'Dude. It's on the beach,' Claire spoke for Jameson.

'I inherited it,' Jameson said humbly and twisted the subject back on track. 'Why do you ask? About antiques that is?'

Vincenzo stood and dusted his trousers. 'Well I was thinking, maybe you like to visit antique market here. Pick up a souvenir of Rome maybe.'

'Are you kidding? Is it far away?'

'We could walk, si. I think we walk to Pantheon next, then to Via de Pellegrino where they have many antique shops. Then maybe, Claire, we could visit the Fontana di Trevi.'

'Trevi Fountain! Right.'

Via de Pellegrino was a long narrow cobbled street running parallel between one of Rome's main thoroughfares, Corso Vittorio Emmanuelle 2nd, and the River Tiber. The area was neat and affluent. The stone buildings, looking to Jameson anywhere between 18th and 19th century, were cool and shaded. Many had the mandatory veneer of cement stucco. On the upper floors windows were shuttered against the heat while at street level decorative wrought iron gates and grates protected the mostly arched entrances and windows. Here, tall and slim potted trees decorated most business entrances.

'Cool, check this out,' Claire said as they passed a wide lane off the main street where an antique market was wrapping up for the day. One trestle groaning under the weight of shiny brass, captured Jameson's attention. He picked up a pocketsize telescope, expanded it to full length and looked through the eyepiece. 'Neat.' He told the other two.

'Ees no antique Jam-eson,' Vincenzo told him. 'I think thees made in India, yesterday.'

'Yeh, I know. But I want one for the bedroom at home.' Jameson read the price tag. 'Eight Euros.'

'Bargain.'

Half a street block further on Vincenzo stopped outside an unobtrusive building with a narrow window onto the street. 'I think you like eet here,' he said. 'The owner, I know him many years. He good man. If you see something I get you good price, si.'

Claire and Jameson looked at the sign. *Cinzia Galleria.* The shop was long and narrow with a low ceiling. The stock, eclectic, from a life sized rearing bear smoker's stand that would have looked more comfortable in Bavaria, to 18th century iron lanterns. Glass cabinets were packed with jewellery, coins, plated silver, pottery and ceramics. The owner, Gastone Salvatore sat at his desk in a corner where a freestanding fan failed to keep the older man cool. He looked up from his laptop and smiled warmly.

'Vincenzo, ciao.' The heat had tired the sixty-year-old and his movements were slow. It was then that Jameson realised the man had been asleep. 'You have brought some wealthy Americans to my gallery have you not?' the dealer said in English with a friendly smile. Vincenzo greeted the man in Italian and introduced them in English. 'And they both from Australia Gastone. No Ameri-can.'

'Oh, please excuse me,' the man said in good English. 'But I get many Americans in here.' He stifled a yawn. 'They are usually looking for ancient antiquities, which, as Vincenzo must have told you, are illegal for me to sell.'

'I think Jameson you know these things,' Vincenzo said.

'I didn't actually.'

'It's such a pity because we have so much of it here,' the antique dealer said. 'Museum spares I call them. Ancient pottery lamps, wine amphora, bronze ware, coins by the hundreds of thousands. The museums don't want them. They get excavated every day either archaeologically or by accident, yet we are forbidden to trade in them.'

An early stiletto dagger caught Jameson's eye. Gastone happily showed the rare piece to Jameson. 'That's 16th century you know.' Jameson felt the weight of the Renaissance dagger with its steel blade and ivory and silver wire handle. He indulged himself briefly, imagining who would have carried such a weapon all those years ago, and right here in the streets of Rome. He caught the price tag, four thousand Euros and handed the weapon back to Gastone who was clearly proud to own such an antique.

'Ever been used?' Claire said cheerfully.

'You would never know,' the dealer said with a wry smile.

Something caught Claire's attention in a shallow glass top cabinet. 'I thought you said you weren't allowed to sell antiquities.' She pointed to half a dozen terracotta oil lamps bunched together at one end. 'What's that then?'

'Have a closer look young lady,' Gastone said. The small oval shaped lamps, no more than one 100mm long, with a 30mm deep oil well and spout at one end for a wick, were all decorated with erotic scenes.

'Nice one.'

'Oh,' Gastone smiled. 'I didn't mean have a closer look for that reason. I meant have a closer look. They are reproductions of originals. See how perfect they are.' Claire nodded sagely. 'I'll take your word for it.'

'The Americans love them. I sell a dozen a week.'

Vincenzo and the dealer exchanged brief words in Italian, culminating in a hasty agreement. 'Okay then,' Vincenzo said. 'Gastone has some-theen to show you, yes. But you must ah ... vow ... ah promise you say notheen to anybody's about thees things.'

'Sounds dangerous.' Jameson said.

'No, no, no dangerous.'

The three watched in silence as the sixty-year-old lifted a shoebox out from under the counter, removed the lid and placed tissue wrapped parcels on the glass top.

'Ah, the good stuff eh?' Claire's eyes brightened.

'Gastone unwrapped several items; terracotta lamps, a silver ladle, two clay votive statues, a grapefruit sized marble head from a damaged bust, three pottery jugs and terra sigilatta dishes with attractive geometric patterns.' Jameson was impressed but confused.

'As I said, it is illegal but every antique dealer has a few pieces.' Gastone looked proud of his little haul. 'All found recently in Campania. I drive down there once a month. I have my contacts see.'

Vincenzo grew serious. 'But you must be silent with these.'

Jameson. 'Of course.'

Claire was less tactful. 'How much?'

'What do you like?' Gastone asked Claire.

'Well not me ... him.' Claire pointed to Jameson who was trying to remain complacent and not too eager. 'You Jam, what rocks ya boat?'

Jameson picked up the larger of the terra sigilatta dishes. 'Well, say this for example.'

'One of the better pieces. You have good taste my friend. It is called Terra sigilatta, very popular tableware in ancient times yes, and it is definitely first century AD. I could let you have that for ... say three hundred.' Jameson put the piece back in the box. 'But everything is negotiable. Make me an offer.'

'I'd pay one hundred, that's about it.'

'I paid more than that for the dish.'

Jameson was an old hand at this game. He picked up a lamp. *Neat* he thought. And in good condition although it hadn't been cleaned and was partly covered in soil and what looked like ash. But that was also half the charm. Freshly dug. You couldn't get any more genuine than that. Gastone sat back at his desk, eager to position himself before the struggling fan. 'That one has some minor damage. It has been in a fire and that ash can't be removed without damaging it further. 'I'll take two hundred for the lamp.'

Jameson inspected the artefact when he noted letters under the dirt. Jameson was aware the Roman potters, who were rightfully proud of their wares, were the first in history to emboss their names on their product. Clearly Gastone had not noticed this for its rarity would be reflected in the price.

'That is also first century and that ash, well it was dug at Campania and I cannot prove this but it is possibly ash from Vesuvio.'

'It's kind of neat,' Jameson understated, and he took the lamp to the shop window into the light where he rubbed at the dirt with his thumb ...

Jameson's heart skipped a beat.

He couldn't believe what he was seeing. Aware that he was being watched he returned nonchalantly to the others, wrapped the lamp in tissue and took two hundred Euros from his wallet. Claire shot Jameson a look ... *not bargaining dude?* Gastone took the money. 'Here, let me wrap it properly for you.'

'It's all good,' Jameson said tapping his pocket, suddenly keen to leave the shop. 'Nice meeting you.'

Gastone watched them leave and had a bad feeling. A feeling dealers have after a quick sale absent of negotiation and followed by a hasty exit.

•   •   •

It was evening by the time the hundred and twenty-kilo tombaroli muscleman and thug Ricco Ricci arrived at Cinzia Galleria in Via del Pellegrino. Ricci hated Rome, and he hated the Romans, preferring to live in Naples, although right at this minute Naples was a city under threat. And the drive north had left him tired and irritable.

He tried the door handle. Locked. He cupped a hand over the window. Without lights the shop was in semi darkness but Ricci could see movement at the rear of the building.

Antique dealer Gastone Salvatore heard the door shake. He peered between the corridor of glass cabinets to the main entrance where a large man stood in the doorway, now knocking. It was clear to Gastone that he had been seen and he was about to call out that he was closed and retire upstairs to his apartment when he had a thought. *Rich American?* Business had been slow. He needed the cash. The knocking grew impatiently louder.

'Venuta ... venuta. Mamma Mia.'

Ricco Ricci stepped away from the door to the street and tried not to look formidable or threatening. He had the right shop and the man he needed to see was here. He felt good about this. Ricci looked up and down Via del Pellegrino. There were few people about. He took a deep breath to relax and forced a rare smile as the antique dealer unlatched the door ...

Because, at all costs, he must retrieve that lamp.

Tunisi Hotel on Via Tunisi on the outskirts of Vatican City. Monday evening.

Elspeth walked into their hotel room and threw herself on the bed, her eyes sparkling from French champagne, intelligent conversation and ecstatic in the knowledge she had made a great impression on Signor Alberto Ferraro of the Museo Nazionale Romano at the meeting and cocktail party.

'Those Italian men,' she grinned over at Jameson busy at the basin in the en suite. 'They certainly know how to treat the ladies.'

'Oh. Went well then.' Jameson answered, clearly preoccupied.

'Well? It was *Magnifico*. And you should have been there to see the marbles. Wow. Australians are in for a treat. The exhibition is going to be a huge success ...' Jameson continued scrubbing in the sink. 'What are you doing in there anyway?'

'Come see.'

'That's my tooth brush Jam.'

'I know, I'll get you another one. It's just that yours is a softer brush than mine ... ' Elspeth immediately recognised the artefact.

'Is that what I think it is.'

'A lamp. Yes.'

'Genuine?' Elspeth smartly answered her own question. 'Of course it is. Jesus Jameson. It's illegal to buy and sell antiquities in Italy. It's a prison offence and I'm here representing the Tasmanian Museum ...'

'Alright, calm down.'

'Calm down! Where did you get it?'

'My eyes are playing up Beth,' Jameson feigned short sightedness. 'What's that say.' He pointed to where he had managed to clean the encrusted ash from the Latin embossing. Elspeth took the lamp and studied it under the bathroom mirror light.

'V-a-t ... Vat ... Vataea. What! Vataea! Where on earth did you find this?' Jameson sat Elspeth on the bed, took a beer from the mini bar and told her the full story. She sat in silence a long moment. 'We have to hand this in,' she finally declared.

'Hang on a sec,' Jameson nearly choked.

Via de Pellegrino. Monday evening.

Gastone Salvatore opened the door to the expensively dressed man at the entrance to his galleria. 'I'm closed,' he said in English, but immediately realised his mistake when the man replied in his own language with a southern accent, Naples maybe.

'Signor Salvatore.'

'Si.'

'May I come in?'

'What's this about?'

'Signor, I do not wish to do business out here on the street.'

Instantly Gastone had a bad feeling about the stranger and reprimanded himself for opening the door. He stood his ground but Ricco Ricci shoved past and walked well into the shop, immediately looking into the cabinets.

'Look signor,' Gastone said. 'I don't know what you are after but now is not a good time ... '

Ricco wheeled about to face the dealer. He was a good 30 cm taller and now he looked threatening. 'Lock the door.'

'Pardon?'

'I said lock the door.' Gastone did not budge. He wanted the door to remain open so he could dash onto the street if need be. Ricco suddenly became aware of his lack in people skills. 'Lock the door, *please*. Because what we have to discuss you may not like passers-by to hear.'

'Like what?'

'Like dealing in stolen, looted antiquities.'

Gastone slammed the door shut. 'Now listen here ...'

'No signor, you listen.' Ricco sat arrogantly at Gastone's desk. He turned on the electric fan. It started lazily enough, making a racket as the blades hit the safety cage, until the fan picked up speed. 'I don't like Rome,' Ricco went on. 'Too hot.'

'And you are from?' Gastone asked.

'That doesn't matter. What does matter is I have come to take back a lamp you purchased from a small-time dealer in Naples, signor Ramazzotti. Oh don't look so glum, I am prepared to pay you for it, and pay handsomely.' Ricci opened his wallet and pressed three one hundred Euro notes onto the leather top desk. But the look on Gastone's face was not one of pleasure. 'What? Not enough? Four hundred then.'

Gastone could see it was no point lying to this man.

Ricci. 'Well?'

'It's not the money signor ... I ... ah ... I sold it.'

'You sold it!' Ricci slammed an open hand onto the desk scattering stationery.

'Only this afternoon as a matter of fact.'

Ricci snatched the money angrily cramming it back into his wallet. He jumped to his feet and walked around the desk to confront the now intimidated dealer. He took a deep breath to calm himself. 'And to whom did you sell it?'

'To this Australian.'

'An Australian!'

'Si. He came in here with another Australian, a young woman, girl-friend maybe, and Vincenzo, a tour guide I have known for a few years. They must have hired him to show them around.'

'And this Australian ... where is he staying?'

'I wouldn't know.'

'The guide? Vincenzo, you said. Vincenzo who?'

'I only know him as Vincenzo. He works in Naples. But sometimes he works in Rome, around the Museo Nazionale mostly.'

'Where can I find him?'

'I don't know ... but wait. Yes. He told me once, he has a sister who works at a bar off Via Gregoriana.'

'What bar?'

Gastone thought a moment. 'L'Oasi ... si, l'Oasi.'

Ricci walked to the door where Gastone followed, eager to lock the stranger out, when curiosity had him ask one last question. He thought of the Australian, Jameson, hurrying off once he purchased the lamp, and the thought he had sold something important and cheaply worried him. 'What's so special about that lamp anyhow?' he asked.

Ricco Ricci turned to face the antique dealer before the door closed in his face.

'That lamp?'

'Yes.'

'Well you rub it see. You rub it real hard and a genie pops out,' Ricci said with a sickly smile. 'And this nasty little genie has long sharp fingernails and he rips the eyes out of antique dealers who can't mind their own business.'

Tunisi Hotel on Via Tunisi on the outskirts of Vatican City.
Monday evening.

'Ya back El?' Claire barged through the unlocked door without knocking. She was barefoot. 'I thought I heard voices.' She saw Elspeth holding the lamp. 'Nice huh?'

Elspeth words were now soft and sober. 'We have to take this to the authorities.'

Claire. 'Jesus El, it's only a lamp ... '

'Only a ...'

Vincenzo's smiling face popped around the hotel door from the corridor, his curly locks and man bun in disarray. He was also barefoot. 'Ciao Elspeth. How was meeting?'

'G-Great. Thanks for asking. Ah ... Vincenzo ...'

'Si.'

'Did you get this for Jameson?' Elspeth turned on the bed to face Jameson who was looking serious, hastily rewrapping the lamp.

'Si.' Vincenzo moved all the way into their room. He closed the door. Elspeth noticed his shirt buttons undone. 'Is only lamp, many antique dealers, they sell these things. Coins, lamps, pottery. They are common in Italy, hardly treasures si?'

'Hardly treasures!' Elspeth raised her voice.

'Ah Beth...' Jameson was now decidedly red-faced.

'An ancient Terracotta lamp,' Elspeth said in a raised voice. 'Stamped with the name of Pompeii's sister city, the lost city of Vataea!'

'Vataea!' Vincenzo and Claire gasped in chorus.

Now Jameson looked decidedly guilty. 'Shit Beth ... '

Elspeth gaped at Jameson, mouth open wide. 'These guys don't know! Do they?'

'Know what?' Claire asked.

Silence.

Vincenzo's mobile interrupted the awkward moment.

'Know what?' Claire said in a persistent tone.

'Tell them,' Elspeth spat at Jameson.

Jameson unwrapped the lamp and passed it to Claire. Vincenzo fumbled in his pocket and swiped his mobile screen. 'Ciao.' He said into the phone at the same moment recognising the one word Claire was gaping at on the lamp ...

Vataea.

'Mamma Mia!' the guide's mouth dropped open.

A female voice cried out from Vincenzo's mobile. 'Vincenzo?'

'Luciana, ciao. Ah … un minuto … ' Vincenzo shrugged his shoulders. 'Ees thees the same lamp from Gastone?' he asked Jameson.

Jameson nodded.

Claire. 'Dude! I wondered why you didn't haggle with that guy.'

Vincenzo frowned into his mobile. 'Luciano, I call you un minuto si … '

Luciana. 'No minuto … questo e urgente … '

'Urgente?'

'Si.'

'I don't believe this,' Claire was almost shouting with excitement. 'And you didn't tell us … '

'I was going to. I just wanted … '

'Vataea dude!'

Vincenzo stabbed a finger in one ear and moved to the en suite. 'Parlare!' He listened to his sister words. His face grew serious.

'When?' he asked. 'Merda … okay, thanks Luciana … keep safe, ciao.'

Claire. 'Everything okay Vin?'

'There has been a man asking for me at the bar.'

'L'Oasi?'

'Si.' Vincenzo's face was grave. 'That was my sister Luciana. She say he was big man with Napoli accent.'

'Police?'

'No polizia. She say Mafiosa.'

'Mafia?'

'Christ … how … '

'He ask for Australians also.'

'Great,' Elspeth grit her teeth and shook her head. 'Brilliant! Now what have you done Jameson Rowley?'

'It must be Gastone,' Vincenzo bit his bottom lip. 'The bast-ard! He must tell this man about us.'

'Clearly,' Jameson said. 'But why?'

'The lamp.'

'Yes, but how the hell would he know about the lamp?'

'Because it was stolen from them, I'm thinking,' Vincenzo's mind was in rapid mode. 'I'm thinking thees men are tombaroli ... '

Claire. 'Tom what?'

'Tombaroli. Tomb raiders,' Jameson told Claire. 'Looters.'

'Si. I'm thinking they have found Vataea. They are looting from the site and this pieces we see in Gastone's shop are from there. Remember he say he come from Napoli with thees things this week.'

'Your right.'

'So now we have the Mafia looking for us,' Elspeth said angrily. 'Brilliant.'

'What did your sister tell him?'

'She not speak to him. Was my friend Aberto. She say he said we were there earlier but we not there now. We must leave ... '

'Leave?'

'Si. We must leave for Napoli. Now.'

'Now!'

'I know thees tombaroli. They bad mans. It will not take thees bad mans much time to find Australians living in Roma hotel, si.'

PART THREE
ROMA TO NAPOLI

CHAPTER NINE

ItaliaRail. Twenty kilometres north of Naples. 11.05PM

The rhythmic clacketty-click of the carriages was calming but no one in the group was able to sleep. Outside the black of night reflected the train's interior. Claire looked at her reflection in the glass and spontaneously smiled. She was reminded of an exhibition she had seen in London; an exhibition for Napoleon Bonaparte artefacts including the General's iconic military hat, the bicorne. Vincenzo caught the smile and Claire told him how she stood in front of the glass case exhibiting the famous hat. 'So I buckled my knees a little until my refection in the glass case was directly under the hat and it looked like it was on *my* head.'

Elspeth sat staring out the carriage window, much the same way as she had the past hour and twenty minutes. She was still trying to figure out how she got herself into this mess. Elspeth mulled over the Tasmanian Museum director's words. 'How would you like to go to Rome?'

'Rome Italy?'

'Where else?'

'The meeting is with Signor Aberto Ferraro at the Museo Nazionale Romano,' her director Charles Bean told her. 'You seal the deal. Enjoy a social evening at a celebratory cocktail party, and then a few days at your leisure to soak up the culture of Rome.'

So what went wrong?

Now she was being pursued by mafia with a hot artefact and a lead to one of the most important archaeological discoveries of the 21st century; jumping from the pot into the fire.

That's an irony. Suddenly the red and yellow glow of fire reflected off the carriage window. Elspeth sat bolt upright. In the distance the unmistakable flare of molten lava silhouetted the outline of Vesuvius. Elspeth looked to the others to draw their attention to the phenomenon but they were already fixated. Eyes wide and gaping at the distant volcano.

'That's the north slope you see,' Vincenzo told them. 'The fire you see is in crater but I'm thinking the lava will burst the crater there and flow down same hill that she do in 1944.'

'Towards San Sabastiano.' Jameson said quietly.

'Si.'

'Then we must get to San Sebastiano a quickly as possible.'

Elspeth's jaw dropped. 'What?'

'The chapel Beth. *You know that.* We must get into the chapel before the lava flow spills.'

'Is late,' Vincenzo said. 'We go to my cousin for sleep. Then first thing, early. We go to San Sebastiano.'

Naploli Termini was in chaos. With thousands of people boarding trains and few passengers alighting in Naples it was an effort to vacate the terminal against the hoards of evacuating people. Cousin Mario – wearing a grubby singlet, shorts and sandals, overweight and with no resemblance to Vincenzo – met them in the Termini car park. Here the sense of urgency in the night air was even stronger and the gang noted the fine layer of ash for the first time. The atmosphere was electric amongst the stink of burning sulphur, the strobing emergency vehicle lights and the constant sirens. Families with piles of luggage were already camping in the car park and surrounds, determined to catch the first available trains. On a positive note, there had been talk of ItaliaRail putting on all night trains.

After hasty introductions Jameson helped Mario toss their packs onto the tray of his pickup. 'Two in back,' Mario ordered. Elspeth climbed in the back with Jameson while Claire and Vincenzo joined Mario in the cabin. This gave Vincenzo opportunity to explain the situation to his cousin. With horns blaring and tempers flaring it took twenty minutes before they had a clear run on a backstreet to the outer Naples suburb of Ercolano where Mario lived.

'It's worse than I thought cousin,' Mario excused himself to Claire and spoke Italian to his cousin who knew little English. Finally Vincenzo explained to Claire, 'a state of emergency has been declared. Pre-alert stage, cousin says. Now the government ... it operates at a national level. He says those who want to leave, the government say they leave now. Naples, Mario says, is under martial law.'

'Jesus.'

'Si. Jesus! He tells me Vesuvio is manned by rescuers. All villages around mountain are being evacuated. Eighteen municipalities, he say, are moved to safer position.'

'Is Mario worried?'

'Mario. No. It happens before. Never bad.'

Mario bounced the pickup from Viale Due Giugno fishtailing onto the Strade Satale. He was speeding and recklessly flouting the law. Polizia flashed by in the opposite direction. No one cared.

Vincenzo looked over his shoulder to Jameson and Elspeth bouncing around in the back and was rewarded with a thumbs up from Jameson, when Claire caught a familiar sign in passing; *Archaeologica di Ercolano.*

'Herculaneum right?'

'Si,' Vincenzo was impressed. 'Is sister city to Pompeii, also buried by Vesuvio in 79AD.'

'Yes I know. I didn't realise we were so close.'

'Oh yes. And Mario, his casa almost on top of Herculaneum.'

'Wow.'

With his sandal flat on the accelerator Mario took the slipway off the highway and made a right turn along Via Mare chased by a vortex of powdery black ash. Minutes later he slowed to negotiate several narrow lanes between what appeared in the dark to be apartment blocks. Mario drove slowly over a street of rectangular tufa blocks, cut like flagstones, and laid in a herringbone pattern. He killed the headlights and stopped outside a large double garage. They all looked about. The only sound in the street was the throbbing V8 engine, distant sirens and the humming of a temperamental streetlight.

Elspeth said quietly to Jameson. 'Hardly five star.' Directly across the street was a tired looking store. *Articolo da Regalo, detersive casalinghi ...* then in English, *Gift shop, detergents and household goods.* 'Hmm. That'll be handy.'

Crumbling cement stucco clung to the tufa block walls in patches. It's narrow entrance looked uninviting with one square window covered in steel mesh. It was closed. Crooked power poles fed the street electricity with sagging wire strung lackadaisically between them. Deserted cars lined one side of the street, some wheelless on blocks; and the black ash did nothing to improve the image. Claire snapped a few shots out the window on her mobile.

Jameson's attention was drawn to ruins on the corner opposite the store. An irregular wall, some three metres high in places, took up the corner block. Behind it earth, peppered with rubbish, created a foundation for shrubbery that grew over the top of the wall. It was one of those nondescript ruins in Italy that could be two hundred years old or two thousand.

'We're close to Herculaneum,' Elspeth said. 'You saw the sign.'

'Right. It's probably right under us.'

'Well they estimate only one third has been excavated and explored.'

'We here,' Vincenzo said nodding to the garage door. 'These is Mario's home.' They can see no evidence of a dwelling. A hand painted sign read *'Meccanico.'* Mario opened the doors with a remote on his key ring and jumped from the driver's seat leaving Vincenzo to slide behind the wheel and drive the pickup forward, parking in darkness. Mario looked up and down the street. It looked deserted.

'Is he married,' Claire asked.

'Yes.'

'Kids?'

'No. Vespa his family. I tell you he have museum. Wait you see.'

The garage doors closed noisily, locking them in total darkness. Elspeth felt a shiver. Mario fumbled in the dark and found the single cord dangling from the light switch. Click! A naked globe tossed out a miserable light, but soon fluorescents backed it up, when Claire's jaw dropped.

'Ya kiddin' me!' Two dozen or more Vespa's were lined neatly in four lines. All looked in immaculate order. All loved. All unusual.

Claire jumped from the pickup. 'This is freakin' awesome.'

'Mario's family yes.'

Mario stood with his hands on his hips beaming proudly. Elspeth and Jameson jumped from the truck tray. 'Impressive,' Jameson walked amongst the two wheelers.

'All original Piaggio manufacture si,' Vincenzo said proudly grinning at his cousin and slapping him on the back with pride. 'These 1946, only 2500 made.'

'Il primo,' Mario beamed, saddling the suitably olive green bike. He checked the bike was in neutral gear and kick-started the motor. It buzzed into life immediately.

'The first one huh? 98cc with top speed of 60kph.' Claire was seriously impressed. 'In 1946, after the war, Italian aircraft manufacture had been restricted, so this clever dude Piaggio designed this pressed steel body that became hugely successful,' Claire lectured the others. 'And called them Vespa.'

'Si Vespa ... she mean wasp in Italiano? Mario, he restore all thees himself, it's ah ... his passion.'

'What's this?' Jameson was drawn to an army green and beige camouflage patterned Vespa in the shadows with a serious gun barrel protruding from the front guard and shield. 'Looks dangerous.'

Mario cut the motor on the Vespa 98 and joined Jameson at the modified army model. He twisted the bare light bulb directing a spot of light over the rarity. Mario looked at Jameson and nodded his head sagely with a cheeky grin. 'Vespa TAP,' Mario said in his gravelly voice. 'Fatto per il Francese.'

'He say made for French army,' Vincenzo translated. 'For troops fighting in Vietnam in the 1960s. Thees Vespa strong. She was parachuted into jungle ... '

'Parachuted?'

'Si. With two troops each one.'

Claire. 'And the gun dude?'

Vincenzo laughed as Mario ran a seductive hand along the barrel of the one metre armour-piercing bazooka. They all took a closer look. The gun was mounted under the seat at a slight angle.

'She carry six large missiles. Mario say 600 of thees Vespa were made.'

'Where would you find such a model,' Elspeth asked.

'Mario buy from another collector who buy factory ... how you say spares ... '

'Surplus.'

'Si, surplus. Back in 1980, yes. It was bad condition when he found eet, but Mario, he restore good, si?'

'It's crazy,' Jameson admired the cannon.

'He even have two missiles.'

'What?'

Vincenzo said something to Mario who slipped an army ammunition box out from under the Vespa stand. He swung back the wooden lid.

'Jesus dude!' Claire went to pick one up.

'No Claire,' Vincenzo signalled for his brother to close the lid. 'Maybe that no good idea'

'Why? Are they alive?'

'Si, of course ... but old yes.'

A sudden tremor unsettled them. It was minor yet unnerving, especially since it was Elspeth, Jameson and Claire's first. Even Mario froze on the spot, starring at the wavering globe hanging from its cord, as if he was awaiting a larger shake to collapse the roof. The shaking passed. The flickering light settled.

'So Mario restores cars too,' Elspeth asked, drawing everyone's attention to a chassis and car body on a stand to one side resting over a mechanic's pit, looking mid restoration.

'Si, he restore cars for special order.' Vincenzo asked Mario a few questions. 'He said thees 1995 Alfa Romeo 164 LS, 210 horse power, V6, 3 litre, 5 speed manual,' Vincenzo translated. 'Big improvement on the '91, '93 he say with its grey cladding whatever this mean.'

Mario said something in rapid Italian to Vincenzo and made a sign for all to follow him.

Vincenzo smiled and nodded. 'Come, Mario say to follow.' Mario led the way through a doorway leading into his living quarters and the delightful aromas of steaming pasta, tomato sauce and Parmesan.

'Mario say, his wife, she make some gnocchi for us.' The moment Mario opened the second door a hairy rat of a dog, maybe a Jack Russel, Claire thought, came yapping down the passage and leapt into Mario's arms.

'Ciao, Silvio.'

'Your dog's called Silvio?' Claire asked.

'Si, after Silvio Berlusconi.'

The short passage widened into a living area of four rooms where a religious theme was maintained with Jesus on the cross and vividly coloured prints of Mother Mary holding baby Jesus to her breast. Other votive statues, mostly plastic, adorned the mantle. Mario's wife Maria knelt on the hearth sweeping with a brush and shovel where a porcelain figure had smashed to the floor in the tremour. She turned to greet them, shyly, and Jameson noticed she held the head of a statue of Mary. She had been crying. On the stove a pot of tomato basil sauce bubbled. Maria was in her mid-thirties but looked older. Mario introduced everyone and gave his wife a consolatory hug. It was clear that Vesuvius was unnerving them.

Tuesday.

They slept in armchairs and on the sofa, if you could call snippets of semi-consciousness sleep. Vincenzo camped on the floor on a blow-up mattress. After their supper of gnocchi and vino Mario snored in his bedroom while Maria's sobs continued. The tremors were becoming eerily more frequent and substantially stronger.

4AM.

Jameson's mobile alarm vibrated on the kitchen table but he was already awake. Jameson was excited. *Damn was he wired.* This was one of the craziest things he had ever done but if he could locate Vataea he mused, he would be up there with Schliemann who discovered Troy, or Carter the Egyptologist who discovered Tutankhamen.

The pungent odour had increased and outside the smoke and ash seemed thicker. The wind was blowing the plume away from the mountain over the bay. But it was still dark and difficult to tell.

Maria made coffee – good and strong Turkish style – on the stovetop. She heated left over gnocchi and turned the flat screen onto the news. Vincenzo switched to the CNN broadcast for his English-speaking friends.

'Hmm. Hasn't got any better.' Jameson took a bowl of pasta and seasoned it with black pepper and Parmesan. It was the best he'd eaten and with thumbs up, he told the woman so.

'It looks to be getting worse,' Elspeth said of Vesuvius. 'Are you sure you want to do this.'

Suddenly *Breaking News* scrolled across the screen over an aerial image from a drone close to the crater. It was still dark outside and the footage was live, but the flames of the volcano revealed a remarkable scene.

'The volcano's lip is about to be broached,' the reporter said. 'Yes. The lava is definitely collapsing the crater and experts have warned should this happen on the north-western slope the lava will undoubtedly head along the old route and for the village of San Sebastiano which was destroyed in 1944 and subsequently rebuilt.' The seventy two year old black and white newsreel footage followed. American News reporters who happened to be in Naples in 1944 to cover the allied landings that forced the German army to evacuate, shot this film, Jameson knew.

Jameson watched the old newsreel a moment. Accompanied by the monotone droning voice of the 1944 news reporter, he watched the ten-metre wall of molten, smouldering rock and rubble roll stubbornly and uncontrollably onto the village of San Sebastiano, destroying all in its path. Buildings simply crumbled and vanished under a walking pace avalanche of volcanic wrath.

'We need to move guys,' Jameson said. 'Now!' He looked to Elspeth. She looked into his eyes a moment. This was probably one of the craziest things she had ever done. 'Ready,' Jameson asked her.

'Yep. Let's do this,' she said with a deep sigh. *Goddam* Jameson thought, *that woman could miss sleep for a week and wear rags and she'd still look great.* Elspeth finished her coffee, electing to give the gnocchi breakfast a miss. She was more at peace this morning as she and Jameson had had a long and meaningful debate. Now she tended to agree. This was a very important find ... *but why,* she asked herself, *did it all unravel as that volcano decided to erupt.* Besides,

Elspeth convinced herself, her main objective was to see the looters arrested and gaoled. That was motivation enough.

Mario was as excited as the rest of them. 'Pronto?' he asked. *Ready?* The man was a regular working class Napolitano who just happened to watch too many Mel Gibson, Arnold Schwarzenegger movies. 'Andiamo.'

Let's go.

L'Oasi Bar and Café. Rome. Tuesday. 5.30AM

In Rome L'Oasi waiter and Vincenzo's acquaintance Aberto looked at himself in his bathroom mirror. One eye was completely closed up. *Why?* He screamed at himself ... *Vincenzo, what have you done now?* Aberto had not slept all night since the beating he had received in an alley near the café. The man was strong as an ox. A henchman. Now Aberto feared the worst. He had weakened and led the thug to his cousin.

Vincenzo where are you?

Aberto had tried calling Vincenzo all night on his mobile. But telecommunication signal towers around Napoli were jamming with the emergency. Calls were not getting through. *Why me* he cried and hit redial ...

5.50AM

The sunrise was spectacular, reminding Jameson of a poached red plum in a sea of egg custard. But drifting smoke threatened to veil the sky with uncertainty. Mario hefted his toolbox into the rear of his V8 and backed out onto the street where the black ash now caked centimetres thick on the ground. Vincenzo closed the garage doors and the others climbed aboard.

'How far?' Jameson asked.

'San Sebastiano is about twenty minutes away,' Vincenzo said. 'Or ten as the Mario flies.'

Vincenzo listened to the car radio and translated as Mario ran lights and enjoyed breaking every road rule in the book. Smoke was thickening. Eyes watered. And the sun struggled to shine through on what would normally be a clear sunny day. Most people were heading north, very few travelled south and no one headed towards the volcano.

'Is at alarm stage he says,' Vincenzo translated the car radio. 'They fear a larger eruption, yes. Already the eighteen municipalities around the north-west slopes, are evacuated ... the entire population of the red zone has been evacuated and operation centres have been set up ... evacuees used their own transport, or public transport under civil protection ...'

'Civil protection! What's that,' Claire asked trying to keep upright with Mario swerving around oncoming traffic and clipping the curb. 'Is it police?'

'Polizia si. And army.'

Claire opened her mouth to speak but Vincenzo held up his hand to silence her, listening to the radio ...

'Use transport routes and main roads access only,' he again translated. Mario slid sideways off the main road bumping onto a poorly gravelled mountain road. The V8 chewed into the rocky skirt and he corrected just in time while Jameson and Elspeth held tight, bouncing about on the pickup tray.

'Jesus!' Jameson held on with both hands. 'If I was only half awake before, I'm awake now.'

Elspeth slid up against Jameson and he anchored them both when suddenly they had a clear view of mighty Vesuvius's crater. It loomed over them with its fiery, thick black smoky plume belching skywards.

'Oh-my-god!' Elspeth cried out. 'Have you ever seen anything so ... so ...'

'So beautiful,' Jameson sighed, seriously in awe.

'I was going to say frightening.'

The short cut avoided roadblocks delivering them to the modern built up suburbs of the red zone. Mario sped through deserted streets where thousands of people lived and worked ...

Once.

But it was now eerily deserted.

Homes, churches and businesses appeared and disappeared as the monster Vesuvius spread her smouldering cloak about them.

'There will be more road blocks further,' Vincenzo told his cousin in Italian. 'We will have to climb the mountain cross country and approach San Sebastiano from the north-west slope.'

'Si, you are right.' Mario hit a hairpin corner with fearless abandon. He dropped back to second gear, corrected the slide and accelerated, climbing the northwest slopes of the volcano with increasing speed. The first armoured vehicle met them on the next corner. Soldiers shouted down at them but Mario floored the accelerator and they passed in opposite directions. The soldiers radioed back to the first roadblock. But thick curtains of sporadic smoke clouds descended upon them and Mario saw the armed soldiers blocking the road ahead before they saw him.

'Un attimo!' Mario screamed out. He spun the wheel.

'What?'

'Hang on!'

The V8 left the road ...

Airborne over a ditch. The F-250 solid axle suspension slammed onto rock. Jarred. Fought back. Jameson and Elspeth travelled across the tray; Jameson gripping the toolbox, and Elspeth the roll-bar.

'Jesus Christ!' In the cabin Claire bounced hitting her head against the roof while Vincenzo crossed himself and gripped the dashboard.

Mario engaged four-wheel drive.

One hundred metres overland Mario skid sideways onto a goat track. 'San Sebastiano,' he cried out through grinding teeth, his pointy elbows jabbing left and right as he clutched the wheel.

'What? Where?'

Mario stabbed a gnarly finger up the goat track.

'This is old peasant track to village,' Vincenzo yelled at Claire. We are now driving over the old 1944 lava flow and will have to approach the village from the mountainside.

Mario snatched a glimpse in his mirror. He saw a pursuing flash of army green vehicle through the smoke. Immediately it was swallowed by a swooping swirl of volcanic steam. It disappeared. A loud crash followed and Mario was certain he saw the army truck roll onto its side.

'This is awesome dude,' Claire cried out wedging her hand against the cabin roof for support. 'Where did your cousin learn to drive?'

Vincenzo shot Claire a wicked eye. 'He drive getaway car for Mafiosi,'

'He what?' Claire was aghast.

'Just jokes yes.'

The track steepened sharply, and levelled. It appeared they were in the wind's direct path. Smoke and steam limited visibility to three or four metres. Another army barricade appeared.

But this one had been abandoned and there was no way around.

They were close.

Mario cut the motor and leapt from the driver's seat. 'Su!' he shouted.

'Out,' Vincenzo translated, pushing Claire out the door.

Mario threw open his toolbox and slammed a sledgehammer into Jameson hand. He collected a spare for himself and handed out facemasks, tying a bandana around his own mouth. With bandana, grubby singlet, shorts and sandals he looked like a Mexican bandit. The five gathered in a circle ...

'What's that sound?' Elspeth aimed her ears into the sulphuric fug rolling towards them.

Claire's face twisted. 'Dude, that sounds like ... '

Jameson squeezed her arm.

Shut it. Listen.

The sound was a distant rumble. A heavy resonance of crashing timber and collapsing masonry. A low thunder of rolling boulders. And the stinging smoke of fires.

Elspeth swallowed hard. 'Is that what I think it is?'

Vincenzo nodded, lines of stress crisscrossing his brow.

'How far to San Sebastiano?' Jameson asked.

'Five hundred metres.'

'Let's go.'

Intermittent gushes of wind cleared patches of smoke. The goat track appeared and disappeared and now they were on what was clearly the 1944 flow field; a gloomy basalt black terrain of no man's land. Either side the rich soil grew plentiful grapes, tomatoes and olives. Within a hundred metres they had arrived at a built-up area. Apartment blocks lined the street culminating in piazzas, a fountain and life-size votive statues of Jesus on the cross or the Virgin Mary. Vines abounded. Olive trees loaded with fruit waved back through the smoke.

'Mamma Mia!' Vincenzo gaped open mouthed. For a brief second the smoke lifted ...

And they all saw it ...

A ten-metre-high hill of burning, hissing, crackling rock and mountain rubble heading directly for them spitting boiling lava. An unstoppable avalanche of death.

It devoured everything in its path.

Crawling like a murderous monster ... one metre every minute.

'Oh ... my ... god!'

Jameson grabbed Elspeth's wrist. 'We have to move ... fast!'

Beneath them the ground was now constantly rumbling, shifting. It was terrifying. Then, as they watched in total disbelief, the first buildings became victims of the crushing rockslide. They watched an apartment block crumble and fold. Four storey walls were mashed like a doll's house. One wall thundered onto another and like dominoes, the buildings fell; their masonry becoming fodder for the gargantuan bulldozer.

'Oh ... shit!' Claire was gobsmacked. She whipped out her mobile and snapped a few shots.

'Claire!'

'Chapel Patiro?' Jameson said abruptly. 'Where is the chapel?'

Vincenzo looked at Mario. They squinted at each other in the blinding smoke. 'Per di qua,' Mario shouted and ran off along via Melloni armed with his sledgehammer. The others turned to follow.

'Arresto!' A voice screamed from further down via Palmeri

'Shit! It's the army!'

'Arresto!' The soldier in full combat gear was instantly joined by others. They gathered two hundred metres further down the sloping street. The soldiers spread out in a combat formation.

'They might think we're looters,' Elspeth said urgently.

'Well I'm not hanging around to find out. Run!' Jameson yelled dragging Elspeth by the arm. Claire tripped after them. 'Run for Christ sake.'

Vincenzo pushed the girls ahead of him and they raced after Mario. A shot was fired. Jameson was certain it was a warning shot – into the air ...

But who would know ... he darted through the piazza.

'Where's Mario?' he said when they caught a breath on the other side of the clearing.

'Psssst!'

They all turned. *Mario!* Mario waved a hand frantically and they ran across the cobbled courtyard, circled a fountain and down a narrow alley to join him. A second shot rang out.

'Now what?'

Mario clamped onto Elspeth arm pushing her into a doorway. He shoved Claire after her. Vincenzo, Jameson and then Mario slipped silently into the dark stifling passageway when ...

A clatter of army boots passed by.

'Mario,' Jameson hissed urgently. 'Where's the chapel ... ah ... Capella de san Patiro?'

Mario spoke to Vincenzo. Vincenzo went white. 'San Patiro?'

'Si ... I mean yes. Yes Patiro. Where is it.'

'Mario, he say he thought you said Matiro.'

'No for Christ's sake. Patiro ... san Patiro. Where is it?' Mario pointed back the way they had come. 'He say up there.' As if a warning from Satan himself the sound of crashing walls was deafeningly close.

'Dude,' Claire said with a nervous twitch. 'We gotta move. That bitch is getting close.'

'There are many capella in all villages in Italy,' Vincenzo apologised for his cousin. Mario shoved past them in the narrow passageway. He listened, and then kicked the door open into the square.

He jerked his head left and right.

All clear.

And signalled them to follow.

Mario was first across the street to the piazza. They all gathered at the fountain where Jameson took a bandana from his pocket and soaked it in the water. Diagonally opposite, another street led towards the mountain. Mario pointed. 'San Patiro, si.'

A horrendous explosion was followed by a boom from the direction they had come. Gaping over their shoulders they watched an entire block of apartments implode as the liquid rock incinerated its foundation. Masonry tumbled into the street creating a thick mushroom of choking smoke and brick dust that channelled its way down the street in a fast-moving cloud towards them. Jameson thought of the collapsing twin towers on 9/11.

'Run!'

They raced across the street the very second the lethal cloud of toxic volcanic fug engulfed the piazza.

'La Cappella, si.' Mario stabbed a finger at the doomed chapel one hundred metres further on.

The small chapel, built over the 1944 ruins of San Sebastiano was the centre of another piazza. It was the size of a small house, made of volcanic rock and *iced* with light blue and white stucco. The Virgin Mary stared down the street towards them, her arms outstretched as if pleading with them. Briefly the smoke lifted ...

'Jesus H Christ!' Claire stammered.

'Oh shit!' Jameson saw it too. The approaching wall of molten lava was towering behind the chapel. Building in strength. Stalking the house of god with satanic determination. Its insatiable hunger preparing to demolish the chapel.

With sledgehammer firmly gripped Jameson sprinted ahead. Mario followed. 'Jameson!' Elspeth screamed.

'Stay there,' Jameson yelled over his shoulder. Behind the chapel a school building crashed to earth. The rumble was followed by a loud hiss of steam and a vortex of smoke sped along the street.

Instantly Jameson and Mario vanished. Elspeth put her hands over her mask. It was becoming increasingly difficult to breath. 'J – Jameson?'

Without warning a high-pitched whirring drew their attention skywards.

'What the ...'

'A drone!'

Claire. 'Is that bitch filming us?'

At that same moment Elspeth noticed blurred legs through the lifting dust ahead. Jameson was safe ...

For the moment.

'It's television right?' Claire asked Vincenzo gaping up at the drone.

'No.' Vincenzo recognised the Matrice 600 DJI drone immediately. 'It is not television.'

They had been spotted. The drone hovered in one position and the camera locked on.

'If it's not television who is it?'

'I don't know. CNN and local networks, they have FREEFLY Alta 6 UAS for thees aerial cinematography ... '

'A what?'

'A Drone Hexacopter.'

'How do you know so much about drones bro,' Claire asked, her watery red eyes mesmerized by the intrusive machine.

'I work with them ... documentary on Pompeii for History Channel, si.'

No one took a second look at the older model Lancia van parked amongst dozens of other deserted vehicles at the side of the road at Via M Falconi on the northern outskirts of San Sebastiano. The van was black and, like everything else in the area, it was caked in black ash. The words *Resina Explosivo* sign written along its sides were near impossible to read. Out of sight in the back of the van Ricco Ricci stared at the monitor. The drone had been a good investment. It had been his idea to search for archaeological sites; mainly Etruscan tomb sites in remote hills of Tuscany and had proved invaluable. Now he was excited at its other uses, hovering over an area far too dangerous to venture into, while he sat in moderate comfort in the van.

'I don't get it,' he said to Silvano Marchetti sitting beside him. 'What in god's name has that lamp they bought in Rome got to do with San Sebastiano? And look at that mountain ... Christ, are they mad?'

Ricci watched the screen with intense interest. At all costs they must protect their find; the lost city of Vataea. Ricci's thoughts went to that cloying waiter at L'Oasi in Rome. He had returned later that evening and waited for the man to leave work. Ricci smiled at how weak the man was, how he squealed like a bitch when he gave him the beating in the dark laneway. Ricci smiled at how easy it was to extract information from the weakling.

Pussy.

And luck had stayed with them. They had positioned themselves in the van outside Vincenzo's cousin's garage on reconnaissance early that morning, and only waited an hour before Mario pulled away with the Australians in the back of the pickup. Yes, Ricci could not believe their good fortune, and now ...

'They're heading to that chapel,' Marchetti's eyes narrowed. 'Zoom in.'

Mount Vesuvius.

Jameson fought through the billowing smoke. He had problems breathing even with a wet bandanna tied about his mouth, and his eyes were red and weeping. The chapel was now only metres away and behind it, through the steam and smoke, he caught momentary glimpses of Vesuvius' crater spewing red lava. Jameson shook his head ...

Crazy ...

This was the craziest thing he had ever done.

Mario appeared. A hot blast of air cleared the smoke overhead a brief moment and both men gaped skywards. The mushroom of smoke expelled from Vesuvius' crater was of Hiroshima proportions. Instantly to one side a modern apartment block teetered, its foundations ravished by molten rock. Boiling lava hit its water mains and Geysers of steam hissed skywards. The rumbling avalanche of rock was deafening. The wall of lava moving at one metre every minute was already at the rear of the stone church.

Jameson and Mario looked each other in the eye.

Faces taught with apprehension.

'Now or never,' Jameson yelled over the racket. Mario understood and nodded solemnly.

Jameson's heart rate was off the charts. Madness. Utter madness. Mario followed Jameson. They stepped up to the tiny church door, their arms up to their faces to protect them from the searing heat. They could hear the lava flow building up at the rear of the building ...

A growling, squealing of metal and tonnes of reinforced concrete as the buildings all about them crumbled.

Either side of the chapel the glowing red semi-liquid rock crept along its walls. Buildings on the north side collapsed and more brick dust billowed skywards.

Jameson charged forward crushing his shoulder into the door. The wooden door flew open. The heat within the confined space was unimaginable. Ahead the altar lay bare. At least, Jameson thought, the locals managed to take the church gold and silver. Several niches high in the walls held life sized effigies of saints. They weren't so lucky. The glass in the baroque style windows had burst from the heat. Smoke was filling the chapel fast. At the entrance the campanologist's ropes dangled freely. A dozen metres above him the single brass bell hung ...

Silently awaiting its detruction.

Jameson knew he had minutes. Two or three at most.

Get in. Get out.

Jameson's head throbbed. His eyes stung and he could feel the molten lava only metres away piling up against the rear wall. He turned a full circle. To Jameson's right a low door led to the vestry ...

Vestry. Vestry. No ...

To the left of the vestry door Jameson saw the pulpit. On the wall nearby he saw the carved marble baptismal font.

Crypt! Where to start? What am I doing here?

'Fretta!' Mario shouted.

Hurry!

Jameson swung about to face Mario standing in the doorway. His legs spread apart, sweat pouring from his brow, muscles flexed and with sledgehammer held horizontally in both hands ready to demolish the house of god. Jameson wanted to laugh hysterically ...

Vulcan himself.

'Jesus Christ!'

Mario jerked his sledgehammer. 'Fretta!'

Hurry!

The back wall split with a thunderous tearing sound. A mighty crevice appeared large enough for a man to step through. Bricks and stonework caved into the church. Crushing the alter. Nothing was sacred to Mount Vesuvius.

'Mamma Mia ...' Mario wasted no time. He rushed to the nearest memorial plaque on the chapel wall and – like a soccer hooligan – he laid into it with his sledgehammer. The marble crumbled to the floor in a dozen pieces. There was nothing behind it.

'Merda!' The mad Italian took to the next plaque and the next.

'Riposte in Pace!' Jameson screamed out. Mario spun about. Jameson stepped back. He had been standing on a crypt in the nave floor. 'Rest in Peace.' He read the name. 'Margareta Parco ... no.'

Jameson sought out others. Skipping from one foot to the other. There were several. 'Riposte in Pace Ferdinando Amedeo ... no ... Arturo Zetticci ... no ... Nicia Sagese ... no ... Jesus!' Jameson shouted in frustration.

'No Jesus,' Mario shouted back.

'Aha!' Jameson danced about tripping on pews. 'Brunelleschi!' he yelled. 'Here. Bernardo Brunelleschi.'

Mario shoved Jameson aside, raised the sledgehammer above his head and bought it down with brute force.

'Bah!' Mario bawled out, his hand jarring violently. Like a warning from the heavens the rear wall shifted forward, moaned hauntingly and surrendered to its fate. The rubble spilt towards them. It seemed a giant bulldozer was out of control. The chancel roof collapsed and masonry dust was shadowed by bubbling boiling lava. The heat was phenomenal as wooden beams and furniture burst into flame.

Jameson exchanged an anxious glance with Mario. Without a word spoken both men took to the crypt like drunken vandals. But the marble was thick. One hundred centimetres at least. Only metres away – three or four – the walls of both side aisles crumbled simultaneously. The masonry tumbled towards them like they were part of some conspiracy ...

A conspiracy to push the trespassers back off the mountain and bury its secrets for eternity.

But Jameson wasn't giving up the fight.

So close.

So damned close.

Immediately they heard a hollow thump. Jameson's hammer broke through first. Beyond the damage lay darkness. A shallow pit. Using the sledgehammer handle he levered the remaining slab. Mario dropped to his knees wrenching at the pieces barehanded as they loosened.

Suddenly the church bell started ringing. Not in an orderly fashion but in sporadic urgency.

Directly behind Mario, Jameson watched the dangling bell ropes dance, as if the very ghost of Bernardo Brunelleschi was threatening them. Masonry was now pushing up against them. Behind Jameson the roof was collapsing in increasingly large sections. The heat was searing. The wailing groans of the dying chapel terrifying ...

And now the damned bell!

Jameson realised the bell tower was about to fall.

Mario threw the last piece of marble aside.

Yes!

In the dusty dark recess Jameson saw a small casket, the size of a shoebox. He lifted it free. At that very moment they heard a thunderous ground shaking crash. Vesuvius' very roots writhed and burrowed beneath them. The last section of the apartment block next to the chapel toppled, crushing against the chapel wall. Immediately pandemonium erupted. Jameson shook himself free of rubble dust clutching the casket to his chest and with Mario's help he staggered to his feet. Overhead the bell protested in deranged peels. The heavy bronze bell pleaded its last. It broke from its mount ...

And pounded through the ceiling in an explosion of splintered timber.

Jameson dived aside the second the bell buried itself in the nave floor, directly where he had stood.

The two men sprang for the door ...

There was no time to look back and they leapt through the arched church entrance the moment it folded and crumbled.

Elspeth, Claire and Vincenzo had seen and heard everything. The encroaching wall of lava, the flames, the chapel roof's cave in ...

'Jameson!' Elspeth screamed out the moment the front of the chapel collapsed into the street and more choking dust spiralled upwards to dance amongst Vesuvius's maelstrom.

'Jameson!'

As they watched, fixated in horror, the two men materialised through the warzone fug appearing to rise from the ashes. They ran towards them. Both men were unrecognisable, caked in dust, ash and grime.

'Jesus Christ,' Jameson had lost his bandanna. He gulped and gasped for clean air. 'That was one hell of a ride.' Jameson swung about to make certain Mario was clear and the two men shook hands and hugged.

'Shit Mario. That was mad mate.'

'Si, si.' Mario grinned, glad to be alive.

'Jameson Rowley,' Elspeth said with relieved anger. 'Don't you ever do anything so mad as that again.'

Claire noticed the dirt-enveloped casket first. 'You got it!' She cried out. 'You actually found it.'

'Of course.'

Immediately the loud whir of a swooping drone sounded over the commotion. They all searched through the smoke above.

'A drone,' Jameson said. 'What the hell's that doing here?'

'We don't know.'

'TV Napoli Uno,' Mario shouted.

'No news, no network. We do not know.'

'Army?'

'Maybe. Let's get out of here.'

For Ricco Ricci and Silvano Marchetti watching the drone's monitor from inside the van one kilometre away, it was edge of the seat drama. Both men were totally astonished.

'What is it?'

'Ossuary from a crypt by the looks of it.'

'They risked their lives for an ossuary of cremated bones?'

'Whose?'

'That's for us to find out. And at all costs we can't have them leading the carabinieri to Vataea.'

The troupe reached Mario's pickup. The drone followed.

'If that is army drone we'd be in troubles by now,' Vincenzo said.

Jameson. 'And you're sure it's not CNN or some other network.'

'Dude,' Claire panted. 'Vincenzo is a drone expert.'

'Si si. No network.'

'So how can we lose it?' Elspeth asked.

'Get in the truck. See if it follows.'

With the evacuation of the red zone complete most roadblocks were deserted. They descended to the lower village, a heavily built up area. Mario driving ...

Fast.

Vincenzo related the news from his mobile. 'They say the eruption is weakening. Maybe not all San Sebastiano buried after all.'

'Dude,' Claire laughed anxiously, 'I don't believe we just did that. And you Mario.' Claire reached across and punched his arm. 'What you and Jam did was awesome.' Mario understood a little. He grinned back through blood shot eyes and blackened face. Claire poked her head out the window to shout to Elspeth. 'Can you see it?' But her question was smartly answered. Claire could see the drone half a kilometre away. It was clearly following them.

Claire. 'Who could it be?'

'I have bad feeling,' Vincenzo said quietly. 'Bad feeling it is mans in Rome who look for us. Now he know we find something in chapel.'

Mario braked. No warning. The pickup fishtailing on the unsealed road. 'Merda.' They all looked straight ahead from the edge of no man's land. Less than half a kilometre away all paths were blockaded and the army and police were present in their hundreds.

Jameson leapt from the tray. 'Now what?'

'Bitch!' Claire shouted. 'Are they looking for us?'

'No.' Vincenzo took binoculars from his cousin's toolbox. 'It look like they allow some peoples back into that part of the San Sebastiano.' Vincenzo and Mario exchanged words in Italian. 'Mario say we must leave truck and we walk. We walk to Ercolona from here.'

'Walk!'

Mario laughed.

Vincenzo. 'He says at least we walk down mountain, not up.'

'And that way we will lose the drone,' Jameson agreed. They all looked back towards the mountain where the tenacious drone hovered. 'First we've got to open this casket.' Jameson took a deep breath and sighed. For the first time in ten minutes the drama and danger caught up with him. He lifted the casket onto the pickup tray and studied the box, with its rusting iron pins on both sides securing the lid in place. Jameson used his blackened hand to rub the years of grime from the lid. 'Yes,' he whispered as the others gathered around. Barely discernable on the lid was a brass plaque engraved with the letters B.B.

'Bernardo Brunelleschi,' Jameson whispered with reverence.

•   •   •   •   •

Ricco Ricci crouched over the drone control monitor in the van. His neck ached. He handed the drone controls to Marchetti while he cricked his stiff neck and for good measure, he cracked his knuckles.

Marchetti flinched. 'I wish you wouldn't do that. It makes me feel ill.'

'You'll get over it,' the ex-commando with the rock-hard face and a jaw like a breakfast cereal carton didn't handle criticism lightly. Marchetti was about to retaliate but thought better of it, when he noticed through clearing smoke that Mario's vehicle had stopped. He watched as everyone in the vehicle gathered about the mysterious box on the pickup tray.

'Hey. They've stopped.'

'Get in closer,' Ricci said in his raw baritone voice.

'We don't want them to see the drone.'

'They've already seen it. We've got to see what's so important in that box.'

'Papers!' Elspeth said excitedly, straining over Jameson shoulder as the casket lid fell aside.

Amongst the cremated remains of Signor Brunelleschi Jameson immediately recognised the 1940s exercise-book paper with its widely spaced faint lines. 'This is definitely torn from Vince Renzo's diary.'

Mario and Vincenzo leant over the casket. Claire pushed forward. 'There's a plan dude, a map or something.'

The loud whir overhead grew closer. 'Jesus!' Jameson grew angry. 'Who-is-that?' He folded the papers and put them carefully into his backpack.

'Come, we walk and we lose them,' Vincenzo said as Mario locked his truck. 'Mario say he come back for truck when things settle down.'

An hour later.

'Yes. I know this man.' Elario Rosellis, small time thief, black marketeer and standover man recognised Mario's stocky shape in the drone's surveillance footage immediately. And the V8 pickup confirmed his suspicions. 'He lives in Ercolano. He is a mechanic, a good one too.'

'Yes we know that. And you know him?'

'We've never met, but yes, I know him. They say he is opposition ...'

'Opposition?'

'Si. He is tombaroli. They say he digs at Herculaneum. But no one knows how.'

Ricci. 'Well that's interesting.'

'It fits with his actions today,' Marchetti agreed. Marchetti looked at Ricci who read his colleague's mind. *That means the Australians are up to no good. They could ruin everything.*

'He also collects Vespas,' Elario said as an after-thought.

'Vespas?' Marchetti asked.

'Yes. He loves the damned things. Has twenty or more I'm told.'

'You've done well Elario. Takes a thief to know a thief huh?' Marchetti looked at Ricci who had suggested they show Elario Rosellis and brother Lazaro the footage in the first place. Ricci acknowledged Marchetti with a subtle nod. Ricco Ricci liked the Rosellis brothers. They were a younger version of himself and, like himself, they were thugs. Elario – with his dark skin of Moroccan Sicilian ancestry, his rich ebony eyes, a square jaw and scarred face rendering him incapable of smiling – dropped out of *Scoula di Napoli Archeologia* to become a tombaroli – tomb robber – instead. Looting antiquities instead of working to preserve Italy's heritage. Brother Lazaro was a loose cannon who enjoyed dishing out pain, money and chasing women – and in that order. Their motto; *Take no prisoners.*

'So you know where he lives?' Ricco asked him.

'Sure,' Elario said. 'He lives at his workshop. Do you want me to rough him up? Thousand Euros.'

Marchetti slipped a silver money clip filled with folded fifty and one hundred Euro notes from his pocket. 'We want you to belt some sense into him and we want you to scare the devil into those Australian tourists with him. We want them so shit scared they will be on the next flight back to kangaroo land. Got it?'

'Sure. But I'll need Lazarro and Remo Angello to help me in that case. And that'll cost you a thousand a piece.'.

Silvano Marchetti and Ricco Ricci new Remo Angello well. They had used him on a number of hits. The twenty-three-year-old gangster was from a small village in Southern Italy and they knew Lazaro and Elario's had met Remo the thug in a Sicilian prison where they did time for extortion. Marchetti peeled off a thousand Euros passing them to Elario who could not conceal his delight. 'One now, the rest tomorrow.'

'It's a pleasure doing business with you signor.'

'One other thing,' Ricci said. The Australian has a backpack, and in that backpack are papers ... '

'Papers signor?'

'Yes. Large pad size. You must retrieve those papers. They were stolen from us,' Ricci lied. 'And there is another thousand in it for the papers. Got it?'

'Si signor.'

Ricci and Marchetti climbed back into their van and drove away from the Rosellis small tomato orchard feeling pleased with themselves. 'You trust him?' Marchetti asked Ricci at the wheel.

'Sure I trust him, in the sense that he would beat up his own mother for money.'

Marchetti smiled at the suggestion then grew serious. 'We cannot be wasting time,' he said. 'According to news updates the volcano is settling. We need to hit Vataea while everything is in turmoil.'

Ricci threw a piece of gum into his mouth. 'If it *is* Vataea you mean.'

'I'll bet my life on it. The site is too big. The grapes are almost ready to harvest. We need to involve more diggers. Get what we can out of there and cover the site to return in a year or so.'

'I could not agree more.'

Meccanico Garage. Erclona. 11.45AM

'Where's Maria?' Jameson asked after Mario's wife as they entered the darkly deserted living quarters.

'Andato a sue madri.'

Vincenzo translated. 'Gone to her mother's?'

Mario threw Jameson a towel and tipped his head to the bathroom where Jameson gave himself a quick wash. Blinds were pulled closed and curtains drawn. Mario flicked the light switch for a single bulb in the centre of the living room. He hit the remote button for the flat screen television and they stood about silently as the screen lit up offering more aerial shots of the disaster.

Jameson looked at the kitchen bench, all neat and tidy. 'Madri huh?'

'Si.' Mario explained through Vincenzo that he had called his wife on his mobile two hours earlier. He had warned her to get out. 'Drone,' he went on. 'Bad.' Mario grabbed a towel and took his turn in the bathroom.

'You had a mobile signal?' Vincenzo said surprised. He walked around the room holding his own mobile high. Suddenly he caught a signal. 'Merda, I have seventeen missed calls from Aberto.' Immediately a call came through. Vincenzo swiped the screen. 'Ciao.'

'Vincenzo!' It was his sister Luciana using Aberto's mobile. 'Are you alright?'

'Yes why?'

'I have been so worried about you.' Luciano told Vincenzo about Aberto's beating.

'Mary mother of Jesus.'

Claire. 'What dude?'

Vincenzo ended the call and explained. He looked to Mario who was back watching the local news channel for the latest on the disaster. Martial law had been declared around the entire base of Mount Vesuvius. But some areas were allowed re-entry to their homes, mostly on the safer southern slopes. Vincenzo explained the phone call to cousin Mario. Mario agreed. He suggested to Vincenzo that the mystery drone was connected to people following his Australian friends and if these people were tombaroli, they were to be feared.

'So we need to get out of here, yes,' Vincenzo said to Claire, Jameson and Elspeth. 'They will find us now for certain.'

Elspeth. 'Who will find us?'

'The same bas-tard what beat my friend Aberto.'

'But go where?'

Mario looked pained, worried for his wife maybe. He spoke quickly to Vincenzo. 'Mario, he say he have safe house. Is friend who has Pizzeria down near the bay, in Via Filangieri Piazza.'

'Pizza?' Claire said, salivating.

Vincenzo. 'Si. Etna Pizzeria. I know thees place.'

'Si, si.' Mario was looking more and more concerned. 'Pronto.'

'But we haven't got any wheels,' Jameson said.

'Oh,' Vincenzo said. 'How you say ... on the contrary.'

Claire's grin was infectious. 'Vespas!'

Mario hurried to the key board, where keys were kept for all his later model electric starters. He handed Jameson the 2013 Vespa GTS 278cc four-stroke one cylinder. Black. Vincenzo took the 2011 Vespa 300 278cc four-stroke piston engine. White.

'These are the faster more reliable bikes,' Vincenzo told them. Mario mounted his precious collectors piece, 1960s Vespa TAP with mounted bazooka. He kick-started the motor and she fired immediately.

'Cool man,' Claire was impressed. But not as impressed as when he loaded a missile into the launcher. 'Dude! Are you serious? That's freakin' awesome. Jameson and Vincenzo started theirs. The 278cc motors buzzed to life ...

When loud banging came from the side lane.

Elspeth. 'What's that?'

Mario dismounted. He hurried to a wire mesh window at the side of the garage. He saw blurred angry figures through the frosted glass. The banging became louder ...

Violent.

'Merda. E' li.'

Vincenzo translated. 'It is them.'

Elspeth. 'Who?'

'You do not want to know. We must leave.'

At that moment the window shattered. But wire re-enforcing held the broken glass in place. Immediately leather gloved fists pounded the window until the glass dropped in one piece to the garage floor.

'Pronto!'

Mario thumbed the remote on his key ring. The garage door rolled aside exposing the street swamped with an eerie blood orange glow. Directly across the street Mario recognised an older model Fiat. He snatched up a large screwdriver, ran across the street and stabbed the tire ...

The tire fizzed and quickly deflated.

'Andare, andare,' Mario yelled at the others.

'Go!'

Jameson - already saddled on his bike – secured his backpack with the casket papers and revved the motor. The 278cc was singing and itching to fly. Elspeth threw a leg over the passenger seat. Jameson shot Vincenzo a look. 'Ready?'

'Si, go!'

Vincenzo cranked the motor on his bike. But it bellowed smoke. Far too much smoke. Claire made to mount the back but Mario screamed an order over the racket.

'Merda!' Vincenzo cursed. 'You must get in Mario's sidecar. He say thees bike no strong for two.'

Claire looked to the window.

The first thug tumbled to the floor.

It was Lazaro Rosellis – wearing a red and white baseball cap, short dreadlocks, face studs and a superman T-shirt – he was hefted inside by his accomplices. Mario heaved an empty petrol can. It bounced off superman's shoulder like a plastic bucket. Another thug, Remo Angello – shaved head, Muhammad beard and geometric pentagon tattoo on his neck hoisted himself over the sill ...

Elario was right behind him.

Mario yelled at Claire. 'Pronto! Pronto!' As the first man sprang to his feet Mario slid onto the seat of his precious war Vespa. Claire made a dash ...

Slipped and fell ...

Landing sideways into the sidecar the moment Mario accelerated. The wheels gripped the concrete. The war Vespa escalated forward while Claire's legs danced over the side. They dashed onto the street as Vincenzo engaged gear, released the clutch and accelerated ...

The back wheel slid dangerously side-ways. Too much throttle. Vincenzo eased off slightly. The bike corrected and he flew past Jameson. In less than a heart beat Jameson was on his tail with Elspeth holding tight. The three thugs were just seconds in their wake. Lazaro ran to the garage entrance pulling a silenced pistol from his belt.

Aimed.

'Are you crazy?' Elario, screamed out. Elario ran to their Fiat out on the street. The front tire was flat.

'Merda!' He watched the Vespas escape.

Mohammed beard. 'Now what?'

Elario raced back into the garage. 'Are you blind? Look at these bikes. Pronto, pick a kick start.'

Immediately the back streets of Ercolano sounded like a motor racecourse on the last lap. Six angry Vespa *wasps* buzzed at maximum speed ...

Through intersections and racing red lights heading for the Bay of Naples. Ash covered shutters were thrown open. Faces appeared at windows.

What was this?

Anarchy?

Mario was used to his Vespa TAP, but also wife Maria for sidecar ballast. Claire didn't have a clue. Awkwardly she righted herself. She had no sense of balance and what was required of the passenger in the bucket. Jameson and Vincenzo easily caught Mario on the straight. They eased ahead, Vincenzo in the lead. They turned left towards Via Mare. Mario approached the ninety-degree corner. He slowed, shifting his body over the sidecar. Claire sat like a statue, frozen with ignorance. And Mario's lack of English didn't help. He managed the turn, opened the throttle and pointed the cannon east but ...

Instantly his TAP was hit from behind.

Mario shot a glance in the side mirror. Superman backed off, accelerated and hit Mario once more. Claire turned feeling useless. Superman darted left, accelerated ...

And came alongside.

He carried a cosh and swung the lead weighted club at Mario hitting his elbow. The pain shot up Mario's arm like an electric bolt. They exchanged curses. Mario found more throttle and the TAP crept forward. At the same instant the man with the Muhammad beard and Elario sped past. Both had 250cc scooters. Power was in their favour. Mohammed cut in front of Mario. He decelerated and Mario ploughed into the back of him. Mohammed's bike shuddered from the impact, the front wheel shaking violently, threatening to eject him ...

But he accelerated and chased after Elario now on Jameson's tail.

On Via Mare the road was clear. A truck here a Fiat there. There was little traffic on the long straight stretch.

In the distance ...

Bay of Naples.

Directly ahead – black ash dust and plenty of it.

Elario – comfortable behind his aviator's sunglasses – raced alongside Jameson and Elspeth, her arms locked about Jameson's waist. They looked about. Elario's face was chiselled.

Hell-bent on victory.

'Backpack!' Elario screamed at Jameson over the whining motors.

'Eat me.' Jameson yelled back and added sauce by swerving at the thug. Elario decelerated and fell in behind Jameson as Mohammed sheared through the ash along his right flank. Vincenzo saw the threat and, spitting ash, he closed in. Mohammed swerved at Jameson, on the attack. But Vincenzo sandwiched him between them. Elspeth kicked out. She connected with Mohammed's wind guard. Vincenzo backed away smartly as Mohammed lost control from the assault. He sheered off across the road as ...

A police car approached ahead. Mohammed's wheels hit the guttering.

The bike slid on its side ...

The rider was dragged along on the road. The police car missed him by centimetres while five other Vespas swarmed by. Mohammed sprang to his feet. He dusted himself while remounting. The police car made a U-turn but Mohammed was already speeding after the others.

'Mamma Mia!' Mario looked in the mirror and saw flashing blue lights. They heard a siren. He may be pursued by thugs but he also knew this was no time for the law.

Vincenzo drew parallel with Jameson and shouted. 'Polizia!'

'I know.'

'Follow me.' Vincenzo hit the slip road and shot down the exit ramp for SS18. Jameson followed while Superman was on his rear guard. Mario was close behind Superman with Elario on his tail. Seconds later Mohammed led the police car down the ramp and onto SS18 ...

The main arterial road into Naples.

Five Vespas, one police car raced along the strata. Traffic was building creating a mist of fine ash. Vincenzo looked desperately for the next exit. The police car was now flashing headlights. Oncoming traffic with impaired visibility pulled to the side of the road. The Vespas managed 80ks ... 90ks ...

'Vincenzo!' Jameson was right on Vincenzo's back wheel. 'Now what?'

'Next left.' Vincenzo gave little warning. He swerved left onto Corso Umberto. The bay was near. Superman anticipated the move and shot between Vincenzo and Jameson. It was close ...

Damned close ...

'Bastard!' Jameson made to ram the man.

Mario saw the turnoff approach. He throttled down forcing the rig to steer left. As the bike turned it pushed against the sidecar. Claire threw her body weight off to the right. Mario cheered. This added traction and Mario twisted the accelerator. Claire felt the wind off the crash barrier and dropped back into her seat. Mario gave her the thumbs up. But Mohammed was again on their tail. Claire spun about to face the man. Mohammed scowled down at her. Teeth grinding. Eyes watering. Then Claire saw the police car in a swirl of ash. It was in her face and pushing to pass them ...

To run them off the road.

Vincenzo maintained the lead, kicking out at Elario who was still wielding the cosh and trying to get close. Jameson came alongside. Elario was now sandwiched. He swung out at Vincenzo but Elspeth reached over snatching the back of his leather jacket. The strike missed. Elario twitched his head right to Elspeth who yanked the thug's jacket towards them as Jameson swerved right. Elario was forced sideways. His handlebars rattled. He had no choice but to brake and avoid crashing.

The police drew alongside, forcing the scooters into single file, penned in against the ramp rail while the cop in the passenger seat made signals for them to pull over. But another slip road led them through an underpass and onto the one way Via Vendetti ...

One-way wrong way.

Five Vespas now made to out race the police. Traffic had increased closer to Naples. Vehicles loomed up at the speeding two wheelers, materialising out of the persistent smoke.

'Accostare ora!' the cop screamed through a PA hailer. 'Pull over now!' Two lanes. One way. Oncoming traffic filed into one lane when they saw the flashing police lights.

'Accostare ... ora!'

Vincenzo saw the Porta del Granatello first. He took the turn and one after the other the single file of singing *wasps* trailed behind. Vincenzo knew the area well. The bay was directly ahead. If he could reach the railway lines running parallel to the shore ...

If ...

POP!

The dull sound of a silenced pistol. It was close. Real close. Mario twisted his neck. Claire followed suite. They heard a screech as the police mashed their brakes. The bullet had exploded their windscreen.

POP!

A blown front tire saw the police car shudder violently. Claire watched on, gobsmacked, as the car broadsided with the safety barrier and stalled. The driver jumped from the car into a cloud of radiator steam and smoke, radio mike in hand.

'Dude,' Claire shouted to Mario now in full flight mode. 'This isn't good.' Mario answered with a twist of the throttle. With the police out of the race Superman sped forward. Elario was well ahead. Superman had the pistol and no one was going to stop him. Claire watched over her shoulder as the last Vespa caught up. 'Christ! Mario!' Mario saw the pistol in his mirror. He swerved left. But with three wheels a bike with sidecar doesn't want to travel in a straight line. Slowing a little creates traction.

POP!

Mario felt the bullet whisper past his ear. He timed his move and jerked the handlebars right as a second shot ripped through the sidecar. Claire suddenly remembered her cayenne pepper. She unzipped her bum bag, took out the spice shaker and uncapped it. Mario caught a glimpse.

Really?

Mario lay as low as possible and gave the scooter full throttle. But Superman was relentless. Mario watched Superman's every move in the side mirror. One-handed, Superman raised the pistol. He aimed. Mario reached 80ks, 85, 90 ...

His steering was jarring ...

The front wheel vibrated furiously.

Mario looked to Claire. *Ready?* Claire jerked her head. *Now or never pal.* Mario eased off the accelerator and *Superman* rode up for the kill. Claire unleashed her secret weapon. The chilli powder escaped the jar in a gust of wind. The dust cloud of blinding cayenne pepper flew directly into the assailant's eyes.

The reaction was instant.

Blinded and one handed the motorcyclist lost control veering off the road ...

Slamming into a barrier.

Claire punched the air as the rider lay twitching at the side of the road. 'Yeha!' she screamed up at Mario. 'Now that's what I'm talkin' 'bout.'

Porto del Granatello was a circular road servicing the port. Vincenzo remained leader. He bounced off the circular road dipping onto a narrow, unsealed road. Ahead were the train tracks. But something was missing. Vincenzo snatched glimpses in his mirror. Jameson was directly behind him and the two aggressors gaining on them once more.

But the cop car?

There was no sign of the police, Mario or the third thug. The dual train tracks were approaching fast. Vincenzo managed to twist about. *Yes!* Mario flew off the circular road ...

Airborne for several metres.

Vincenzo snapped his head forward, took a last check in his quivering mirror. He caught blurred visions of Claire's bright red hair. *She was safe.* The plan was to lose the police on the train tracks.

But there were no police!

Vincenzo turned onto the tracks, racing parallel to the waterfront. Jameson and Elspeth followed but Mohammed and Elario knew the area. They took a service road parallel to the tracks. They were now gaining.

Mario careered over the train tracks executing a right-hand turn onto the service track. He now sped after Elario and Mohammed. Jameson and Vincenzo juddered over the railway sleepers. Sixty kilometres an hour over sleepers was not sustainable. 'Got – to – get – off – these - tracks,' Jameson yelled to Elspeth who felt her entire body was on some crazy exercise machine.

'Where's he taking us?'

'Christ knows. I thought we were going for pizza,' Jameson tried to make light of the situation.

'Ah Jameson ... is that what I think it is?'

Train ahead ...

'Oh shit.'

The tourist train normally on the Pompeii run was packed with army personnel. It came into view on a long bend one hundred metres ahead. Jameson vision was blurred, jarring as they rattled over the sleepers.

Vincenzo saw the train.

Now level with him on the service road Elario and Mohammed saw their chance. Jameson brain was scrambling. He had seconds to react. But Vincenzo suddenly turned towards the bay, jerking his front wheel so it cleared the train rail. His rear end slid on the inside of the track. The train siren blared a warning. Twenty metres ...

Ten, five ...

Vincenzo gave the Vespa full throttle. The rear tire slammed against a sleeper and the rear end bounced over the rail in a shower of gravel. Jameson passed the train in the opposite direction. It was on the dual track. Elspeth feared her hair would turn white. 'You knew!' She screamed out in relief. 'You knew the whole time we were on another track ... '

'Well not really. Not until the last minute ... '

'Jesus Jam!'

Jameson managed a brief wave to the hundred faces gaping from the carriages. To their left Vincenzo bounced over rocky terrain. He was angry. But he was now in control. He knew what he must do. As Jameson and Elspeth cleared the train they watched Vincenzo bounce through overgrown shrubbery. His scooter picked up speed down an embankment and to the war cry of an attacking barbarian he slammed into Mohammed's rear guard. Mohammed was propelled into a three-sixty spin. The Vespa slammed into an abandoned coal carriage and the rider wheeled over the handlebars. Vincenzo continued on unsteadily.

Elspeth squeezed her arms about Jameson's waist and as the last carriage passed Jameson executed Vincenzo's manoeuver.

'Hang on!' he screamed over his shoulder.

Elspeth squeezed harder. Jameson hooked the front wheel over the rail and the rear wheel followed. Elspeth was almost thrown free but Jameson opened the throttle fully and steered the Vespa down the embankment.

Elario's plan to cut in front of Mario and slow him for Mohammed went out the window as Elario caught a glimpse of his accomplice somersaulting through the air. Mario pulled back slightly allowing Vincenzo and Mario to catch up. Elario was alone. He accelerated to escape ...

The hunter had become the hunted.

Mario checked his mirror. The other two were closing in fast. Then he saw the flashing lights. Two police cars had picked up the chase. They slid around the corner sliding broadside in the gravel before racing onto the service road ...

And were closing the gap between them ...

Fast.

Mario looked ahead. He needed to negotiate the Napoli waterfront docks and cut up towards Via Filangiera Piazza. But immediately ahead was the deserted baroque palace Villa Elboeuf. Mario knew the gigantic five-storey 18th century hundred-room villa was earmarked for restoration, although now it looked more like demolition. In fact, much of the historic Napoli Bay waterfront was in disrepair. But money was tight these days. Developers had toyed with the project for years. One hundred and twenty apartments ...

But still it lay unloved.

Elario saw his chance. He passed through the damaged security fence jarring up the exterior stairs like a scrambler bike on a mountain slope. He entered the south wing. Mario followed while Claire in the sidecar held on for her life. Vincenzo and Jameson were right behind them. The police had little choice but to take an arterial road a hundred metres north. But if they were fast enough ...

If they were savvy ...

They might cut the bikers off at the villa's exit point.

The villa's first floor corridor was a minefield of building debris. Elario picked up speed. Rooms left and right flashed by at frightening speed. A glimpse in his shuddering mirror saw Mario leaning over the bars of his 250cc TAB. The echoed buzz in the confined space was ear-splitting. Vincenzo and Jameson negotiated the grand staircase and screamed after the others, dodging plaster and loose floorboards. The northern entrance loomed with little warning. Elario, now fearing for his life, careered out the exit the instant ...

On the ground floor below ...

The first police car chatted over the rail lines, slid sideways across the garden, and blocked the bottom of the stone stairway.

Elario was airborne ...

The two officers gaped through their windscreen as the Vespa sailed mid-air towards them. Elario crashed onto the car roof in an exploding thump bouncing to the ground. The second police car broadside into the first the moment Mario's three-wheeler with sidecar slammed onto the same roof. Claire's wide eyed, gaping mouth and fire engine red hair was but a blur. But Mario skilfully executed the challenge. He bounced to the ground and sped after Elario. Jameson and Vincenzo were less confident. They braked and their Vespas slid sideways to a standstill at the top of the steps. They gaped down at the police, revving motors at the top of the grand staircase. The first cop jumped from his car and pulled his pistol screaming.

'Attendzione!'

Vincenzo. 'Merda! Follow me.'

Vincenzo twisted the throttle, dropped the clutch and to the squeal of burning rubber he retraced their path. Jameson followed. A warning shot sheared the lip on an ancient jardinière. At the rear of the abandoned palace they bumped back down the steps and jumped the train tracks to enter a car park of overgrown pines, firs and shrubs.

The police cars retraced their route along the waterfront. Now the sirens were heard from the docks as Mario and Claire raced after Elario onto the container wharf. Vincenzo led Jameson between buildings. They buzzed a narrow lane, recrossed the rail lines ...

'There!' Vincenzo pointed to Mario three hundred metres away as he disappeared between the shipping containers. Thirty seconds later all four bikes hurtled between the containers stacked in formation ready for loading, creating a small village with lanes and streets. The docks were deserted.

A security guard appeared. He screamed a warning from his first-floor office. The door flew open and he was waving frantically, a radio in his hand. At the east end of the container dock another security guard opened the gates and the two police cars entered at speed.

It didn't look good. The police were gaining. Mario managed 100ks per hour. A terrifying speed between containers. Claire closed her eyes. But the smaller bikes were faster. Abruptly the containers ended. They leapt into the open, racing up an exit slip lane and once more they were on a public road; Via Cristoro Colombo. Here Neapolitans were venturing back onto the streets. Army and civil service personnel were starting the clean-up while behind them a glimpse of Vesuvio showed a weakening plume. Jameson watched Elario disappear behind administration buildings. Mario followed. A moment later Mario reappeared. No Elario. Mario's head pivoted. Hunting. There was no time to stop. No time to go back or search. He was clearly miffed but two other police cars had joined the chase. Fishtailing onto Colombo off Piazza Municipio. Mario weaved around vehicles, desperate to lose the police in the city.

'Oh – my – god!' Elspeth stiffened.

'I see them,' Jameson yelled back.

'Stop,' she shouted. 'We can explain to them ... Jameson?'

'Stop! Are you kiddin' me. They took a shot at us back there.'

Vincenzo looked over his shoulder. 'Nearly there,' he cried out. Ahead Jameson recognised Castel Nouvo the 13th century castle. They flew along Via Acton in front of the castle. Passing the Royal Palace they scootered across the pedestrian Piazza del Plebiscito with its fifty-three metre high Pantheon style dome. Nervous Neapolitans were gathered in small groups. They discussed one thing only.

Vesuvio.

Until ...

Leaving a trail of ash dust Vincenzo and Jameson sped across the square when out of nowhere Elario cut in front of them. They crossed paths centimetres apart. Elario turned a tight circle and was quickly on their tail. He slid a machete from a sheath on his leg and accelerated. Mario entered the piazza from a narrow lane. Saw Elario closing in. This was his moment. With the 9 pound American M-20 armour piercing warhead already loaded all that was left to do was aim. This wasn't as easy as it seemed. Mario opened the throttle closing in on Elario. Elario closed in on Jameson. He raised his machete. At this range he could slice Elspeth's back open.

'Do it do it!' Claire screamed at Mario.

But a hundred metres still separated them.

Now or never.

Mario released the missile.

It launched from the sixty-inch aluminium barrel in a jet stream of smoke and steam. It was a long shot. Groups of people scattered. Screaming. Panicking. Claire grabbed at her hair. If this went wrong ...

The missile bounced off the rear of Elario's Vespa forcing his bike into a spin. Elario fell to the ground somersaulting across the paving stones. The rocket continued on towards the Church of San Francesco di Paola. All watched in horror as the missile whipped between pillars, flew through the open church door, skipped along the marble floor towards the altar and stopped with a clunk.

Nothing.

It was a dud.

Mario was horrified. 'Merda!'

Elario made a dash on foot and dissolved into the crowd the moment four police cars entered the pedestrian piazza. Sirens screaming. Horns blaring. People ducked and dodged, terrified.

'Terroristi!' Someone shouted.

At the northern wing of the famous crescent shaped church, tall narrow apartment buildings watched over the street below. Upmarket dwellings. Vincenzo lead the other two between dozens of parked cars and were immediately swallowed by a narrow alley ...

An alley too narrow for police cars.

• • •

Parked outside the Museo Di Anatomia Umana at number 5 Via Luciano Armanni, carabiniere Dino Abandonato listened to the police radio in their unmarked car. Vice Sovrintendente Renato Di Stefano crossed the street to join him. He carried two espressos from a portable van making the most of the closed cafes. In his wake he left heavy footprints in the ash while further up the street army bulldozers were already clearing the carbonated mess. As he walked

Di Stefano's attention was drawn to Mount Vesuvio in the distance and his immediate thoughts were she was losing her puff.

'You need to listen to this sir,' Abandonato said. 'The traffic boys have had a incident.'

'Incident?'

'A police car was shot at by a gunman on a Vespa ...'

'Vespa! That's a first.'

'Yes. But the thing is they have taken the man prisoner. He's been hospitalised but he talked. There is a stakeout being organised and ... wait for it, at Etna Pizzeria.'

'Etna!'

'Yes.'

• • • • •

Etna Pizzeria was closed. Vincenzo slapped the security roller doors protecting the windows. They rattled noisily. Augusto, the pizzeria owner was waiting. And angry. The side door opened. 'Put the bikes around the back, hurry!' he spat. 'I listen to police band radio, they are looking for you. Jesus Mario! What have you done?'

They pushed the Vespas up a narrow side lane where Augusto opened a gate leading to a cramped back yard. He threw a tarp over the bikes. 'Inside. Hurry.'

Claire was wired. 'Man did you see the dude I got with the cayenne pepper?'

'You're on girl,' Elspeth said. 'I'm getting some of that.'

'Dam right. Terrorist bitch.' Claire pulled the lidless jar from her jeans where what remained spilt into the bottom of her pocket. 'And I'll be needing more too.'

'Inside,' Vincenzo pleaded. 'Quickly. Inside.'

Claire was first into the kitchen. She froze. In the ill lit kitchen a Rottweiler stood guard. It was over a metre high, sitting on its haunches. A deep slow growl greeted her.

'What's that?'

'A dog,' Elspeth whispered as Jameson and Vincenzo joined them.

'Jesus H Christ I know it's a friggin' dog. But ... '

The dog was on edge, wary of strangers. Another low rumbling growl was accompanied by slobbery jowls and gnashing teeth from the shadows. It barked, making a statement.

'Jam,' Claire said without moving her lips, or any other part of her body. 'There's a dog in the kitchen ... *The Health Department wouldn't like that back home.*

'That's not a dog,' Jameson hissed from the corner of his mouth. 'That's Kong.'

'How you know he is called Kong?' Vincenzo asked, impressed. 'He is Augusto's dog si ... Kong.' Vincenzo pushed into the tiny kitchen and gave the animal a vigorous head massage with both hands while serenading the beast with *doggy* talk. Kong wagged his tail. Good sign. And came to sniff the others.

Augusto locked the doors and hurried behind Mario into the kitchen. He took hold of Mario's singlet and threw him against the wall. 'The police are *here*,' he said angrily in his native tongue. 'You brought the police here.'

'We lost them,' Mario shook the cook free. 'Jesus Augusto, Easy ...'

'Easy! The police are outside.'

'I don't understand,' Vincenzo asked. 'How?'

Jameson understood one word instantly. *Polizia.* 'The police are here? What's going on? We lost them.'

'Then someone must have talked yes?' Augusto said in English. Elspeth. 'But Who?'

Jameson. 'The guy the police caught. The guy with the pistol.'

Augusto. 'Pistol?'

Tell you later amico,' Vincenzo said.

'Attenzione,' the police loudspeaker resonated through the walls. 'Apri la porta ...

'Open the door!' Vincenzo translated. 'Not likely.'

Claire. 'I guess there's no pizza for lunch then huh?'

Instantly more police cars screeched to a halt outside in the piazza. Police surrounded the building. The security roller door covering the shop window rattled. Another loudspeaker boomed.

'Apri la porta. Questo e la polizia.'

'Police!' Elspeth shook her head. 'How do you do this Jameson Rowley. Everywhere we go you attract trouble.'

'Yeh well,' Jameson said contemplatively. 'I don't mean to ...'

'But you do.'

'Come. Argue later,' Vincenzo said. Follow Augusto.'

Elspeth. 'Now where?'

'Escape polizia!'

'Escape! Escape the police. Are you nuts. We should ...'

'These Italy,' Vincenzo said. 'The polizia shoot and ask questions after. They stand over your dead body and say ...'

'Yes. I get the picture.'

'Especially now Napoli in emergenza,' Vincenzo added. 'Now please bella.'

Vincenzo. 'To the toilets si?'

Augusto. 'Si.'

'Claire. 'Toilets?'

'Yes. Hurry.'

Like most down-market bars and cafes in Italy Etna Pizzeria's toilets were underground. The cost of real estate dictates why. A spiral stair led to the confined and unventilated conveniences. There was no turning back. Kong was on their heels.

Augusto pulled the cord on a single bare light bulb dangling from the ceiling on a short wire. It threw out a dim light dancing shadows as the group gathered around Augusto.

'Give me hand,' August ordered. He dropped to his knees. He slid back a two-metre strip of old worn linoleum and began fumbling with an iron ring handle recessed into what they could now see was a trap door.

'W-What's this?' Clare asked wide-eyed.

Vincenzo. 'Catacombs.'

'Ca – catacombs!'

'Si. I tell you I do Guide Book of Secret Naples.'

'You mean like catacombs ... as in cemetery?'

'Yes. They are many many theengs underground here. Napoli, she built on volcanic rock. Is easy to carve under ground. Our ancestors, they build wine cellar, larder, they make grotto like chapel ...'

'And catacombs!' Augusto interrupted. 'Now please.' He nodded to the trap door.

'First I've gotta go to the little girls room,' Claire said eyeing the sign *Donne* along the corridor.

'Little girls room?' Vincenzo screwed up his face. But Claire was gone. 'Oh ... hurry please.'

Augusto turned the iron ring to a resounding echo. Iron bars beneath them slid sideways and the trapdoor dropped inwards like a hangman's drop. A cool stale musty draught beckoned them and everyone peered into the black void of Naples' underworld.

•   •   •   •   •

Augusto had rigged a single light bulb to light the immediate entrance. After that they would have to rely on a nine-volt torch he kept at the top of a steel ladder that took them four metres down to the tenth century entrance.

'Silenzioso,' Augusto demanded. Everyone froze and listened. On the floor above they heard bolt cutters snip the locked roller door over the main entrance. And then the unmistakable sound of the steel roller being wrenched open.

Claire re-joined them. 'Hear that?"

Augusto shot Mario, descending first, an angry look. Augusto watched the others climb down the rusted ladder then, after a few consolatory words to Kong, he closed the trapdoor, bolting it locked from underneath. The linoleum sheet fastened to the floor would hopefully settle back in position hiding the entrance. Besides, Kong would keep the police occupied a while.

At the base of the ladder several narrow-arched passageways carved out of the soft tufa, like one would carve foam, snaked off into the blackness ...

Into the afterlife.

There were dozens of corridors and if a person did not know where they were going they would be lost down here for eternity ... at one, with the ghosts of thousands of Neapolitans before them. Vincenzo saw the apprehension in Jameson, Elspeth and Claire's faces.

'These tunnels, they go for kilometres si,' Vincenzo told them matter-of-factly. 'There are many of thees catacombs under Napoli. Thees one, she date from 2nd century, and further away I show you Byzantine paintings ... ah frescoes you know ... 9th and 10th century.'

Augusto walked quickly. The electric bulb soon became of soft glow and then a memory as their impromptu guide switched to torchlight.

'Jesus dude,' Claire's excited voice was laced with elements of doubt. 'Does he know where we're going?'

'Si, is good thees catacombs,' Vincenzo took the opportunity to take Claire's hand. 'Police never find us here.'

'Fine. But ... ah ... Augusto?' Claire said quietly to Vincenzo as Augusto was in no mood to talk. 'Where's he taking us?'

Elspeth. 'Good question.'

'Under the church. These catacombs were part of a basilica, now gone, where the Church of San Francesco di Paola is now ... '

'The one we passed by.'

'You mean the one Mario nearly destroyed with a missile!' Jameson said from the end of the file.

'Si. But never you mind. Augusto knows thees passages. We make exit in hundred metres or more. Ah look.' Vincenzo pointed to a widening ahead where Augusto's torch exposed a beautiful fresco of what was clearly a wealthy family. Mother and father stood either side of a young girl. Their angelic expressions staring back at the explorers.

'That is tomb of, we say arcosolia,' Vincenzo slipped into guide mode. 'These arched tomb were for wealthy family. See their clothes and their jewels they wear?'

All about them empty horizontal niches denoted where the bodies once rested. Vincenzo explained how they were walled in with wet clay. But sometime in antiquity the graves were robbed for the very jewellery portrayed in the frescoes.

'So where's the bones Vin?" Claire asked, while Vincenzo led her along a particularly narrow and tapering passage lined with yet more niches, some undisturbed and sealed. Suddenly Claire stepped on something underfoot with a snap and crunch.

'You just step on some, yes?'

'Argh! Ya kiddin' me?'

'No, I not kid you.'

Elspeth followed the torchlight aimed briefly at their feet. To one side was a small skull with a section of cranium missing.

'Child yes.'

Elspeth. 'Gross.'

Claire. 'This is so cool.'

Jameson. 'Indiana Jones eat your heart out.'

Without warning Augusto's torch failed. 'Merda!' Augusto cursed. In the stygian blackness they heard Augusto banging the torch on his thigh; the universal standby tactic for any malfunctioning electrical appliance. Finally, Augusto's terrifying analysis echoed through the pitch darkness. 'The battery.'

'Da-dar!' Claire's mobile screen lit the immediate area. She found the torch APP. 'Thank Christ for modern technology,' she said cheerily. 'There's no signal down here but.'

Augusto led the troupe to a steady incline where they made an exit from the catacombs into what was a disused 19th century sewer. Jameson guessed they had travelled two hundred, maybe three hundred metres along the sewer when they came to a broached brick wall. This dropped knee deep into a disused cellar where a faint but welcome natural light seeped in from somewhere.

'Light!' Claire exclaimed. 'Thank Christ.'

'Quiet!' Augusto ordered. They all listened. Augusto found his bearings and hurried to a second room where an iron grate, and the source of the light, led to the street.

'Where are we?' Jameson asked.

'Via Toledo,' Augusto said. 'Follow.'

With the grate pushed out onto the street the six made their exit. Augusto replaced the grate and they all dusted themselves free of ash. Passers-by took little notice.

'The traffic's picked up,' Vincenzo noted, and switched to Italian to join Augusto and Mario, clearly planning their next move.

Jameson. 'What's happening?'

'We're walking to Stazione Napoli Centrale where we'll catch the train to Ercolano. 'We are returning to Mario's.'

Elspeth. 'Is that wise?'

'Mario, he must return. His wife yes?' Vincenzo said.

Mario was desperately trying for a mobile signal.

'The city, Napoli yes, the signal towers are all busy. Too many peoples use mobile. Now you come with me ... us four – and Augusto and Mario meet us, later yes. We must separate for polizia, they look for us.'

The train terminal was busy with as many people appearing to leave as were returning, for most Neapolitans knew Mount Vesuvius to be temperamental. Vincenzo purchased tickets on the Scavi line and fifteen minutes later they disembarked walking Via IV Novembre back to Ercolano and Mario's garage apartment.

As they skirted the archaeological site of Herculaneum, enclosed behind a tall wire fence, Jameson's enthusiasm returned. 'It seems a crime to be so close to Herculaneum and not to visit the ruins.'

The four stood a moment, gaping through the wire down at the ancient port, Pompeii's sister town. The half a square kilometre area of excavated buildings, some three storeys high,, sat exposed in what seemed a huge quarry. With the solidified volcanic mud creating a stonewall about the town, it appeared to have been carved out of rock, a little like ancient Petra in Jordan. Even more surreal was the sight of streets and buildings simply disappearing into the quarry face, almost organic; as though mother earth was offering a teasing glimpse, and no more, of life thousands of years ago ...

And modern Erclona built on top of the buried ruins made future excavation difficult, if not impossible for the foreseeable future.

'Seventy-five per cent ees still hidden,' Vincenzo said. 'Many public buildings including the forum are still buried.'

'Crazy!' Claire's gaze followed neat cobbled stone streets, with grooves worn by chariot wheels and oxen carts two thousand years earlier, clearly discernable. And to make the site even more spectacular a fine coating of Vesuvius' latest outpouring of ash had settled over the ruins.

'When was it discovered?' Elspeth asked staring through the wire in reverent awe.

'1709 I believe,' Jameson said.

'Si. Some peoples here in Erclona, farmers, in the 18th century, they know thees ruins are buried deep and some tunnel into their ... how you say ... '

'Backyard.'

'Exactly. Backyard. Many treasures were lost thees way. But in 1738 a Spanish engineer, Rocque Joaquin de Alcubierre, he dig here and publish a book, *The Antiquities of Herculaneum.* Thees book brings visitors from afar. But digging here was difficult, yes. Twenty metres deep thees Herculaneum, but Pompeii was only four metres deep and the ground soft, no hard like thees.' Vincenzo picked up a chunk of tufa and rolled it about his fingers. 'So digging here stopped and peoples dig at Pompeii instead.'

'It wasn't until 1861 that excavations under archaeologist Giuseppe Florelli were taken seriously in Pompeii,' Jameson added. 'I mean academically, isn't that right Vin.'

'You know your history amico.'

'It's a bit of a passion mate.'

'Passion!' Elspeth said. 'More an obsession.'

'So when was this all dug out?' Claire asked.

'Early last century.'

'Twentieth century?'

'Si.'

'You can tell by the trees growing amongst the ruins,' Elspeth said of the fully mature pine and fir trees nearly a century old. 'Look, there's even palms. It's been exposed some time.'

'You know recently they excavate the boat houses to the south,' Vincenzo said, and pointed towards what in all appearances was a moat but was in fact a deep gully between modern archaeological administration buildings and the 2000-year-old waterfront. 'Here three hundred skeletons were found, all ... how you say ... bunched up ... '

'Huddled.'

'Yes. They hide in boathouses when pyroclastic blast hit them. Some, their brains boil and explode inside skull.'

'Gross.'

'Is true. The skeletons still there for peoples to see. Womans, child, mans.'

'Yes,' Jameson said. 'I read about it in *World Archaeology*. The water's edge is now 400 metres further west than it was in 79AD, eh.'

'Come,' Vincenzo threw the tufa aside and rubbed his hand free of ash onto his trousers. 'We must hurry.

Mario's garage was one street removed from the ruins, running parallel. It was a poorer suburb with graffiti vandalised apartment blocks, neglected infrastructure and streets of trash co-inhabiting with a World Heritage Site. It was an eyesore after the ruins.

'I for one,' Jameson muttered. 'Would happily bulldoze this lot to get at Herculaneum.' And he waved a hand towards the decrepit late twentieth century residences, home to several thousand locals.

'Maybe Mario,' Vincenzo warned. 'He is not happy to hear this.'

'When will the site re-open for tourists?' Elspeth asked Vincenzo.

'Maybe one week. If Vesuvio, she behave.'

'You'll have to come back babe,' Claire sighed. 'It's pretty cool huh?'

'You can say that again.'

'We nearly there.' Vincenzo slowed and surveyed the neighbourhood. Nothing appeared untoward. 'Two hundred metre, yes.'

Mario was like a bear with a sore head. 'Three Vespa,' he spat at Vincenzo in Italian when he opened the garage door. 'Three of my later models. Mamma Mia, two thousand Euros, easy.'

'Lucky they did not do more damage here in the garage,' Augusto said looking about. Then repeated the comment in Italian for Mario's benefit. 'What about my pizzeria, Huh?'

'I am so sorry about your restaurant Augusto,' Elspeth said in all seriousness. Claire nodded vigorously. 'What will happen now, I mean with the cops an' all?'

'The polizia, they have nothing on me,' Augusto said solemnly.

'What I'd like to know is how did the police find us at your pizzeria,' Jameson asked.

'The men on the Vespa,' Vincenzo answered for Mario. 'I see them before, in Pompeii maybe. They are hired thugs and I suspect are tombaroli. They knew where to find Mario here and might come back.'

'Is everyone around here antiquity looters?' Elspeth spat in disgust. 'It's a wonder Italy has any treasures left.'

The room went quiet.

'Two were caught by the cops,' Claire finally said. 'They must have known where you work too Augusto.'

'Exactly,' Jameson said. 'They anticipated where we were headed.'

Mario threw his arms about in animated conversation as only passionate Italians do. All in the garage listened and watched the roller door close.

'What's he saying,' Claire asked Vincenzo.

Vincenzo. 'He say thees men are thugs and he thinks they were sent by whoever flew the drone.'

'Well that's a no brainer.'

'Si. And Mario says they come back, as long as you Australians here ...'

'Jesus.'

'Yes. He says we not see last of them.'

'Two are in police custody are they not?' Elspeth said.

'Means nothing here in Naples. They pay moneys to polizia and go free.'

'What is it with you Italians and corruption?'

Vincenzo could only apologise when Silvio, the hairy Jack Russel, came yapping from the apartment. 'How is Maria?' Vincenzo asked his cousin.

Mario turned his back on Elspeth, Jack and Claire and said in Italian. 'I'm holding you accountable cousin.'

Vincenzo looked at the others and forced a smile. 'Non parlano italiano,' Mario went on.

'Dopo,' Vincenzo said. 'Later Mario.'

A brief and animated conversation continued followed by uncomfortable silence. Vincenzo looked a little red in the face.

'What's happening dude,' Claire asked.

'Mario, he say you can stay one night. Then we must leave.'

'We'll go *now* Vin,' Jameson insisted, shrugging apologetically at Mario to say he understood. Vincenzo and Mario exchanged more words in rapid Italian.

'No, no. Is not safe tonight. We leave tomorrow, si. Why don't we look at the map and documents?'

Jameson sighed. There was now another set of eyes in the room, Augusto's, and he would prefer to scrutinise the chapel find alone with Elspeth and Claire, with Vincenzo to translate. 'Maybe we should ... ' But Mario walked over to Jameson and tugged at his backpack muttering in Italian.

'Mario,' Vincenzo said. 'He insist. He say he has risked his home, his wife and now lost three Vespas si.'

Jameson looked at Elspeth who knew they had little choice. Claire returned a subtle shrug. Reluctantly Jameson unsaddled the backpack and Mario smiled warmly.

They all retired to the kitchen where Maria was preparing a simple but plentiful late lunch of pasta. Claire was immediately drawn to the stove with thoughts of *that* pizza lunch that never materialised. Mario cleared the table for Jameson while Claire's finger dipped into the bubbling tomato basil sauce.

'Oh – my – god!' Claire salivated.

'We eat after, sorry,' Vincenzo translated for Mario.

Vincenzo sat at the table and took his time, reading the papers slowly while Mario and Augusto watched on. The writing was old school, a little untidy. Maybe written in haste he thought.

'It look like thees Victor Renzo,' Vincenzo finally said. 'He write this page quickly... fast.'

'In a hurry eh?'

'Si ... in hurry.'

Elspeth. 'Well if things were as urgent as they were today I wouldn't blame him.'

'These part here,' Vincenzo pointed to a scrawled paragraph near the bottom of the first page. 'He saying he hid these for future generations ...'

'That's us dude,' Claire put her hand on Vincenzo to peer over his shoulders.

'He say thees is most important discovery for 20th century.'

'And he must have thought he'd never return.'

'Maybe.'

Vincenzo continued. 'He say the Germans, they dig at site.'

'What site goddam it,' Claire exploded. 'Does it say Vataea?'

'Vataea!' Mario and Augusto's eyes widened.

Jameson groaned. Claire bit her tongue.

Augusto. 'You say Vataea?'

'Si,' Vincenzo said more reverently. The word demanded respect as it represented one of the most important archaeological sites yet to be discovered.

Mario pored over the papers and he located the magic word. 'Vataea,' he said again, hypnotised by the thought of such a find.

'Are you trying to say these pieces of paper are going to lead *us* to Vataea?' Augusto muttered inquisitively.

Us!

Jameson's felt the entire venture collapsing beneath him. He looked at Elspeth who read his thoughts.

'We have little choice,' Elspeth said to Jameson. 'We find this place first for the glory of discovery then go to the authorities. Right?'

'No authority!' Augusto said a little too forcefully. 'I mean, we should find this place first. Where is map?'

There were four sheets of exercise book paper in the total cache. All appeared to have been torn roughly from the book. The last page was a hand drawn map of Campania drawn in pencil. The chart was busy with detail and scrawled notes in a left-hand column.

Vincenzo tapped a finger on the map. 'There's Vesuvio.' The aerial sketch of a volcano was unmistakable. Pompeii was represented by a few parallel and adjacent lines denoting the already excavated town.

'Vataea … Vataea? Can't see it written anywhere,' Augusto said.

'But there is a cross of sorts,' Elspeth pointed out. 'Right there.'

They all leant over the table. Sure enough a second, albeit faint, pencil mark was scratched at what would be ten kilometres roughly south-east of Vesuvius, Jameson thought.

'X never marks the spot!' Claire said. 'That's a treasure map fantasy started by Robert Louis Stevenson in his 1883 novel *Treasure Island*.'

Jameson and Elspeth shared a moment. Only the year before they found gold on the island of Jamaica. 17th century Spanish gold no less. And X was definitely a defining factor in the discovery.

'1883 huh?' Vincenzo was impressed.

'Yes,' Claire smiled. 'I studied the author once for an essay.'

'Keep reading Vincenzo,' Elspeth said. 'That first page.'

Vincenzo read on in silence a brief moment then ... 'Aha. Thees answer question I ask myself. If German's dig at Vataea why not whole world know about it?'

'Well?'

'Because the Germans only know about Vataea one week. But they did not realise it as Vataea. They think large villa maybe. And they dig one week only before the Americans come ... '

'You mean the allied amphibious landing at Salerno in 1943,' Jameson's face lit up. There was hope yet.

'Si. 9th September ... I know these. And it say here on paper ... 13th September, 1943.' And Vincenzo pointed out the date. 'Four days later.'

'So there definitely was a Vataea,' Augusto's brow furrowed.

'Read on,' Jameson ordered Vincenzo.

'Okay ... so ... it say here that the German man Vince Renzo took orders from, was a commander in the 15th Panzer Grenadier Division ...'

'Tanks.'

'Si tanks. The German commander, his name Franz Berchtold. Vince say the man was *spietato* ... ah ... ruthless. Hard man. Very bad man. He dig what they think was Villa but Vince knew better than theses things. He know ... in he's blood, that they find Vataea. He say he dig with five other mans from village. Thees Franz Berchtold, he threaten everyone's family.'

'And all this while there was a war on,' Elspeth said.

Claire. 'So this Nazi dude was looting.'

'Many Nazi Claire. Vince say ten Germans involved. Other commanders and soldiers.'

'So how did the Germans find it I wonder?' Elspeth asked.

'It say they dig trench for war,' Vincenzo noted. 'For defence.'

Jameson. 'That makes sense.'

Vince read the remaining page. 'Vince, he say here he co-operate because Germans threaten his family. He say he poor ... his shoes were home-made of sheep's skin and his coat and trousers made from sail cloth. Then on 9th of September Americans attack at Salerno and Vince, he hide thees pages with map of Vataea in the chapel on 13th September, yes.'

'What bloody map?' Jameson shook his head at the four pages of 1940s exercise book paper; two were written on by Vince Renzo, one mostly blank and one with the pencil drawing of Vesuvius and Pompeii with an X in the middle of nowhere. *What clue was that?*

Vince looked up at the others. 'This not good. Vince was scared for his life. The German soldiers killed his comrades who dig at Vataea with him when allies land. They were all shot in village before Germans escape.'

'And that's when his son was killed,' Elspeth suggested.

'Oh Christ,' Claire scratched at her bright red hair.

'But Vince, he escape.'

Jameson. 'Does it say how he escaped?'

'Vince say here that he knew Germans booby trap buildings in Napoli before they evacuated. He overheard Germans talk of thees things ...'

'He must have spoken some German.'

'Or understood enough for the German commander to pick him as a digger in the first place.'

'Anyways, Vince, he try to warn Americans. He was away from village when Panzer attack it as they escape Napoli.'

'And that's the only reason he wasn't shot.'

'Si. Buildings were booby trapped by Nazis,' Vincenzo confirmed. 'The Post Office building in Napoli for example. Many civilians die ... '

Mario ordered Maria to serve up the pasta and excused himself, returning to the garage to repair the broken window. Augusto followed.

'I wonder if Vince Renzo was seen as a Nazi sympathiser,' Jameson thought aloud. 'Because, as the rest of the diary tells us, he came to Australia as an immigrant.'

'He continued to dig at Vataea though, after the war, didn't he?' Elspeth asked.

'Absolutely. He was the only one who knew and kept it all to himself.'

'Freakin' awesome!' Claire grinned. 'Imagine that. Imagine digging at Pompeii all on your lonesome.'

'But he eventually came to Australia with only a few souvenirs,' Jameson said. 'That's why he put his talents to work making forgeries.'

Now it was Maria's turn to be the centre of attention. Jameson carefully folded the papers and put them away safely in his backpack with the rest of the diary; together for the first time in seventy years. Elspeth cleared the table. Claire arranged the chairs, helped with the plates and cutlery and sat herself down. Maria placed a huge platter of thick ribbon fettuccine with tomato basil sauce in the centre of the table.

'Jesus that smells fan-bloody-tastic,' Claire smacked her lips unashamedly. Maria understood one word.

Jesus.

And took it as a divine grace. Maria crossed herself and went looking for her husband. Vincenzo passed Claire a bowl of halved lemons. 'Limone?'

'On my pasta?'

'Si. Is good with Parmesan. Watch Jameson, he knows.'

Jameson scooped a soupspoon of grated Parmesan onto his plate. He squeezed the juicy lemon onto it, mixing it well before forking it through his pasta.

'The acid of the lemon goes great with pungent sweetness of the mature cheese,' Jameson told Claire. Claire imitated Jameson's moves. 'Good,' Jameson approved. 'Now plenty of cracked black pepper.'

'Ah you like lemon with your pasta I see,' Augusto said returning to the table. He and Mario sat. Maria sat with Elspeth.

'I do yes. And your lemons in Italy, they are so juicy,' Jameson made polite conversation at the same time nodding enthusiastically to Maria for her efforts.

'One thing Italy grows in abundance,' Vincenzo said. 'Ees lemons. Lemons, olives and tomatoes.'

Immediately Jameson was hit with a revelation. *One thing Italy grows in abundance ... lemons ...* The words triggered a notion and suddenly Jameson thought Vataea's secret location was in his backpack after all.

'Say Parmesan!' Claire laughed, and framed a selfie with them all at the table. Jameson finished his third glass of Campania vino roso.

'What are your plans then?' Elspeth asked Augusto, still feeling guilty about the damage to his pizzeria.

'My plans?' Augusto's confidence was nourished by a full belly and wine. 'I'll return to the Pizzeria tomorrow like ... ah ... like notheen happen, si. Notheen. Now Vesuvio finish her anger, I re-open for pizza. Best Margarita in Napoli si?'

'Salute,' Vincenzo cheered. Mario filled all glasses.

'You're too kind Mario,' Jameson thanked his host. The atmosphere had grown festive. Mario, it seemed, was more forgiving than Jameson had expected and although he checked the street outside several times, he appeared to relax. The wine helped and Jameson found the full-bodied red wine was most palatable even if it did come in a four-litre glass jar.

'Vincenzo,' Elspeth asked. 'Please tell Mario we are really sorry about his Vespas but will try and make good. Maybe send some money when we are back home. And thank Maria also for her hospitality.'

Mario listened to Vincenzo and shrugged. 'He say, eet not really your problem.'

'Salute,' Mario said. Some things like sharing the dining table crossed all borders and fused friendships. The flagon was passed around again while Claire helped herself to her second square of polenta sultana cake.

Outside grew dark while the flat screen television played softly in the background. The general consensus was that the volcano had run out of steam. Martial law had been lifted from Vesuvius's surrounding villages and some normality returned. The city breathed a sigh of relief. Miraculously only the northern end of San Sebastiano had been destroyed. But for residents in the area this had been devastating. Vincenzo switched to CNN news and cranked the volume.

'... the area is returning to the pre-alert phase,' the reporter stood facing the camera with smouldering ruins of the worst effected, upper San Sebastiano in the background. 'The people here were temporarily housed in shelters in the Campania region and while many will be able to return in the weeks to follow just as many have lost their homes. The scientific community, I have been assured, are constantly monitoring the volcano and the damage effected areas are being assessed. Civil protection throughout the emergency has been a priority and all necessary measures have been taken to safeguard life and property in the area at risk ... '

'Hmm,' Jameson added with a grin. 'Nothing about crazy Australians looting the chapel.'

Mario returned to the table with a litre bottle of clear spirit. Eight shots were already poured.

'Aha,' Vincenzo flushed with rosy cheeks. 'Grappa.' He exchanged words with Maria. 'Si, si. Thees grappa,' Vincenzo told them. 'Ees made by Maria's papa, Roberto.' Vincenzo's accent grew stronger with every drink. 'He make it under hees casa.'

'Salute,' Mario shouted.

'Salute.'

There is nothing like shots of forty per cent home distilled grappa to calm the nerves after a hectic day. Eventually, with their hosts retired to bed, Elspeth tried to talk to Jameson about their future plans but the days crazy events, chased with grappa, sent

Jameson into a deep sleep. Elspeth pulled a blanket up around her shoulders and nestled into the armchair. She was aware that she was fighting fatigue but listened a moment to the laboured snores of Jameson in the opposite armchair, Vincenzo on a blow-up mattress on the floor and Claire on the sofa. Somewhere in another dark corner she knew Augusto was curled on a makeshift mattress. Finally, Elspeth drifted off herself, into a deep sleep peppered with dreams of Rome and it's amazing past.

Initially Claire dropped into a deep sleep, aware that she was snoring. But twenty minutes later she woke with stomach cramps; a violent sharp pain worse than any IBS she had suffered in the past. About her everyone slept. Guided by the soft light from the television screen Claire rushed to the toilet and proceeded to empty the contents of her stomach. She groaned, on her knees in front of the porcelain bowl, heaving until there was nothing remaining. Twenty minutes later Claire crawled back onto the sofa, exhausted. And fell into a deep sleep.

Some time later a distant sound woke Claire. A disturbance somewhere in the garage-apartment. The television had been turned off and the room was dark. Feeling decidedly better Claire looked down at Vincenzo; a dark motionless shape on the floor. He had a rattling snore. Jameson's was not much better and Elspeth sat semi-reclined with her head to one side, pouting in dreamland. But something wasn't right. For one thing Augusto's improvised bed in the corner on the floor looked deserted and there were no sounds of snoring coming from the hosts bedroom, not like last night. Claire's eyes adjusted to the dark. Mario's door was ajar. She crept over and peeped into their bedroom. The night was warm and the bedclothes appeared to have been thrown aside. Maria was sound asleep, dead to the world. Even Silvio the dog slept soundly, cuddled alongside Maria. But there was no sign of Mario. Claire stole towards Augusto's bed. As she suspected, it was empty. Then Claire heard a disturbance coming from the direction of the garage; a metallic sound like someone dropping a wrench.

Pulling on her jeans and runners Claire felt her way along the dark passage to the garage. The door was unlocked. She entered. Claire could just make out the window smashed by the attackers that afternoon. It had been boarded up. Off to one side a faint light caught Claire's attention, rising from the floor, which Claire now realised was the mechanic's pit. The Alfa Romeo under repair had been shifted to one side and soft echoes came from the pit. Claire crept silently to the edge.

At the bottom of the pit Claire saw another trapdoor. It was open. Immediately Vincenzo's words earlier that day at the pizzeria repeat themselves; *'I tell you I do Guide Book of Secret Naples. They are many many theengs underground here. Napoli, she built on volcanic rock si. Is easy to carve underground. Our ancestors, they build wine cellar, larder, they make grotto like chapel ... '*

Against her better judgement, Claire decended the ladder. It was a strong modern ladder well fitted and bolted firmly to the tufa wall, descending to what appeared to be a landing. Beyond that another ladder disappeared into semi-darkness. This appeared to lead to a horizontal tunnel where Claire heard the muffled sounds ... vague voices.

'Jesus! Claire gasped. 'I don't believe this.'

Claire hurried back to Vincenzo. 'Vincenzo, wake .... Vincenzo.' The man was in a dead sleep. 'Jameson ... Jam ... ' Same response. 'El ... Elspeth ... wake up for god's sake.' Claire put an ear to Elspeth mouth. She pouted back. 'Drugged! Must be.' Claire remembered the first round of grappa was already poured when Mario brought them to the table. She had vomited soon after. Then slept soundly.

'Shit! Jam ... El ... ' Claire's eyes swam with worry. She hurried into Maria. Sound asleep. 'He drugged his own wife?' Claire said loudly. 'Christ what sort of guy does that?'

Claire lifted Jameson's head off the armrest and shook him roughly. 'Wake up for Christ's sake.' Jameson answered with a growl and incoherent murmur before crashing back into unconsciousness.

'Shit!' Claire stared down the passageway towards the garage. All was quiet while about her were only the snores of stupefied sleepers.

Claire returned to the garage and listened. Nothing. Confident all was clear she swung her legs backwards onto the ladder and climbed down into the unknown. The shaft was circular, and crudely dug. Like a well. Following a dangling cord of low wattage LED lights, Claire dropped to the landing four metres below the mechanic's pit. The landing was welded steel, professionally made and semi-permanent. The warm globes gave the walls a golden hue and now Claire noticed other bolts in the shaft; old rusted iron bolts that appeared blacksmith made and possibly once held a wooden ladder. Clearly Mario and Augusto had not dug this volcanic rock themselves.

Claire waited in silence. She could feel her heart thumping. Low voices seemed distant but the echo of the underground was deceiving. Claire silently descended the second ladder down to a horizontal tunnel. She listened once more. Behind her the tunnel tapered off into blackness but the lights, stapled to the low tunnel roof, led forward and disappeared around a bend some ten metres further on. The tunnel was cramped and Claire had to drop to her knees and crawl.

What am I doing?

Am I insane?

At the corner, thankfully, the tunnel widened and the ceiling was raised high enough to walk in a stoop. But the voices had faded away.

Was this a good thing or bad?

Claire pushed her back against the tunnel wall craning her neck in concentration. Nothing. She was certain she was alone. She continued on, taking short soundless steps. Here the tunnel ceiling was vaulted and roughly chiselled. The light became sparingly dim and Claire was once more forced to crawl on her hands and knees. Ten, maybe fifteen metres further Claire encountered her first structure. The crude tunnel breached the wall of a man-made construction. To her left were two Roman era arches, side by side, one and a half metres high and two metres wide. Part of a waterway system ... an aqueduct maybe. Claire recognised the flat Roman bricks 200 mm long, 90 mm and 70 mm thick. Bricks that built an empire. Suddenly Claire realised their importance.

Herculaneum!

She was entering the ancient town and in a most unconventional manner; via a looter's tunnel. Claire knew Herculaneum was close by, but not *this* close by. The LEDs became sparser still and the Roman structure, whatever it may be, was in near darkness.

But there was light at the end of the tunnel.

Claire squinted off into the gloom. The arched aqueduct, if that's what it was, opened into muted light further along. Another twenty metres she guessed. Claire was parched, thirsty. She tried to moisten her lips and took deep slow breaths. *I've come this far,* she whispered to herself ... *this is crazy, surreal ... almost dreamlike.*

At the far end, the tunnel had collapsed forcing Claire to crawl over fallen rubble. She had less than half a metre of headroom and for the first time Claire could see where the looters had broached the original Roman brickwork. It appeared to have been bricked up some time ago but recently reopened. Claire rolled awkwardly off the brick pile when in the darkness ...

A face stared back.

Cold shallow eyes glared into her own. A stern white marble face. *Freakin' hell!*

Claire blew out her cheeks in relief. The marble head was slightly larger than life-size, an orator or someone of importance. Someone important in ancient times. Someone valuable in the 21st century. The bust sat on a canvas sled and had been dragged here recently for removal. 'The bastards,' Claire heard herself say. *Mario and Augusto are stealing from Herculaneum. I never saw that coming.*

Beyond the bust the LEDs were either turned off or non-existent. Claire waited. Her heartbeat settled. Slightly. As her eyes adjusted she could see faint moonlight casting diagonal shafts of light through what appeared to be branches and leaves. Claire crept towards the opening. The moonlight now illuminated the walls either side of her, while the leafy bushes hiding the exit cast sinister shadows. This was not a normal day for an archivist. She was surprised at her own daring. Claire found herself inside a ruined building where the crumbling brickwork was held firmly in position by the mudflow that solidified two thousand years ago. The exit was irregular in shape. It was never a proper entrance. Claire pushed through the foliage, relieved to be in the fresh night air, although Vesuvius's sulphuric stink still lingered.

Claire stood shaking fine black ash from her clothes. The bush covering the opening, in what she could now see was a quarry, was a crimson rose.. From the outside it hid the opening perfectly. Claire had read extensively about Herculaneum and Pompeii on her flight from London and knew that tunellers – treasure seekers – of the 18th century, dug many tunnels into the volcanic rock. But these were bricked up later in the 19th century as serious archaeologists treated the site with respect.

Claire stood behind a two-metre wire fence, designed to keep tourists away from exactly where she had made her exit, and gaped into the historic site. The town of Herculaneum – or at least the portion that had been excavated and explored since its discovery in 1709 – was situated in a huge, more or less rectangular basin.

The modern metropolis was built above it so that today's ground level is fifteen to twenty metres higher than in 79AD. Today visitors to the site stand at rails and peer down into the archaeological gem, before walking down a grand earthen ramp to walk the streets and wander amongst the ancient structures, most of which remain to the second and third storeys. Taverns, bakeries, brothels, villas, merchants, fullers, public latrines, bath houses and much more; all intact and abandoned as they were two thousand years ago when disaster struck.

An enormous time capsule.

Claire thought she heard voices. Either side of her were ancient brick walls. She was trapped in what essentially was an alleyway.

Were there security people here at the ruins? Surely. But with all the panic lately. All the Vesuvius activity – maybe not. Under cover of darkness Claire rushed to the wire fence. If Mario came this way there had to be a way through she reasoned.

There was.

Two metres along one side of the wire fence a subtle hole had been cut close to the ground with wire cutters. She dropped to her hands and knees and crawled through. Claire crossed the ancient stone paved road to a doorway that took her into a tavern. The three remaining walls of the building bore no roof but at least she had cover. Claire slipped behind the brick and stone counter where the remains of terracotta amphora were still fused into vertical recesses within the stone bar top. As crazy as it seemed Claire easily imagined the Romans supping wine with honey and eating hot snacks like roasted dormice with garum –fermented fish sauce ...

Right here where she cowered.

The voices had disappeared. *If* she had heard voices at all. Claire crept out and back to the street.

The street!

An ancient Roman street!

Claire dared stand in the middle of the moonlit thoroughfare. For two hundred metres to the north-east she could make out the shape of buildings ... shops, dwellings and public structures of the town. Some had balcony's – the wood carbonised and preserved for millennia – where Claire imagined chariots riding by or carts of amphorae full of wine, olives or garum being hauled by bullocks.

The enormity and excitement of where she stood threatened to cloud Claire's judgement and dull her perception of the danger she was in. With Vesuvius's plume depleted the half-moon swamped the ancient ruins with an eerie, yet welcome veiled light. Claire ran an eye over her surroundings. The streets of modern Ercolano above and around the perimeter were almost empty; it was early morning after all. However the odd vehicle passed by, affecting the most surreal atmosphere down here with the ghosts of antiquity. Yet somewhere amongst all this history Mario and Augusto were up to mischief. The thought of her drugged friends snapped Claire from her reverie.

But ... where to start?

Claire knew she was near the north-eastern perimeter. A sign in Latin read CARDO III. She hurried to the first *intersection* ...

Huh! Claire laughed at her analogy ... *intersection*. All about her, ancient met modern.

Concentrate girl.

At the intersection another street ran south-east. The sign read DECUMANUS INFERIOR. This led to CARDO V.

Claire heard a vague sound. An electric drill? The low buzz sounded as though it came from the south quarry wall. She shot across the street. This one was wider than most and Claire thought it was possibly a main avenue. She saw a shortcut through what was clearly a wealthy villa. Claire entered through a tall and wide front entrance and padded across a magnificent mosaic floor with a scene of sea creatures; dolphin, octopus, fish and even a shark – all meticulously created with tesserae, or tiny squares of coloured marble and stone. She slipped through a door way and below frescoed walls suddenly realising the two-thousand-year-old wooden door itself was still in situ; propped against the wall of hardened lava that had preserved it in position all these years. This led through to the internal peristyle, common in Roman villas with vines, fruit trees, exotic gardens and statuary.

Back in the street once more Claire followed the sound of the drill. But another sound disturbed her path ahead, and Claire ducked into what she realised was a bathhouse. The ceiling was vaulted with a corrugated pattern, an unusual feature in Roman architecture. A muted moonbeam highlighted a stone washbasin resting on a plinth with the head of the goddess Diana overseeing the ablutions. The two-thousand-year-old bronze faucet protruded from the goddess's chest. The pencil of light on the marble head was simply too much for Claire's artistic side. She slipped her mobile from her jean's pocket.

Still no signal.

She checked the flash was off, and snapped a shot of the basin and Diana. The high resolution of her Apple iPhone 5s was perfect. She smiled inwardly ... *a National Geo shot if I do say so myself.*

An idea.

Selfie time. Claire took three more photos, and then slipped back to the avenue where she again heard the faintest sound of an electric drill. It was coming from the direction of CARDO IV. Fuelled on adrenalin Claire crossed over CARDO IV. The drilling was emanating from the southern quarry wall. It must be coming from underground she surmised. A sign to her left read VESTIBOLO and another on her right pointed to INSULAORIENTALIS.

'*Insulaorientalis,*' she muttered. 'Whatever the bloody hell that is.' But a narrow and ancient alleyway ran between the buildings at this point. A makeshift modern wooden gate closed the entrance and Claire could only guess the sign, *divieto di ingress*, meant *no entry*.

Claire felt at the top of the gate where she thought she saw a bolt in the hazy light. And entered.

As she suspected the narrow alley led to the exterior quarry wall where thick vegetation disguised the original excavation of centuries past. The alleyway came to nothing; just more overgrown flowering foliage sprouting from the quarry face of solidified lava, now a tufa wall that signified the enormity of that ancient eruption. To Claire it reminded her of a vertical fifteen-metre surf wave suddenly frozen in motion. Overhead Claire knew, was the site's main entrance and ticket office and grounds that led to the modern car park.

Defeated, Claire was about to return the way she had come when she again heard the distant drilling sound ...

Faint but distinct.

She gazed into the undergrowth when she saw the slightest flicker of artificial light. It came through the thickest of the bushes. Claire crept forward and pushed back the greenery and there, at ground level, she saw an entrance no bigger than a crawl space for a small person. An exceptionally large flagstone had been dragged aside. *This was the simple cover that must have eluded authorities for god knows how long.*

Claire listened.

The drilling was consistent.

Certain that she was not being observed, Claire climbed into the space with visions of Alice in Wonderland. The crawl space was two metres long before, thankfully, widening into a standing space. This Claire noticed was a hand-hewn passage, similar to the others, and apparently carved by looters a long time ago. Mario and Augusto must have discovered this old means of access. The tombaroli's light seeped into the passage from up ahead. Five metres further and Claire stood before an ancient room lit with a battery-operated lantern. It was magnificent, part of a temple perhaps. The vaulted ceiling was richly decorated in ochres, carmines and blues in both stucco and frescoes. Painted into the plaster were mythological figures that Claire recognised as Griffins, centaurs and lions. Another frieze showed Priam appearing before Achilles to claim the body of Hector. And yet another portrayed Paris choosing one of the beautiful goddesses. The detail was stunning.

The artwork priceless.

Claire stumbled over bricks and debris and stepped into the chamber; now realising she had entered through a wall that had been breached, destroying a fresco of Hercules being received at Mount Olympus. In the corner Claire saw a stepladder and a carry bag of tools including saws. Her jaw dropped open.

No!

Surely they weren't about to cut the work from the ceiling. Claire reigned in her anger as she heard voices. They were close. She stole forward, stalked by her own ghoulish shadows cast across the walls.

Entering a wide arched doorway Claire passed frescos, undisturbed for millennia, in brilliant colours, condition and artistry. The wall of boiling mud had not managed to penetrate the interior of this temple and had solidified preserving the interior like it had been deserted yesterday. Claire was sick with excitement. Giddy with veneration. Ahead stairs led down into the semi-darkness. Stairs last trodden by the ancient citizens of Herculaneum ...

Immediately Claire recognised Mario's baritone voice. The two men were nearby. They appeared excited. With heart racing, she descended the stairs. Unhurried. One at a time. Here was a much larger chamber with a domed ceiling; a miniature version of the Pantheon in Rome and lit with another electric lantern. In the centre of the dome was the circular opening once open to the elements but now *corked* with solidified lava. Claire imagined the initial lava flow had hardened before this magnificent building filled with molten mud and rock. A brighter light and voices emanated from an antechamber to the left off the main dome building. They were talking in echoed, hushed tones ... but in Italian. A language she did not understand.

Claire could not believe her situation. Common sense told her to retreat but sense of duty strengthened her resolve. Claire inched soundlessly across the irregular flag stoned floor, careful to avoid scattered broken pottery and amphora. The voices were close now ...

Too close.

She dropped to her knees and peered around the corner. The antechamber was rectangular but lining each side of the walls Claire recognised stone pigeonholes – shelving – storing thousand upon thousands of charred scrolls stacked neatly in horizontal triangular pockets. It was an ancient library.

A library not known to the scholars!

The enormity of such a discovery was incalculable. Claire watched the two men at the far end of the vaulted room. They seemed uninterested in the scrolls; probably as they knew how fragile the treasures were and how impossible it would be to remove them safely. The two men worked quickly. Efficiently. Eager to evacuate artefacts before sunup. In the light of another battery lantern they busily drilled beneath a metre high bronze statue of a dancing faun, loosening the footing on its marble plinth. If there was anything positive about their scandalous actions, Claire considered, it was the fact that they took care not to damage the artefact. Claire bit down on her lip, desperately trying to figure what to do.

Already prepared for removal was another bronze, this one Claire recognised as the goddess of the underworld, the goddess Gaea. She lay on a canvas stretcher, awaiting removal like the bust back at the other entrance point. Now, Claire realised, they were making the most of the lack of security on the site with the Vesuvius emergency. One last haul before the authorities closed in on the garage, maybe.

Instantly the statue came loose. The men let out a hushed cheer. They lifted the bronze carefully to the ground and turned. Claire ducked from sight only to step on a pottery shard. It broke with an echoed snap. Claire froze. Silence. The men stiffened ...

They stared at each other. They said nothing and waited. The silence was deafening. Claire pushed herself hard against the wall, praying they had not heard her. Thirty seconds ...

Forty-five ...

Silence.

Claire daren't breath. Immediately she heard the sound of the two men proceeding to prepare the statues for removal. She recognised urgency in their voices and the hollow clunk as the two pieces were wrapped hastily in the canvas. Wary of more shards Claire scampered back to the looter's opening. She crawled back into the night air and gasped at its balmy freshness. With voices approaching the exit Claire dashed down the ancient alleyway, closed the gate behind her and rushed along the stone paved CARDO V to the moonlit DECUMANUS INFERIOR when ...

An irresistible sense of responsibility overcame her. Claire needed evidence. She must at all costs take a photo of the men with the artefacts …

In transit *and* on the streets of Herculaneum.

Claire dissolved into the black corners of an ancient bakery, recognisable to her by its grinding stones for crushing grain, and the wall ovens with their hinged iron doors in situ. Not unlike wood-fired pizza ovens today she mused. With Vesuvius' fading plume drifting north the moon was free to bath the historic street in soft blue light.

Claire waited. Motionless. Surprisingly calm.

It was not long before the two men could be heard scuffling awkwardly along the avenue with their heavy booty. Claire checked once more that the mobile flash had not inadvertently been activated. She positioned herself low at the edge of the baker's counter. She took a deep breath … and held it …

The men came into sight …

Eight metres distant.

Their cargo was heavy. They moved slowly. Claire zoomed in on her screen, tightening the shot, waited for auto-focus and snapped as many shots as possible before the two passed out of view. There was just enough ambient light that the men did not notice the red light on the camera – something Claire had totally overlooked. They continued on and Claire finally breathed. She checked the shots. They were soft focus and a little grainy under the poor photographic conditions but Claire was confident Mario was recognisable. The stolen antiquities were most definitely recognisable. Claire made to enlarge the last shot when the screen went black. The battery had died.

Allowing a head start Claire finally followed, watching from a safe distance. Beyond the wire fence the two darkened figures carried their spoils into the underground and disappeared. The faint light vanished with them. When she considered it safe, Claire approached the secret entrance …

But it had vanished. There was no sign of where she had entered the archaeological site forty minutes earlier. Fighting panic Claire pulled back the bushes and searched. Nothing. There was no trace. The entrance was well concealed ...

Too well concealed.

Suddenly Claire felt alone and vulnerable. Escaping the site unseen was a priority. Claire walked the gently inclining ramp at the south-west perimeter. There were security cameras everywhere but clearly, because of the emergency, they weren't being monitored otherwise she would have been arrested by now. Between the ticket office gift shop and the main gate was an entrance path to the site with an unloved garden of olive trees both sides. Claire made her way to the wire fence. It was over two metres and topped with barbed wire. Feeling trapped and powerless she proceeded on a path parallel with the fence in a wild hope she would find a hole in the poorly maintained grounds.

Suddenly outside spotlights sent a flood of light over the garden. Night was day. Claire rushed to the semi-darkness of the grounds periphery and froze hard against the trunk of a mature olive tree. She daren't move.

But she had been seen.

'Arresto!' a voice shouted. So there *was* a security guard on the premises. The man stepped from the gift shop waving a police issue torch. Claire saw her chance. The tree she stood under offered a branch reaching out over the wire fence. The guard knew his quarry was close by. He swept the beam in oscillating arcs towards her. Claire climbed ...

'Arresto!'

Claire crawled out on the branch.

'Arresto!'

Not likely.

'Stop ... Arresto!'

Claire had visions of a prison cell in Naples. She inched along the tapering branch...

It bowed.

The security guard was tall and lean, but beyond retirement age. He reached the olive tree shouting curses while gasping breaths the moment the branch surrendered to Claire's intrusion. It snapped. Claire fell two metres thankfully landing on turf. Instantly she was hit with blinding torchlight. But a wire fence stood between them. 'Cossa stai facendo donna?' he shouted.

'Sorry matey,' Claire answered grinning anxiously. 'No speak Italiano, si.' She bounced to her feet and before the man could unlock the main gate to pursue her Claire was lost amongst the apartments of modern day Ercolano.

Twenty minutes later ...

'Where's the mouthy one,' Augusto whispered to Mario in his native tongue. They stood silently at Mario's bedroom door where the early morning sun was already lighting the apartment. Everyone slept. But the sofa was empty. Claire was missing. Mario jerked his head silently towards the toilet. Augusto checked. He made a sign across the room. 'Empty.' Mario looked at his watch. 5.10AM.

'Merda! Where is the bitch?'

The two men searched the apartment. There wasn't much to search. Two rooms Mario kept locked. Empty. The living area come kitchen, the toilet, the bathroom and the bedroom – where Maria slept soundly. There was nowhere to hide and the only entrance and exit was the roller door. Although it had a manual button the door was securely locked.

'You don't think she ... ' And Augusto nodded down the passageway towards the mechanic's pit.

'How?'

'I don't know. But where else could she be?'

'Jesus!'

Mario was about to lock the passage door and re-open the trapdoor at the bottom of the mechanic's pit when Maria appeared, groggy and yawning.

'Where have you been?' she asked timidly.

'Pack your things, take the dog and go to your mothers,' he hissed.

'But you haven't even slept ... '

'Mind your business woman. Now pack Maria! Don't make me repeat myself.'

The two men waited. Maria packed an overnight bag, something she did often, and made her way to the garage. Mario used his remote to open the roller door enough for Maria to exit when the squeaking door woke Vincenzo.

'Maria, is that you?' Mario heard Vincenzo call from his bed on the floor. Mario took her by the shoulder and pushed her towards the exit.

'Go!' he snapped.

The two men watched Maria and the dog cross the garage floor and hurried back into the living area to *greet* the others. Elspeth and Jameson sat stiffly, stretching awake.

Maria slipped through the garage door onto the street. Claire slipped inside. The women exchanged simple greetings. Having no English Maria said nothing and scurried away quietly.

Claire had seconds to plan her next move. The garage door opening was most fortuitous but now what? Claire noticed the Alfa Romeo chassis had been placed back in position over the mechanic's pit. She rushed across to the barricaded window repaired by Mario the day before and tore the loose boards free before dragging a plastic milk crate beneath it for a step ...

'Cosa fai?'

Claire spun about. Mario was standing with his fists balled at his side. Angry.

'I ... ah ... I was just ...'

'Cosa fai?'

Vincenzo appeared. 'He says what are you doing?'

'Oh.' Claire tried to sound complacent. This had given her the briefest of respites to make some excuse. 'I was just putting the boards back.' Mario and Vincenzo exchanged rapid dialogue. 'Mario, he ask why?'

'Because I went out for some fresh air last night. The garage door was locked ... I got claustrophobic and needed a walk ... '

'You went walking outside last night?' Vincenzo asked incredulous.

'Yes. Why not?'

'And you climbed out the window?'

'Yes.' Claire held Mario's gaze, looking suitably apologetic. 'Sorry Mario, I just get anxiety attacks ... claustrophobia you see.'

Vincenzo translated. 'Why use the window Mario asks. Why you not use button, there.' And Vincenzo pointed to a green button the size of a cherry tomato on the wall beside the roller door.

'Huh!' Claire forced a laugh, feigning ignorance. 'Stupid me. Didn't see it ... stupido si?'

Mario looked at Claire without expression. He knew she lied. At that moment Elspeth and Jameson dawdled into the garage feeling dazed. 'Jesus Mario, that's the last time I'm drinking grappa.'

Mario frowned. 'Che-cosa?'

Vincenzo interpreted. Instantly Mario let out a forced laugh. He walked over to Claire slapping her on the back. The tension relaxed. While Augusto took a power drill to the window the others returned to the living area where Mario prepared coffee on the stove and ordered Vincenzo to lay out some prosciutto, cheese and day old ciabatta. Elspeth was starting to realise the apartment seemed unorganised and very temporary. 'Where's Maria?' She asked.

Vincenzo related Mario's answer. 'Gone to her mothers.'

'Yeh Beth,' Claire said as she fossicked through her overnight bag. 'I passed her on my way in.'

'Way in?' Beth suddenly remembered. Her brain was slow this morning. 'Where did you go anyway?'

Mario hovered.

'We need to talk,' Claire whispered to Elspeth, confident Mario could not understand. 'Urgently.'

'Why?' Elspeth continued the reticent tone. Claire was about to answer when Augusto joined them. Jameson returned from the bathroom and immediately helped by cutting the bread. 'What's the plan for today then?' Jameson asked Vincenzo noisily rinsing coffee cups in the sink. The innocent diversion was perfect for Claire. 'Have you got your mobile power adaptor here?'

Elspeth. 'No. It's back in Rome. Jam and I only bought our overnight kit. Why do you ask?'

'Christ Beth!'

'Why? Where's yours?'

'Lost it.'

'How?'

'I dunno. I musta left it plugged into the power point in the hotel in Rome.'

Elspeth understood. Claire would lose her head if it weren't attached to her shoulders. Mario took the opportunity to visit the bathroom. Claire squeezed Elspeth's arm and dragged her down the passage. When she thought it was safe she whispered to Elspeth hastily in as few words as possible what had happened.

Elspeth was gobsmacked. 'They what? Drugged us?' Elspeth head ached. 'But Claire ... You what? Herculaneum! Claire!'

'They're tomb robbers Beth.'

'I ... ah ... Are you certain?'

'Why would I bullshit. What'll we do?'

'But Jesus Claire ... that's serious crap.'

'No shit! Tell me about it ... '

Elspeth found it too hard to believe. 'You were there ... in Herculaneum?'

'Yes, for Christ's sake. I told you already.'

'Jesus ... but ... '

'I've got proof on my phone Beth, but the battery's died.'

'Does Vincenzo know?'

'No. Because they drugged him also.'

'No wonder I've got a sore head. Alright let's have it out with them ...'

'Are you nuts? These guys are pros Beth. They'll kill us, or worse ...'

Augusto appeared in the passageway. 'Colazione ... ah Breakfast is ready, si.' He delivered an insincere smile delivering his words directly at Claire. 'Come.'

Jameson, Vincenzo and Mario were already eating at the table.

'Nice of you to join us,' Jameson said with an innocent grin and a mouthful of bread and prosciutto.

'I've gotta go to the shop,' Claire said out of the blue.

'Shop?' Jameson mulched. His appetite particularly sharp this early morning. Jameson noticed the time on Mario's watch. 6.05AM

'Yeh,' Claire said. 'I need a European power adaptor for my phone.'

Jameson. 'Use ours.'

Elspeth. 'It's in Rome.'

Claire checked her purse was in her bum bag. 'Back in a jiffy,' she said with forced cheer. 'The shop across the street's open, I saw it.'

'I'll come with you,' Vincenzo offered, but half-heartedly. He too was hungry.

But Claire was still uncertain about Vincenzo's motives. 'You eat Vin. I'll be right back.'

Elspeth joined the others at the table while Claire left for the garage. Augusto followed, ostensibly to open the roller door for Claire.

Claire crossed the street; her footsteps remaining in the volcanic ash covering the herringbone-patterned flagstone road. Moments later she reappeared from the shop carrying her brand-new adapter in its plastic sheath. Claire crossed the street, more occupied with opening the packet than paying attention to her surroundings ...

Without warning the van cut in front of her. She jumped to attention. 'Augusto!' she cried out.

Bloody idiot nearly ran me over.

Augusto pounced from the driver's seat, motor running. Without a word he clamped a fist about Claire's arm and she was thrown bodily into the rear of the van. Taken totally by surprise she was speechless.

Augusto!

She wanted to yell. The van doors slammed in her face. Locked. Instantly the van raced away from Ercolano. It took less than one minute. No one had seen them.

Now she screamed.

'Where's Claire?' Elspeth was beginning to worry.

Vincenzo. 'The shop, maybe they no have thees adaptor and send her elsewhere.'

Elspeth grew increasingly suspicious, especially in the light of what Claire had told her. 'Where's Augusto?'

Mario pushed his chair back dropping his plate noisily into the sink. With his back to the others he fumbled in the cutlery drawer.

'Mario,' Elspeth raised her voice. 'Where's Augusto?' Vincenzo's eyes widened. But Mario was uncooperative.

'Easy El,' Jameson was feeling decisively uncomfortable. Without warning Elspeth leapt to her feet and the chair flew across the room.

'Mario,' she shouted. 'I said where's Aug ... '

Mario spun on his heels and aimed a pistol point blank at Elspeth's head. She froze. Mouth open.

Eyes swollen in shock.

'Jesus!' Jameson was about to jump to his feet. The pistol rounded on him. He sank back into his chair. 'Easy mate for Christ's sake. Is that thing loaded?'

'Mario?' Vincenzo was gobsmacked. 'Cousin? What are you doing?' he asked in the only language Mario understood.

Mario told Vincenzo. 'Sorry you had to get involved in this Vin but this is my livelihood. There's good money to be made and damned if I'm not having my share.'

'Share in what?'

'You must have suspected all along.'

'Suspected what ... Mario?'

Mario stepped back waving the gun to give him wider coverage. He jerked the pistol at Jameson signalling him to join Elspeth. Jameson recognised the pistol as a 9mm World War II German military Luger. A collector's piece left over from Nazi occupation of Naples he guessed. Jameson stood by Elspeth pushing her gently behind him.

'Mario,' Vincenzo was growing angry. 'Suspected what?'

Mario said nothing but ordered them into the garage ahead of him. He made the three stand against the wall facing the Alfa Romeo over the mechanic's pit. Mario took a key from his pocket and flipped the boot of the vintage restoration. The three craned their necks in curiosity.

'I'm not getting in the boot of that car,' Elspeth said defiantly. Mario seemed to understand and began laughing. 'Guarda!' he said to Vincenzo.

'Look?' Vincenzo translated.

'Si, guarda.'

Vincenzo stepped into a position to peer into the boot and sucked in a short breath ...

'Claire!' Elspeth shouted fearing the worst. Mario laughed harder. Elspeth and Jameson hurried forward and stood gaping at the Roman marble bust and the bronzes of the dancing faun and the goddess Gaia. 'Claire told me you were thieves!' Elspeth's eyes narrowed. 'Tombaroli,' she said in disgust.

'Si, si. Claire,' Mario understood enough. 'Claire cause this problem,' he told Vincenzo in Italian. 'And you cousin, are you with us or against us?' Mario waved the Luger aiming it directly at Jameson's heart.

'Mario,' Vincenzo said. 'What have you done?'

'Are you with us or against us I ask?' Mario demanded. 'A simple question cousin.'

'Of course I'm against you, you fool. I am a tourist guide. I work to protect our heritage I make good money ... honest money ... '

'Bah!'

Although Jameson and Elspeth did not understand Italian they gleaned enough to know they had Vincenzo on their side.

'Back inside.' Mario kept the pistol aimed directly at Jameson. 'Back. Now.'

Vincenzo lead the way back to the passageway. At gunpoint, the three were forced to hand over mobiles and herded into one of the locked rooms off the passage. The window was boarded over but a single low wattage light bulb bathed the room in a dull light. Jameson and Elspeth soon realised the room had been used for storage and crating of the artefacts, although little remained except for a metre high marble statue of a headless horse that would need heavy lifting equipment.

The door slammed shut behind them and the key turned in the lock.

'The bast-ard,' Vincenzo swore. 'I never suspect nothing ... nothing at all. I thought he sell some marihuana sometimes, but never antiquities. The bast-ard.'

Elspeth sat on a crate, sinking into a huge roll of bubble wrap and put her head in her hands. 'Claire told me. She tried to warn me ... '

Jameson. 'What do you mean?'

Elspeth told Jameson and Vincenzo all she knew. They listened in amazed silence.

'I always thought Claire was crazy but now this,' Jameson shook his head in disbelief. 'Christ!'

'She also said she took photos of them moving the bronzes ...'

'That I've got to see.'

'Jesus Claire ... where are you?'

'Mario and Augusto are looters, thieves, tombaroli, si,' Vincenzo finally said. 'But I do not believe they harm her.'

Elspeth. 'How well do you know this cousin of yours?'

'Not well enough I am thinking,' Vincenzo shook his head. 'Now I know why he rent this old garage. He is mechanic si, and a good one. But he use this building as a ... how you say ... '

'Front.'

'Si, front.'

'How long has he rented this building?'

'Two year maybe.'

'So god knows what he has stolen.'

Vincenzo looked embarrassed by his cousin's crimes. 'He buy and sell Vespa too. I never thought there was too much moneys in that. Huh!'

Jameson considered their position, still trying to understand how everything had suddenly turned from the prospects of a peaceful breakfast to this. 'And we are standing on top of one of the world's most treasured ancient sites. Can you imagine the goodies down there?'

Elspeth. 'Goodies?'

'Well antiquities then.'

'That's why Mario so interested to help you in San Sebastiano chapel,' Vincenzo told Jameson. 'Herculaneum is well guarded, well supposedly, and Vataea, well she has never been re-located.' He tut-tutted again. 'Bas-tard!'

'And maybe it never will,' Elspeth said. 'Maybe it's best left alone.'

'Si,' Vincenzo agreed. 'We have remaining diary from crypt but still no map. Just a pencil mark made by looter many years ago on a hand drawn map. Is useless. Campania is big place, yes. And maybe now there be village on top of Roman town.'

'But we know someone has recently dug there,' Elspeth reminded them. 'The lamp for starters ... '

Jameson grinned from ear to ear.

Elspeth recognised *that* grin. 'What?'

'Well,' Jameson said matter-of-fact. 'I think the directions *are* there on the papers, but they are hidden by ... '

Immediately they heard the clack of the key in the door. Mario entered waving the Luger.

'Tu,' he scowled at Jameson and pushed the door wide open, stepping back to allow Jameson only to exit. Avoiding eye contact with Vincenzo Mario relocked the door. He pushed Jameson hard in the back with the pistol barrel. In the living room Jameson's backpack had been emptied onto the table.

'Vataea.' Mario grunted. 'Vataea. Dove si trova?'

Jameson understood the question, even in Italian. And Mario understood his answer. 'Wouldn't have a clue dickhead.'

Jameson didn't see the slap coming. He reeled back in shock. Angry. He made to retaliate but instantly Jameson had a Luger barrel creating a deep welt in his brow. Mario's eyes narrowed. They looked darker, beadier. Jameson held his gaze answering the tombaroli with a defiant stare.

'Vataea,' Mario shouted. And this time took Jameson's prized lamp from his cargo trouser pocket. He held the lamp high in his fingers so that Jameson could read the letters like a medallion. 'Vataea, si? Vataea, Vataea!'

'You sound like a parrot ... '

Smack! Mario didn't hesitate. He used the pistol to give Jameson a clout. Metal on bone. The pain pierced the side of Jameson's head like a lance.

'Christ!'

'Christo! Christo!' Mario moved fast to club Jameson a second time. But he was not fast enough ...

Jameson's left hand exploded ...

Up towards the pistol arm. He clamped Mario's wrist, forcing the Luger towards the ceiling.

The gun fired.

And a neat hole appeared in the plasterboard.

At that same millisecond Jameson's right fist balled. Twisted for an undercut. And pounded Mario in the liver. Breathless, Mario folded double with a groan. Jameson's knee rose striking Mario in the mouth. A hit hard enough to send the man crashing to the floor unconscious. The Luger chatted along the floorboards. Jameson finished his move with a stamp to the back of Mario's head pinning him down.

Stillness invaded the room.

Jameson checked Mario's pulse. The bastard was alive thank god. Jameson rolled Mario onto his side so he could breathe. The man's face was covered in blood and Jameson was certain he had a broken tooth or two. Satisfied, Jameson marched along the passage to Elspeth and Vincenzo. Pumped with fury his second kick ripped the door of its door jam.

Elspeth rushed forward. 'Jameson! What happened? I heard a shot. I ...'

'Hurry, we need to vacate this joint in case someone heard the gunshot.'

Vincenzo rushed into the living area. 'What happened,' he cried out. 'Where's Mario?'

'What?' Jameson raced back along the passage and into the main room. 'He was right here. Where is the bastard? I knocked him out ... oh Christ!'

'Now what?'

'The pistol's gone.' Immediately Jameson threw a finger to his lips. He made a hand signal for Vincenzo to check the bathroom and toilet. 'There's only one way out of here,' Jameson whispered to Elspeth. 'Through the garage. Stand behind me.' With Elspeth pushing up against him Jameson led them slowly, silently down the passage. Vincenzo caught up with them, and not so quietly.

'Mario, he not here. He's gone.'

Jameson slapped his finger against his lips hissing. 'Keep it down will you.'

Vincenzo. 'He's gone I say.'

'Jesus Vin, he's got a gun for Christ sake.'

'Gun maybe. But no bullets.' Vincenzo held up the magazine. 'On floor si.' The magazine had fallen out when he dropped it.

The three hurried into the garage ready for any challenge but the garage horizontal roller door was open. The bird had flown. Jameson ran to the roadway and sighed.

'We must leave now,' Vincenzo said.

'No kidding,' Jameson said more causticly than intended.

'Mario, he has friends near here. Big friends. We must leave.'

'We can't go anywhere until we find Claire,' Elspeth demanded.

'I know where Claire is,' Vincenzo said.

'Augusto's Pizzeria?'

'Si.'

'Where's our mobiles?' Elspeth searched the kitchen. 'Surely he wouldn't take four mobiles with him.'

'Who knows. Check the drawers, cupboards ... check his bedroom.' Jameson stuffed his belongings back into his pack. 'Oh you're kidding me!'

'Now what?'

Jameson found the precious Vataea lamp on the floor in two pieces. It had fallen in their struggle. He carefully wrapped the pieces back in bubble wrap and buried it amongst his change of clothing in his backpack.

'We must go,' Vincenzo said nervously.

'Mobiles? Can't leave without mobiles.' Elspeth turned over the bedroom and returned to the living quarters where she rifled through drawers. 'Huh!' she yelled in relief. The mobiles had been thrown into a cutlery drawer. 'And look what I found.' Elspeth held up an *Apple* recharger with the Italian 220 volt power connection.

'Must be Mario's.'

'Plug Claire's mobile into the power.'

'What? Now?'

'Quickly yes.'

Thirty seconds recharge sucked enough juice into the phone to check *photo stream.*

'What's her code?'

'1-9-9-5.'

'Birth date?' Jameson said with a wink. 'Now how would I have ever guessed?' He swiped the screen. 'Dam that girls got nerve.' They stared at shot after shot of Herculaneum.

'There, what's that?' Elspeth cried out. Jameson enlarged the shot. 'That's Mario and you can clearly see the bronze of Gaia that's in the boot of the Alfa.'

'Bingo. Got him.'

'Oh man,' Elspeth was ecstatic. 'You can't get better evidence than that.'

'Please,' Vincenzo was growing increasingly nervous. 'We go now.'

CHAPTER TEN

The municipal train into Stazione Napoli Centrale was packed with commuters. The sombre mood smothering the locals had lifted, as had the threatening ash and acidic smoke. Neapolitans were returning slowly to their daily business. Life was returning to normal and although San Sebastiano was partly destroyed, the attitude was one of relief.

'Mario and Augusto aren't working alone,' Vincenzo said as the three were forced to stand on the train for the fifteen-minute journey. 'But you know thees, yes.'

'I can imagine they belong to a larger syndicate,' Elspeth agreed. 'It's so sad you Italians want to sell your incredible heritage like that.'

Vincenzo was immediately defensive. 'Eet is a big problema. I agree. But Italy's economy is bad right now. Many people suffer.'

'No excuse,' Elspeth snapped. 'Sorry Vincenzo, I don't buy that.'

'What you know about thees looting anyhow,' he asked, his face reddening with frustration and embarrassment.

'The tombaroli,' Jameson answered.

'You know thees word? Is Italiano.'

'Yes. Tomb raider,' Elspeth persisted in disgust. 'It's such a popular profession that you have an Italian name for it.'

'What do *I* know?' Jameson held his pack tight as the packed carriage wobbled on a bend. 'I know what I read before flying to Europe,' Jameson said. 'It's a huge problem here and not only tombs, as we have seen with Mario and Augusto in Herculaneum, no site is sacred, huh.'

'Si. I am ashamed of my fellow Italiano,' Vincenzo sighed. 'And my cousin. I thought I know him better.'

Out the window to their right Vesuvius looked exhausted and Jameson had a moment to dream of what else lay buried under its sweeping foothills. His attitude towards the looters was slightly more understanding than Elspeths. Certainly, stealing the nations treasures was unacceptable – the unique pieces belonged in museums. But hey ... what was so bad about selling off the *museum spares*, as Jameson liked to call them. If an institution had ten votive statues of Bacchus eating grapes, then why not sell a few off, help fund the museum's future excavations.

Right?

Wrong, apparently.

Jameson cut short his reverie. 'The Etruscan ruins and tombs have really been copping it haven't they,' he said, speaking of the remarkably industrious Etruscan civilisation that thrived from 800BC until 300BC. It stretched from Pisa on the central west coast, down to Rome and pre-dated the Imperial Romans. Grave robbers found their tombs particularly interesting for the Etruscans believed that the dead should be reminded of the pleasures in life and decorated their tomb walls with scenes of banqueting, music, dancing and hunting whilst filling the tombs with treasured possessions.

'Si,' Vincenzo sighed. 'Looting thees tombs is big problem.'

'But with some Apulian vases fetching hundreds of thousands of Euros,' Jameson suggested. 'It's a no brainer why they risk their freedom to loot these places.'

'And what about Mortantina?' Elspeth said of the two-and-a-half-thousand-year-old Sicilian city. 'Raped and pillaged for decades and it's still going on.'

Vincenzo grew defensive once more. 'The Tombaroli carabinieri – that ees the tomb robber polizia – they have had budgets cut, si. They cannot police the thousands of sites in Italy and Sicily. Ees too much. Then we have bad polizia who take ... ah ... moneys ...'

'Bribes.'

'Si. And looters, they know thees things. Sometimes I am ashamed to say I am Italiano.' Vincenzo craned his neck around the commuters wedging them into the carriage as the train slowed. 'We here at termini. Come.'

Tree lined Corso Umberto was returning to business as usual. Jameson, Elspeth and Vincenzo walked briskly from the station, through the Piazza Garibaldi and down the main thoroughfare leading them to Via Filangieri, Piazza Martiri and towards Etna Pizzeria.

The car horns were back, as was the exhaust smoke, weaving scooters, shouting hawkers, shopkeepers sweeping ash from doorways and the general hustle and bustle of a city quick to forget nature's threats. Overhead Elspeth watched mammas hang washing on balconies or hook canary cages back on their pegs, all grateful to enjoy the sun once more. Elspeth found the residential buildings of central Naples so uniform. So staid. Vincenzo had told her these buildings replaced the damaged treasures of antiquity destroyed by the earthquake of 1805. They were ordered demolished and new buildings were built by Napoleon Bonaparte. The simple but practical architecture of a dictator.

Jameson stepped into a doorway out of the path of hurried pedestrians. 'We need a plan,' he said. 'We can't just barge in to the pizzeria.'

'You're right,' Elspeth agreed. 'And anyhow what if the shop is still closed ... you know, the roller doors shut?'

'No, no,' Vincenzo shook his head. 'We go through underground. The way we escape before. More better, yes?'

Jameson. 'Why didn't I think of that?'

'Quickly, thees way.'

• • • • • •

Mario crashed through Etna Pizzeria's front door breathless. He had caught the train to Stazione Napoli Centrale and ran the two kilometres to the pizzeria where Augusto's sister Jina had set restaurant tables and was busy sweeping ash from the front. Kong the rottweiler basked on the pavement in the welcome midday sun now unobstructed by Vesuvius. Inside Augusto was preoccupied preparing food to open for lunch service. The polizia may return and he needed his alibi, his front.

Business as usual.

'What are you doing?' Mario asked Augusto who rolled a pizza wheel through a Neapolitan pizza baked fresh from the oven, trialling the oven's heat.

'What's it look like I'm doing? Do want a slice.'

Mario hurried behind the counter and took Augusto firmly by the arm. 'Where's the girl?' he hissed in a whisper.

Augusto looked at his sister who was busy with the broom, content in her chores with earplugs firmly in place listening to an Ex-Otago concert.

Mario's grip tightened. Augusto brow furrowed. 'Easy Mario.' The heat from the wood fired oven was too much. Mario dragged Augusto aside. 'The girl. Where is she?'

'Claire? She is down stairs.'

'Merda! Christo! The polizia were here yesterday and you bring the girl back here.'

Augusto's eyes narrowed. 'I took her like you told me and she's in the store.' Immediately he grinned. 'She's sleeping like a babe. The polizia found nothing yesterday?'

'We have to leave.' Mario went on to explain what had happened back at the garage.

The blood drained from Augusto's face. 'Jesus Mario! You pulled a gun on your own cousin.'

'He's family. I don't think he will go to the polizia.'

'And why not?'

'Well he is a tourist guide yes. He does not want to get mixed up in all this. And as I said, he's family. But the Australians ... We need to relocate that mouthy bitch downstairs and I need your help to sort out last night's haul.'

'I just opened the pizzeria Mario. It is our cover remember.'

'Listen to me,' Mario leant in close, his breath stale from the night before. 'They know about us, right. And ...'

'The Australians?'

'Yes.'

'How much do they know?'

'Enough to get us arrested. And I'm certain they are on their way here looking for Claire. Now let's get rid of this girl.'

•   •   •   •   •

Three people removing an iron grate at street level on a busy avenue was always going to attract attention. But not when a waste bin miraculously caught fire. They had a ten second window. Vincenzo lit papers in the bin with a cigarette lighter. It flared and smoked drawing attention while they dropped back into the abandoned cellar.

Jameson wedged the bars back into place. 'Well that was fun.'

'Do you always carry a lighter Vincenzo?' Elspeth asked.

'Si. For the ladies' cigarettes,' Vincenzo smiled cheekily and led the way back into the disused sewer. Vincenzo's mobile torch light cast a beam of moderate light from wall to wall. Securing their backpacks, Jameson and Elspeth followed single file for one hundred metres when Vincenzo located the breach in the stonework. Using the discarded blocks for leverage they re-entered the catacombs.

Elspeth immediately had a sense of foreboding.

She felt the hairs on the nape of her neck bristle. In the shadows three passageways beckoned. 'W-which way Vincenzo?'

The Italian guide swept the light before him into the tunnel on the right. The beam was promptly devoured by blackness. 'This way.'

'Are you sure?'

'Sure, I am sure,' he said with the confidence of a used car salesman, and promptly stepped into the stone arched corridor on the right. Jameson and Elspeth dutifully followed and they entered the unmapped labyrinth of ancient tunnels and mass graves.

Next passage right ...

Second left ...

'Are you sure you're sure?' Jameson was now having doubts. Nothing seemed familiar from their first visit. But then again ... dark passageways *all* look the same. 'I mean ... ah ... I don't recognise this passage.'

'Jameson my friend, have some ... how you said ... faith,' Vincenzo said over his shoulder and he led them deeper into the gloom. 'I tell you, I am guide, I do tours of catacombs ...'

'What? These catacombs?'

'No these. Thees new to me but old. I do tours in North Naples, San Gennaro. They bigger, taller roof, wider, si.' And Vincenzo bowed his head to enter an even tighter corridor. 'And in Rome, same same yes ... I tell you sometheen, I been to Paris catacomb and they have six hundred kilometres of catacombs under there. Six hundreds, I say. Down one hundred metres some of them and carved out of tufa 200, 300BC. People get lost in them and ...'

'Vincenzo!'

'Si?'

'Just get us out of here, okay.'

'Okay my friend.'

A draft caught Vincenzo's neck and he panned his light to a hole at head height where someone, a grave robber maybe, in centuries gone by, had broken into an ossuary. Vincenzo held his light high so they could see inside.

'Oh god!' Elspeth shuddered staring directly at a skull with loose mandible staring back at her in a macabre grin. The chamber was piled with bones, the remains of hundreds of people just discarded like garbage. There was no sign amongst the mound of human remains to show where the floor level may be. Fibula and tibia leg bones being the strongest bones were the most predominant, along with pelves and crushed skulls.

'They say thees is the portal to hell,' Vincenzo said casually, ever the guide.

'So you *have* been down here before, I mean along this passage?' Elspeth said feeling a sense of assurance.

'Here?'

'Yes.'

'No, I say no. Thees I have not seen Bella.'

'Jesus Vincenzo, I hope you know where we are going.'

'Si, si. I also hear in nineteenth century medical students, here in Napoli, they have market for bones you see. To study for doctors.'

'They stole the bones ... you're saying?'

'Si.'

Elspeth. 'Charming.'

Minutes later the pace slowed accompanied by gnawing doubt. Vincenzo stopped.

'What's up?'

'I do not theenk we come thees way.'

'Vincenzo!'

'You said you knew the way ...'

'Si si. But one catacomb now look like another catacomb.'

'What?' Jameson groaned. 'Are you trying to tell us ... '

Elspeth felt a lump in her throat. Her heart beat faster. 'Are you saying we're lost?'

• • • • •

Claire woke with a screaming headache. Her mouth parched with thirst. Wherever she was she was lying on a floor in total darkness. Claire reached for her head to massage the pain but her wrists were tied. She made to sit up but her ankles were tethered. Instantly she started hyperventilating. An anxiety attack. With disciplined difficulty Claire slowed her breathing and forced herself to relax. Her mind was racing.

What had happened?

Where was she?

Claire remembered Augusto abducting her in the street outside Mario's garage. She remembered fighting the man but he was too strong ...

She recalled being thrown into the back of the van. Then blankness. What happened? Immediately Claire had a flashback of Augusto forcing her to swallow a pill ... yes! A pill. *He forced it into my mouth and held my nose until I swallowed.*

I've been drugged ...

Again!

Bastards.

Claire screamed out. The ploy worked. Footsteps could be heard padding along the corridor outside. A metallic sound echoed in the room. A key turned in the lock. The door swung open and Claire recognised Augusto's slim physique silhouetted in the doorway across the room. Standing next to him was Kong the rottweiler. Both smelt sweaty.

'Bastard!' She shouted. Augusto said nothing. He just stood there. Kong growled, drooling from his jowls. A second later they were joined by another familiar figure ... Mario. Hasty words were exchanged in Italian.

'Untie me,' she screamed out.

'Shout all you want,' Augusto finally spoke in English. 'No one hear you down here.'

'Why are you doing this?'

'You know too much.'

'Know what? I know nothing. Untie me ... please.'

'You lie. You follow us last night.'

'I don't know what you're talking about.'

'Liar!'

Claire knew no Italian but she gauged they were discussing what to do with her. And none of it seemed hopeful.

'Please. Just untie me.'

'Silenzioso!' Mario yelled back.

Claire shrieked. 'HELP!'

Augusto strode across the room and slapped Claire a backhander while Kong barked and snapped forcing Mario to restrain the beast by the collar.

'Shut it, you stupid bitch.' Augusto leant over Claire, his fist balled and ready to strike again if she opened her mouth. Claire fell silent, her eyes welling up with tears and as the door was relocked her nostrils twitched. She could smell the unmistakable aroma of baking pizza; basil, tomato sauce and mozzarella and at least now she realised where she was ...

Etna Pizzeria.

•   •   •

'We're lost aren't we?' Elspeth felt the anxiety rise in her throat.

'No Bella. Vincenzo ees guide yes?' Darkness disguised his uncertainty. The passageway was tight. He pushed past Jameson and Elspeth to return along the passage they had just travelled. 'These way.'

They followed.

Out of the left passage and into a chamber of burial niches recently traversed. Vincenzo swept the light around the ancient gravesite.

'Ah, which way we just come,' he asked nonchalantly puzzled. The three gaped back at the three openings; all the same size and shape and all leading off into the unknown underground.

'Which way? Are you kidding?'

'To the right,' Jameson waved a hand in that direction.

'We just walked out of that one,' Elspeth nodded left, her voice noticeably fragile.

'No Beth, it was right.'

'I'm positive it was that one.' Elspeth wheeled around to Vincenzo who was looking uncomfortably confused. She felt the anxiety pressing on her chest.

Vincenzo turned back to face the other direction. To collect his bearings. 'I theenk we come from middle one, because I walked right to that one. He cast the light over the passage they had vacated. Jameson shone his mobile torch towards his feet.

'We should have left footsteps right?'

But there were no footsteps.

The solid stone floor gave no clues.

'Jesus Vincenzo,' Elspeth fought claustrophobia. 'Don't do this. You said ... '

'Si, si, we come from thees one.' Vincenzo bowed his head slightly and entered the middle tunnel.

'Vincenzo,' Elspeth tugged his shirttail. 'Stop ... stop and think this through.' She turned to Jameson. 'What do you think?'

'I don't know what to think. Bloody hell Beth I'm disorientated.'

'We haven't passed the fresco ... you know the one of the wealthy family and the young girl that we saw yesterday.'

'That thees way,' Vincenzo was keen to continue along the middle passage.

'But if it was, we would have seen it a moment ago. Jesus Vincenzo, think.'

The guide took the middle passageway. Elspeth and Jameson could only follow. And foreboding stalked after them.

Fifty metres on they approached a gentle bend, which came to a T-junction. Vincenzo turned right. 'Si, si, thees ees it ... ' They stared at a large chalked Christian sign, like an elongated letter P with a diagonal cross over the vertical stroke, drawn on the wall in antiquity

Elspeth and Jameson trailed after him; conserving their own mobile batteries. Humidity increased marginally and Jameson wiped beads of sweat from his brow cursing drinking Mario's grappa the night before when ...

Dead-end.

'Aha!' Vincenzo cast his light down a steep, narrow stone stairway carved out of the rock. 'Buona ... good.'

'Good? But it goes deeper underground.'

'Si, we must go down to go up.'

'Jesus Mario ... that sounds like bullshit to me,' Jameson said curtly.

Elspeth. 'We're lost. It's best we backtrack ...'

'No lost, no ... what you said ... backtrack ... trust Vincenzo.'

The three took the stairs, one behind the other, towards the pitch-blackness of the underworld. At the bottom step Vincenzo raised his light. They gaped at two passageways.

'Oh Christ!' Jameson was unnerved. 'Left or Right?'

'Right of course.' Unaware of Vincenzo's uncertainty they continued. The air seemed staler and cooler although the humidity was high. It was now impossible to take a step without crushing human bones underfoot. Vincenzo slowed ...

And stopped dead.

Ahead was a circle of blackness on the floor, maybe a metre in diameter.

'What is it?' Elspeth asked not knowing what to expect.

'It looks like water,' Vincenzo said. But immediately he realised the terrifying truth that the black circle was the entrance to a vertical shaft ...

And Vincenzo was only centimetres away from stepping into it.

He swallowed hard and crossed himself.

'Back, back,' Vincenzo said urgently. He dropped to his knees and crawled to the edge shining his torch down the shaft. It seemed bottomless. He certainly couldn't see the base. Jameson stood behind him dropping a bone over his head. They waited.

Jameson counted. 'One thousand ... two thousand ... three thousand ... four ... ' Finally, the faintest of echoes as the bone bounced at twenty or more metres below. A chilling shiver sparked through his body.

'Eet is airshaft for more catacombs,' Vincenzo decided.

'Bit big for an air shaft isn't is,' Elspeth said.

'Si.'

Jameson. 'We'll have to jump across.'

Vincenzo aimed his light beyond the shaft opening, to where it highlighted more catacombs. But the beam of light was feeble in the inky shadows ...

And disappeared into the coal-black of the unknown.

'Let's do this,' Jameson said stepping back for the run up.

Elspeth. 'I say we go back the way we came.'

'Go back and we lost.' This was the first time that Vincenzo used the 'L' word.

'L-lost?' Elspeth jaw dropped.

'Si.'

'Are you admitting we're lost?' Elspeth said agitated.

'No, no. I say go back we lost. Go this way we come to Pizzeria.'

'Jesus you better be right Vin,' Jameson said. 'Cos I don't fancy starving to death down here.'

Jameson took three hurried steps and jumped the shaft. 'Hey! That was easy. Beth, you're next.' He held his hands out to catch her. 'Just don't look down.'

'Your sister Jina,' Mario asked Augusto. 'She can cook pizza can she not?'

'Yes of course. Everything is ready. And Liliana her friend starts at midday.'

'Good. Then back the van up to the fire exit and we will take this nosy bitch to the village. Either way you and me need to make ourselves scarce. And we were lucky we had no pieces here when the polizia came, just plain lucky. So now we go by the garage and move the latest finds and abandon that address. Okay?'

'But Herculaneum has been so good to us.'

'And it will again in the future. But for now we need to clear it, cement over the entrance and we need to find Vincenzo and his friend with the map of Vataea.'

'But I thought you said the map showed nothing.'

'On the contrary. The location is there, it's just a matter of solving it and I suspect that Australian, Jameson, has worked it out.'

'What will we do with the girl, at the village that is?'

'For all I care she can fall down a well. We're making good money now. Really good money and I for one am not throwing it away because of some busybody tourists.'

•　　•　　•　　•　　•

'Go.'

Elspeth made the terrifying jump across the plunging shaft and vowed *if and when they got out of here she would never go in a mine or catacombs or a cave ever again.*

On the far side of the shaft the passages widened where ossuary were exposed on both sides. All had been vandalised by grave robbers, which gave Elspeth a renewed hope that if the grave robbers made a safe exit so would they.

'Do you recognise this ossuary?' she asked Vincenzo.

'Sorry Bella, I no see before.' Suppressing their fears Elspeth and Jameson kept close on Vincenzo's heels. Vincenzo picked up the pace and Jameson hoped he wasn't panicking.

'Someone once told me,' Jameson said. 'If you are ever lost in a maze always take the left turn. Eventually it ... '

'Please Jam,' Elspeth sounded aggravated. 'No talk of mazes ... okay?'

'Fine.'

'Because I can tell you ... '

Without warning blackness.

Total stygian darkness.

Vincenzo's mobile phone battery cut out. The torch failed.

Elspeth stumbled up against Jameson. 'Please! No!'

'Merda! I was thinking it last a long time ... '

'What!' Elspeth grew angry. 'You didn't check the battery before we came down here ... Christ Vincenzo ...'

'Easy guys.' Instantly the total blackness was swamped with light from Jameson's mobile. 'How's that.'

'Don't do that to me,' Elspeth cried out.

'Sorry Bella. Eet will not happen again ...'

'Dam right it won't. When I get out of here I'm never going underground again. Never, ever, nowhere ... you hear me ...'

'Mamma Mia!' Vincenzo screamed out. Eyes bulging off into the shadows.

Jameson wheeled around. 'Shit!' Disorientated by the brief seconds of blackness no one had seen the chamber off to their left. Now they stared in horrified awe at a wall of mummified cadavers.

'Oh-my-god!' Elspeth gaped at the bodies hanging on hooks from the ceiling. They were all incredibly well preserved and dressed in the clothes they had died in – boots and all. Ghoulish faces of desiccated skin gazed back down at them fixedly. 'Please-tell me-I-am-dreaming.'

'You no dream,' Vincenzo sighed gaping along the lifeless assembly.

Jameson held his light well above his head illuminating a long corridor with dozens, if not a hundred, bodies of the long dead hanging neatly in two rows, one either side of the chamber. The slightest movement of light cast phantom shadows amongst the mummies. Ghostly shapes. Open jaws. Spectral eye sockets appeared to dare them enter.

'This is like the Palermo burial chambers,' Jameson finally said trying to calm an extraordinary situation.

Silence.

'You know the Palermo burial chambers ... Vin?'

'Si. Yes. I have been there. Thees is ah ... no one seen thees before. I am certain of thees.'

'Then we *are* lost,' Elspeth's voice sounded choked.

'Not yet we aren't,' Jameson took the lead with his torch APP. 'There is another entrance or exit at the far end ... let's do this.'

'Have you been to Palermo?' Vincenzo asked Jameson, his words slightly fragmented with unease as he made casual conversation to hide his worst fear ...

The fact that they *were* lost.

'No. But I've seen a doco on it and I've read heaps about it.'

'Oh.'

'Yes,' Jameson continued as he led the others through the macabre alley. 'Started by the Carpathian monks in the 1500s I believe, and the last body was of a young girl in 1920s I think it was. Rosalie her name was. She's in a glass case and is so well preserved she looks like she died yesterday.'

'Amazing, yes. I see thees Rosalie.'

'There was some bloke, a mortician or doctor who injected ... '

'Can we talk about something else?' Elspeth interjected.

'Sure. How about I can see steps ahead.'

'Oh, thank god.'

The steps led to catacombs overhead. They ascended and filed along another passage when Elspeth stubbed her foot on a skull.

'Huh!' she nearly screamed for joy gaping down at the skittled skull. Jameson and Vincenzo watched the skull scatter across the path before them.

'Are you alright Beth?' Jameson asked Elspeth who was laughing hysterically.

'That skull. That's the kid's skull we passed yesterday. The skull with the piece of cranium missing. See?' It was clearly recognisable with the circular chunk of bone missing. Elspeth switched on *her* mobile torch and headed off enthusiastically down another corridor. 'Yes!' She shrieked pumping the air. 'Yes! Yes! Yes!'

Jameson and Vincenzo rushed to her side. 'There.' Elspeth waved her torch beam back and forth into a familiar vaulted chamber where the fresco of the man and woman with their young daughter stared back at them complacently, immortalised in paint and plaster.

'We here,' Vincenzo said retracing their steps with confidence. He led them along a familiar corridor. 'We must be quiet now. Turn off your lights.' Instantly they stood silently in darkness. At first they could not see their hands before their faces.

Elspeth. 'What are we doing?'

'Look up front,' Vincenzo ordered. As their eyes accustomed to the blackness the faintest smear of light could be seen ahead. 'Augusto, it seem, he forget to switch lights out.'

'Thank god for that,' Elspeth sighed with relief.

'I smell pizza,' Vincenzo smiled. 'Augusto, he re-open pizzeria.'

'Well he would, wouldn't he?' Jameson said hanging beneath Vincenzo on the ladder leading to the pizzeria trapdoor. 'That's his cover isn't it?'

'Cover?'

'To fool the police,' Elspeth explained, hanging below Jameson.

'Si, si. Now I understand. Yes. Pizzeria is cover.'

The three dangled on the ladder beneath the trapdoor, one atop the other, and waited in the welcome illumination of the low wattage globe. Augusto apparently, had forgotten to switch it off.

'Can you hear anything?' Jameson said quietly.

Before Vincenzo could answer they all heard loud footsteps crossing the pizzeria cellar floor above. Vincenzo froze. If Augusto opened the trapdoor now they were sprung ...

Worst scenario – escape the way they had come and risk being lost for ever once more in the tunnels of ghosts and ghouls. Vincenzo looked down at Jameson and Elspeth who daren't breath. He displayed two fingers, a silent sign to acknowledge there were two people above. The steps grew closer and closer and stopped. And then the lights went out plunging them back into darkness ...

'You left the catacomb light on,' Mario noted as he passed the switch on the passage wall; which he knew was Augusto's own handyman electrics hidden amongst the other cellar light switches. He flicked it off. Augusto unlocked the storeroom, pushed the door open and switched the light on. Mario followed him into the storeroom closing the door behind him in case Jina should become curious. Claire blinked furiously as if something was in her eye.

'I need to go to the toilet,' Claire said instantly.

'Piss in your jeans,' Augusto said coldly.

'I don't need to piss,' Claire replied sourly.

Augusto translated. Mario shrugged his shoulders and muttered something in Italian. Augusto shook his head in annoyance and crossed the room heaving Claire to her feet. Mario took her arm so she wouldn't fall while Augusto untied her ankles. He jerked his head towards the passage door where the pizzeria toilets waited.

'No funny business,' he said in a low growl.

Claire held her wrists up. 'I can hardly go with my hands tied can I?'

• • • • •

In the darkness below Jameson, Elspeth and Vincenzo waited silently, once again in *damned* darkness.

'Is all silenzioso si,' Vincenzo called down the ladder in a whisper. 'The footsteps, they gone.'

'Gone where?'

'They move back to pizzeria I am theenking.'

'Then move it Vin, hurry,' Jameson grew impatient. 'Let's get out of here.'

Vincenzo slipped the iron bolts holding the trapdoor in position. He let it open slightly to peer out. Although a single naked light bulb lit the passageway above it remained gloomy. Vincenzo slipped the linoleum cover aside. When he was certain it was safe he silently allowed the trapdoor drop open. The three climbed free, cumbersome with their backpacks, and gathered in the passageway, listening, anxiously in the stillness. A sound came from the storeroom opposite the toilets. Muffled voices. Immediately the door handle rattled.

'Merda!' Vincenzo waved his hands about in a sudden panic. He pointed frantically to the toilet ...

'Hurry!' Vincenzo instinctively hit the passageway switch and the hall darkened as the three crushed into the *men's* toilet – a single cubicle, and prayed they weren't heard.

'Where's the damned light?' Mario snapped in Italian as he stepped into the corridor holding Claire firmly by the arm.

Augusto. 'The globe must have blown.'

Mario shoved Claire roughly before him.

'How am I supposed to know where the toilet is in the dark?' Claire asked.

'First door on your left,' Augusto told her. 'Hurry.' Mario pushed Claire across the hallway where Claire felt her way along the wall to the ladies. She slipped inside and felt about blindly until she touched the switch. The cubicle filled with light. Her heart sank. There was no window. No exit but back through the door she had entered.

'Watch her,' Mario ordered Augusto.

'Where are you going?'

'I'm going to get the van. Then we'll take this bitch to ... '

Mario plummeted through the open trapdoor.

The shock was so sudden, so unexpected, he didn't even scream out. Augusto heard a distant sickening thud ...

And then silence.

Augusto stepped out into the corridor where the faintest of light spilt from the store. 'Mario!' he called out. He hurried to the trapdoor. Suddenly realising what had happened he carefully stepped around the opening. 'Who opened this? Jina?' He felt for the light switches and immediately the passage and the catacomb lights illuminated his surroundings.

'What the ... ?' He realised the passage light had been switched off deliberately.

'What the hell was that?' Jameson whispered in the dark confines of the men's toilet.

'We left the trapdoor open.'

'Oh Jesus!'

'Mario!' Augusto yelled down the ladder. Mario's body was twisted at the first landing four metres down the shaft. His leg was impossibly buckled half way up his back. If he was alive he was unconscious and Augusto knew if he *was* alive his leg was fractured badly. 'Mario!' Augusto heard the slightest of groans. 'Mario!' He mounted the ladder and descended. At the landing Augusto saw Mario's fracture was serious. The shinbone had snapped in half and the bone pierced through his skin and flesh protruding out of his torn bloodied trousers – like a severed branch.

'Merda.' Augusto stood over Mario, a leg either side. His mind racing. *What to do?* Mario. Can you hear me?'

Mario groaned. His eyes opened. Suddenly he coughed blood from an internal wound and, eyes bulging, he managed to point one finger skywards. 'Guarda, guarda.'

Augusto turned to look up over his shoulder. Staring back at him were three ill lit faces - Jameson, Elspeth and Vincenzo.

'You!' he roared, and started back up the ladder.

'I'll call an ambulance,' Vincenzo shouted down to his cousin in Italian leaning in and pulling the trapdoor shut. He twisted the iron ring sliding the bolts across, locking them in position, but the mechanism was under the trapdoor. Immediately Augusto was directly beneath him, frantically trying to escape when someone shouted ...

'Kong!'

The snarling, slavering growls of Kong approached at speed, bounding down the stairs from the pizzeria.

'Oh shit!' Jameson cried out. 'Beth! Into the toilet.' Vincenzo dived back into the men's bathroom.

But Jameson was trapped.

The corridor was a dead end. The toilets unreachable. Kong hit the passageway at a sprint ...

Teeth gnashing ...

A split second before Kong struck, Jameson slammed heavily against the storeroom door. It flew open. He dived inside. The monster, propelled by fury, overshot the entrance. It braked ...

Its massive weight skidded across the smooth floorboards. The dog turned in frenzied anger. Its paws clawing for traction. Jameson leapt behind the door. Kong rebuilt his momentum. He rounded the storeroom entrance, teeth bristling with salivating fury. Jameson gave the beast a half second. It realised the room was empty. The animal whirled about ...

Saw Jameson.

But Jameson rushed back out from behind the door wrenching it shut. The door shook as the massive dog threw its full weight against it, frantic to shred Jameson's throat. Jameson twisted the key, imprisoning the Rottweiler.

'Jameson!' Elspeth rushed from the ladies.

'Oh Christ!' Jameson panted. 'I hate dogs.'

'Jameson. Are you alright?'

Claire stepped into the passageway. 'Claire?' Jameson's jaw dropped. 'Where the hell did you come from?'

'She was in the toilet,' Elspeth yelled over the barking.

'In the toilet! Of course she was,' Jameson shook his head amazed. 'What were you ... '

'Later.'

Behind the store door Kong was crazed; thrashing at the wooden door like he was devouring it. 'We have to get out of here.' Everything was happening fast. Vincenzo's head appeared around the men's toilet door into the corridor just as Augusto managed to open the trapdoor a fraction. Vincenzo clamped onto the iron ring. He pulled it shut.

'You're a dead man Vincenzo,' Augusto cried out in Italian. 'A dead man. You hear me?' Vincenzo looked about but other than the pull ring there was nothing with which to hold the door closed. The storeroom door rattled. Kong's persistence was weakening it.

'Go, go, go!' Vincenzo shouted to the others.

Jameson pushed Elspeth forward and shoved Claire after her. They stepped around the trapdoor, now opening and jarring shut as Augusto and Vincenzo played at tug of war. But Vincenzo was no match for the angry tomb raider. Augusto yanked the trapdoor open, enough to clamp Vincenzo's wrist. Jameson ploughed his Blundstone boot into Augusto's arm. Augusto cried out in pain releasing his grip. Jameson leant down and wrenched the iron hoop snapping the hatch closed.

'Go Vin. Get the girls outta here.'

Vincenzo didn't argue. He took to the stairs, chasing Elspeth and Claire up to street level. The trapdoor rattled like a gorilla cage. Jameson yanked on the trapdoor one last time and stepped off after the others when the trapdoor flew open and Augusto's hand lunged ...

He gripped Jameson's ankle. Jameson tripped and fell. Augusto's lean athletic body rose from the catacomb like a stalking leopard. Jameson rolled onto his backpack as Augusto prepared to land on top of his adversary but Jameson brought his boot up and crushed Augusto in the side of his head.

The wasp's nest had been shaken.

A second kick sent Augusto crashing to the floor. He landed heavily. Jameson saw his chance and ran for the stairs.

Two treads at a time ...

Four, six, eight ...

Augusto leapt after Jameson catching his other ankle. Jameson tripped cracking his head on the upper treads. Augusto tugged Jameson back towards him. But Jameson slammed the sole of his boot into Augusto's face. Augusto cried out clutching a bloodied nose. Jameson crawled on all fours to the top of the stairs, stood groggily and staggered to the tiny dining area. The door to the street had been latched. Jina, Augusto's sister had heard the commotion and locked it. Jameson swung around. The room was intolerably hot with the door and windows shut and the wood fired oven smouldering away. Immediately a hand slapped the window from outside.

'Beth!' Jameson called out. 'Where the hell ... Vincenzo?' The others were out in the piazza. They had taken the fire exit.

The fire exit!

Jameson turned again for the exit only to have Augusto enter from the top of the stairs. His face bloodied from a broken nose. The crazed Italian cook kicked the door shut leading to the exit ...

And bolted it.

Augusto swept up a twelve-inch cook's knife. 'Now we see who is tough guy yes?' Augusto wiped blood from his nose onto his sleeve, and stepped out to meet Jameson in the open dining area – his legs splayed apart and back hunched. Augusto tossed the knife from one hand to the other – and back again – and Jameson had no doubts about the pizza cook's knife skills. Jameson took a defensive stance himself. However he was unarmed. And one slash from that twelve-inch blade would be the end of him.

'No!' he heard a scream out on the footpath as Elspeth stood watching. Helpless. Vincenzo and Claire tried to re-enter the pizzeria via the exit. But the door was bolted.

'Well tough boy,' Augusto eyes had yellowed and his face was smothered with his own blood. 'What's it to be? One finger at a time. Yes that's it. I'll chop off one finger at a time.'

Jameson kept his cool. Stayed alert. Eyes dancing about his surroundings. Then he saw his weapon of choice. *His only weapon of choice.*

The pizza-slicing wheel.

It sat behind the serving counter. Jameson conducted a faux leap right. Augusto met the move. But fast as Mohammed Ali Jameson skipped left, negotiated the counter and scooped up the pizza wheel. At the same moment he snatched an apron from the hatstand.

'Huh! And what do you think you will cut with that?' Augusto was buying time. Planning his move.

'How about I start by slicing that smirk of your face.'

'Bah!' Augusto dived in a forward stab. Jameson dodged and parried with his wheel.

'You're English is good Augusto,' Jameson said as a diversion. 'Where did you learn it?'

'I learn it talking with English pig tourists like you.'

'But I'm Australian Augusto.'

'Australian ... English. All same pig.'

'What about the Americans?'

'Argh! The Americanos are the biggest pig of the lot.'

'But you like pig,' Jameson dodged a second knife lunge and threw himself back behind the counter. 'You love pig don't you?' Jameson forced a grin. He scooped up a handful of prosciutto, heaving it at Augusto. This he followed with green olives, tomato slices and grated mozzarella until Augusto slashed furiously once more, chasing Jameson from behind the glass food cabinet.

'Bas-tard.'

The dining area was becoming unbearably hot and beads of sweat poured down Jameson's cheeks, soaking his shirt. Augusto was more acclimatised. He circled Jameson with the advantage of the long blade.

And lunged.

Jameson parried.

Augusto hit back with an immediate right hand thrust. He slashed Jameson's shirt. Jameson felt a warm trickle of blood. He jumped aside putting tables and chairs between them but Augusto hoed his foot into the plastic furniture. It scattered across the floor like doll's house fittings. With the longer weapon Augusto stepped into a fencing stance ...

Arm outstretched.

Jameson danced back. Augusto lunged. Jameson stumbled backwards only to crash hard with his backpack against the tiled wall. He was trapped. He lashed out with the pizza wheel, its circular blade spinning on its axle.

Augusto made several stabs, holding the knife like a legionnaire would hold his gladius. He thrust forward in an assured and violent stab but slipped in some tomatoe. Jameson twisted his body aside and Augusto's powerful arm stabbed the tiles with such violence the blade snapped. Steel tinkered across the floor.

Jameson's reaction was swift. He pushed away from the wall and made several rapid horizontal slashes. The serrated wheel blade finally swiping his opponent's chest. The pizza cook's white shirt instantly reddened with blood. Augusto, fearing the worst, fell onto his knees. He dropped what was left of his knife and grasped at his chest.

Jameson kicked the knife across the floor. 'Had enough?' he said between snatching breaths. Augusto tore at his shirt exposing his pounding hairy chest and his bloodied wound. Whilst the cut was 20 centimetres across, the depth was minimal. The wound was more to Augusto's pride. Frantic slapping at the window was accompanied by the sound of sirens.

'Jameson, hurry,' Elspeth shouted. Passers-by were stopping. Gawking in the window. 'Now!'

Jameson stepped around Augusto whose face and chest were a bloodied mess.

'What have you done?' Augusto babbled. 'You slashed me.' The man cried with self-pity. Jameson ignored the plea and unbolted the exit door where Vincenzo and Claire waited on the other side.

'Jesus dude,' Claire said to Jameson when she saw the bare-chested blood smothered Augusto. 'Is he ... ah ... is he gonna live?'

'Of course,' Jameson pushed his way towards the back entrance.

'Christ he looks like one of those dudes outa the Evil Dead movie.'

'Call an ambulance,' Jameson ordered Vincenzo.

'I already call one for Mario, yes. But looks like Augusto need one too.'

'That was awesome Jam,' Claire called out tripping after Jameson. They crossed by the fountain and disappeared up an alleyway the moment the ambulance entered the piazza.

'Do you still hate dogs? Claire asked Jameson.

'Only that big bastard Kong.'

•   •   •   •   •

Café Romeo. Ten minute walk from Etna Pizzeria.

The four sat nervously around a corner table in the café. Claire rubbed her wrists where the tethers had chaffed her skin. 'Doped twice in one day,' Claire said angrily and skulled her second tall glass of water. 'I can tell you where I would stick those pills if I had half a chance.'

'Look on the positive side,' Jameson said as the waiter skilfully unloaded four espressos onto their table. 'At least *you* got to see Herculaneum up close and personal.'

'I am so sorry,' Vincenzo apologised, dropping three sugar cubes into his coffee. 'I had no idea Mario was mixed in thees Tombaroli busi-ness.'

'How long did you say he's been renting that garage?' Jameson asked Vincenzo.

'Two years.. On top of ruins. I should have ... how you English say ... smell a rat.'

'Well he's paying for it now,' Elspeth said. 'He's lucky that fall didn't kill him.'

'I think it nearly did.'

'What I want to know,' Elspeth said. 'Is why did Mario lead us to Augusto's pizzeria in the first place, you know, when those other looter thugs crashed our party?'

'Well, for one thing he knew about the map didn't he?' Claire said. 'And he thought if we holed up at Augusto's he would have a better chance of getting it.'

'That makes sense.' Jameson settled his backpack on the table and fished out the diary pages. 'Now let's move forward.'

Elspeth manoeuvred her chair to look closely at the documents. 'You said you had an idea.' She leant forward and said in a plotting whisper, 'where Vataea is located.'

Jameson ironed the creases out of the page in question with the ball of his hand. Besides a topographic symbol for Vesuvius and a few words in Italian there was not a great deal on the paper.

Jameson looked at their Italian guide. 'Vincenzo,' he said with a sly smile.

'Si.'

'Lighter if you please.' Jameson presented his hand, open palm upwards. Vincenzo passed him the cigarette lighter and joined Claire and Elspeth with inquisitive patience. Jameson sparked a flame and gently waved it beneath the horizontal page, careful to warm the paper without burning it. Immediately letters became clear, then a representation of what was plainly a map. 'What does Italy have plenty of?' Jameson mused as his experiment became a resounding success.

'Ruins,' Elspeth said.

'Hunky men,' Claire grinned, squeezing Vincenzo's knee.

'Yes, what else?' Jameson asked.

Vincenzo. 'Olives.'

'Close,' Jameson grinned. 'Lemons.'

'Ah,' Elspeth understood immediately. 'The old invisible writing technique.'

'Exactly. Vince Renzo wrote in lemon juice.'

'Invisible ink.'

'That's kid's stuff,' Claire said.

'Sure. But in the conditions available to Vince in 1944 it was perfect.'

'Okay Sherlock,' Claire was now enthused. 'What have we got here?'

At the top left of the page was a rough bird's eye view of the volcano, with its crater circled in the centre and the slopes portrayed as reclining lines snaking away from the centre. An arrow, written in lemon juice and now visible on the page as a sepia marking, pointed south-east. Vincenzo translated the rest, although it was not difficult to understand.

3kms from Pompeii. Mariconda Village. Three hundred metres southwest. Bordered by Via Fondu della Rocca.

'Google maps!' Elspeth took out her iPhone. The Wi-Fi password stuck to the wall with yellowing tape read *CaféRomeo96*. A satellite image over Italy appeared, finally concentrating on Campania. 'Cool, so that's what Vesuvius looks like from above.'

'Yes, but a little flatter down the north-west slope, after this week's eruption.' 'And here ... ' Modern day Mariconda came up as an industrial area with its most dominant feature being a huge truck depot.

'Si,' Vincenzo said excitedly. 'Yes, yes. I know thees area. Mariconda ees near Via Bonifica which follow canal. Thees canal ees joining Via Molinelle canal, which pass near Mariconda. See ... ' Vincenzo pointed to the canals marked in the lemon juice. 'And yes, now I theenk of eet there ees vineyards south-east of Mariconda.'

'Vineyards?'

'Si. Maybe five hundred square metre of grapes.'

'Enough area for looters to dig.'

Vincenzo. 'The grape, they be ready to pick soon.'

'When?'

'October, maybe earlier with thees weather.'

'So the looters have only until October. Four or five weeks maybe.'

'Si.'

Jameson rearranged his pack and slung it over his shoulder jumping to his feet.

'Claire,' he said with a chuckle.

'Huh.'

'Since we saved your arse,' Jameson took the bill out of the glass where it was rolled up awaiting settlement. 'Here.'

'Please,' Vincenzo reached for the docket. 'Let me pay thees, yes.'

'No Vin. As Jam said you saved my arse.' Claire passed the hovering waiter a ten Euro note. He smiled and walked away, clearly expecting the change was a tip. 'Jesus no change,' Claire frowned. 'I'm getting shafted from every angle today.'

CHAPTER ELEVEN

Bus Interchange S.M. Carita 255. Three hundred metres southeast of Mariconda.

Claire popped a Tic-tac in her mouth and passed them around. The others took a mint each and watched their bus continue on to the village of Mariconda further up the rural road. Here inland it was hot, and the air still.

'Bit hard to imagine eh,' Claire lifted her baseball cap from her shock of bright red hair, scratched the top of her head and pulled the shade back down once more against the early afternoon heat. The sky had cleared and the sun was back with a vengeance. 'I mean it's hard to imagine there was a town like Pompeii here two thousand years ago.' She frowned at the unexceptional landscape.

Jameson's eyes searched about. It didn't look promising. 'Yes, supposedly. But where?'

'Well there's your vineyards.' Elspeth nodded to hectares of grape vines unfenced except for a shallow canal bordering the property, directly behind the bus stop. Beyond the vineyards, some two hundred metres northeast was Mariconda main village, although the area was pretty much built up all the way back to the Mediterranean. The roads, filled with mended potholes like bad dentistry, were lined here and there with umbrella pines. The homes bordering the road were in need of love with rusting iron balconies supporting air conditioners on precarious brackets. Blistering paintwork exposed stucco over the volcanic tufa block buildings where the occupants lived above their shops and businesses on the ground floor – much like the ancient Romans thousands of years earlier. Jameson noted a

Farmacia with its green cross neon hanging at an angle. Beyond the pharmacy were cafes and a faded torn canopy protected a greengrocer's stock from the fierce sun. There were several cars passing by and it seemed impossible for the tombaroli to operate here without drawing attention to themselves. Across the road from the grocer was the chapel of the miraculous virgin, wedged in between a farm equipment business and a clothes store. At the peak of the chapel's gable a concrete Mother Mary stared across the village in stony, yet angelic, silence.

Nearby a one storey building backed onto the closest vineyard and appeared to Jameson to be a large farm shed with few windows at the sides. These were blocked out with what looked like black plastic sheets. The front of the building was scaffolded to above the roofline and the scaffold covered with builder's tarps. It looked in all appearances to have been an abandoned building project.

'So where do we start?' Elspeth took a tug at her water bottle passing it to Jameson.

'Maybe I ask questions,' Vincenzo suggested. 'Maybe we visit some peoples who live in the houses near vineyards, yes.'

'Good idea,' Claire agreed. 'Let's do it.' Claire stepped off the road and was about to negotiate the ditch to take a shortcut through the nearest vineyard when a man appeared from behind the farm building wearing a black T-shirt with white writing; *Resina Explosivo.*

'Questa e proprieta, private,' he shouted out storming towards them with purpose flicking the back of his hands in a shooing motion.

'Scusa,' Vincenzo said in Italian. 'Sorry. We were just going to take a short cut to the houses over there.'

'No, no, no. Can't you see this is private property.' The man stabbed a finger at a sign they had all missed.

Proprieta private tenere fuori attenzione

Vincenzo. 'Yes. I see now. Sorry. But normally this is not a problem.'

The man, with thickset eyebrows meeting above a purple wine lover's nose with a round, sun freckled face and double chin was clearly paid security. He stood between them and the vines.

'You want to visit those homes you must walk to Via Fondu della Rocca, hundred metres that way,' he pointed down the road. 'Now leave.'

'What's the big deal.' Vincenzo asked annoyed at the man's attitude.

'Big deal. Big deal!' The security guard pushed his chest out angrily. 'There's unexploded ordinance from the war lying in this vineyard and I have been ordered to keep meddling onlookers away. And that means you. So leave.' Then as an after-thought he added. 'It's dangerous.'

Vincenzo translated to the team and they looked across the thick row of vines to where subtle green tarpaulins were draped over a large area.

'Explosives?' Jameson asked.

Vincenzo. 'Si.'

'Bombs dropped by the allies in Word War II?' Jameson reiterated.

'Si.'

The security guard became impatient. 'Andare, andare ... go ... leave ... '

'Alright,' Claire shot the man a sour look. 'Keep ya shirt on.'

'Some bombs fell on Pompeii I believe,' Elspeth said straining for a better look at the tarp covers some hundred metres from the roadway as they walked away.

'Yes,' Jameson shook his head in disgust. Pompeii was one of Jameson's special interests and he had read up on it only recently. '*Operation Avalanche* it was called. American and British bombers were trying to dislodge the German army from Naples and block their resupply routes. Unfortunately many bridges, railways and overpasses were near the archaeological site and bombing accuracy wasn't what it is today. Pompeii took several hits.'

'Jesus,' Claire was sickened. 'Didn't you say before that one bomb hit the House of the Faun?'

'Yes. One of the best and most important villas of Pompeii.'

'Why was it called The House of the Faun?' Claire asked.

'Because … ' Jameson and Vincenzo said in chorus.

'You go Vin,' Jameson bowed to the tour guide.

Vincenzo returned a humble shrug. 'Because in 1830 a bronze figure of a dancing faun was discovered in the centre of the peristyle by German archaeologists. Eet is in the Napoli Museo of Archaeology. The one at Pompeii is a copy yes.'

'You see,' Jameson added. 'We don't know who lived at these specific villas, well some we do but not many, so they are given a name according to some interesting discovery on the site … House of the Faun …'

'Or House of the Mosaic Atrium,' Vincenzo said. 'House of Faun was a luxurious villa. Eet belonging to someone important. Eet was also built and ah … decorated in the Roman Republic era so already over one hundred years when Vesuvio erupt in 79AD, si.'

'You know the famous mosaic of Alexander the Great at the Battle of Issus in 333BC?' Jameson asked.

Claire. 'Isis?'

Vincenzo. 'No Isis. They barbarian cowards and butchers. I-S-S-U-S. Thees was Alexander the Great's second conquest for Asia against Darius the Third of Persia.'

Jameson. 'You'd know the famous mosaic the moment you saw it Claire.'

'And don't tell me, it's in the museum.'

'Yep. The one at Pompeii's a … '

'Copy!'

Claire stopped suddenly. 'What's going on over there?' As they watched two men pushed wheelbarrows of dirt between the rows of vines and onto a spoil heap nearby. 'They hardly look like bomb disposal guys.'

They had walked the two hundred metres to the intersection off Via Mariconda and travelled another hundred metres northwest along Via Fondu della Rocca. This affectively placed them in a position for a rear view across at the green tarps covering the vines where the bombs were being excavated, and also the rear of the huge vineyard farm building. From here they had a good view the two hundred metres across to the diggings whilst the low-lying road dipped below the tallest vines.

'That's a lot of dirt removed looking for a bomb, or bombs, that you would assume had already been located.'

'You're right.'

'Let's take a closer look.'

Vincenzo had caught the attention of a nosey resident living nearby, apparently curious to why four young people were so interested in goings on at the vineyard.

'Scusami, buon pomeriggio,' Vincenzo greeted the woman, who was well into her seventies and walked to her boundary with an arthritic gait. She nodded warily. Vincenzo turned on his charm and spoke to her in the only language she knew. 'We are looking for work, picking grapes,' he lied.

'You're too early. One more month.'

'Yes we just realised. I have friends from Australia you see.' There was an awkward silence. 'Tell me, did you know about the unexploded bombs in the vineyard.'

'Yes,' the old lady answered, and it was now Vincenzo realised the woman either had no teeth or had removed her dentures. 'I wish they would hurry and find them. They keep me awake at night you see, and I am seventy-eight and need my rest.'

'At night! They work late then?'

'They work all night. Signor Bianchi would not be happy.'

'Signor Bianchi?'

'He owns the vineyard you understand. But he has moved to Positana to his sister Maria's until they dig the bombs out and remove them.'

'How long have these ... ah ... men, been digging here?'

'More than two weeks now.'

'That's rather a long time do you not think?'

'Yes.'

'Well thank you for your time.'

'You know,' the old lady was warming to the charismatic young Italian with the man bun and northern accent. 'It's the trucks that keep me awake.'

'Trucks?'

'Yes. Big trucks that drive here and there at all hours of the night and day.'

'Well, nice talking to you. Buona giornata.'

Satisfied that the young people in her street offered no threat the old lady sauntered back into the shade of her home, which Vincenzo realised was the source of the delicious tomato pasta sauce he could smell.

Claire. 'What was that all about?'

'Very interesting.' Vincenzo relayed his conversation.

'We're here guys,' Jameson said with that glint of success sparkling his handsome blue eyes. 'Welcome to Vataea.'

Elspeth. 'You really think so?'

'What else could it be?'

'What about the bombs?' Claire said. 'I mean look, these dudes have got *Resina Explosivo* T-shirts. They kinda look legit.'

'Are you kiddin' me?'

'I am with Jameson,' Vincenzo enthused.

'You guys lay low,' Jameson told Elspeth and Claire. 'Vin and I'll go in for a looksee.'

Elspeth. 'We need a signal in case someone comes.'

'Jameson. 'Text me. My mobiles on silent it'll vibrate in my jeans pocket. I'll feel it.'

'Cool.'

'And if someone stops us and asks why we are loitering?'

'Say what I tell old woman. We backpackers looking for work grape picking.'

'Brilliant.'

Elspeth and Claire took shelter beneath the shade of an umbrella pine and shared a bottle of warm water. The air was still and the sound of crickets relaxing. From this position they watched Jameson and Vincenzo drop into the canal bordering the vineyard and followed them until their heads vanished from view.

'What is your plan?' Vincenzo asked Jameson as the two crawled on their stomachs up the embankment and manoeuvred between the vines.

'Plan?'

'Si.'

'I don't know yet. You got any ideas?'

'Hmm. Not at thees minute.'

'Great. Let's just get closer.'

Fifty metres closer. 'Merda! What ees these?' Crawling low they were stopped by a temporary fence; steel posts driven into the ground were wrapped with re-enforced plastic sheeting. Green to match the vines. Double layers. Jameson tried to lift the base to crawl beneath it but someone had gone to a lot of trouble to tent peg the bottom flaps. They rose carefully to peer over the top.

'Jesus Vin,' Jameson hissed in astonishment. 'Will you look at that?' Vincenzo saw it too. Not twenty metres away two men struggled with what appeared to be a marble splash back from an ancient fountain. Clearly the artefact had only recently surfaced.

'I knew it, I bloody knew it!' Jameson said excitedly. They could just make out the raised carving of a naked maiden tipping water from a jug. It was certainly Roman and in perfect condition. It was also desirable, rare and extremely valuable.

'Looters,' Vincenzo mumbled angrily. 'Bas-tards.'

'That's Vataea mate. It's gotta be. We're standing on it!'

'It certainly looks like eet … bas-tards. Merda.'

'What else could it be?' Jameson dropped back from sight. 'We need confirmation. We need proof.'

'Then what?'

'We go to the police.'

'Polizia. No Jameson. You do not know thees Italiano polizia.'

'As long as we get the credit for this discovery I'm not going to argue over it. Let's get the evidence we need first.' But Vincenzo held back. He was less enthused. 'Vin. Are you up for it?'

'I don't know. Thees men ... they have guns I'm thinking.'

Jameson bit his lip in thought. 'How many men did you see?'

'Ah two with the dirt. I am thinking two more digging ...'

'And the guard. That makes five. And there's probably a couple in that building. We'll keep our heads low. If we don't do this now we'll never know and I don't fancy flying home to Australia without knowing.'

Vincenzo looked at Jameson long and hard. 'We keep our heads low, yes?'

'Yes mate. Real low.'

Following the fence for fifteen metres Jameson found a join, a weakness in the barrier. He stretched the bottom half horizontally, enough to snake through on his belly. Vincenzo followed. They knew immediately that they were within the boundaries of the clandestine excavation. What they witnessed now was a stepped-up operation. While two were transporting artefacts to the farm building another two labourers manned the wheelbarrows of excavated earth to the growing spoil heap. All men wore the *Resina Explosivo* tee-shirt. White writing on black.

Deep trenches – hidden from aerial reconnaissance by green camouflage tarpaulins – were carved in systematic rows in a south-east to north-west direction. Luckily for the looters the protective vines were in full leaf and heavily laden with fruit, almost ready for harvest. Jameson and Vincenzo inched to within metres of the first trench and, under cover of the vines, they watched.

It was clear that Vataea had succumbed to the same fate as Pompeii; as in being buried under volcanic ash and pumice and not like Herculaneum which was buried under solidified volcanic mud – now hard as rock.

The looters had uncovered the beginnings of a street with the ruins of a tavern to one side – easily recognisable like the taverns of Pompeii; two storey stone buildings with L shaped counters hard on the pedestrian pavement. These counters bore deep circular repositories for holding the amphora full of wine that passers-by could purchase. Others, Jameson knew, held hot or cold food, as Romans loved snacking. The pumice had mostly destroyed the owner's residence above. Evidence of several other small residences stood either side of the street; many being shops with apartments overhead. Now Jameson realised why the trenches were dug in the same direction as the street.

'These ees criminal,' Vincenzo whispered. 'Tell me thees ees not happening.'

'Oh it's happening alright.'

As they watched the two wheelbarrows were rolled down a wooden plank to a landing carved out of the ground. Here another plank led to the ancient street level where the tufa flagstones were exposed, showing grooves from chariot and cartwheel use. The two with the barrows shovelled soil and staggered with heavy loads back to ground level.

Jameson could have wept. Two-handled pointy-bottomed amphora were thrown aside from where they were excavated behind the tavern counter. Clearly the looters kept only the better ones.

There's $3000 each Jameson thought to himself. Vincenzo shook his head, disbelieving what he was witnessing. Jameson positioned himself to watch two men excavating. He was mortified. They were digging with the finesse of road workers. More amphoras were destroyed as they worked frantically to excavate a skeleton protruding further underground. Jameson guessed they were looking for gold, silver or jewellery, as many human remains of citizens killed in Pompeii were carrying their valuables as they tried to escape.

The other pair who had carried the marble fountain to the warehouse returned. They descended into the second trench out of sight only to reappear with what Jameson guessed was more of the fountain.

'These ees Vataea, yes?' Vincenzo said softly.

'That's the lost town all right. And look at the location.' The two turned to Vesuvius thirteen kilometres north-west, her wisping pinnacle barely in view from the vineyard. 'And exactly where our mapmaking friend Renzo said it was.'

The warning signal from a reversing truck captured their attention. Jameson lifted himself onto his knees carefully parting vine leaves. 'Now what?'

The older model Cardi semi-trailer reversed off Via Mariconda positioning itself parallel with the vineyard building. Emblazoned along one side were the words *Resina Explosivo – Montava. Italia.*

'What are you thinking,' Vincenzo asked quietly.

'That's not what it appears.'

'Oh?'

'I've seen my share of food trucks in my time and that is a food transport truck. So why does it say explosives along the side?'

'How do you know thees?'

'See the front wall between the cab and the trailer,' Jameson whispered.

'Si.'

'Well there's a section missing. And if you look carefully you can see traces of old brackets. Those brackets were to hold a refrigeration unit.'

'Could be ... how you say ... ah, second hand.'

'Sure it is. But it's not for explosives either.'

As the two watched the hydraulic ramp at the rear was lowered and a tarpaulin screen draped around the rear of the trailer.

'No! Don't tell me ...'

'What? What ees eet Jameson?'

'Don't tell me they have looted enough treasures to fill that bloody truck. Because that's what it looks like.'

'You are right. Bas-tards.'

As they watched the truck driver jumped from the cabin, landing with the grace of a leopard.

Square jawed, rock-faced Ricco Ricci landed from the cabin next to the truck with his commando boots stirring up a wisp of ash cloud. He stifled a yawn. They had been working around the clock and today was the day. His business partner ten years his senior, the charismatic Silvano Marchetti joined him, turning his head slightly to one side to accommodate his blind left eye.

'You weren't followed?'

'Not possible,' Ricci said. 'I kept off the main routes and backtracked several times to be certain.'

'Good, come inside.' Neither man was enthusiastic about working the site during the daylight hours but they had stepped up the operation and had both agreed it would be wise to rebury the site today. Leave it for a year and come back when things had settled. A mole in the carabinieri had warned them of information reaching the police HQ about stolen antiquities of remarkable quality turning up in London, Paris and Frankfurt. It was time to disappear for a while.

The two men walked into the warehouse. Ricco Ricci sucked in a sharp involuntary gulp. The dazzling hoard of statuary was mind-boggling and this was the first occasion he had had to see it laid out before him as one collection. Thirteen full sized marbles of Roman Imperial sculpture alone; lay on pallets. They had all been bubble wrapped awaiting the forklift but the works of art were clearly visible.

Priceless works of ancient art ...

'Priceless' but sold for eight million Euros to the secretive Man of Mirrors.

Ricci believed he and Marchetti had cut a great deal. Sell the collection as a lot and let another worry about its dispersal. All the same his greedy mind wondered what the black marketeer would be paid for – say – the life-size marble statue of the god Mercury or the larger than life-size Herakles or the marble of the wealthy Roman in the toga. *Absolutely stunning* Ricci sighed inwardly. And worth a fortune to the right discreet collector. A reclining marble figure of the river god, Tiber, was of immense value. The Getty Museum in Las Angeles might be persuaded, with the right documentation of course, to pay a few million for that one alone.

'This is quality Silvano, pure quality,' he said discreetly to Marchetti whose blind eye wept from the ash. For the first time in weeks they both took the time to appreciate what they had achieved: Greco-Roman busts, already antiques when Vesuvio erupted in 79AD lay waiting next to a portrait head of Mars, the god of war, and a limestone figure of Palmyra. The 1st century bust of a woman wearing a veil, and of extraordinary beauty, lay beside a marble sarcophagus decorated with griffins. The statue of Aphrodite even missing his head would fetch in excess of fifty thousand Euros. Ricci felt his heart hasten. The bronze statuary was his favourite. Before him on a trestle were figures of a nude Hermes as Mercury, Mithras, Eros and Asklepios, the god of medicine.

It was mind-blowing. In all his years as a tombaroli he had never come anywhere near as rich a site as this. And his family, a long line of tomb raiders and looters could never dream of such luck ...

And there was more ...

Much much more.

Ricci had already been eyeing a modern villa on the north coast of Sicily, half way between Palermo and the beach coast of Cefalu, for sale at three million Euros. It now seemed within reach ...

Hell, he might even decorate it with a few ancient marbles.

Ricci let his hand caress the figure of a togatus. The one metre female bronze had the rich patina of antiquity, akin to the magnificent pieces excavated at Pompeii that he had admired in the

Museo Archeologico Nazionale di Napoli. It was all a little overwhelming. Even overwhelming for Ricci the ex-Comando Subacquei ed Incursori – known in English as the Raiders and Divers Group. A special force formed in Italy in 1952, like the US Navy Seals or the British S.A.S.

Marchetti hitched his boot onto the horizontal marble torso of a nymph found in the private baths of the first villa uncovered; the villa that had started this venture. He began rethreading his bootlace.

'That sarcophagus alone should fetch one and a half,' Marchetti said quietly so as not to be heard by the hired help. Ricci knew he was talking millions. 'Marcel has received the photos and is preparing each provenance as we speak.'

Ricci said nothing. He knew each of the larger items would need a provenance for them to be sold freely on the world market. The bigger buyers like the museums would demand it. Most provenances would guarantee the items had been in private collections for decades, well before it became illegal to deal in this irreplaceable heritage. And the beauty of all these treasures was that none had seen the light of day in 2000 years so a provenance was simple to concoct. Marcel in Frankfurt, Ricci knew, was one of the best forgers in the business and his fee of one hundred thousand Euros to prepare counterfeit paper work and guarantee his silence was a bargain.

Ricci continued to gloat on their exceptional haul. Eight million for the larger pieces but the smaller items they would move themselves. Ricci cast an eye along the trestles of 'smalls,' as they called the less important artefacts like terracotta pots and lamps, jugs, glassware, coins and everyday Roman utensils of bronze and silver. Hell, they had even found weaponry such as a gladius ...

The gladius would fetch five grand!

Each of the smalls on the trestles alone would sell for, on average, a few hundred Euros apiece. And there must be two or three thousand of them. Ricci felt a warm feeling, some would call avarice, flood through his veins.

'I've spoken to the Indian woman,' Marchetti said of the Man of Mirrors partner Drishya. 'We must be at the rendezvous tonight. She expects a call as we enter Venice.'

'Good. We'll be there.'

The conversation was interrupted by the two workers fitting together the fourth and last piece of the piazza fountain. Ricco watched as they placed the marble blocks together, like a puzzle. He was pleased with his decision to bring working class men from Sicily for the dig. They were small time crooks who would have to return to Sicily, and it was doubtful they would try to return to this site until he and Marchetti ordered them. His biggest mistake was to hire the local, Fulvia, who stole from them. Bastard! What cheek. But now he was dead. Ricci smiled at the memory of the grape press squashing the man's brains; when a voice interrupted his thoughts.

'Signor Ricci,' the worker named Piero, a most unfortunate looking man with a small head and greasy hair, a full beard and a large MMX tattooed on his neck, called out. 'The fountain is complete,' he said. 'It is all there. Shall we start the back fill?'

'Yes. And be certain all pottery shards, all evidence of the villa has been reburied and covered up.'

Piero paid no attention to the word villa. Signor Marchetti and Signor Ricci had been insisting they were excavating a one only ancient villa, but he was not stupid. Villas did not have streets and piazzas with fountains. But they were being paid fifty thousand Euros each for the few weeks work. Certainly it had been hard work but this was hard cash. And they were promised more cash in the future. It was best to keep quiet, do the work and get out. Besides they all had prison records and the slightest problem could see them back inside.

Marchetti tightened the lace on his other boot and scowled at the two workmen lingering longer than he found necessary. 'Move it you two. We haven't got all day.'

'Si signor.'

'Piero.'

'Si.'

'Tell Cecco and Christofano to back fill without delay. Use the Bobcat. The four of you should manage the work by nightfall alright?'

'Yes boss.'

With all the activity Jameson and Vincenzo found a better location by crawling along the northern perimeter to a centuries old deserted shepherd's cottage. The whitewashed brick building was tiny; one wooden door, one window – boarded up – with a loft sporting a shuttered hatch in the gabled roof. The vines grew up to and against the building with wild vines creeping up its walls. The ground floor had been used in the distant past as a store for wooden wine barrels. Now forgotten, their dried staves shrank allowing the metal hoops to drop like the belt off a dieting fat man. In the loft Jameson and Vincenzo had the perfect sniper's nest thirty metres away from the warehouse.

From here they could make out a small opening in the tarpaulin pulled over the rear of the semi-trailer with a commanding view of the two trenches. A black Lancia van was in view also and they clearly read *Resina Explosivo* on its side.

'This is criminal,' Jameson was secretly envious. 'Look there, behind the big bastard with the square shoulders.' It was the purple-nosed security guard who had told them to move along.

'Listen,' Vincenzo said. They heard a motor and watched as a puff of smoke spiralled out from behind the tarpaulin.

'Forklift,' Jameson said, noticing the familiar vehicle as it traipsed back and forth across the gap in the tarpaulin. 'They're loading goodies into the truck.'

At the same moment they watched Piero drive the Bobcat mechanical shovel towards the excavation.

Jameson. 'They're filling the site in.'

'I theenk you are right. And what ees thees van I am thinking?'

'Hey!' Jameson said scavenging through his backpack. 'I nearly forgot.' He pulled the small eight Euro telescopic eyeglass from the pack.

Vincenzo was impressed. 'Ah. The eye glass you buy in Rome.'

Jameson extended the glass. 'Now what's he up to?' he watched Marchetti walk towards the black van. As they watched the rear doors of the Lancia were thrown open.

'Look like van is office or sometheen like these,' Vincenzo whispered.

Jameson closed his left eye and positioned the telescope over his right. 'Jesus!'

'What?'

Jameson passed the scope to Vincenzo. 'What do you see sitting on the shelf just inside the black van?'

'Ees drone! Mamma Mia, do you theenk ... '

'That's exactly what I think. And that means they were the ones who sent those thugs to Mario's garage.'

'Bas-tards.'

Jameson took back the eyeglass. 'Oh man! You should see the marble statues being packed into that truck. They're wrapped in bubble wrap but I can still see heads and feet.'

As they watched through cracks in the loft hatch Marchetti and Ricci both carried piles of blankets from the van into the semi-trailer.

'The men, they must be wrapping them for transport, yes.'

'Spot on Sherlock.'

'Sherlock?'

'Don't' worry about it. It's an English thing.'

'Oh, you means thees Sherlock Holmes the English detective.'

'Hmm. So now do you think ... ' Jameson turned as Vincenzo was climbing silently down the ladder to the ground floor. 'Where're you going?

'I must ... how you said ... pee.'

'What now?'

'Si. Un momento.'

'Jesus. Be quick and be careful.' Jameson squinted back into the scope. The square set shorter man was now operating the forklift and Jameson only caught glimpses of the other man busy with blankets. 'We should really be going to the cops,' he muttered to no one out the corner of his mouth, the glass glued to his eye.

'Oh I do not think that will be necessary.'

Jameson wheeled about so fast he cricked his neck. 'Jesus!'

'Not quite Jesus, as far as you are concerned I am more like the devil,' the Italian spoke perfect English.

'Who ... what?'

'Get up. And slowly. Keep your hands where I can see them.' Marchetti pointed his IMI Desert Eagle semi-automatic handgun at Jameson's face. The lightweight pistol with its gas operated rotating bolt for its nine-round magazine was produced by Magnum Research Inc. in the United States. And was deadly accurate for two hundred metres.

'Jesus man,' Jameson's face reddened. 'Point that to the side would you.'

'Are you deaf? Get up.'

Once at the bottom of the ladder Marchetti shoved Jameson at gunpoint from the cottage. 'Who else is with you?'

'No one.'

Crack!

The pistol may have been lightweight but used as a club it bloody hurt.

'I will ask you one more time. Who else is with you?'

'No one ... ' The pistol arm rose again. 'Easy.' Jameson tried to step backwards only to stumble and drop the telescope.

'You think you are so clever Englishman.'

'I'm Australian.'

'Australian. Then you are as big a fool as the English. Pick up your precious telescope. You may like to know that is how you were caught.'

'The sun huh?'

'Si. The glass glinting in the sun, saying to me, come and catch me. Fool.'

The afternoon's shadow stalking the umbrella pine at the edge of Via Fondu della Roccas had shifted considerably. If Elspeth and Claire had been Girl Guides they may have realised that an hour had passed. Until now they had kept a low profile, sitting with their backs leaning against the tree trunk. Without warning Vincenzo appeared. He was hot, bothered and animated.

'Christ!' Claire sprang to her feet dusting the parched volcanic soil from the back of her jeans. 'Took ya time Vin. We heard a truck arrive. We were starting to ... '

'Where's Jameson?' Elspeth jumped up, peering anxiously over his shoulder.'

'The men, they got him.'

'Got Jameson! How? What happened ... '

Vincenzo explained how he had climbed down from the loft to relieve himself when he heard rustling outside the cottage, like someone was stealing up on them. He had seconds to react. He climbed inside one of the horizontal barrels and Vincenzo shuddered at the thought of the cobwebs clinging to his clothes.

'And?'

'It was one of the boss mans. He had a gun ... '

'Oh Christ!'

'Si. A hand gun. Sorry Bella. I could do nothing.'

Elspeth. 'So where is Jameson?'

'They take him to the warehouse.'

'Then we must get the police.'

'No polizia. Polizia bad mans. Corrupt. We must get message to the Tombaroli Polizia.'

'The tomb robber police?'

'Si. There is one man who can help us. Honest man. He work with museums. He hate thees looters.'

'Argh!' Claire jumped. 'What's that dude?' She pointed to a large grey spider crawling slowly up Vincenzo's arm towards his face. 'Don't move.'

'What ees it?' Vincenzo froze. But he knew. The cobwebs, the barrel, the darkness and the earth floor of the cottage. 'Claire?'

'Don't move.' Claire's eyes darted about for a stick or some other weapon.

'Claire.' Vincenzo suppressed a terror-stricken squeal. 'Claire?'

'Ah ... it's a spider dude. Big bastard. Don't move.'

Vincenzo turned his head ever so slightly, straining his eyes to steal a peek. The ugly ash grey arachnid with its armour-plated abdomen like a spiky nut crawled slowly onto his shoulder. Vincenzo was beside himself in fear.

'Don't move Vin,' Claire found a vine twig that would barely swipe the spider, let alone dislodge it.

'Oh you pussies,' Elspeth had had enough. She stepped forward with a swipe of the hand flicking the frightened creature. It landed on the gravel road scurrying for cover.

'Oh thank you so much,' Vincenzo's relief was palpable. 'I've always had fear of thees theengs ... '

'Forget the damned spider,' Elspeth said, face red from the heat and angry. 'Who is this police man?'

'Vice Sovrintendente Renato Di Stefano.'

Claire. 'Sounds important ... '

Elspeth. 'Where can we find him?'

'Palazzo della Questura. Via Medina. Napoli.'

Claire. 'Sounds like the Italian Inquisition.'

'Claire!' Elspeth scowled.

'Sorry.'

'Di Stefano, he is boss man for tombaroli carabinieri. But like many polizia in Napoli they are corrupt.'

'But you just said this ... this Vice Sov ... '

'Vice Sovrintendente Renato Di Stefano ... '

'Yes Di Stefano ... you said he was a good man.'

'Si, Si. Di Stefano is good man. But amongst corrupt mans he ees renegade. Yes, that ees a word I remember ... renegade.'

'I think you mean maverick,' Elspeth corrected. 'So call him.'

'Now!'

'No in a week's time when Jameson is dead! Stupido! Yes Vincenzo ... Now!'

• • • • • •

In the warehouse Ricco Ricci pinioned Jameson's arms from behind with a cold hard stare. Marchetti circled aiming the IMI Desert Eagle semi-automatic directly at Jameson's face demanding answers.

'I told you already,' Jameson insisted. 'I'm working alone. I am a freelance reporter doing a story on the vineyards of Campania when I stumbled on you guys. Serious.'

'What magazine?' Marchetti asked.

Jameson didn't falter. *40° Degrees South*.'

'Where's that?'

'It's a Tasmanian magazine. Tasmania Australia ... '

'I know where Tasmania is. Why would they send you to Italy.'

'I'm doing a comparison essay on Campania wines to Tasmanian wines,' Jameson lied brilliantly, his life depending on it.

'So you wine expert huh?' Ricci said. 'Tell us more.'

'Ah,' Jameson stalled for time. 'What did you want to know?' This wasn't a question Jameson offered lightly but fortunately his knowledge of Tasmanian wines was passable, being a chef and he had read an article on the overseas flight about Italian wines.

'Tell me your favourite Campania wine?' Marchetti asked waving the gun towards the vines.

'My favourite Campania wine? Oh that's easily the Falanghina made from the light skinned grape with its honeyed sweetness. But it must be well chilled ... '

'Of course.'

'It's the rich volcanic ash in the soil that grows these fine grapes. I read somewhere Pliny the Elder ... you know Pliny the Elder 2000 years ago ... yes course you do, well he loved a similar wine. But I like the Fiano and the Greco too, believe me. Now,' Jameson rattled on with confidence. 'The Tasmanian wines. Well. We have a cooler climate down there which makes our island wines distinctly different to the wines of the rest of Australia ... '

'Enough!'

'What are you really doing here?'

'Look. I know nothing,' Jameson said as calmly as he could. 'I don't give a rat's arse what you're up to. I'll just go my way and keep my mouth shut.'

'Not likely,' Marchetti pounded his balled right fist into Jameson's gut so hard Jameson thought he would faint from the pain.

'What – did – you – do – that - for?' Jameson stammered breathless, angry, defiant.

'You were in Rome recently and bought a lamp. A special lamp. We know these things. Where is this lamp?'

'I don't know what you're talking about.'

The second punch was as brutal as the first. Jameson sucked in a breath biting down on his lip.

'Well. The lamp. What did you do with it?'

'I rubbed it to clean it,' Jameson protested. 'And this genie popped out and said fuck you.' Marchetti pulled back his fist to strike. 'Wait,' Jameson cried out. 'Wait. It's in my backpack. It's in two pieces, broken.'

Ricco Ricci clamped an open hand over Jameson's head forcing him to sit on the truck's rear hydraulic platform. He checked the backpack. Marchetti kept the pistol aimed at Jameson's head. 'You have friends here. We know this. Where are they?'

At that moment Domenico, a hired thug, walked back into the warehouse. He shook his head. 'I found no one,' he said in Italian.

'See that this site is cleared in half the time,' Marchetti ordered the guard in the same language. 'We leave within the hour.'

Ricci waited for Domenico to walk out of earshot. 'Here.' Ricci held up the two pieces of ancient lamp. Under any other circumstances the artefact would have had appeal. But with a semi-trailer full of priceless antiquities the item was somewhat superfluous. 'And there's our culprit.' Ricci read the inscription in a reverent hushed voice. 'Vataea.'

'But that alone did not bring you here,' Marchetti shot a cold eye back to Jameson. 'What was so important in that chapel.'

'Ah ... ' Jameson said. 'So that *was* you up there. The eye in the sky.'

'Answer the question.'

To Jameson it appeared there was no point in holding back the information. It could hardly hurt now. Besides he wanted to avoid another crushing blow.

Marchetti. 'Well?'

'We found a map there. A map of Vataea with an X marks the spot.'

'A map?'

'Yes. That's the truth as simple as it sounds. Are Mario and Augusto a part of your racket?'

'Mario and Augusto?' Marchetti huffed. 'You mean those small time tombaroli from Ercolano?'

Jameson nodded. 'But I wouldn't say robbing Herculaneum was small time.'

'What. Herculaneum you say.'

'Yes.' Jameson felt good about this. He knew something they didn't for a change. 'That garage you sent your monkeys to is actually a front. They've dug through the tufa, underneath the roadway and tapped into older 18th or 19th century diggings to get into the ancient town. They have been robbing it blind without the authorities knowing.'

The twitch in Marchetti's eye told Jameson a lot. 'Get in the truck,' Marchetti's anger returned and he stabbed a finger on the hydraulic button. The tray shuddered as Jameson was elevated.

'What the ... ?'

'Now move back into the truck.' Anything seemed safer than having a gun pointed at your head Jameson thought. He capitulated. 'Move down the back.' Ricci threw Jameson's backpack after him. 'And don't look so worried. You are in the company of some of Italy's finest in there.' Ricci saluted the treasures with a nod.

Jameson stepped around the crates and pallets of bubble wrapped antiquities. He was trapped. 'What are you doing,' he asked, his confidence melting. He prepared himself for the worst, staring at Marchetti. At least if he was going to be shot, he would be staring his murderer in the eye.

'Further in. Move it ... oh don't worry, I am not going to kill you ... not yet. You're going for a little journey.'

'Where?'

'Somewhere nice,' Marchetti chuckled. 'Oh, I nearly forgot.' Marchetti put his hand out. 'Mobile thank you.' To hurry things along he waved the pistol about. Jameson threw him his phone. Immediately Ricci used the forklift to place a false wall into the rear of the semi-trailer. Like a tight-fitting lid on the inside of a shoebox. Jameson would never know, but if the truck was stopped for any reason, and searched, the first two metres was effectively indiscernible. The four-cornered custom-fitting prop, like a movie set piece, was bolted into place and the space filled with second hand furniture. While Jameson familiarised himself in his dark surroundings Ricci fixed the finishing touches to the sides of the trailer with new signage reading Traslochi Hercules. Milan.

Hercules Removals. Milan.

Ricci watched Domenico with a keen eye as he went about his business. Out of all of their hired help Ricci liked the educated dark-skinned Sicilian Domenico Rosellis. In a way he was like Ricci; short, stocky, square jawed and tough. The only thing that Ricci wouldn't trust the man with, was his woman. But that was not an issue today as Ricci didn't have a woman. Ricci waited until he was alone with Marchetti. When he was satisfied, he joined his partner in the rear of the observation van.

'Silvano. We need to continue this discussion we had the other night.'

'Oh,' Marchetti's mouth curled in a sly smile. 'Changed your mind at last.'

'Yes.'

Marchetti knew where the conversation was headed. For years the two men had been the middlemen, doing the labouring, the dangerous part, robbing tombs and archaeological sites in the middle of the night, supplying the likes of this ghost, Man of Mirrors, as he was known. It was time they stepped up the ladder. They had contacts now. They could sell direct and quadruple their earnings.

'So, is eight million Euros for this lot not enough for you?' Marchetti asked quietly.

'For this truck load? I'll accept the eight million. But you know as well as I do that what we have here is unique. This site here will never be equalled again. There are hundreds of millions buried beneath us here.'

'Yes. There is.' Marchetti eyed his partner carefully. 'Close the doors.' Ricci pulled the van doors shut behind him. 'So what brought you around to my way of thinking.'

'This.' Ricci handed his partner a newspaper cutting from Rome's *la Repubblica*. The article showed a photo of a 1st century AD statue of Bacchus with provenance to prove it had been in a private Belgium collection since 1956. It had sold to a wealthy American collector in Houston for eight hundred and twenty thousand Euros.

'I know,' Marchetti's brow furrowed. 'Sickening I agree.'

'And what did this Man of Mirrors pay us for it?' Ricci spat. But Marchetti knew only too well. 'Fifty thousand! Fifty thousand miserable US dollars and he sold it for over eight hundred thousand. Bastard!' Ricci tapped an angry finger at the article. 'Did you read it?'

'Yes of course.'

'All of it?'

'Yes. What are you getting at?'

'Well it says there that the provenance is legit and there is nothing the Italian government can do about the sale. It's legal. And now ... ' Ricci dropped his voice. 'Along comes this idiot who tries to tell us he's a wine journalist. He is perfect. We call Man of Mirrors wolfhound – this woman Drishya – and tell her we have a prisoner who threatens our project ... threatens everyone for that matter, including Man of Mirrors, and that we need their advice.'

'Yes. And?'

'Then, after our rendezvous tonight we hand over our prisoner. All going to plan they will take him with their new purchases to wherever. We will make certain he has his mobile in his pocket but switched on silent. Then ... ' Ricci nodded to their own GPS satellite connection. 'Between the Australian bait and our drone we will easily locate wherever this Man of Mirrors has his headquarters.'

'It's close to Venice I'm certain,' Marchetti liked the idea. 'I used to think they sent the artefacts directly out to a ship but now I am thinking he has a headquarters closer to Venice. And you know the risks?'

'Of course.'

'So now you want to play with the big boys?'

'You know I do. I'm ready. I'm sick of playing second fiddle.'

Marchetti turned his head slightly to accommodate his good eye. He had known Ricco Ricci some time. They worked well together. Sure, they argued sometimes. But not all partnerships were perfect. 'Good. I'm glad you have made this commitment. It's about time I agree.'

'Okay. So for now, let's get rid of this lot.'

CHAPTER TWELVE

Claire took one look at the handsome charismatic Vice Sovrintendente Renato Di Stefano and sighed. At 1,850 centimetres the clean-shaven, tremendously fit forty-one-year-old policeman was a hunk. He walked into the Nero Café in Mariconda with his trusted assistant, Dino Abandonato, a twenty-six-year-old Special Forces policeman with the Tombaroli Carabinieri. Both men wore black; black slacks, black roll neck, black sports jacket, black shoes. Their badges were hidden but not their personalities.

Di Stefano's eyes were drawn to Claire. She reminded him of his wife when she was younger; a little on the tubby side with a bubbly nature. 'Ciao.' He offered her his hand.

'I'm Claire,' Claire said in her most charming voice.

'Vice Super Di Stefano,' he said in good English, abbreviating the title Sovrintendente. 'I am sorry we could not make it sooner but, like I tell you on the phone, we have been held up on the Isle of Capri where we were sent on a lead. But to no success.' He looked to Vincenzo. 'And you must be the man who called me, yes?'

'Si, Vincenzo.'

'This is my assistant Dino Abandonato. So please, tell me everything.'

It took five minutes for Claire to tell the quick version of accounts. Di Stefano sat fascinated but not surprised. 'Scusami,' he finally said. 'I need espresso,' he called across the café to the owner.

'Closed signor, the machine, she is switched off.'

'No coffee!' Di Stefano looked at his watch. 5.10PM. He had not realised the time. 'So where is this ... Elspeth woman?' he asked.

'Well that's the thing Stefano,' Claire said. 'She should be calling me any minute.' Claire waved her mobile.

'Calling you. Why?'

'She is following the semi-trailer.'

'Mother Mary of Jesus! Are you serious?'

'She was beside herself with worry ... about Jameson.'

'Do you know who you are dealing with?' The polizie looked at his colleague who had been making notes, and took a deep breath.

'What is she following in if you don't mind me asking,' Dino Abandonato's English was as good as his supers.

Claire and Vincenzo nodded to a small car hire yard across the street from the café.

'I don't know whether to applaud you or lock you up,' Di Stefano said frowning at the caryard owner who was also closing up for the afternoon. 'So here's the story. Yes we knew about you coming from Roma. I know all about the Vespa business in Napoli, how you did not kill anybody I do not know.'

'How did you know?' Claire asked.

'We've suspected that Mario and Augusto for some time now. And another looter captured recently told me that Etna Pizzeria was a fence for stolen art treasures. I was there the day you escaped from the polizia after the chase. Now I know *how* you escaped. Catacombs huh. I must check it out personally. If there was not an emergency underway with Vesuvio, there would be a lot more police on the case and you would most certainly have been arrested.'

'Not all polizia are as helpful as us,' Abandonato added.

'We drove by the vineyard in question on the way here. There is nothing there.'

'If you look closely you'll find the ground recently dug.'

'Vataea you say.'

Vincenzo. 'Si.'

'Do you realise how important that site is. Why it would be the most important archaeological discovery since Egypt's Tutankhamen in 1922.'

'Believe me, we know.'

Di Stefano looked across the table at his understudy. 'Get the local policia involved. I want the site made secure. No one, and I mean no one, is to touch anything. Find out who owns the land and bring him in for questioning.' He turned back to Claire. 'For now though, we need to find this shipment before it leaves Italy. You say this Elspeth is calling you?'

'She said she would call at six.'

'Jameson. Does he have a mobile?'

'Of course, but he's not answering.'

'I wonder why?' Abandonato muttered.

'Enough of the pessimism Dino. Now get the car out front. We're all going for a ride.'

'Ride?'

'Yes. To the police headquarters. We can start by trying to track this truck with Jameson's mobile GPS.'

Claire. 'Assuming he has it with him.'

Abandonato. 'But if he did he would call, no?'

'Maybe its been taken from him,' Di Stefano said. 'But it is still on board the truck ... who knows we can only try?'

On the outskirts of Naples.

Claire's mobile sang. It was Elspeth. 'You're twenty minutes late girl,' Claire said. 'Where are you?'

'The traffic's bad,' Elspeth said. 'I think they're headed to the Autostrada ... '

'Then where?'

'How would I know?'

'Jesus Beth. Do you know what you're doing?'

'Jameson's in that truck.'

'We're with the police.'

'Good ... Oh no!'

'What?'

'They're turning off. Gotta go Claire ... I'll call you.'

'Call me soon ... Dam!' Claire checked her screen. 'Line's dead.'

Climbing the stairs to Di Stefano's office on the fourth floor Claire was short of breath. 'You gotta lift?'

'Si, but walking better for you.'

'Are you saying I'm fat?'

'No. No.'

'Are you sure?'

Di Stefano palmed open the glass door to his office. 'Good, you are still here,' he said in Italian to one of his more dedicated late workers. 'Antonio.' Abandonato, Claire and Vincenzo filed in behind him. Antonio sat before a bank of computer screens. In his mid-twenties Claire thought the man a handsome nerd. He had the physique of someone who could devour whole trays of tiramisu without gaining weight. Tall, slim and with unkempt red hair.

'Si signor,' Antonio said without taking his eyes from the screen.

'I need a GPS search on this mobile number.' He passed Antonio Claire's mobile. 'Second number from the top. Name Jameson.'

'Si, si.'

'And hurry, lives depend on it. Not to mention National art treasures.'

'How the hell's this work,' Claire asked, watching Antonio's experienced fingers tap furiously on the computer keyboard using the investigation bureau's network analysis software.

'How's this work? Tell them Maestro,' Di Stefano ordered his subordinate.

'Well ... in each cellular service area many cell service towers maintain bi-directional communication with nearby wireless phones.' Antonio's English was also perfect.

Claire was both impressed and embarrassed that she did not speak a second language. 'Dude, you sound ... well ... English.'

'I grew up in Surrey.'

'Oh, that'd do it.'

'Do you understand so far?'

Vincenzo. 'Si.'

Claire. 'I think so.'

'So,' Antonio continued. 'When a mobile phone is switched on, its signal is picked up by two, three or more nearby wireless towers known as cells. When that mobile makes or receives a call the cell network pinpoints the mobiles position and records which of these towers, or cells, is best positioned to provide the wireless service ...'

'Got ya.'

'As a result of this overlapping service coverage, any mobile switched on maintains connections with several towers. The phone does not have to be actively engaged in a call to be connected to the cells, but it must be turned on. Mobiles turned off or with dead batteries cannot be tracked.'

'So are we getting a signal?' Di Stefano asked Antonio.

'Not yet,' Antonio concentrated on the screen before elaborating. 'You see we rely on the signal triangulation to track down the phone in question. Because the cellular network allows the mobile to communicate with a number of cell towers at the same time. Towers close to each other that is. And for each cell to be evaluated according to the strength of the mobile our network analysis software here can estimate the distance of the phone from each tower.'

Di Stefano. 'Savvy?'

'Si, si,' Vincenzo nodded his head vigorously. 'Savvy.'

'Hence the triangulation system. Got it?'

'Uh-huh.'

'This same software then estimates the geographic position ... '

'Like Google Earth.'

'Hmm. Using this software we are able to, usually, pinpoint a cell phone and its user to within fifteen metres. Having said that, however, most modern mobiles carry GPS in their handsets for a much more accurate reading. Rather than rely on three local cells these use the aid of twelve or more low-Earth orbit satellites. This is far more precise.'

'Wow.'

'Yes ... aha! Got it!' As they all watched the screen they watched a tiny dot moving slowly north on the computer map. 'They're heading north on the E45 and are passing Caianello as we speak.'

'E45?' Claire shrugged.

'Si.' Di Stefano said. 'They are headed for Roma ... Dino.'

'Yes sir.'

'Call your beautiful wife and tell her you will not be home tonight.' Di Stefano turned to Claire and Vincenzo. 'Do you both have your tooth brushes?'

'In my pack,' Claire brightened at the thought. Vincenzo nodded.

'I need you to stay online,' Di Stefano ordered Antonio. 'Call in Salvadore to share the shifts.'

'Si signor.'

PART FOUR
NAPOLI TO VENEZIA

6.45PM Rolling north on the Napoli to Roma express rail.

Di Stefano's budget allowed second-class tickets but he paid for an upgrade to first class for the four of them on his own credit card. Somehow, later, he would figure out how to reclaim it. At least this way he could have a freshen up in the W.C.

Dino Abandonato starred into blackness outside the carriage window, his thoughts returning to his tolerant wife Norlina. Sometimes, he thought, she must wonder who she had married, Dino or the polizia. He caught Di Stefano's reflection returning from the bathroom.

'I hope you are right about Roma,' he said as his super re-joined them, wiping his face dry with paper serviettes. They had called Antonio only twenty-five minutes earlier from Stazione Napoli Centrale for the latest triangulation reading.

'They passed Frosinone which is half way between Napoli and Roma,' Di Stefano said of the GPS. 'They are going to Roma that is for certain.'

Instantly Claire's mobile sounded a highland jig. 'Elspeth!'

'I think we must be half way to Rome,' Elspeth said. 'I hope they don't realise I'm following.'

'Why don't you answer when I call?' Claire asked.

'I'm not getting your calls Claire.'

'Well that's weird.'

'Maybe it's a poor signal ... '

'Listen. We are on the express train to Rome ... '

'You're what? Rome?'

'Yes. We're with the cops. And the cops are tracking Jameson's mobile and your right on the money girl. They can see where the trucks headed to.'

'You're on your way to Rome?'

'Yes. Express. We'll get there about the same time as you I'm thinking.'

• • • • •

Jameson had a bad feeling about this. He was trapped in the back of a semi-trailer with millions of dollar's worth of looted antiquities. It was pitch black. But at least, now that they were moving, the humidity had backed off and somewhere he could feel a draught. Trying to take his mind off the situation his thoughts went to blind people and how they coped. As he sat on a horizontal marble figure he ran fingers over the exposed face of one, trying to assess the sex and then the specifics of the statue. The enormity of the discovery in part distracted him from the dire situation he was in. The only saving grace being that if they wanted him dead he would be dead by now, but he was kidnapped for whatever reason.

Since arriving in Rome four days ago Jameson's life had been turned upside down and he reprimanded himself for putting Elspeth and Claire's life in danger. He correctly guessed, as their speed was consistent, the route continuous and the travelling smooth with gentle bends that they were on a main highway ... *but travelling south or north?*

The draught grew stronger.

Jameson felt his way through the maze of ancient art drowned in stygian blackness. More than once he cracked a shin or stubbed a foot on a pallet or an ancient treasure. He squeezed by one particularly large crate that he guessed was the marble sarcophagus decorated with griffins. Then, towards the rear of the trailer, nearest the cabin, Jameson noticed the faintest of light. The night sky? Over the whine of the 430 horsepower diesel motor he heard the sound of other vehicles. A busy Autostrada.

Jameson remembered noticing the truck's missing refrigeration unit, missing from when the truck had been converted from food transportation to illegal antiquity smuggling. Suddenly Jameson had a thought he might end up in Switzerland or worse, somewhere like Russia.

With renewed determination Jameson mounted the crates closest to the far wall near the truck's cabin, where load-locks criss-crossed vertical crates. Here, near the ceiling, the air was fresh, but bitter-sweet as the rectangular opening left by the removal of the refrigeration fan grate, was covered with pot-riveted steel mesh.

Marchetti slouched against the semi-trailer passenger window, his mouth wide open and snoring like an exhausted miner. The last few days had been hectic. He and Ricco Ricci had had little sleep working harder on this dig than on any dig before ... but hey!

They had done it.

They had successfully excavated a small portion of the ancient lost city of Vataea – if one can call ploughing deep test trenches excavating. And no one would ever know. They had painstakingly replanted vines over the trenches – kept alive within tubs of earth. Ricci smiled at the ingenuity of it all. They had even located large rusted shrapnel shards of exploded World War II bombs and left them in a neat pile on the outskirts of the vineyard near the main road, for all to see. Ricci had personally doorknocked the homes in the immediate area with the news that the live bomb had been removed for destruction, telling the simple country folk that the area was now safe.

Brilliant.

Ricci listened to Marchetti's snores and smiled. The older man needed a rest he grinned to himself. *Christ he was nearly fifty.* Ricci watched the eternal white line of the Autostrada slip beneath the semi-trailer with monotonous consistency. His mind wandered to how he and Marchetti first met – over the sale of some Etruscan

Jewellery in a back-alley café in Pisa, not too far from the famous leaning tower. A friend of a friend had introduced them and Marchetti paid Ricci three hundred Euro to shadow him as hired muscle, should the deal go awry. The Arab buyer proved a slippery contact. He argued over the agreed price and Ricci smiled to himself at the memory of flattening the man's face against the café table. He slammed it so hard he broke his big fat Arab nose. And now, Ricci had shadowed Marchetti ever since and Marchetti soon realised that in Ricci he had a solid partner. Now, several years later, they had proven to be a good team and had made a lot of money.

Yes we're a good team Marchetti and me. Marchetti the negotiator and Ricci the muscle.

But there was a great deal more to be made and Ricci wanted it all. This was just the tip of the iceberg.

The simple farmer and vineyard owner Signor Bianchi was happy with his five thousand Euros. He could return to harvest his grapes in a week's time and be none the wiser. *Oh,* Marchetti had thought, *he's not totally stupid, but he was under the impression we were digging for pocket money spoils.* He even doubted there was anything under his property. Once this settled down they would invite a third party to negotiate the purchase of the vineyard. Then they would have total control.

And the workers were paid well for their efforts and had returned to Sicily. Marchetti had seen to it that they were all of the impression they had exposed a lone villa. Why not? Vesuvio buried heaps of villas all those years ago.

As for the grasping fool Fulvia Conte; he deserved to die. Ricci smiled at the thought of his original demise, squashed to death in the grape press, now his juices were pushing up vines, where they had tossed his carcass into one of the back-filled trenches.

All they had to do now was make the rendezvous at the Venice dockyards, collect a briefcase of cash and then, maybe, start with a cruise on one of the hundreds of cruise ships leaving Venice each summer.

Ricci's grin returned as he thought of the eight million Euro deal. The deal with this ghost, this entity only known as the Man of Mirrors.

'She is one of the most beautiful women I have ever met,' Marchetti told Ricci of Man of Mirrors dark-skinned assistant with whom he had negotiated the deal. A woman called Drishya. 'Stunning. But don't be fooled. The woman is tough and not to be trifled with.'

Ricci kept to the right-hand lane, the slow lane, sitting on one hundred kilometres an hour. He felt like Caesar himself propped up in the driver's seat of the semi-trailer. He enjoyed driving the powerful Cardi. It made him feel even more macho he thought, more macho than he already was. Traffic tonight on the Autostrada wasn't too bad either. The odd traffic police had passed in both directions but he was cautious. This made for a relaxing trip, seven hours; eight with rest stops. He looked to the driver's consul where Marchetti's IMI Desert Eagle semi-automatic lay next to their prisoner's mobile, and Ricci threw a road map over the offending weapon, in case they were stopped by the police.

• • •

Jameson balanced on the top of the crates. They were secured by load-locks to the rear trailer wall. Here the faintest of night light filtered through the wire mesh grate and he figured he had about half a metre of width to manoeuver on top of the crates here. Jameson worked his fingers through the tight gaps in the mesh. It had been screwed into place from the outside, so if he kicked hard enough there was a chance he could dislodge the 400 by 300cm rectangular grate. He rolled onto his back and bunched his legs for leverage and began slamming the soles of his feet into the mesh. After half a dozen solid strikes he felt the metal frame loosening. Jameson was making a hell of a racket, but with all the other din about him he thought it safe; when on the seventh kick he loosened the top right hand screws ... and the mesh bent a fraction.

Jameson's luck was holding.

In the cabin Ricco Ricci listened to a Ricky Martin CD. He couldn't be happier. His thoughts drifted to the villa he fancied buying on the north coast of Sicily halfway between Cefulu and Palermo. The oncoming traffic felt rhythmic. The white line on the road ahead continued its monotonous journey. Ricci's eyelids grew heavy. He was fighting sleep and the nearest espresso stop was still thirty kilometres away.

Bah!

He shook his head vigorously to wake himself. The Ricky Martin ballad *A Medio Vivir* filled the cabin. The song was slow and relaxing. Ricco Ricci's eyelids grew heavier and heavier and fight all he could, fatigue finally prevailed ...

Three slow blinks pre-empted a nod ...

And Ricco Ricci dozed off.

The sound of the first blaring car horn did nothing to snap the man from his sleep. Nor did the others. The semi-trailer with its 28,750KG payload veered across the three northbound lanes. It forced a Fiat sedan and an intercity bus to swerve sharply. The semi-trailer slammed into the left-hand guardrail. Sparks flew up off the front guard. Ricci snapped awake. He crushed the brake. The truck started a skid. Ricci realised his mistake. He eased the brake and turned the wheel into the skid and promptly out of it. The bus and fiat narrowly missed each other ... but continued on.

Jameson rolled off the crates. He fell two metres to the floor where his head sideswiped a marble statue and he was knocked unconscious.

Marchetti woke into a nightmare. His head slammed against the window. His eyes bulged. The landscape ahead reared up through the windscreen. Somewhere out of the corner of his eye he saw sparks. His body juddered violently. The truck jack-knifed coming to a rest half in the fast lane and half in the middle lane. No vehicles stopped. All traffic swerved and continued off into darkness. Luckily for Ricci the semi-trailer suffered minimal damage. With hazard lights blinking their warning, Ricci rolled the rig into the slow lane once more ...

When a blue light flashed in his side mirror.

'Polizia!'

'Merda!'

'What happened,' Marchetti said groggily. 'What have you done?'

There was no time to argue. The traffic cop was at the driver's door. He signalled for Ricci to open the window. 'Are you alright? Anyone hurt,' the cop asked.

'No officer,' Ricci said in a combination of subserviency and shock.

'Licence,' the cop held out his hand.

Ricci flipped open his wallet. 'Here.'

The cop took the wallet. 'There is a rest stop three hundred metres further on. Get this rig off the Autostrada pull in there.'

'That's one way to look after people's property,' the cop said panning his torch off the truck's removal sign and into Ricci's face where they parked at the rest stop.

Ricci. 'What was that?'

'You're removalists are you not. I hope everything in the back of this truck is well stowed.'

'Oh,' Ricci laughed. A forced laugh of relief. 'Yes, yes it is.'

'Then let's take a look.'

Marchetti was aware another policeman was on his side of the cabin, standing back at a safe distance and prepared to draw his pistol if need be. Marchetti looked briefly at the console and noticed a roadmap hid his pistol.

'Both of you get out of the truck,' the first policeman ordered. The polizia looked carefully at Marchetti. 'You're a little old to be a removalist, aren't you?'

'Oh there are some young bucks following us,' Marchetti assured him. 'They're the muscle men.'

'Oh really. Open up the back please.'

'What for?'

'Routine.'

Elspeth had witnessed everything. Being on the Autosrada she had managed to drop back and follow safely at a discreet distance. She saw the accident unfold and it looked to her like the driver had fallen asleep as the truck had veered slowly across the lanes. She passed on by the crash scene and pulled into the first rest stop she came to.

And waited.

Ricci unlocked the rear doors to the semi-trailer and prayed they would not hear Jameson. The first policeman climbed onto the rear bumper bar and shone his torch into a crammed space of household furniture. The false alcove, only two metres deep was packed with furniture. And should the law insist on delving further, the false back wall was a painted facade of realistic painted cartons ... a trompe l'oeil.

'The owners are very frugal officer,' Marchetti said, unaware that beads of sweat pooled on his forehead. 'They throw nothing away, as you can see.'

The officer with the torch shone the light directly in Marchetti's face. 'You're sweating. Is everything alright?' Marchetti whipped a handkerchief from his pocket and mopped his brow. The cop's eyes narrowed. 'Well?'

'I think I'm coming down with a fever,' Marchetti put a hand to his face to cut the torch beam. Ricci stepped away from the truck. His thoughts racing to Jameson.

'Stay where you are sir,' the other cop said to Ricci, and placed his hand on his holstered pistol.

'Do we have a problem officer?' Ricci tried to hide his anxiety and held the man's gaze.

'Problem? Now why would we have a problem?' The second cop walked over to Ricci and leant in, twitching his nose ever so subtly fishing for evidence of alcohol.

Jameson woke with a thumping headache. At first anxiety threatened – laying on a hard floor in pitch darkness he feared that he had been blinded. Slowly he remembered he had been kidnapped and he was in the back of the semi-trailer full of looted antiquities. He felt about him and sat upright groggily, his immediate thoughts being, that he had fallen asleep on the flat-tray floor. But then he remembered the sharp swerve of the truck, the violent thump as they crashed into something and the memory of tumbling from his perch up near the steel grate. A warm trickle ran down from his brow.

Blood!

He felt his head. Rubbing his fingers together he knew the sticky substance was his own blood. He had cracked his head on a marble statue and had been unconscious, not asleep. But for how long?

It was deathly still ...

Ghostly quiet.

• • • •

'Is there a reason we should have a problem?' the cop reiterated, content that driving under the influence of alcohol was not an issue.

'No,' Ricci assured the man. 'It's just ... Well we have a deadline see. The owner wants her property delivered by the morning.'

'Deadline huh? Where?'

'Rome.'

'Where in Rome?'

'Via del Foro Italico,' Ricci said without missing a beat. 'Near Quartiere district.'

The cop on the bumper concentrated his light amongst the furniture. 'Who is the owner anyway?'

'Sig.ra Mancini,' Ricci thought of his old school head mistress. 'A mean old bat with a moustache and attitude.'

This comment fetched a smile. 'Fair enough. It looks like a load of crap anyway. She must have a lot of it to fill a truck this size.'

'Oh she has apartments she rents see, so she needs loads of crap.'

Jameson heard muted sounds. He concentrated, listening intently in the empty darkness. He heard muffled voices, but in Italian. And all male. Jameson wanted to thump on the side of the truck, scream out ...

But a sense of fear and the unknown possessed him.

And he remained in silent.

'What happened to you then,' the first policeman asked, handing Ricci back his trucker's licence.

Ricci. 'I must have fallen asleep. I've been working hard lately, long hours.'

'No excuse,' the cop who was several years younger than Ricci threw his authority about in a most humiliating manner. 'You're lucky you didn't roll the truck ... '

'Or luckier still no one was hurt,' the other cop said. 'There's a café up ahead. I suggest you stop for coffee. Or better still take a rest.'

'Yes officer,' Ricci took the wiser, subservient, attitude.

The rest stop where Elspeth had pulled over was several hundred metres long, a crescent shaped nature park for long hauling trailers and family car's alike. A public toilet block lit by a single streetlamp stood at the centre. Elspeth was the only car parked, at the far end near the exit back onto the Autostrada. She watched the semi-trailer in her side mirror. It parked several hundred metres back along the dark turnoff. She watched the drivers climb from the cabin where they were joined by two other figures at the rear of the trailer. But it was ill lit and the figures were just that ... figures. And Elspeth felt it safer to observe rather than approach the truck. Eventually, after ten minutes respite, the flat-bed's motor roared back to life and in a hiss of air-brakes the massive truck rolled by while Elspeth sat silently in the ill lit car park. Elspeth allowed the truck a half kilometre head start, took a deep breath, and pulled back onto the highway.

The world about Jameson tipped and jerked in total darkness. They were on the move again. For the time being he could only nurse his sore head, and positioned himself sitting on the trailer floor, his back pressed hard against a horizontal statue.

•••••

Di Stefano ended his call. 'Antonio, he say they stop for nearly fifteen minutes at a rest stop but now we have major problem.'

'What problem?' Claire frowned.

'Well they have continued on the Autosrada E45.'

'So?'

'Well if they were going to Roma they should have turned off onto the EB21.'

'Are you saying they are not driving to Rome?'

'Si.'

'Well where's E45 go to.'

Vincenzo confirmed. 'E45, she go to east coast.'

'Of Italy?'

'Si, Italy.'

'And the problem is,' Di Stefano said deep in thought. 'There are many ports on the east coast where the antiquities could be freighted overseas.'

'Unless thees peoples, they go to Venice.' Vincenzo suggested. 'Where I was born.'

'Venice.' Di Stefano rubbed his chin. 'There was a small container of antiquities found at a storage facility recently in Venice. It was destined for Switzerland.' The tombarilo caribinieri consulted Google Maps on his mobile. 'If they continue E45 towards Bologna and then take the ring road A13 there is a strong chance you are correct. Then they would turn onto the E70 which becomes A57 to Venezia.'

'But we have one problem,' Claire muttered.

'Yes I know,' Vincenzo smiled. 'We are heading to Roma. No matter. We change at Roma and travel onto Venezia. I show you my home.'

Claire. 'How long is the train to Venice from Rome?'

'Nearly four hours.'

'And driving ... Naples to Venice?'

'Seven hours about.'

'So if we can get a connecting train quickly we can get to Venice first huh?'

'Maybe.'

Claire's mobile called. She put the mobile on speakerphone and lay it on the table for all to hear. 'El, thank God. Now listen, you are on speakerphone, all right. I'm with superintendent Di Stefano and another policeman. Where are you?'

Elspeth immediately launched into the accident she had witnessed. 'I'm scared for Jameson!'

'So that's what happened,' Claire said. 'We knew they had stopped.'

'Really? Is the GPS working that well?'

'Yes girl. But they are on the move again, right?'

'Yes.'

'Jam'll be fine. Where are you now but?'

'On the E45. But they didn't turn off to Rome.'

'We know that too. We think they are heading to Venice ... '

'Venice! Jesus Claire. I'm going to need fuel.'

Di Stefano leant over the mobile. 'This is Renato Di Stefano. Elspeth, how much gas have you got left?'

'Quarter tank.'

'Can you see the trailer?'

'Yes, about half a kilometre ahead.'

'Good. Is better you stop at next gas station and fill up on Autostrada. You soon catch them up because we know they're average speed is eighty kilometres and you drive Fiat 500 si?'

'Si, I mean yes.'

'Bene ... Good. Full tank from there will see you to Venezia, okay?'

'Okay. But then what?'

'We are changing trains in Roma for Venezia,' Vincenzo said.

'Oh boy, what a mess,' Elspeth sighed. And what if they aren't going to Venice?'

Claire. 'Then we're screwed.'

'Jesus!'

'Do not worry miss Elspeth,' Di Stefano deflected panic. 'I would bet my life on eet.'

'Oh no!' Elspeth gasped.

'What?'

'My battery is really low, in the red.'

'Turn it off, conserve eet,' Vincenzo advised.

Claire. 'Drive safe babe.'

10.30PM Roma Termini

Claire struggled for breath. 'There's – one – thing – I – really – really – hate - Vinny,' she complained as they rushed from platform seven out through the gate and against the tide of people to platform sixteen only to scramble blindly aboard the 10.35PM to Venice.

'What ees that?'

'Running – from – one – train – to – the – next.'

'We have not much choice,' Di Stefano answered for Vincenzo. 'If we want to catch the last train for the day.'

'I – know ... I - was – just – sayin' ... that's – all.'

ItaliaRail was on time. The electric driven Nuovo Transporto Viaggiatori locomotive was capable of nearly 200 kilometres per hour meaning they were three hours and ten minutes from Venice.

Di Stefano finished his call to police headquarters. 'I am certain we have made the correct decision,' he said. Abandonato, Claire and Vincenzo looked up from their seats to the older man. 'Antonio, he say thees truck we chase has bypassed Firenze and Bologna and ees on the A13.'

Abandonato. 'Good.'

Claire. 'That's to Venice right?'

Vincenzo. 'A13 takes truck to Padua. But after Padua, if GPS shows they are on E70, all is good because E70, eet become A57 all the way to Venezia.'

'Jesus,' Claire frowned. 'That sounded all gobbligook to me.'

'Yes. There is a very good chance they go to Venezia.' Di Stefano dropped onto the seat opposite Claire. 'We arrive at 1.45AM,' Di Stefano said. 'We should sleep a little.' The downside was they had to buy second-class tickets online as Di Stefano's budget blew out on the first leg. The good news was that at this late hour their carriage was near empty. Claire took a moment to admire the athletic, square jawed, charismatic cop sitting opposite her. She thought he wasn't unlike Brad Pitt, but taller. The culture commando, as she knew he liked to be called, caught her starring.

Di Stefano smiled. 'Your friends ... they will be okay. We will see to this.'

Claire shared a half smile and nodded silently. 'Tell me,' she said. 'You're going to call more cops to help us in Venice aren't you?'

'Si si. But first I must do ground work. Find out where these tombaroli are hiding. Find their rendezvous, save the treasures. Unfortunately there are too many bad polizia in Italy. I want information first before these people can be ... what you say in English ... tipped off.'

'Are you packing a weapon,' Claire had picked up too much movie culture.

'Packing?'

'Carrying a gun?'

Di Stefano looked about discreetly and then lifted his left trouser leg slightly to reveal a light-weight service Glok in its shin holster. The other double barrel semi-automatic handgun was in a shoulder holster. Claire looked to his subordinate, Dino Abandonato, whose smile told a similar story. Claire wasn't certain whether this made her feel safer or not.

'So, what made you become a culture cop?' she asked hoping a chat would calm her nerves.

'Because I care about herit-age. Italia is unique with eets histories. The Itailio-Celtic tribes, Greeks, the Etruscans, Illyrians and of course the most important Romans ...'

'Not to forget the earlier Neolithic, Copper Age, Bronze Age, Iron Age.' Abandonato added.

'Si. But we have many peoples here, Italiano peoples who are poor or greedy and do not care for herit-age. They dig at night. Digging, digging, digging.'

'And,' Abandonato added. 'They take pottery from tombs and smash what they think is not worth much money. They break skeletons looking for jewellery and have no regard for the dead.'

'We recently travelled to Switzerland,' Di Stefano pointed with his chin to Abandonato who was leaning forward intently, with his hands on his knees. 'My colleague here and I were sent to identify and repatriate hundreds of stolen works of art. Have you ever heard of The Geneva Freeport?'

'Uh-uh.'

'No, I suppose not. It is a Swiss warehouse where goods of any description can be stored safely without query or incurring taxes or duties. No one knows what it holds behind its vaulted walls. One museum curator from France told me that if its contents were to be exhibited it would undoubtedly be the best museum in the world.'

'So how did you get onto it?'

'It was joint co-operation between the State of Geneva ...'

'Who by the way,' Abandonato said. 'Are the largest shareholders in this tax haven storehouse.'

'Yes exactly, *and* the Italian government. We have suspected for some time that illegal art works and antiquities were being smuggled to Switzerland. Then a haul was discovered in a store, searched because the rent had not been paid for sixteen years.'

Abandonato. 'A store in the name of a London art dealer called Robert Mueller.'

'Yes. There were forty-seven crates. Some marked 'Statuary' others 'Terracotta.'

'We found Etruscan antiquities, pots, coins, carvings, marbles, frescoes and a magnificent mosaic from Pompeii ... Pompeii for god's sake,' Abandonato said in disgust.

Di Stefano. 'There were representatives from museums worldwide. One man was there from India ... '

'After a huge stone Buddha.'

'China ...'

'A terracotta horseman.'

'We met curators from Iraq, Cambodia and Yemen,' Di Stefano said. 'It was an amazing haul. *We*, Dino and me, we organise the return of the Italiano antiquities.'

'What has happened ... ah to this man Mueller?' Vincenzo asked.

'He is under house arrest in New York where he has a gallery, until we can build a case against him. He is a many times millionaire and the man will use his stolen millions to defend himself in court.'

'I read recently in a library article,' Claire said. 'That Italy put a lot of legal pressure on The Metropolitan Museum of Art in New York to return a stolen Etruscan piece, worth millions.'

'Si. That was us,' Di Stefano crowed proudly. 'It was the Euphronios krater – a wine mixing bowl of incredible beauty looted from a previously undiscovered Etruscan tomb twenty years ago. I believe the museum paid nearly two million U.S. dollars for it. But it was eventually handed back.'

'And,' Vincenzo spoke for Italy. 'The museums, they get no money.'

'Exactly,' Abandonato nodded agreeably. 'Repatriation. You buy stolen property and get caught, you lose everything, yes.'

'Now that Vataea has been discovered, well, that ees the most exciting news in archaeology for the 21st century,' Di Stefano said. 'Just imagine the treasures to be found. You may not get the credit for eets discovery but I will see you get all the credit for saving eet from robbery.'

Claire's face melted with pride.

Without warning the southbound express passed in the opposite direction. The pressure created by the passing forces at high speed snapped them all to attention briefly until the other train continued on in a quivering blur.

'It was legal once wasn't it?' Claire asked after composing herself. 'I mean trafficking in antiquities?'

'If an item has provenance before 1970 it is legally owned,' Vincenzo said.

'How do you get provenance?' Claire asked.

'Auction catalogues are usually the best source. See many items, they change hands back in early 20th century at auction houses like Christies, Sotheby's or Bonham's. The better antiquities have a photo. And this is the best evidence that the object existed in a private collection before 1970.'

Vincenzo. 'Papers can be forged, but not catalogues or the written record.'

'Exactly,' Abandonato said. 'And in the 19th century for instance many Europeans visit Pompeii and they all take souvenirs. Sellers in the ruins sold freely you see. There was no tombaroli polizia then.'

'And you must remember,' Vincenzo offered. 'That when a tombaroli take from tomb or looter take from ground, like thees Vataea site, there ees no provenance because the archaeological context has been damaged. No matter how attractive thees item look eet has been looted and not recorded by professionals ...'

'Exactly.'

Di Stefano cast an eye over his charges, all three in his company were under the age of thirty. He yawned. 'May I suggest we take some sleep for eet is going to be a long night?'

Jameson remembered the grate and climbed awkwardly back onto the vertical crates closest to the truck cabin ...

But again his heart sank.

The crash had caused the grate to slam back into position. It was stuck fast. Only this time any light was totally blocked out. Jameson felt sick in the gut. There was nothing else he could do to help himself, except wait.

Exhausted and fighting sleep Elspeth followed the distant semi-trailer taillights along the A57, which, in turn, became the SR11, or main artery into Venice, praying she had not been noticed tailing all the way from Naples. Fortunately she had been able to maintain a reasonable distance between them, but now they approached Venice she wasn't so certain. Then, two kilometres before the causeway that crossed the lagoon to ancient Venice, the looters turned right, onto Porto Marghera, the industrial waterfront.

On the dockside road Via delle Industrie the gap between them narrowed. It was after 2AM and immediately she felt alone, vulnerable. With enough illumination spilling from security lights Elspeth turned off her headlights and cruised slowly in the dark. They passed cranes, warehouses and slip yards eventually reaching what appeared to be an abandoned and derelict warehouse of gigantic proportions. Finally, after nearly eight hours, the truck had reached its destination. Elspeth parked off the road some three hundred metres further back, hiding the hire car behind disused shipping containers. She turned on her mobile. The phone struggled; eventually the signal bar reappeared.

'I'm in Venice,' Elspeth blurted into the receiver the moment Claire answered. Where are you?'

Claire. 'On the trai ... '

Dead.

'No!' Elspeth stared at her mobile in disbelief. *You're kidding me.* There was no option. For Jameson's sake she would have to follow on alone.

A weather battered sign gave Elspeth a clue to the former use of the ramshackle deserted plant. *Fabbrica di cement.* The disused cement factory loomed over the skyline, much of its twenty-metre-high roof missing and open to the elements. Across the Canale Industriale Nord, Elspeth watched the warm lights of old Venice and thought no two locations could be romantically further apart. Off to the west, further along the docks, grain silos stood silently guarding the waterfront. Otherwise the entire area seemed deserted.

Elspeth waited in the shadows. Listening. Watching. The truck had disappeared into the bowels of this monolithic building. All about her was silence except for the distant hum of Venice. Somewhere in the distance she heard an eerie tune play as a gentle breeze strummed the wire rigging of yachts moored at a marina. Or the drunken shouts of the odd late night commuters on the canals where the sounds travelled over water clear as the telegraph.

Elspeth approached the building. There were several points of entry; sheets of missing iron or exit doors kicked in by vandals. The building clearly awaited the demolition crews. Over her shoulder was the Canale Industriale Nord and alongside the cement factory dockside several empty refuse barges were docked one next to the other, tied bow to stern for several hundred metres. One particular barge caught her attention as a lone figure, a lean muscular black man, stood on board giving away his position with the glow of a cigarette.

Instantly activity nearby forced Elspeth into the darkness of what remained of a supervisor's office. Through a missing panel she could see the dark shape of the semi-trailer fifty metres away and observed the glow of a mobile screen as one of the men from the truck made a call. Immediately the men stepped from the shadows and onto the dock to meet a launch fast approaching from the inky darkness that was the Venice Lagoon. Elspeth watched as the craft tied up alongside the guarded barge. Two athletic figures leapt from the launch, crossed the deck of the empty barge and effortlessly climbed up onto the dock. Both figures were dressed in black and Elspeth now noted one was a woman, with a fine curved figure.

Ricco Ricci the ex-commando frogman had only met their buyer's spokesperson once before. And he was impressed. The ravishing twenty-something Anglo-Indian was a dish he would certainly like to know better. Ricci walked in front Marchetti; to welcome Drishya with what he thought was Ricci's charisma. One-eyed Marchetti was more wary. He knew the reputation of this Man of Mirrors, and trifling with this woman was not an option. Drishya stood, legs apart, eyeing the two men carefully as they approached, her milk chocolate skin lost in the night where they stood on the docks.

'Buongiorno,' Ricci gushed.

'Drishya nodded sharply. Not a smile. Her accomplice, carrying a small suitcase Elspeth now noticed, stood at her side and made it clear he was armed. The barge skipper dragged on the last of his cigarette and flicked the butt into the water before joining them.

'Let's get this over,' Drishya said in their native tongue.

'Sure.' Ricci and Marchetti led the way back into the blackness of the factory. Elspeth manoeuvred herself silently into a better position to view the opening of the truck, praying that Jameson wasn't harmed. Praying he would step from the trailer unscathed.

With a faded smile, Ricco Ricci unlocked and opened the back of the trailer. Marchetti hit the contents of old furniture with a torch beam. 'I trust you organised a forklift.'

'Of course.' Drishya tipped her head towards a shape lost in the shadows. Seconds later the quietness of the night was disturbed by the motor of the forklift as Ricci hastily dragged the furniture from the two-metre space between them and the false wall.

Inside, Jameson was unnerved by the darkness. The truck had stopped and silence prevailed. He heard soft voices and now the sound of crashing furniture penetrated his senses. Anxiety pressed on his chest but determination to come out fighting sent Jameson into a defensive mood and he started pounding on the partition.

'He's alive then,' Drishya said dryly. She had agreed to deal with the prisoner after her phone conversation with Marchetti the afternoon before. This Australian, Drishya realised, knew of the whereabouts of this allusive Roman town Vataea and was a valuable asset and must be detained at all costs.

Marchetti unscrewed the brackets holding the partition in place. It fell forward and Jameson followed like a ringside boxer. Ricci shone the flashlight in Jameson's face causing him to cower from the sudden brightness.

'What's going on?' Jameson shouted behind an open palm blocking the light.

'Jameson!' Elspeth gasped silently.

'Where am I?' Jameson demanded desperately trying to peer through narrow gaps in his fingers.

'Shut it and get down,' Marchetti said in English as he lowered the hydraulic tray. Jameson refused to move. 'Now!' Marchetti ordered.

Jameson figured if they wanted to kill him he'd be dead by now. With the torch beam trained on his body Jameson stepped forward and was lowered to the ground where he stood amongst the discarded furniture. Immediately he was aware of others close by. The attractive woman caught his attention first, flanked by two men and then his kidnappers.

'What's going on?' he asked in a more civil tone, conscious that he was being scrutinised by the woman. Jameson blinked, his eyes slowly becoming accustomed to the light around him. He considered making a dash for it but was pushed in the back by Marchetti armed with his pistol.

'What's the matter? Cat your tongues?' Jameson asked of their silence.

'What happened to his head?' The woman enquired. Jameson's gash from the fall had thankfully dried. But it needed attention and looked as though it could become septic.

'How would I know,' Marchetti scowled at Jameson. 'Self abuse by the look of it. So where do you want him?'

'You got restraints?' Drishya asked in Italian.

'Yes.'

'Then zip tie him.'

Marchetti forced Jameson's hands behind his back and shackled his wrists with a zip tie. Jameson took a deep breath. *Be calm. Stay on top of this* he told himself. The woman with the exotic appearance stared intently into Jameson's eyes. He held her stare and sensed something besides curiosity. *Was it desire in her eyes?* 'Now blindfold him and lock him in the launch.' Drishya threw Marchetti a scarf. Jameson was crudely blindfolded and shoved again in the back. 'Giorgio,' Drishya called after her launch skipper. She nodded to the small suitcase and Giorgio stepped forward passing the case to his superior. 'Lock him in the launch below decks, see he gets first aid on that cut and return here smartly. I want you on the crane.'

'Si signora.'

'You,' Drishya snapped at Ricci and Marchetti. 'I want to inspect each piece before loading onto the barge. Quickly now.

Elspeth wanted to scream out Jameson's name. She glared through the missing panel from her dark confinement not knowing what to do next. Elspeth stepped to the rear of the deserted office space squatting amongst old filing cabinets and turned on her mobile. She was rewarded with an illuminated screen and the red battery bar.

'Yes, yes!'

Then darkness.

'No. You're kidding me.' Elspeth thrust the mobile into the crook of her armpit; she had read somewhere that batteries needed warmth. Elspeth repositioned herself once more, now in a position to observe both the truck and the stumbling figure of Jameson being dragged blindfold and shackled to the launch moored next to the barge. Her mind raced.

Should she make a dash for help?

But the highway was a kilometre away and when she drove in here there was not a soul on the docks at this hour. While she watched, the crates and pallets in the rear of the trailer were forklifted to the dock next to the barge where the barge skipper operated a purpose-built crane to lift the treasures on board the floating dumpster.

They can't be going too far on a barge Elspeth correctly deduced. *Maybe they are in transit to a ship to take them out of the country.* This is crazy Elspeth admonished herself. She looked back across at Venice. This was crazier still. Here she was in Venice, Italy, with its canals, museums, galleries and romantic restaurants. Where Gondoliers serenade and masked balls are a regular event, and here she is in dire straits. She was powerless. Helpless. As Elspeth looked across the lagoon at the old city a late train sped across the causeway into Venice.

Claire?

Elspeth caught her mobile as it slipped from her armpit. It felt warm. She pushed the *on* button. Surprisingly the screen immediately lit up and Elspeth crouched, covering the screen with her body. The red bar held. She hit *Claire* ... redial.

Claire answered immediately on speakerphone. 'Babe! Where are you?'

'Venice.'

'Yes. But where in Venice.'

'The docks. Look they've put Jameson on a boat.'

'Where?'

'The docks. I don't know exactly. My batteries about to die ... '

Di Stefano cut in immediately 'Meet us at Saint Mark's Basilica we'll wait for you at the... '

'At the what?' Elspeth blurted. But at that same moment she realised her mobile was dead.

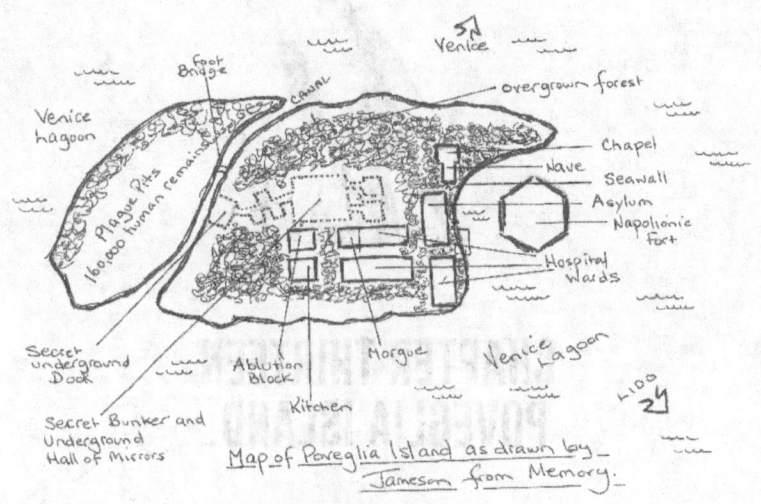

Map of Poveglia Island as drawn by
Jameson from Memory.

Labels on map: Venice; Overgrown forest; Foot Bridge; Canal; Chapel; Nave; Seawall; Asylum; Napolionic Fort; Hospital Wards; Venice Lagoon; Morgue; Kitchen; Ablution Block; Secret Bunker and Underground Hall of Mirrors; Secret underground Dock; Plague Pits 160,000 human remains; Venice Lagoon; LIDO 24

PART FIVE
POVEGLIAISLAND5

CHAPTER THIRTEEN
POVEGLIA ISLAND.

Written up in the history books as the most cursed island on the planet, five-hundred-year-old Poveglia Island was an asylum and much more until it was eventually abandoned in the 1960s. Now the deserted island served as the perfect front for covert operations.

The mega wealthy antiquity black marketeer, Cambino Salvi Cardinale, known only as Man of Mirrors to outsiders, was where he loved to be most. Relaxing amongst his Hall of Mirrors in his underground bunker. His magnificent collection of antique mirrors were hung in such a manner that while sitting in the centre of this room he could stare into the infinity of mirrors reflecting mirrors. The effect was as thought provoking as it was astounding. *Infinity* the terminally ill man managed to smile.

Just think about it.

The only item besides his precious mirrors was a life size marble statue of the Roman Emperor Hadrian, circa 130 AD he believed. Removed from Hadrian's own villa, Villa Adriana, thirty kilometres east of Rome in the eighteenth century, Man of Mirrors had been smitten by the brilliantly carved statue. And the irony was that he had legitimately purchased the artefact in the 1980s from Christies in London. Hadrian kept the Man of Mirrors humble. He never tired of its presence with the emperor's head turned slightly to face him, with his characteristic wavy hair combed forward and corkscrewing curls along his forehead. With cropped beard, gently arching brows, convex eyes, standing in a chiastic pose with the weight on the right leg, right arm raised, and wearing a voluminous mantle around the lower part of his muscular body and over the left arm.

Man of Mirrors sighed at its beauty.

Without warning he coughed and the pain from his cancerous bowel shocked through his abdomen like a savage electric charge. He reclined in his moose leather upholstered armchair made by Yves Saint Laurent in 1919. When observed from the front the sculpted wood frame was not unlike elephant tusks in appearance. This he purchased at Christies Rare Furniture Auction – three hundred thousand Euros. Cambino relaxed to Johann Strauss's Blue Danube Waltz, which sounded unbelievable on his Bloomberg Stereo with its Goldmund Epilogue Speakers and stage lighting. Stereo half a million Euros. Speakers one hundred thousand each.

I so wish Johann could share this moment he thought to himself as he aimed the remote to tweak the volume while sipping his Baron de Castelneau Armagnac, 1978. Nine thousand Euros a bottle.

Poveglia Island had been a godsend. *The most cursed island on the planet* wrote some journalists. *Sensationalists all of them.* The truth of the matter was; that the abandoned and neglected Poveglia Island, a half hour water taxi ride from the Grand Canal in Venice, was for many centuries a repository for the diseased and dying.

A plague quarantine station.

As early as 1403 authorities marooned anyone on the island who looked remotely ill for fear of the plague. It was rumoured that the remains of as many as one hundred and sixty thousand humans were interred here, and the irony was that the land where the bodies were buried was the land that best grew the vegetables to sustain the living. The Man of Mirrors chuckled at the thought.

Yes, the island had been a bargain.

And he had read in one mid 20th century publication that *the souls of the plague-stricken roam the island in such large numbers that they have disturbed the minds of the living.*

Bah!

It was the perfect ruse. The perfect front for his nefarious activities. After decades of deterioration the small island of only a few hectares had been offered up by the cash strapped Italian Government for four hundred thousand Euros. No takers. Man of Mirrors had encouraged the ghoulish rumours of hauntings and poltergeist sightings. To this end there were no buyers for the small island, separated into two parts by a narrow canal. Dilapidated abandoned buildings dating back to the 18th century, their roofs collapsing, were left to decay. The island had been a hospital and then an asylum for the mentally ill where it was rumoured the inmates were the victims of crude lobotomy experiments conducted by a doctor who was himself mad. Indeed, the doctor threw himself to his death from the spire of a bell tower, still prominent on the island. The buildings were finally boarded up and the island forsaken in 1968.

An island of angry ghosts, one reporter wrote. Cambino approved the title …

Island of angry ghosts.

After languishing for years on the books of Venice's real estate agents, finally, five years earlier, the government had accepted an anonymous offer for two hundred thousand Euros, et viola! Here he was, Man of Mirrors listening to Strauss with only vanished spirits for company …

And the contents of his Armagnac bottle.

Cambino's attention was drawn to his state of the art security panel. He had earlier watched his launch skipper skilfully cruise out from the underground bunker and into the narrow canal that divides the island before spilling into the vast Venice Lagoon. The entrance to the underground dock, half-way along the canal, was disguised as part of the embankment. It was like a remote controlled garage door that closed behind the launch. Cambino marvelled at the engineering. A huge part of the embankment had been removed and the canal dredged and widened. A steel frame with hydraulics was built to the same dimensions of the removed earth and a false, *movie set* style replacement now resembled solid land.

In fact, the entire operation was one large movie set. It had cost Man of Mirrors over ten million Euros to build the perfect front for his illegal operations. Vast rooms and chambers were excavated beneath the old asylum buildings and chapel. Engineers from Dubai and the Middle East, sworn to secrecy and bribed handsomely, pile drove foundations and supports into the ground to secure the old buildings. Once fortified they created a labyrinth of storerooms and living quarters underground, while maintaining the neglected integrity of the haunted island. A museum quality antiquity conservation laboratory was created along with a photographic facility to record and eventually aid in the sale of the artefacts. All sales were conducted online, all exchanges encrypted. All transactions and freight details secret. And very few trusted people knew of its existence.

Cambino sipped his Armagnac. He was rightly proud of his achievements. He had even submitted plans for a small exclusive resort to the Venetian City Planners which was readily approved – fast tracked with baksheesh. And conveniently, after substantial groundwork had been completed, which was really the foundations for his enterprise. this company conveniently went bankrupt and the operations closed down. The perfect ruse to continue building in secret.

The excavated earth was taken at night by barges and dumped kilometres away in the lagoon. Extra workers were also brought from Saudi Arabia, Pakistan and India. They were paid triple wages. They were flown into Venice, taken to the docks at night, secured on barges undercover, and without a clue to where they were going they were taken to Poveglia Island. Many were specialist workers; plumbers, electricians, plasterers, painters and any other tradesmen required for the fit out. Power was generated by diesel motors on the island; the diesel fuel delivered like most things, in darkness.

But the piece-de-resistance;

Two million Euros alone was spent on an elaborate system of 'wires, smoke and mirrors', as the special effects expert from Las Angeles called his booby-trapped island set pieces.

'Oh sure,' Joe Berry chuckled to Drishya when she explained what she wanted for the island at a private meeting in a Rome hotel. 'Ya want ghosts ma'am, I'm ya man.' Another million was spent guaranteeing sealed lips. Along with only two assistants Joe Berry built false walls and secret trapdoors within the ruins. High tech visual art, camera and sound equipment was installed to scare off the most sceptical trespassers. Using holograms and subtle artificial mists, apparitions could be summoned at the push of a button. Not over the top phantoms but low-key visions and effects. More moving shadows, and mind games.

Of course the island, now private property, boasted a wire fence around its perimeter accompanied by several older style warning signs. However Man of Mirrors was aware there would always be the young or adventurous ghost hunter prepared to trespass.

Despite the charade the island projected a sense of brooding. The sense of being watched was constant.

And things *did* go bump in the night.

The Pakistanis and Indians were the most disturbed. Being naturally a spiritual people they feared the island from day one. They only worked (and slept) together in teams. Some demanded to be sent home even after the threat of not being paid.

And Joe Berry the special effects expert found the work challenging. Equipment would go missing only to turn up elsewhere, power tools would turn themselves on or off mysteriously and sights and sounds beyond even his control confronted him. By the time his work was completed he was convinced the island *was* haunted.

'And why shouldn't it be,' he muttered taking an anxious last look over his shoulder as the launch took him and his assistants back towards Venice. 'Look at the misery of that place and all the dead deserted there.'

Man of Mirrors smiled to himself at the thought. Timorous gullible fools, all of them. He, of course was a sceptic.

Ghosts.

Humbug.

With the Vataea treasures safely transferred from the semi-trailer to the barge Drishya ordered Gabriel, the black barge skipper to return to Poveglia Island before hefting the small suitcase onto the hydraulic tray at the rear of the semi. 'Check it,' she ordered the tombaroli without a smile or any warmth in her voice. The launch skipper Giorgio stowed the crane and stood by. Marchetti was a little more impatient to sight the money than Ricci who stepped back allowing his partner to count the notes. Ricci kept a sharp eye. It was now clear there was no love lost between him and this creature of beauty and if anything untoward was about to happen, now would be the time. Marchetti counted the money; bundles only. Eight million Euros.

'Happy?' Drishya asked. Marchetti turned to Ricci, his face silhouetted by what little light reflected from the docks outside the factory, and nodded.

'Yes. Happy,' Ricci told Drishya.

'Good. Then we will resume business as soon as we see fit. We will contact you in three months.' Drishya swivelled on the spot and made to step away when Marchetti pulled something from his pocket.

'You might be wanting this,' he said. Giorgio pulled a Glok free.

'Easy cowboy,' Ricci bristled.

Marchetti passed Drishya Jameson's mobile. 'You might find what you're looking for on this.'

Drishya stared a moment at the mobile in the palm of his hand. She allowed the subtlest of smiles, plucked it from his palm and made her exit for the launch.

The older model black Lancia van rolled quietly into the factory, parking next to the semi-trailer.

'Where the hell have you been?' Ricco Ricci yanked the driver's door open the moment Domenico killed the motor.

'Sorry boss, I had fuel issues. This heap of shit is more thirsty than my granddaddy on the grappa.'

'Save your smartarse comments. Get the back open.'

'I've got to ask you something,' Domenico said.

'Not now.'

'But boss. I think ... '

'Later! Now open the van up.'

Ricco Ricci's skill with the drone had the Matrice 600 DJI with its Panasonic GH4 camera in the air within six minutes. From the dark shadows of Venice's industrial dockside he elevated the drone to two hundred metres and flew out over the Venice lagoon in search of the speeding launch, which unfortunately had dissolved into black waters. Ricci was about to take a swipe at Domenico for his tardiness when he noted the barge, struggling to manage three or four knots with its payload of marble, limestone and terracotta. Ricci nodded a satisfied smile. This slow craft should lead them directly to this enigma ... this Man of Mirrors.

And access to his riches.

Man of Mirrors observed the launch's return on the monitor. He switched cameras to the underground dock and watched Drishya's toned body vault from the stern of the craft and onto the landing stage. Their guest was not so nimble, being man handled and blindfolded. Man of Mirrors kept his eye on Drishya while she marched their prisoner to one of the holding cells he had had made for this very purpose.

Salah Attalah, Cambino's manservant poured his master a fresh Armagnac. The Moroccan was a deaf-mute and difficult to communicate with, unless one knew sign language. But Salah was a brilliant and talented cook. Trained by French cooks in Marrakesh in the French Embassy and in the home of a French diplomat, he had cooked for many dignitaries including the French President Francois Hollande in 2013. Man of Mirrors found his Burgundy Coq au Vin particularly stunning. An award winning slow braise of rooster, mushrooms, lardons and red wine; its juices thickened before serving with the blood of the rooster.

Drishya had heard of Salah Attalah while she was on a visit to Morocco. She heard he was looking to broaden his horizons for he was also a talented forger with an eye for Islamic antiques, which would make him a good conservator. And as good fortune accompanied good timing for both parties, Salah Attalah had upset authorities in Fez by selling the Dar Batha Museum a 13th century unglazed ewer. Unfortunately it was recognised as a one-year-old copy. It was time to leave his beloved Morocco poste haste.

Salah Attalah followed Drishya's screen image over his employer's shoulder. She crossed several security monitors on her way to the inner sanctum, as she had affectionately named the mirrored nucleus of her boss's labyrinth. Moments later a soft tap at the door heralded her entry.

'Cambino,' she purred in that husky voice the Man of Mirrors found beguiling. And Drishya was one of the very, very few who knew the man by the name his mother gave him.

'Drishya.' The Armagnac and painkillers for his cancer had made Cambino alert. Salah Attalah need not be told. He stepped before the Man of Mirrors and bowed slightly, his eyes awaiting orders. 'Go to bed Salah,' Man of Mirrors signed. 'An early breakfast I should think, and for three. We have a guest. And after that we will require your services in transportation.'

The Moroccan nodded without smiling and retired. Although the man was deaf Drishya waited until he left the study before speaking. 'We have the prisoner secured.'

'So I saw. Very good.'

'But he is Australian. He will be missed and I am certain he has a flight booked to return soon.'

'And you are happy with the delivery,' Cambino asked, without acknowledging Drishya's concern about their prisoner.

'It is astounding. Much, much better quality than I expected. And the good news is most of it does not need conservation, not by us anyhow. I suggest the traces of Vesuvio's scars on the better statues will aid in their provenance.'

'So we will ship them on tomorrow without delay.'

'I think it best, yes.' Drishya studied her beloved mentor. 'How is the pain?'

'I'm fine,' he lied, raising his chin in defiance of death. 'Now I think I shall retire. I should sleep well after my nightcap.'

'Then I will see you to bed,' she said, and wheeled the man to his bedroom.

Jameson paced his cell. He was hungry, tired and angry. At least the wrist restraints were removed along with the blindfold and the room was comfortable enough. Four metres long, three metres wide with a narrow, yet comfortable single bed. Near the ceiling an air vent circulated air. The smooth solid concrete walls smelt of new paint and it was clean, new even. A single bunker light burnt high overhead and out of reach. But stranger still was a skinny door-less shower, all stainless steel with a stainless steel toilet bowl, no seat and a tiny basin. Jameson tried the tap. The water smelt okay. He drank greedily.

Jameson imagined a map of Italy and was pleased his geographical memory was intact. He tried to guess his location. After a long drive he had been taken across water. He was on an island maybe. He had spent half a day or night in the semi-trailer on an open highway. Driving south? He thought not. That would put him on Sicily. North meant Genoa, maybe, or Florence ... no not Florence. Venice?

Although he had no answers he felt convinced his captors wanted him alive. Jameson took another drink, relieved his bladder, splashed water on his face and collapsed onto the bed.

• • • •

Domenico hovered impatiently about the rear of the black Lancia trying to get the attention of Ricci and Marchetti but they were pre-occupied, their eyes focussed on the monitor.

'Jesus!' Ricco Ricci cursed. 'The drone's almost out of range.'

Marchetti's brow creased. 'What is the range?'

'Six kilometres thereabouts … wait … ' the three men studied the drone's camera monitor. 'The barge is going straight for that island.' As they watched the dark shape of Poveglia Island – with its distinct narrow and shallow canal cutting the island in two – crept into the top of frame.

'What island is that?' Ricci asked, his eyes narrowing as he maintained a safe hovering height of two hundred metres. 'Check GPS against the map.'

'Poveglia Island.'

'No!'

'Why?'

Poveglia Island. Haven't you heard of Poveglia Island?'

'Try me … '

'Ah signor Ricci,' Domenico stepped up interrupting, 'Signor Marchetti.'

Ricci. 'What now?'

'Did you think you may have been followed?'

'Followed?'

'Yes. Followed from Napoli.'

'Good god no. Why?'

'Well I'm certain a red Fiat Panda's been following you all the way … a female driver.'

'Are you serious?'

'Yes.'

'Why didn't you say something earlier?'

'You wouldn't let me.'

'Bah! How certain are you?'

'Well when you had the accident and the polizia stopped you she was waiting in the rest stop. When you left she followed. Later she stopped for gas, and then raced to catch up with you, and then she slowed to follow you.'

'How can you be certain?'

'Well she passed me, then pulled in between us and followed. But I got caught at an intersection coming into outer Venice and lost her. I knew where you were going so didn't worry.'

'And?'

'Well I haven't seen her since.'

Marchetti looked at Ricci. 'What do you think?'

'Could be his girlfriend or it could be a coincidence.' Ricci's sharp eye caught the long dark shape on the black screen of the barge as it squeezed into the canal. 'Hello, will you look at that.' As they all squinted at the grainy image the barge appeared to be swallowed by the canal embankment. 'Did you see that?'

'Yes I did. What exactly happened?'

'Look. The barge has disappeared completely.'

'I think we need to take the truck to Sandros for the paint job,' Ricco said recalling the drone with a sharp manoeuver. 'Then get some sleep and send the drone back over that island first thing in the morning.'

•   •   •   •   •

The bells of Saint Mark's Basilica tolled 4AM, waking pigeons in its tower and reverberating about Saint Mark's Square and across the open canals. With the last restaurants and bars closing at 2AM the alleyways and Piazzas of Venice were deserted. Superintendent Di Stefano and Dino Abandonato, constantly in contact with Antonio back in Naples police HQ, stood under the basilicas entrance deep in conversation, when Antonio's final call came through.

'I think they have stopped.'

'Where?'

'It's an island on the lagoon.'

'What island?'

• • • •

'Jesus,' Claire said to Vincenzo, stifling a yawn. 'Even Hobart's waterfront is busier at this hour.' They had waited one and a half hours and the basilica's steps were giving Claire, in her own words, a numb bum.

'Hobart ees an island too ees it not,' Vincenzo asked.

'Yeh dude. I thought Venice would rock at this hour ...'

Suddenly a lone figure ran out of Calle de la Canonica and into the Piazza san Marco.

It was Elspeth.

Breathless.

'Claire!' Elspeth rushed into the square spinning in complete circles yelling out frantically.

'Claire! Claire!'

'El ... babe.' Claire ran to greet her.

'Thank god you're here,' Elspeth snatched breaths of air. She had parked the hire car in a high-rise car park near Stazione de Venezia, crossed into old Venice on the footbridge Ponte degli Scalzi and literally rushed down Venice's labyrinth of alleyways stopping every now and again to ask directions from night staff wherever she found a hotel foyer light burning. The two friends hugged.

The polizia joined them. 'I am so happy you safe,' Di Stefano said. Abandonato agreed. Di Stefano introduced himself and his colleague. 'Si ... very happy you are safe, yes. You must never chase criminals on your own like thees, okay?'

'They've taken Jameson away on a motor boat,' Elspeth blurted. 'But I don't think it can be too far because they put all the looted artefacts on a slow barge ... maybe they are taking it to meet a ship. And Jameson too. Kidnapped!'

'They put the antiquities on a barge?' Di Stefano looked intrigued.

'Yes. Quickly, I can show you where ... '

'It is alright,' Abandonato said calmly. 'Slow down your breathing. We know where your Jameson is.' He held up his mobile.

'You have a signal? Where?'

'Poveglia Island.'

'Poveglia Island?' Vincenzo's looked deadly serious.

'Why dude?' Claire shrugged. 'What is Povagilly Island?'

Vincenzo said nothing a moment. He looked at Di Stefano who was also thinking out loud. 'Ah ... '

Elspeth. 'What is it?'

'What's the big deal about Povagilly Island?' Claire insisted.

'Poveglia Claire,' Vincenzo said. 'It ees Poveglia Island.'

'So?'

'All Venetians ... they know of thees island.'

'Well I'm not Venetian *Charlie*.'

'Thees island,' Di Stefano offered. 'Ees home to ghosts. They say the souls of the dead, who die centuries ago of plague, leprosy or abandonment, roam the island like gangs of demons out to recruit any living persons who may have ventured on its shores.'

Claire. 'Ya mean Haunted?'

'Si, haunted.'

'No one,' Vincenzo said. 'No Venetian, no Italiano they go there. Very dark history. Very bad place, si.'

'No I don't see,' Elspeth grew angry. 'Jameson's life is at risk.' There followed a brief awkward moment of silence. 'Please don't tell me you macho policemen believe in ghosts.'

Dino Abandonato started. 'Well ... ah ... ees like these. Is quarantine station in old days. Many peoples die there. Now their spirits ... their ghosts, so peoples say, haunt thees island.' He crossed himself.

'There ees a little more than that I must say,' Vincenzo said in a soft reverent voice. 'I wrote a paper for the Archaeological College in Roma ... to qualify as guide yes. And I did a paper on Poveglia Island. The thing is there is very little written record. Eet is as if all records were destroyed.'

Elspeth. 'Have you ever been there?'

'I pass in small boat once, ten year earlier. But I never visit. No.'

Di Stefano. 'No one ever visits Poveglia Island.'

'Si.'

'So tell us dude,' Claire turned on Vincenzo. 'What's so special about a tiny island?'

'Ah ... well ... the island is first mentioned in chronicles of 421AD, when people from Padua and Este fled there to escape the barbarian invasions,' Vincenzo the tour guide went on. 'And by 9th century more and more peoples inhabit thees island. Then in 1370s these peoples come under attack by Genoans and people of Poveglia flee to Giudecca ... '

'Today thees Giudecca ees residential area of Venice for many working class living in apartments,' Di Stefano elaborated.

'Exactly. Then in the 1640s and 50s, the Venetians build eight sided forts on many islands to protect Venice Lagoon ... '

Elspeth. 'That's the sea around Venice right ... it's called the Lagoon?'

'Yes.'

'Octagon Forts they were called. Today only four remain and one ees part of Poveglia Island. And then in 1776 the island was used as checking point for ships coming to Venice. They were checking for diseases on people or in the cargo ... looking for plague. In 1793 many plagues, they come by sea so Poveglia Island then become a ... what you say ... sickness prison ... '

'Quarantine.'

'Si, si. Quarantine. Many many sick persons were left there to die.'

'Oh, now I'm getting the picture,' Claire said. 'Isle of the dead!'

'Then in 1805 Napoleon Bonaparte came to Venice and he continued quarantine on the island but he make the church tower ... ah church spire, into a lighthouse for shipping. Then in 1814 quarantine, she finish. In 1922 the existing buildings were converted to make lunatic asylum. These closed in late 1968. Some agriculture happen here but soon after the island was abandoned ...'

'Left to the ghosts huh?' Elspeth was sounding decidedly sceptical.

'There are three islands really. A narrow canal runs between the two largest with a small bridge connecting them. It ees on thees second island where the plague burial pits are.'

'Burial pits?'

'Si. Thees ees where the plague victims were disposed. They say more than 160,000 peoples are buried here on thees tiny island ...'

'The hill on the island ees all bodies.'

'Gross.'

Elspeth. 'And the third island?'

'Oh that ees the 1640s fort.'

'Tell them about the doctor,' Di Stefano told Vincenzo.

'Si, the doc-tor. In 1922 when the island was a hospital for the insane the head doctor, it ees said, perform operations on the patients ...'

'Lobotomies.'

'Si. Lobotomies. Crude experiments you understand. Then later he became mad himself, or maybe remorseful and he climb the church spire and jump.'

'They say he was driven mad by ghosts.'

'Great!'

'In 2009 the Italian State offered the island for sale on a 99 year lease hoping someone build luxury hotel there but no one was interested,' Di Stefano said. 'Then in early 2011 I hear some foreigner has taken the challenge. He buy for less than 200,000 Euros and has lease ... but nothing happen.'

'He started to build but all ees a mystery once again. The ghosts it seems, have taken over once more.'

Elspeth. 'You don't believe that crap, do you?'

'Poveglia Island, eet has a long reputation for being haunted. No one goes there. No one ever goes there. Is dark, brooding, evil place.'

'And now Jameson's mobile signal is coming from that island. I'll go on my own if I have to.'

'No Bella,' Di Stefano grabbed Elspeth's arm. 'We must do thees the police way.'

Elspeth shook her arm free. 'Which is?'

'Is dark still,' Abandonato said. 'We wait for light.'

'Si.'

'Then we must a find boat, yes.'

'I can help with thees things,' Vincenzo's enthused. 'I have cousin who runs small café along Calle Megio, near the Grand Canal. He will be preparing now to open at 5AM. We go there now, have some espresso and pastries. Then I have uncle who has fishing boat okay?'

Di Stefano looked at his watch. Dawn was almost two hours away and breakfast with several coffees sounded good. 'This boat. Where exactly?'

'Squero di San Trovaso.'

'The gondola boatyards?'

'Si.'

CHAPTER FOURTEEN

Jameson slept better than he expected. He had no concept of time. The electric light still burned brightly but surged from time to time hinting at locally generated power. He swung his legs over the side of the bed and waited for his throbbing head to settle. It was then that he realised a disturbance on the other side of his prison cell door had awakened him. The latch was dragged across and the door opened.

'Buongiorno.' It was his beautiful kidnapper.

'Where am I?'

Drishya stared back.

'Well?' Jameson persisted.

'Here.' Without entering Drishya threw a clear plastic parcel onto the bed.

'Well if you aren't going to tell me where I am you could at least have the decency to tell me what you're going to do with me.'

The corners of Drishya's mouth curled in annoying silence. Finally she nodded to the parcel. 'Shower. You smell.'

Jameson looked at the parcel that contained clothes and a bathing sponge bag.

'And there's a fresh bandage and antiseptic cream in there too. Ten minutes. Then you can eat.'

'Shower! But ... '

The door slammed shut. Locked. Jameson showered quickly and dressed. It certainly felt better.

Ten minutes later the door opened. 'Come.'

'Where are we going?'

'You will see. Now walk.'

Jameson had to squeeze by the woman to vacate his cell, the door opening being no more than 500mm wide. Jameson guessed at the manner in which the woman carried herself that she was proficient at self-defence. More than likely into martial arts, and he thought it best to find out more about his situation before he did anything foolish. As he pushed by she did not flinch. Their bodies rubbed together and her smile returned. Jameson thought she smelt of lavender oil and her sweet warm breath sharp with spearmint.

She allowed a compliment. 'You smell much better.'

'Yeh well,' Jameson refused to accept her smile. 'You'd stink too if some crazy locked you in a stinking semi-trailer for god knows how long. What time is it anyhow?'

'Breakfast time. Now move.' Drishya followed Jameson along a tight corridor where they passed other cell doors before arriving at another locked door. Drishya brushed past Jameson, unlocking the door with a four-digit code. Beyond, Jameson caught the salty smell of the sea. Surely they weren't on a ship of some sort. Another corridor, two more locked doors and they walked into a moderate, sterile room some six metres by four; a dining room with plainly dressed walls of aluminium sheeting. A smoky glass-topped dining table for up to six with stainless steel carver chairs was the only furniture. It all looked expensive. The lighting was soft except for a large bay type window at the far end. But Jameson's hopes were short lived. The window was backlit with artificial light. They were in the bows a ship ... maybe. Or underground, he wasn't certain.

'Sit.' Drishya pressured Jameson's left shoulder guiding him into a comfortable throne like chair at one end of the table. He sat. Instantly his senses were bombarded with the aromas of delicious food and Jameson realised how hungry he was. With the panache of a conjurer Drishya levitated a silk cloth exposing a magnificent breakfast. Prosciutto, thinly sliced cold cuts of roasted meats, a salver of scrambled eggs with ham and shallots, warm crusty bread, olives, vine ripened tomatoes, salmon – both smoked and gravlax – and a selection of cheeses was expertly presented on polished stainless steel platters. Jameson hesitated. Was this a trap? His stomach rumbled betraying his hunger.

Drishya sat next to Jameson and passed him a clean dinner plate as the far door opened and in wheeled the man he would learn was his host ... even if Jameson was a reluctant guest.

The man in the wheelchair was in his late fifties. He was dressed in a white Panama suit, open neck shirt and shiny black leather shoes. He looked wealthy. A wealthy gentleman with a taste for the good life Jameson assessed.

'Good morning Jameson Rowley,' the man smiled warmly and took the seat at the other end of the table. 'Please start. You must be starving.'

'Who are you?'

'You can call me John, Jameson.'

'How do you know my name? My full name that is.'

'Oh ... the Internet is a wonderful tool Jameson. I know all about you. But first, please, eat.'

Jameson had a hundred questions and felt inclined to tell the man to shove his food where the sun don't shine. But the sound of the dark-skinned woman next to him tearing warm bread with her long-nailed fingers, and the smell of the prosciutto as she placed it between crusts, was too much. He ate greedily, not caring for table manners. *If I am a captive I'll damn well behave like one.*

'So where am I … John … if that's your real name.' Jameson spoke with a mouth full of egg and bread. Damn he was hungry. 'Well? We're underground huh?'

'Maybe.'

'Where? Genoa? Venice? Pisa maybe?' He popped an olive in his mouth and slapped prosciutto between bread tossing a cherry tomato in for good measure.

'It is not important where you are Jameson. The important thing is that you help us. Help us and we will make you a rich man.'

'So you're the big cheese, huh?' Jameson spoke with a mouth full of food. 'I'm not going to help you steal Italy's heritage, if that's your caper.'

'Caper? What is this caper?'

'Your thieving act, mate.'

'Oh, this tiresome old argument. Don't you people realise there is plenty of heritage, as you so eloquently put it, for everyone,' Man of Mirrors said patiently sipping espresso. 'Italy has plenty to go around. So much of it is repetitious and languishes in museum storerooms never to be seen. I fulfil a service. I fill a gap in the market, a market for connoisseurs who appreciate the fine arts. They protect these items, cherish them, look after them with kid gloves for future generations.'

Jameson could relate to this. There was a certain, ever so slight, amount of envy for the man. Jameson thought of his pitiful broken lamp from Vataea and thought how much he would love a marble or a small bronze or a …

'It's wrong and you know it,' Jameson answered, but his voice lacked conviction.

•   •   •   •   •

Claire wiped Madeira cake crumbs from around her mouth and hurried after the others along Calle Megio towards Squero di San

Trovaso, refreshed on espresso and pastries at Vincenzo's friend's café. Dawn had arrived and it was time for action.

'Bloody hell that was good,' Claire panted catching up to Elspeth rushing along the narrow canal paths. 'What was it called again?'

'Zuccotto.'

'Zuccotto huh,' Claire said of her breakfast of almond, hazelnut, chocolate, liqueur, candy fruit and cream desert. 'Total mouth-gasm I'm tellin' you,'

Now that another hot summer's day dawned on northern Italy the alleyways and canals of Venice were washed in a gorgeous orange dawn. Claire's head swivelled about swallowing the view.

Venice! She was in Venice.

It's all a bit much. She would have to return another day to appreciate it. Claire shook her head in frustration as they passed specialty shop windows of Italian fashion, shoes, handbags, luxury stationery and confectioner's shop fronts that she knew would soon be piled high with colourful treats. Thankfully it was early and all the shops closed. Claire was drawn to one window crammed with masks. The Venetians love their masked balls and the one in particular that caught Claire's attention was the plague doctor mask, a bird-beak-like mask worn by 17th century doctors to protect them from airborne diseases. The beak, Claire knew, was filled with herbs, often lavender, to filter the bad air. Worn with a facemask and monk like habit it must have been a terrifying sight for the inflicted or dying.

'Much further?' Elspeth asked Vincenzo, catching her breath.

'Close.'

They had followed a dozen canals, walked two kilometres of cobbled laneways and crossed a dozen footbridges with their fancy filigree iron balustrades. Either side of the brackish canals six and seven storey brick and stone buildings – many centuries old – vied for the best positions, crammed along the waterways in tight but romantically uniform symmetry. But it was 6AM and the windows mostly shuttered. The lucky ones sitting on canal corners had a better view, attracted more sun and supported bay windows sitting out over the water; a little like castle garderobes of medieval times. Who knows, Claire wondered, they may have done their business over the canals in years gone by, and she had a quiet chuckle to herself imagining bare bums exposed through horizontal porthole seats.

Vincenzo led them along the pedestrian walk that followed Rio de S. Trovaso canal to the gondola boatyards of Squero di San Trovaso. It was still early and the alleyways and canals deserted. Venice would not come alive for four hours. The only Venetians out and about were the laden pushbikes delivering the fresh baked bread and pastries to the breakfast cafes. Or the odd gondolier poling his craft along the back canals and heading to the Grand Canal where he would dock between the red and yellow striped posts to await the tourists. The only other craft they saw was the garbage barge. This overloaded rubbish barge sat low in the water motoring slowly through Venice heading out towards the lagoon where it would rendezvous with landfill.

The 18th and 19th century brick and timber gondola boat slips were a tourist attraction in their own right. Here the shipwright workshops bordered a long narrow slip yard with a boat-ramp into the Rio de S. Trovaso Canal. A vertical board boathouse with its conventional gabled roof hugged a three-storey building of red orange brick boasting a five-storey chimney. The chimney discarded spent smoke well above the terracotta tiled roofs of the residences penned in all about it. This building, Vincenzo told them, was the carpentry shop. Here the fir, oak, cherry, walnut, elm, mahogany, larch and lime wood were prepared for gondola construction.

'That's eight different woods!'

'Si. Two hundred and eighty different pieces go into a gondola construction.'

'Well bugger me.' Claire was impressed.

To all intents and purposes, Elspeth thought, this could be a scene from a century ago. It was here that the freshly painted gondolas were launched. Four long sleek gondolas in varying degrees of manufacture or repair sat perched on custom built wooden horses. No doubt in an hour's time the yard would be alive with activity but for now it was unattended.

'Looks deserted,' Di Stefano said looking across the canal at the slips.

'Luigi, he will be there somewhere,' Vincenzo assured them. And as if to acknowledge Vincenzo, an invisible raucous laugh skipped across the water from the boathouse.

The group crossed on a footbridge at the mouth of the canal where it met the lagoon. They hurried along the opposite canal boardwalk, crossed another narrow footbridge over Rio del Ognissanti Canal and entered the unfenced boat yard.

'Wait here,' Vincenzo ordered the others, and headed to the workshops.

'Did you know,' Abandonato said leaning against a nearly completed gondola. 'That the left side ... '

'Port side.'

'Si. Is longer than the right side. Thees is because the gondolier, he use oar to push on left side.'

'Fascinating,' Claire rolled her eyes and whispered to Elspeth. 'Not.'

Moments later Vincenzo appeared with his uncle.

Luigi Marinos Villani could have stepped from the film set of *Crocodile Dundee*. At one hundred and ninety centimetres he was tanned and ruggedly handsome with dark blonde dreadlocks pulled back tightly in a ponytail. He wore cut-off jeans to the size of boxer shorts and a loose sleeveless Denim waistcoat, bleached by sun and adventure, exposing a tanned six-pack. About his neck he wore a sweat cloth the size of a small tablecloth. Who knows Elspeth thought; it probably was a tablecloth. A spare sweat cloth was hooked through his leather belt and hanging to one side down to his knee. For a man well into his forties he had an athletic body with long thin muscular legs and arms to match. There were tattoos on both. He wore above ankle length army boots, no laces no socks. Both wrists were adorned with manly bracelets of twisted leather and cheap silver. But most important of all, he wore a friendly smile.

'Ciao,' he waved as he walked ahead of Vincenzo from the shadows of the boathouse. He stopped a moment, only a metre from Elspeth and Claire and looked them up and down smiling warmly. This was inspection time. There was nothing sleazy in his behaviour. Vincenzo introduced them all. Elspeth offered her hand and Luigi took it, only to pull her close for a friendly hug. Claire was rewarded the same treatment. While Luigi greeted Di Stefano and Abandonato, with less verve, Claire and Elspeth stole a glance at each other. Claire waved her hand in front of her nose ...

Fresh sweat, beer and pheromones.

'Vincenzo,' Luigi started in good English. 'He tell me what you want. He tell me your amico ... your friend, he be prisoner on Poveglia Island.'

'Yes,' Elspeth said impatiently. 'Can you help us?'

Luigi's head tipped on an angle and he looked Di Stefano in the eye. 'You polizia, si?' he asked in Italian.

'Si.'

'I will help your friends but I need one thing from you.'

Di Stefano stiffened. *Here we go, a barterer.* 'I am not in a position to negotiate Signor Villani.'

'Oh there is no negotiation here signor polizia,' Luigi continued in their native language. 'It is a simple matter of you scratch my back and I scratch yours.'

'Time is running out. What do you want?'

'My tourist charter licence has been revoked. I want you to un-revoke it.'

'But that is a matter for ...'

'It's a matter for *you* signor polizia.'

'I'll see what I can do.'

Luigi's right hand shot out. 'Man to man, deal?'

'Si.'

Di Stefano took the skipper's hand. Luigi crushed it, and dragging the policeman towards him he gave him a man hug. Abandonato stepped away and made himself otherwise engaged.

'Better we move now,' Abandonato told the others in English. 'Ah … which way is your boat signor Villani.'

'Please,' Luigi reverted to English. 'My boat, she is on Giudecca,' he said of the Venetian island only a stone's throw across the lagoon to the south where many marinas and boat yards snuggled close to shore. 'We take *Constanza*, si.'

'*Constanza?*' Claire whispered to Vincenzo.

'Yes. Luigi, he like to give all his boats woman's name. *Constanza* is … how you call, a tender.'

With six sitting in a three-metre wooden dinghy – made by Luigi's shipwright mates – and a 1960s one horsepower Squalitalia clamped to the stern, it was a good thing the lagoon crossing at this point was only a few hundred metres. Elspeth held the port side gunwale. There was so little freeboard the water lapped her fingers.

'Where's the life jackets dude?' Claire asked anxiously watching the opposite shore approach.

Vincenzo's brow furrowed. 'Life jacket?'

'You know what I mean. Life Jacket … you wrap 'em around you so you can float if you end up in the drink.'

'Drink?'

'Ah … ah forget it.'

'Thees Poveglia Island,' Luigi called out over the squealing motor. 'You know about thees things yes?'

'If you mean do we know it is supposed to be haunted,' Elspeth answered over her shoulder. 'Then the answer is yes.'

'Haunted … si.'

Brief silence followed as they thankfully completed the crossing to Giudecca without mishap, weaving amongst other water traffic going in every direction. Now Luigi steered *Constanza* through the island on a canal that sectioned it. Beyond was the wide-open Venice Lagoon.

'Ah ... signor Villani,' Elspeth called back, her look of consternation hidden to their skipper as she faced the bow.

'Luigi, Bella, call me Luigi.'

'Ah Luigi. Please tell me we aren't crossing to Poveglia Island in this?'

'In *Constanza*!' he roared with laughter. 'No Bella. We go to *Olga*. *Olga* take us to island.'

If anything afloat should have a woman's name like *Olga* ... it was *Olga*. Luigi Villani's fishing trawler was ... well ... a *tetanus bucket* as Claire christened the twelve and a half metre, rusted steel hull *Herodotus*, built in Piraeus in 1971. She sported twin 25 horsepower diesel engines, two propellers and VHS radio. The recently added fly bridge, ten years earlier, was built by Luigi's shipwright mates for his charter passengers. Luigi caught the staring, open mouths and assured everyone she was at least reliable, with a cruising speed of fifteen knots. However, a shallow keel for the lagoon made Olga a little unstable.

'Christ!' Claire whispered to Elspeth. 'Will you look at that thing?'

With the dawn sun low on the eastern horizon *Olga's* blood orange hull was the colour of sunset ...

'Or is that rust?' Elspeth asked Claire.

As they watched their skipper jump on board and kick a short gangplank over the side for his passengers, shards of corroded steel broke free from the hull dropping into the dock.

'*Olga* huh!' Elspeth said of the ugly duckling amongst a marina of classier vessels.

'Si. *Olga*,' Villani said proudly. And Elspeth imagined the boat being named after some fat fraulein Luigi had met in a Munich beer hall, carrying trays of slopping tankards. Elspeth managed a smile. For the first time she felt confident. At least she knew where Jameson was and they had the police with them.

'Well he got the reliable bit right,' Claire said to Vincenzo as the twin diesels roared to life amongst a purge of black smoke ejected from the stack. Luigi seemed surprised himself. He stood at the helm in the wheelhouse, an oxidising cabin of varying shades of corrosion with its six portholes wrapped in a semi-circle; front, port and starboard. Elspeth now understood why *Olga* was so ugly. At some stage she had been a trawler but the trawler gear had been replaced with davits for a tender and a grubby Italian flag on a two metre pole. Once used in the deeper Mediterranean by Greek sponge divers before she was a trawler, the bow was steep and proud as if she was permanently tackling a big wave. Elspeth imagined if Jameson's skipper friend Barrie Duggan in Hobart spotted her on the River Derwent, he would call *Olga* a mongrel.

A visitor to Poveglia Island does not have to believe in ghosts to be moved by the experience.

Isola dei Morti.

Isle of the Dead in the distance appeared harmless enough. Elspeth and Claire fell into silence as they approached – the rhythmic thrumming of the engines beneath them comforting, while leaning on the bow rail and starring ahead in anticipation

The most predominant structure rising from the floating graveyard was the thirty-metre bell tower rising up out of thick forest growth that threatened to devour the entire island. Originally belonging to the 12th century Church of San Vitale, which was demolished by Napoleon in 1806 except for the bell tower with its pointed steeple, which was used as a lighthouse in Napoleonic times.

'See the steeple?' Claire asked as Vincenzo joined them. 'That's where that nutty doctor threw himself off isn't it?'

'Si,' Vincenzo nodded solemnly. 'Many bad theengs, they happen here.'

For a summer morning Elspeth felt a chill. She turned to look at Di Stefano and Abandonato who were deep in discussion with Luigi in the wheelhouse.

'What's the plan?' Elspeth asked Vincenzo.

The guide shrugged. 'We better go find out, yes.'

They say the way to a man's heart is through his stomach and Jameson had certainly mellowed now he had a full belly. He sat back with an air of cocky confidence and sipped his second espresso. 'So, you steal the great treasures of Italy and sell them to unscrupulous buyers ... where? United States, oil sheiks in Saudi, London dealers.'

'I sell to the highest bidder,' Man of Mirrors was amused by Jameson audacity. But if Cambino were to discover the location of Vataea for himself he would soon uncover the whereabouts of the House of Cethegus, the centurion trusted to guard the bronze lance head used to pierce the side of Jesus while he hung dying on the cross. For the scrolls Cambino had read were specific, written in haste by Cethegus himself only hours before he was roasted alive by the pyroclastic wrath of Vesuvio. Cethegus told where, exactly, he had hidden the spearhead, in a wall cavity of his humble home. And Jameson knew the whereabouts of Vataea.

'Highest bidder,' Jameson scoffed. 'You mean the most wealthy thief don't you? I don't know how you get up in the morning and look yourself in the mirror.'

Suddenly his host and his beautiful warder burst into laughter, spontaneous heartfelt laughter.

'That is good. Yes,' Man of Mirrors chuckled. 'I like that.'

While Jameson struggled to see the joke Drishya changed the subject. 'So Jameson Alexander Rowley ... '

Jameson flinched but immediately guessed since they had his mobile a name check had been easy.

'Yes,' Drishya went on. 'We Googled your name. You're a famous chef.'

Jameson shrugged modestly. 'Hardly famous.'

'Oh but on the contrary. You are a chef and treasure hunter.'

'Treasure hunter! Where'd you get that idea?'

'On the net. Your success in France and Jamaica were in your local newspaper with online windows directing your history to

Belgium, French newspapers and again in Jamaica. Yes. You're quite famous.'

'Ah.'

'But it is your cooking we are interested in,' Drishya said. 'Whilst we enjoy the French and Italian cuisine of Salah our Moroccan chef, *John* here fancies some local seafood cooked with the flair of an award-winning chef like yourself.'

'Local seafood? And what might local be?'

'I am not stupid. All I will tell you is we have fresh sea bass, clams and mussels.' Drishya poured herself a second green tea squeezing the end of a juicy lemon on top of the steaming brew with forefinger and thumb without taking her eyes off Jameson.

'So,' Cambino asked patiently. 'What are you going to do with our sea bass for lunch?'

'I'm on holidays.'

Drishya's response to his insolence was instant. She leapt to her feet tossing her orange silk scarf over her shoulder and leant in close to Jameson clamping her fingers either side of his throat. 'Look at me,' she hissed starring at Jameson with her rich dark brown eyes. 'You have a choice. Back in that cell or you can have free time in the galley and prepare John his sea bass. What's it to be?'

Jameson's eye twitched. He was being throttled. He felt his breath slipping away. He coughed. Drishya released her grasp. 'Well?'

'Galley,' Jameson said in a croak. The woman was dangerous Jameson knew ... stunningly beautiful with skin as smooth as a peeled boiled egg ... yet very dangerous.

The galley was an underground kitchen six metres long and four metres wide. Just like the galley on a ship. Jameson was impressed. Everything looked new. Everything was stainless steel, the equipment electric and top of the range. A hotel quality extractor hood hung over the cooking stove, oven and fryer to clear the galley of unwanted smoke and steam. Jameson opened kitchen drawers noting they were professionally stocked with everything a good cook could possibly want.

Drishya opened the double doors of an upright stainless-steel food chiller and slipped a tray free holding two sea bass. Their fish eyes were glassy wet, the skin soft and the product very fresh. Jameson looked in the larder where every spice and herb was stored in glass jars with all their labels facing forward and stored in alphabetical order. This Salah, Jameson acknowledged, was an orderly cook. Jameson brushed by Drishya to inspect the vegetable racks where there appeared to be a strong Asian influence; bok choy, garlic, lemongrass, coriander and bamboo shoots. But the Mediterranean was also well represented. He took the lemon grass, a red chilli, two limes, a nob of ginger, garlic and kaffir lime leaves from the fridge.

Drishya approved. 'Well, what's it to be ... chef?' She said loosening her long jet-black hair and shaking it free.

'Baked sea bass with garlic, lemongrass and ginger,' Jameson answered putting the ingredients on a chopping board on the workbench.

'You're keeping it simple. I like that.' Drishya refused to budge from where she was clearly in Jameson's path. 'Because we don't want to dominate that magnificent fish with overpowering influences ... now do we.' The siren with the hourglass figure allowed her toga to fall away, exposing a silk wrap-around loosely held with a silver dragon broach. Her breasts were not large but Jameson could clearly see they were firm and magnificently curved with dark chocolate nipples supple but firm.

'You know something Jameson,' Drishya's voice softened. She smelt so clean and her breath fresh from the lemon tea. 'Do you know what I really like?' Drishya licked her long slender forefinger and – unbuttoning Jameson's shirt – she ran her sharp fingernail down his exposed chest. Jameson swallowed hard. *This bitch was too much.*

'Do you Jameson? Do you know what I really, really like?'

Jameson shook his head soberly.

'I just *love* men who can cook,' her voice was barely a whisper. Drishya floated her face close to Jameson's who found himself leaning awkwardly backwards against the workbench. Suddenly she popped the broach and her wrap fell to the tiled floor. Drishya hefted one leg up wrapping it around Jameson. She pushed her love hard against his and with her hands clamping his face she stole a kiss. Jameson pushed her away catching a breath and noted she was wearing Moroccan slippers, pink, with a yellow geometric design ...

But nothing else.

'Take me,' she demanded. Her husky voice full of desire. And she pulled Jameson's face towards hers once more.

'Jesus!' Jameson grew irritated. 'Enough already ... shit!'

At that moment Salah entered the galley. He was not fazed. With his eyes trained low he fiddled senselessly until the woman re-dressed. Drishya tied her hair back in a ponytail.

'Get on with lunch, *chef.*' Her mood had soured. 'And don't even think of trying to escape. This place is like Fort Knox, all doors are monitored, all areas under surveillance and even if you did make it to ground level there is no escape.'

'So we *are* on an island?'

Drishya looked upon Jameson with renewed contempt. She ignored his comment. 'Get cooking, you have one and a half hours.' The mistress walked sulkily through the galley to Salah who looked at her as if all was well with the world. 'See he's got what he needs,' she signed to the deaf mute. 'Then join us at the conservation lab.'

Jameson watched as she tapped the code into the lock panel, careful to block his view. The door swung open on an electronic hinge, closing with an audible click the moment she had stepped into the corridor beyond.

It had been a waiting game, and one that was nerve-raking for Elspeth. The *Olga* anchored off the island under the guise of a charter vessel that had anchored for some repairs. Luigi fiddled about on deck, nonchalantly unconcerned with the island whilst, armed with a large wrench, he pretended to work on the hold cover. The others kept their heads low as they observed the island. They were anchored to the south, three hundred metres from the hexagonal 17th century fortress. Directly behind the fortress was a narrow channel where the original landing steps for the old asylum were still in place. The island had been fenced in places with several clear signs. Di Stefano trained Luigi's binoculars on signage on the island. *Attenzione tenere fuori private.* He sighed. If the looters *were* on the island somewhere they certainly would be watching the fishing boat.

There appeared to be no life on Poveglia. No movement. Not even birds in the trees. The ruins looked ominous, deserted and uninviting and the islands reputation played heavily on everyone's mind.

'We can't stay here all day,' Elspeth said in frustration.

'I know,' Di Stefano said. 'But we must wait for confirmation on the GPS triangulation. I am sorry.' He looked to Abandonato who held his mobile ready. They were crouched in the wheelhouse out of sight, when the mobile vibrated.

'Si. Antonio,' Abandonato answered. He listened, nodding his head silently. Then terminated the call. 'Mr Rowley's mobile is definitely on that island.' He gestured out a wheelhouse porthole.

'Then we search the island, yes?' Elspeth said impatiently.

'Si. We search the island,' Di Stefano capitulated. 'But thees is not a game. We just can't all rush ashore like army men. We must expect they are watching us. We must expect they have weapons and are dangerous.'

'So me and El will go,' Claire offered without thinking. 'Who would suspect a couple of girlies. Then when we find the bastards we'll tear 'em a new one.' Claire pumped the air.

'No Bella. Is not good plan. You do not know these people.' Di Stefano thought a moment. 'Miss Poole.'

Elspeth. 'Yes.'

'You and I will go to the island. We will carry a fishing tackle box and a fishing pole each. We look like father and daughter go fishing okay?'

'Sounds good to me ... anything ... now let's do this.'

'Wait. Take it easy. Do not look so ... how you say ... eager.'

•   •   •

The car ferry transported Ricco Ricci and Silvano Marchetti and their black Lancia van to the northern coast of the eleven-kilometre long Venetian sandbar, now an island suburb known as the Lido. From here it was only a fifteen-minute drive along the main route of Via Malamocco to the exclusive Associazione Tennis Club Ca Del Moro where Marchetti pulled the Lancia van up amongst tree cover on a waterfront nature reserve. From here the two men could clearly see Poveglia Island, some kilometres away, out on the Venice Lagoon.

It was mid-morning and the day was shaping up to be a warm summer's day with a clear sky and perfect flying conditions for their drone with its Panasonic GH4 camera.

Ricci wasted no time. With fully charged batteries he had a half-hour window. Once certain they were alone Ricci ascended the drone to 120 metres and maintained a 30 kilometres per hour flying speed in a wide semi-circle around the island. Marchetti watched the drone's progress through binoculars, with his one good eye. 'The island looks deserted,' Marchetti muttered.

Ricci concentrated on the monitor. Flying in a wide arc so as not to attract attention he flew the drone in from the north, maintaining a 120 metres altitude. The camera's view never failed to impress the ex-commando. He flew in low on the approach and buzzed the church steeple before ascending once more.

'It's not a toy,' Marchetti said tartly from the corner of his mouth.

'Okay then,' Ricci said. 'I'm flying over that canal where we saw the barge disappear.'

Marchetti joined Ricci at the monitor. 'Nothing. There's nothing to give us a clue. We'll have to visit the island and check it first-hand.' Ricci descended the drone to fifty metres when the *Olga* came into frame.

'Hey,' Ricci said. 'There's a fishing boat anchored off the island, I wonder if that belongs to our Man of Mirrors.'

'That's interesting,' Marchetti checked with the binoculars. 'I can just make out its stern. Looks like someone's lowering the tender.'

As casually as possible the superintendent polizia carabanieri and Elspeth revealed themselves on deck. Di Stefano disguised himself as best as possible wearing a diesel-scented jumper borrowed from Luigi. With the help of the skipper they lowered the tender *Constanza* into the water from the stern davits and, armed with their props of fishing rods and tackle box, Di Stefano and Elspeth motored towards the island.

Di Stefano's only comfort was the fact that he would take the credit, at last, for taking down Italy's most elusive and prolific antiquities thief. He looked discreetly to Elspeth whose beautiful eyes were fixed on the island, and hoped he had made the right decision bringing her along.

Moments later they approached the landing. Di Stefano's felt his double-barrelled semi-automatic handgun under Luigi's jumper and an element of confidence returned.

'They're definitely going to the island,' Marchetti acknowledged, his good eye remaining fastened to his binoculars. 'You better back off with the drone.'

But Ricci was already onto it. As the strangers motored up to the old dock he pulled the Matrice 600 back half a kilometre and used the long lens on the camera.

Di Stefano cut the outboard and Elspeth jumped ashore onto a decrepit concrete dock. She caught *Constanza's* mooring rope and tied it to a length of rusted re-enforcing steel protruding treacherously from the dock wall.

They stood a moment ...

In silence.

And gazed up at the nearest building, the two-storey hospital. Just beyond the hospital to the north-east the ominous church steeple stared down at the unwelcome strangers. Elspeth looked at the policeman and they shared a moment ... an unexplainable sense of doom had swamped over them.

The island was deserted, eerie, forlorn.

Poveglia – within sight of one of the world's most romantic cities – was unwelcoming ...

Strangely threatening.

There were no birds chirping. The air was still, warm and humid. Even the waters surrounding the island seemed void of life.

'You feel that?' Elspeth asked Di Stefano.

'Unfortunately yes. Is not nice place thees island. Many many bad things, they happen here.'

Elspeth's chest heaved with uncertainty. Framed by an opening in the forest, like a giant wreath, the wary trespassers noted an overgrown path leading towards the hospital wards and further on the crumbling red brick medieval style windows of the chapel. The morning's sun behind the ruins created silhouetted dark, threatening shapes. There was no breeze yet shadows appeared to cast movement before them.

'Let's get this over with.'

Di Stefano could not agree more. He had been in many dire situations throughout his career and never had he felt such unease.

Stepping away from the narrow dock they pushed through tangled undergrowth towards the hospital. The wire fence they had seen from *Olga* was in disrepair, clearly not erected recently. Ignoring 'Keep Out' signs the two finally found a breach in the fence, well hidden behind bushes and possibly made by vandals years ago. After a deep breath, Di Stefano climbed through the gap. Elspeth took a last look behind her, and followed.

The hospital itself was enclosed with its original head-height iron spiked fence. They eventually found a gate, well hidden by vegetation. Here a pair of hooded crows, the first wildlife they encountered, voiced their displeasure at the intrusion and flew off towards the church spire.

The two stood at the entrance to the asylum administration. Stone steps led up to grand arched double doors, supported either side by gothic pillars. The steps were overgrown with thorny vines creeping half way up the main entrance. But the doors were boarded with thick planks crudely nailed across the entrance.

'There's no getting in that way,' Elspeth looked about for another path.

'No. But maybe ... ' crushed undergrowth to their right seemed to lead off along the perimeter of the building. 'Maybe here,' Di Stefano led on, forcing a path through the thicket where eventually, around the western boundary, they climbed through a damaged window and into a lower floor ward. Here tangled rusted iron beds were shoved aside against walls. Vandals had contributed their labours also, wrenching doors from hinges and trashing the walls with graffiti. Elspeth stepped over old hospital equipment. Corkscrew shaped bed springs curled about discarded clothing and in places the floors were piled with debris from collapsed sections of ceiling.

It immediately became clear that the building was not safe.

The roof had collapsed in many places and masonry littered the wards where vegetation had taken root. At one end of the ward solid cast iron radiators were strewn about, torn from their plumbing and discarded where they fell. Other wards, corridors and the matron's office were all in the same state of disrepair. There was no sign of life beyond scurrying rats and the timid flutters of birds nesting in the roof.

'Where could they be?' Elspeth looked disconcerted. 'I mean there is no sign of recent occupation. Does the GPS pinpoint exactly where on the island the mobile is?'

'No. It is only accurate to within, say, twenty metres. But your friend's mobile is definitely on this island.'

Di Stefano stepped into a corridor. The windows had been shuttered and only pencils of dust-speckled light pierced through cracks creating a purplish hue from the reddish-blue walls. Treading carefully around missing floorboards the polizia took out his pocket torch and led Elspeth the full length of the passageway. Double doors blocked their pathway. Di Stefano read the faded sign through the blistering paint over the door – Obitorio – but said nothing to Elspeth.

He pushed the doors.

Both were stuck.

Shouldering the right door it opened enough for him to notice a thin tree root twisting up through broken floorboards; enough to jam the wooden door. Three further shoves and the root severed. The door creaked open into a windowless room where they were both assaulted by a musty, cold darkness. Elspeth followed the policeman into the room, no more than six metres by eight. Here the ceiling was low and Di Stefano's torchlight struggled to cut through the morbid blackness and into the darkest corners where half a dozen narrow peeling chrome stretcher beds were jammed hard against the walls. The beds Elspeth noticed were all furnished with leather straps. Elspeth's eyes focussed slowly. She swallowed hard. 'What is this room?'

'The morgue.'

Elspeth felt an involuntary, chilling shiver. 'Nothing here ... let's go.'

Di Stefano couldn't agree more.

They turned to leave. But the door slammed shut in their faces ...

They stood frozen in total darkness.

'Merda!' Di Stefano swung a tight circle of torchlight over the closed door.

'No,' Elspeth felt a chill in the air. 'Did you ...?'

'No Bella,' Di Stefano said unnerved himself. 'No I did not ... I am standing here with you.' He rushed to the door. Snatched the handle. There was no resistance. The doors opened on protesting, squealing hinges. Di Stefano shook his head at his own dread and held one door open for Elspeth. 'Must have been wind ... or a spring or something,' he said to comfort them.

'Sure.'

They negotiated the rubble and passed quickly back down the corridor to the far end. Matching double doors waited. Di Stefano caught Elspeth's anguish in the soft edge of his torch beam. 'Are you alright?'

'Yes, yes. I'm fine. Let's just get this over with.'

With torch in left hand the polizia pushed the right door. It opened with a groan on corroded hinges. He shone the light about the sobering ward. Here cell like doors occupied both sides of the room. Three either side.

'Cells?'

Elspeth frowned.

Di Stefano said nothing and tried the first door. It opened outwards. They both followed the faint light into the cramped gloom. The upholstered walls were weathered and torn padded leather, with its horsehair stuffing, had spilled onto the floor.

'Solitary cells for the insane,' Di Stefano muttered.

Elspeth was certain she recognised claw marks cut into the covering. 'This place gives me the creeps,' she started ...

When the torchlight blinked.

Instantly they were thrown into blackness. 'Merda.' Di Stefano shook the torch. 'I put new batteries in this yesterday.' Further along the ward Elspeth was certain she heard scraping.

'Did you hear that?'

'Rats!' The polizia said in an uncertain shallow voice. 'Come Bella.' He took Elspeth's arm and they back stepped awkwardly in the dark. The moment they re-entered the corridor the torch sparked to life. But Di Stefano's sigh of relief did nothing to console Elspeth. She sensed a presence she could not explain when thankfully they saw natural light further ahead.

'Thank god!'

They stepped into a courtyard at the rear of the hospital where they noticed a door leading from the overgrown courtyard into the *dispensario*. The slim 19th century double doors – weather-beaten grey – were totally imprisoned by ivy, twisting and curling like slow moving serpents through the missing glass panels of the doors. Inside, a three-metre tree had buried its roots under the damaged floorboards. Now it reached for an area of collapsed roof while passing through missing treads of a spiral staircase. Di Stefano cupped his eyes from the sun to peer inside the dispensary ...

'Jesus!'

He jerked back.

'What?'

The policeman stood silent a moment. Trying to be rational and analysing what he saw.

'What is it?'

Di Stefano composed himself. He slowly peered back through the panels, beyond the snaking vines on the stair and into the shadows of the dispensary where he was certain he saw a figure. A faceless shape undoubtedly starring right back at him.

Nothing.

'Superintendent. What is it?'

'N-nothing.'

'What do you mean nothing? You just jumped out of your skin.'

'It was nothing Bella ... I ... just got something in my eye.' He pulled back from the entrance and feigned rubbing at a sore eye. 'It is all good.'

'Eye?'

'Si. Sorry. Come.'

They made their way through waist high weeds and debris to administration buildings. Here ivy vines snaked through the broken glass windows reaching out across the rooms, entwining rusted iron banisters and coaxing stucco from brick walls.

'Nothing! No one has been here for years,' Elspeth protested.

'Maybe there is something over the canal on the other part of the island.'

'You mean the plague pits?'

'Si.' It was a word he did not wish to use. But suddenly the policeman became aware of a foreign sound. A low thrumming. A motor, possibly.

•   •   •   •   •   •

'Shut down the air-conditioning. Now.' Man of Mirrors kept his gaze fixed on the security screens before him. The male intruder appeared to be listening for something and as well disguised and insulated as the air-conditioning units were, there was a possibility they could be sensed by an astute ear.

'Do you think he is polizia?' Drishya kept a sharp eye on the monitors.

'Who knows. Why do you bring fishing poles ashore and then stalk about like thieves in the night?'

'She is very pretty.'

'So?'

'Well maybe she has come looking for her chef.'

'How?'

Drishya suddenly looked contemplative. 'Yes. How could I be so stupid?'

'Why? What have you done?'

'Ricci and Marchetti ... '

'Yes?'

'They gave me the prisoner's mobile. Said it may have information we could use.'

'GPS!'

'Yes.'

'How could you make a mistake like that? So stupid.'

Drishya stiffened. Angry with herself and angry Uomo di Specchi should call her stupid.

'Then that is undoubtedly polizia.'

'But that fishing boat,' Drishya reasoned. 'It is hardly a police boat.'

'Take the spyglass to the steeple. See if there is anyone else on board that boat while I try and distract them.'

'What can you hear,' Elspeth asked Di Stefano who now stood on the crest of the old wooden footbridge that joined the main part of the island to the plague pits.

'Hear? I thought I could hear a motor running, a generator maybe.'

'And?'

'Nothing. It's gone.'

'Passing boat?'

'Maybe.' Di Stefano stepped onto the sandy soil overgrown with vegetation that he knew were the plague pits where thousands upon thousands of victim's bodies were burnt in open ditches. But then he realised it wasn't sand. It was ash. The huge mounds that appeared to be sand hills were knolls of human remains. A piece of a skull with its tell-tale eye socket exposed itself as he passed.

'Oh ... really,' Elspeth was horrified. 'Are you kidding me?'

'No Miss Poole. Thees whole part of the island ees made up of human remains.'

Elspeth stood fixed to the spot, as if she was about to be swallowed by quicksand. There was nowhere to tread without stepping on some poor devil who had died pitifully, centuries earlier. Di Stefano saw her discomfort. He looked about them hastily. The plague pits were on a section of Poveglia that was a quarter of the site. The mounds themselves were mostly matted with sea grass and weeds with some forestation on the northwest shoreline. It was quite clear that no development had been undertaken here; in antiquity or recently. Di Stefano reached for Elspeth's hand. 'Come.'

They retraced their steps across the bridge, walking back into the overgrown woodland returning in the direction of the asylum hospital.

'I wonder if they threw the mobile onto the island in passing last night,' Elspeth suggested. 'I mean, if they realised it could be traced like.'

'Maybe. But the policeman in me tells me there is more to this island than we think.'

'You're telling me. It's damn spooky.'

'I want to check all the buildings.' Di Stefano looked back at the collection of buildings and rubbed his chin. Under normal circumstances the view from here would be scenic. 'Come. We will start with the chapel.'

Elspeth was the first to step away from the path through the woodlands. Brushing cobwebs from her hair she paused in a shaded space and looked up. The thirty-metre church tower watched over her like some unholy ogre. There was something decidedly ungodly about the structure.

Evil even.

To her right the two storey asylum wards led to the derelict chapel. The only doorway in was blocked completely by twisted gnarly vines and a blistering wooden sign on the wall read *Reparto Psichiatria.*

Di Stefano quietly joined her. 'Eet looks like we must climb in a window ... again.'

Inside, the ward leading to the chapel nave entrance was long and narrow. The forest outside masked much of the light so the shades and shadows of the decaying ward were blacks and greys. On the shoreline side of the building the sun's rays penetrated the broken window frames, painting the floor in squares of bright light while casting sinister shadows and twisted shapes over the rubbish strewn floor.

Suddenly Elspeth felt specks of dirt and filth.

It sprinkled onto her head.

She looked up. Di Stefano saw it too. A fine dust falling towards them backlit by shafts of sunlight. Then they heard them ...

Footsteps!

Heavy footsteps walking with haste on the rotting floorboards above them. Di Stefano pulled his pistol.

'Wait here,' he whispered and hurried stealthily to stairs at the far end of the ward. Elspeth stood silently numb in a pool of sunlight; false security from anything on the dark side.

She hardly breathed.

Elspeth watched Di Stefano disappear through a doorway into a hallway. She heard him take to the rickety stairs.

Three treads at a time.

As she watched, the falling dust above shifted quickly ...

Rushing in Di Stefano's direction!

She heard the superintendent enter the first floor ward above. Immediately the dust stopped. Then, as Di Stefano ran across the floor overhead dusty steps followed. Elspeth heard the policeman falter ...

Directly in the centre of the ward. Directly overhead. She waited for the sound of a confrontation ...

Nothing.

Silence.

Elspeth stood rigidly. Rooted to the centre of the ground floor ward like one of the encroaching trees.

'S-Stefano ... ' she called softly.

Deathly silence.

'Stefano ... Renato,' now louder.

Silence.

'No!' Elspeth looked about for a weapon. She found comfort in a length of iron from a bed head loose on the floor. She plucked it up, juggled it into a comfortable grip for clubbing ...

And stole quietly across the floor and into the hall towards the stairs. The stairs were spiral with a curled iron banister. Once ornate the fancy ironwork reminded Elspeth of the devil's horns, now throwing terrifying shapes onto the rickety decaying wooden treads. There was no natural light on the stairs. Forest grew over the roof masking the skylight. Elspeth took one step at a time. Slowly. Measured breathing. The treads protested ...

Three steps... five ...

Suddenly Elspeth's leg disappeared from under her. The tread had splintered. Rotten. She snatched the banister pulling back before her other leg failed her ...

Elspeth prayed her short sharp shriek wasn't heard.

She didn't move a muscle. Listening.

Silence. Damned silence.

With any element of surprise deserting her Elspeth rushed to the top. 'Stefano ... Renato ... where are you?'

She felt her heart thump. Taking short sharp breaths Elspeth crossed the upper landing. She raised her club. She crashed through the door into the ward ...

And froze ...

Nothing.

No one.

'Jesus. Renato ... Christ!' Elspeth ran to the centre of the twenty-metre long ward. She wheeled about. The man had disappeared. Footsteps remained in the dust. One set only. Fresh. Di Stefano's?

Shadows in dark corners played on her imagination. Shifting shapes. More subtle footsteps. A distant cry ...

Seabird or human?

Elspeth felt the hairs on the nape of her neck bristle. Just the thought of returning down the spiral stair and negotiating the old asylum ward intimidated her.

But where the hell was Di Stefano?

Elspeth descended back down the stairs. She re-entered the ground floor ward and stood silently in the gloom, her back to one wall ...

And listened.

Silence.

Elspeth squeezed the iron bar firmer than ever. Then a sound drew her attention to the far wall at the other end of the ward. It was more a moan.

'No!' Elspeth felt her heart quicken. She gaped into the shadows. As she watched, a black mist descended from the ceiling, dissolving through the floorboards from the ward above. The vision had the appearance of ink spilt into a bathtub. Tentacle like. As Elspeth stood dumbstruck, riveted to the spot the haze took on a human form ...

A headless human form.

The phantom's feet touched the floor. Elspeth sucked back and the entity drifted towards her.

Elspeth felt paralysed.

She couldn't move.

Immediately she felt a sting on her cheek. Then another, like someone pea-shooting rice at her face. She blinked. The approaching image reared. Try hard as she could Elspeth was disabled. Another sting to the face. Elspeth involuntarily blinked. The apparition drew closer and closer. Another nip, this time at her eye lid. Elspeth closed her eyes, stifling a scream ...

Petrified.

The only sound was her laboured breathing. The pea-shooter stopped. Elspeth forced open her eyes.

The spectre was gone.

Vanished.

Elspeth's taught muscles eased. She swivelled about searching for answers. But there were none. Nothing. The vision had melted away. Elspeth felt mentally drained. She stood with her feet fixed to the floor. Gobsmacked. Was she going crazy?

'Stefano!' she finally shouted and climbed clumsily back through the window to the courtyard.

'No! No!' Looking about it appeared she was standing in a central courtyard. There were no exits. 'You're kidding me.' The only possible way out was to re-enter the buildings. Elspeth was certain she had noted a path alongside the ward earlier, leading to sunlight. But where? And the other courtyard seemed larger. A lot larger.

'Jesus!' Elspeth felt a stab of claustrophobia. Anxiety rose in her stomach. Suddenly she was parched. She felt a pain in her chest. She twisted about. A low door, unnoticed before, appeared amongst the wild growth. Shoving dead branches and leafy vines aside she stepped back into semi-darkness crawling into the space followed by despair and shadows.

Elspeth had entered the old hospital kitchen.

Like the rest of the buildings abandoned in the 1960s, the floor was strewn with broken furniture and machinery. The walls were yellow tiled to head height and painted a depressing pale blue above that. The collapsing ceiling also showed evidence of pale blue paint. In the centre of the kitchen the skeleton of a kitchen flue hung menacingly on loose corroded brackets. The cast iron wood fuelled stoves and ovens remained in situ, too heavy for the most enthusiastic of vandals.

Then Elspeth saw an exit at the west wing.

She hurried towards the light.

To her right an exterior porch hugged the kitchen wall leading, Elspeth fervently hoped, to the water's edge. She ran along its length where rows of shuttered windows were open to the elements. On the other side ... a concrete wall. It felt more a prison than a hospital ...

A hospital for the insane.

Elspeth smelt the sea air. The end approached. She dropped her iron club and broke into a sprint ...

'Woh!'

She ploughed into Di Stefano.

'Easy there.' The man shouted.

'Thank god!' Elspeth screamed in the man's ear. 'Where have you been?'

'I could ask you the same thing.'

'You left me ... you went upstairs and disappeared.'

'I went upstairs and *you* disappeared,' he insisted.

'No I ...' Elspeth made to protest but thought better of it. 'Let's get out of here. This place gives me the creeps.'

'I know what you mean.' And then he said in a whisper. 'I have the sensation we are being watched. Come. We go back to *Olga* and speak with others.'

•   •   •   •   •

'What on earth is going on?' Marchetti dropped the binoculars to his side and gazed at the drone's camera monitor from the comfort of the van. They had successfully hovered the drone out of sight watching the man and the woman on the island.

'It has to be the girlfriend,' Ricci's face was tight. 'The woman Domenico said was driving the red Fiat Panda.'

'But how did she find out about Poveglia Island.'

'God knows but we have to move fast if we're going to do this.' He faced Marchetti. 'The way I see it they found nothing. But we know better, right? So, as we discussed. Are you in?'

'Are you kidding me. I want this as bad as you do.'

'Good. Then we search the island tonight starting with that canal.'

•   •   •   •   •

Man of Mirrors tweaked the joystick of camera 26 covering the landing dock and although the pain was worse today he managed a smile. He had been more than happy with his X-Vision High Definition speed domes with their times twenty optical lens security cameras. Hidden amongst the ruins, disguised with cobwebs or decaying timber, not even the most vigilant person would spot them. Drishya joined him at the bank of split screens where more than forty cameras worked twenty-four seven.

'I am so impressed with our electronic supernatural friends,' Cambino managed a smile for Drishya. The special effects set up five years earlier were rarely used but when they were they worked a treat. 'You should have seen the reaction when I manifested Leonardo,' as Man of Mirrors called the misted headless torso spectre that so alarmed Elspeth. Cambino gave all his special effects a pet name. 'She scurried into the courtyard like a scared mouse. And the footsteps on the upper floor of the asylum ward,' Cambino smiled up at his beautiful assistant. 'When were they installed? I hadn't used them before. Did you operate those from the observation spire? Very effective.'

'Footsteps?'

'Yes. On the floorboards of the first floor. The dust fell. It looked fantastic. Very scary. Very realistic.'

'No Cambino, I controlled nothing. There are no effects installed on the floorboards upstairs in the asylum ward closest to the chapel.' The two exchanged a look of confused concern. This wasn't the first time Drishya had been spooked on this island.

'I told you this place gives me the creeps,' Drishya said. 'I have seen things too, out of the corner of my eye. I'd be happier if we moved on somewhere.' But the moment Drishya said this she knew it was a futile comment. Drishya felt a pang of guilt towards the man who had saved her from a life of abuse and poverty.

Cambino Cardinale looked at her with the yellow sickly eyes of a dying man. He was clearly going nowhere and read her thoughts.

'There is an explanation for everything Drishya. Besides I ... ' He wanted to say I will die soon but could not bring himself to do so.

'I wish I could agree with that,' Drishya said. 'I know some people are more susceptible to the supernatural. More so than others. And I fear I am one of them.'

'That's your exotic background. Try not to think about it. So,' he asked Drishya of her time in the spire observatory. 'Did you see anyone else on that fishing boat?'

'I saw movement below deck but could not determine who or how many.'

'Polizia?'

'Possibly. How else would she have access to a GPS search.' They watched the soundless vision in silence a moment as the small tender returned to the fishing boat. 'They found nothing. Maybe we were wrong about the mobile and GPS. I just hope we don't see them again in a hurry,' Drishya said.

'Nonetheless I want the Vataea hoard moved on tonight. We have the advantage of a quarter moon, it will be dark. And have Salah complete cleaning the smaller artefacts from last week's Baiae purchase, we don't need him in the kitchen today, not with our new chef.'

'Speaking of which,' Drishya said. 'I think we are going to have to cause this Jameson some pain. He knows where Vataea lies.'

'I agree, but I would like a little more time to convince the man to our way of thinking first. Without the torture. I trained you too well.'

Drishya studied the sickly man a moment and let her guard down showing an emotional side she rarely exposed. 'I love you,' she said softly.

'I love you too.' Cambino returned the maternal sentiment. 'We have come through a lot together. We have achieved great things.'

'I ... I don't know ... ' A single tear rolled down Drishya's cheek.

'Don't know what?' But the second Cambino said this, he knew.

'I ... I ...'

'You don't know what you'll do when I am gone,' Cambino answered for her.

Drishya nodded solemnly. She felt ashamed of herself all of a sudden.

'You'll take over this empire. You must promise me that Drishya. We have built too much to simply let it go.'

'We must find Vataea,' Drishya regained her red-blooded stamina. 'We must find this spear ... the lance of destiny. It will cure you ...'

'Maybe ... maybe not. I am starting to think I won't make it.'

Cambino Salvi Cardinale's tired eyes followed his adoring Drishya as she made to leave the room. He watched the steel framed mirror door close silently behind her on its vacuum controlled arm. It was the way he like things. Silent. Except for his precious music.

He picked up the remote, released pause, and continued playing Beethoven's Moonlight Sonata trying not to stress about the mysterious visitors. Five years he had lived on this island without a problem. Sure, he shared the island with the supernatural; it was inevitable that a spirit or two may be trapped here on this island with its miserable past. But Cambino had learned to live with them. Half the time he thought it his imagination, but he felt safe here, running his empire in anonymity. Besides he had a more pressing problem, his own mortality. He coughed into his handkerchief ...

Blood.

Immediately darker thoughts clouded his judgement. He had never killed another human and he questioned himself how far he would go to protect Drishya's future and his empire. A sudden movement on the screen drew his attention. The fishing boat was weighing anchor. They were leaving. Excellent.

Cambino relaxed and found himself admiring his latest mirror, an original 18th century Venetian mirror taken from the salon decorations in a Venetian Bordello. It was in its original condition, never touched or restored and backed with its original mercury. Twelve thousand Euros, Sotheby's Milan.

He recalled the first time he was seduced by the magnetism of antique mirrors – in the Versailles' Hall of Mirrors. He was only twenty-one. The very thought of who stood before these centuries old mirrors, powdering their wigs or dabbing rouge on aging cheeks fascinated him. Kings, Queens, ambassadors, courtesans, guards, servants; they would have all taken side-glances at the mirrored glass in the famous hall at Versailles.

Cambino turned the volume higher and gazed into *his* mirrors. Sitting as he was in the centre of the room and with mirrors covering every inch of wall, he could peer magically into eternity. His image was repetitious but the mirrors were unique. Each had its own story. Centre stage was the fine Napoleon III gilt bronze mirror, tall as a man, with its early bevelled edges. A favourite. Coming a close second was his 18th century Louis XVI mirror with its gilded frame of cherubs. Not all were antique. Placed where he could enjoy it was his 1969 Robert Goossens spectacular rectangular dressing mirror with its unique frame of coral like bronze. Cambino enjoyed over three hundred looking glasses in this underground bunker of mirrors; from Rococo to Chippendale and he adored them all.

CHAPTER FIFTEEN

Elspeth was hoisted aboard *Olga* by Luigi. She hurried below deck where Claire and Abandonato waited.

'Well?' Claire asked.

'I'm worried,' Elspeth paced the tiny galley amidships below the wheelhouse where it was difficult to avoid the stink of diesel fumes and stale fish. 'There's no sign of life on that island.'

'No?'

'Nothing. So why's Jameson's mobile signal pinging from there. God I wish GPS was hundred per cent accurate. At least we could then find the damned thing.' Elspeth was holding back tears. 'Jesus Claire, where is he?'

'We'll find him babe.'

Di Stefano sympathised. 'We will find him. Do not worry.' He climbed backwards down the companionway where Claire rounded on him. 'We need to go to the cops dude.'

'We are the cops,' Abandonato almost laughed.

'Look,' Claire said. 'I know you are saying there are heaps of crooked cops in Italy but a man's life's at stake. He's our friend.'

Di Stefano drank from his water bottle. 'Twenty-four hours is all I ask. I have been chasing this criminal for years and I have never been this close ... '

'Close to what,' Elspeth snapped. 'There's nothing there except ghosts ... '

'Ghosts! You saw ghosts?' Claire and Vincenzo cried out together.

'I saw *a* ghost.'

Claire. 'Cool.'

'Well I think it was a ghost,' Elspeth was shaking her head in utter confusion. 'It was all this mist in the shape of a man and ... '

'Forget ghosts,' Di Stefano said. 'This is just stories, legend, si?'

'Well I've news for you,' Elspeth looked genuinely upset. 'That's the most scary damned island I have ever set foot on.'

'Please Luigi, take us from here,' Di Stefano said in Italian.

'Where to?'

'Anywhere where we can't be seen. Make it look like we have left for good but we're coming back.'

Elspeth wondered what the polizia knew that they didn't.

'Remember I say, there is more to this island than meets the eye?'

'Yes.'

Di Stefano. 'And I hear a motor, yes?'

Elspeth. 'But we thought it could be a passing boat.'

'Yes. But then when I was looking for you I could smell cookeen.'

'My god!' Elspeth had a revelation. 'You're so right. So did I. I was so damned scared, I forgot.'

'Si. I smell cookeen fish, with garlic.'

'That's why it was so familiar. Jameson's always cooking fish with heaps of garlic.'

'What are you trying to say,' Claire frowned. 'That Jameson's in some kind of spook kitchen cooking fish and garlic?'

'I am theenkin, that the island has more secrets than we imagine. Certainly the island is abandoned, yes? But I am thinkeen, well is there underground chambers where they hide Jameson.'

Elspeth coughed a laugh. 'And he's cooking them lunch? Hardly.'

• • • • • •

'Lunch is served,' Jameson said proudly. Prisoner or not there was one thing he always took pride in. And that was his cooking, and in particular his specialty; seafood. Before him on a stainless-steel platter the two baked sea bass *swam* in opposite directions on a sea of steamed jasmine rice surrounded with stir-fry bok choy and bean shoots with garlic.

'Looks good,' Drishya said begrudgingly. 'Smells good. I hope you haven't overdone the garlic.' The beautiful woman was not accustomed to having her advances rejected. Jameson had hit a nerve and rejecters beware.

'Come. *John* insists you join us for lunch.' Drishya tapped the numbers into the kitchen door security panel and it hissed open on compressed air.

'What's his real name,' Jameson asked as he squeezed by with the platter. 'It's not John.'

'If I told you that I would have to kill you.' Drishya waited on the other side for the door to relock itself and glared back. 'Now move it. *John* is waiting for his lunch.'

Man of Mirrors heard the dining room door hiss open and closed his laptop lid. Maybe Vataea *was* within his reach. And maybe the Lance of Destiny *could* be found and his cancer cured. If only. He washed down more painkillers with Perrier from an 18th century Venetian glass baluster facon; one thousand Euros from a Florence antique glass dealer. The pain was worse today but Cambino was determined to hide it.

Once again Drishya opened the door to the underground dining room and Jameson was immediately taken by the false window with its artificial afternoon sun pouring through the pearled glass. At least he *thought* it was afternoon. But trapped here underground he would never know and was rapidly losing sense of time.

'That smells delicious,' Cambino complimented Jameson as Jameson slid the porcelain platter onto the dining table. He was more than impressed and insisted Jameson join them in savouring his efforts.

'Wine?' Drishya held a familiar bottle for Jameson to read the label.

'Dalrymple pinot noir,' Jameson read aloud. 'Tasmanian. I'm impressed.'

'There are many Tasmanian wines available in Italy if one knows where to look,' Man of Mirrors said proudly. 'As we have a Tasmanian guest I thought it appropriate.' He waited while Jameson's wine was poured and then his own. 'Besides I enjoy your island's vibrant ruby coloured wine with its hint of summer plums and cherry confiture. And the subtle complexities of five spice goes so well with this sea bass, don't you think?'

Jameson. 'You read the label.'

His comment went ignored. Jameson was inclined to believe they wanted him to join them for lunch to prove he had done nothing untoward to their meal but as the conversation progressed he realised the man's motives.

'So,' Man of Mirrors wiped his mouth gracefully on a starched serviette. 'Have you had enough time to consider our proposal?'

'Proposal?'

'Yes. You direct us to this archaeological site where you observed your captors at work, and I will make you a rich man.'

'You'll let me walk, right?'

'Of course. We are not murderers.'

Jameson was desperate to buy time. He had no doubt these people would kill him once they had the information they required. 'And what's in it for me?'

'Now you are talking sense.' Man of Mirrors smiled at Drishya sipping mineral water. She had hardly touched her meal. 'One hundred thousand.'

Jameson whistled.

'I will wire the amount into your account immediately.'

Jameson. 'One hundred thousand huh?'

'Yes.'

'Euros?'

'Of course.'

Jameson sat upright and pushed his half-finished meal aside. 'Find me a map of Campania.'

'Mariconda!' Cambino could not contain his excitement. 'Mariconda ... I knew it. I suspected it was around that area.'

'Then you were correct, *John*,' Jameson said with a twist of derision. He had indeed pinpointed the village of Mariconda but had conveniently located the illegal diggings of Vataea five hundred metres northeast.

'May I go now?' Jameson almost laughed at his own request. It came out as a throw-away line. *May I go now?* He made to stand, pushing back his chair. Drishya was fast. Poised like a cobra about to strike. She jumped to her feet clamping Jameson's shoulder forcing him back in his seat. 'Not so fast.'

Man of Mirrors opened his laptop and Google Earthed the location. Jameson swallowed hard and prayed the satellite images were old. They were. 'You are saying here?' Man of Mirrors pointed a manicured fingernail at the location Jameson had drawn on the Campania map. The shot was taken during winter and the vines were neat rows of naked bushes.

'Yes,' Jameson lied. He too pointed, making out contours and landmarks further away than the real location.

'It looks like most of it is under Mariconda,' Drishya said.

'True,' Jameson agreed. 'But there is still one hell of a lot under the vineyard, here.'

'What are you like at making gnocchi?' Man of Mirrors asked Jameson.

'Gnocchi!'

'Yes, gnocchi.'

'Why?'

'Because gnocchi is one of my favourite meals.'

'But you said ...'

'Once we verify this location you will be set free and as I promised you will have one hundred thousand Euros wired to your account. But for now you will remain in the galley.'

'*John's* favourite is gnocchi with gorgonzola and walnuts in a cream sauce,' Drishya smiled. 'Isn't it *John*?'

'Yes my dear.'

Jameson looked on defiant.

'Unless you want to spend the time in your cell,' Drishya spread her legs in a threatening stance, balling her fists in preparation for conflict. 'Well ... chef? Galley or cell ... cell or galley?'

'Galley.'

• • • • •

Jameson had searched every square centimetre of the sterile stainless kitchen. There was only one door. Exit come entrance. Always locked by a coded panel. There were no windows, however the kitchen was well ventilated. The range hood filters were only 200mm by 200mm so there was no escaping up the flue. The floor was terracotta tile and the benches all bolted down.

Claustrophobia haunted Jameson.

Now the deaf-mute Salah had been sent to keep an eye on him. The man busied himself grilling bell peppers with a blowtorch and painstakingly peeled them in preparation for preserving them in glass jars of brine.

Biding time, Jameson prepared the gnocchi; his method of pushing the cooked potato through a mouli and *then* mixing with sifted flour, salt and Parmesan was happily accepted by Salah who offered the odd nod of approval. Under normal circumstances, Jameson felt, he could bond with this man.

Finally, some time later Salah pushed past Jameson in the narrow galley and tapped in his exit code. The door hissed open and the Moroccan slipped out into the corridor. He didn't look back. The hydraulic door arm juddered, before automatically closing ...

Jameson didn't hesitate.

He threw a sack of flour onto the floor jamming the door open in a burst of flour dust. The door protested, hissing loudly with a succession of noisy clicks attempting to re-lock.

Jameson's luck held.

Deaf Salah punched in his code at the far end of the ill lit corridor. Jameson skipped over the flour sack squeezing through the gap and raced to the next self-closing portal. With less than a second to spare Jameson slammed his shoulder between the door jam and the door ...

Again, the sliding panel protested.

Again, Salah did not turn back.

Jameson slammed his back to the wall. He waited ... heart pounding. Salah turned a corner and vanished from sight.

It was all too easy and Jameson feared a trap. He held back. He listened. He took several deep slow breaths.

Now what?

Hugging the passageway wall Jameson crept to the corner. Here the corridors forked off. He hurried along the corridor Salah had taken ...

'No!'

Too late. The door had re-locked.

He tried the other passage. It too was locked. Jameson was trapped between secured doorways in a poorly lit corridor. He guessed there would be security cameras although he couldn't see any. Jameson backtracked; something caught his attention in the first passageway. He pushed his body against its walls spreading his fingers and feeling its construction.

Aluminium tread plate. Industrial. Raised pattern for slip resistance. Same material used on ships.

Jameson placed his cheek against the cold metal. He could barely make out a low humming. Motors? Generators maybe. *Surely he wasn't on a ship. There was no movement for a ship. Maybe it was moored somewhere.* He suspected not.

Underground more likely.

Jameson sensed a draught. An inconsistent breeze that he was certain was not air-conditioning. He felt his way along the corridor towards semi-darkness when his fingertips detected an anomaly in the panelling.

A gap.

A scarcely discernable gap.

And the panel was loose.

Jameson managed to claw his fingers into the tight space and was rewarded with movement. The panel was hinged. It opened outwards freely. Suddenly a sensor light, a soft nightlight, exposed the pitch darkness beyond. The darkness of another passage that gave Jameson hope.

So John, or whatever you're name is, you're a man who loves secrets.

Jameson repositioned the concealed panel. He made his way along the corridor. A door to one side presented a small sign.

Generatore.

He tried the handle. The door opened. Inside two diesel generators thrummed softly. But the room was small and went nowhere. A room opposite faintly displayed another sign. *Negozio.*

Locked.

Running fingers along one wall Jameson felt his way to a ...

Dead end.

It didn't make sense. In near darkness he ran his hands over the aluminium plates. He dared to tap the panels ...

When one returned a hollowed tone.

A room on the other side maybe?

Jameson pushed gently. This hinged panel opened inwards when ...

He heard voices.

Drishya and *John.*

Noiselessly Jameson shuffled forward. Before him was a blackened partition. It was hard to tell in the dark but it was apparent the other side was well lit. More importantly the voices were clear ...

And so was their intension.

'My sickness is worsening Drishya. If we are to do this it must be done quickly.'

'You really do believe in the lances healing powers?'

'I have faith Drishya. Faith in the Lord. Yes, I believe it will heal.'

'Then I will go to Napoli tomorrow Cambino, and confirm Vataea's location.'

'And then what?'

'We make the vineyard owner an offer he cannot possibly refuse and excavate immediately. The Herculaneum scrolls are very specific where this Aulis Cethegus lived. I will find this lance. Believe me, I will find you the lance of destiny.'

Lance of Destiny!

Jameson could hardly believe what he was hearing. The Lance of Destiny, Jameson knew, was one of the holy relics sought by men of god for generations.

'And the Australian?' *John* asked.

Jameson stiffened.

'Leave him to me.'

'Pity, he's a good cook. And how will you deal with him?'

'I'll burn him like the others and hide his ashes in the plague pits. No one will ever know.'

Jameson was weighing up options when he heard a commotion. He heard what he could only imagine was a guttural howling; an incoherent panic ...

Salah!

'What is it?' Drishya yelled at the mute Salah as he crashed uninvited into their presence. More incoherent garble accompanied frantic signing.

'Escaped! How?' But Drishya didn't wait for an answer. Jameson heard the door hiss open and the room went silent.

Drishya swept along the corridors, a spectre with her fine orange silk shawl chasing after her, flying on anger. Cambino rolled after her in his wheelchair. They came to the galley door, it's automatic arm still hissing and jarring as it tried to close. She saw the burst flour bag and turned to the terrified Moroccan swiping his face with an open claw. Man of Mirrors own anger, temporarily sated with that single, lethal strike, added his wraith.

'Get up top,' he yelled at Salah while signing. 'Now! Fetch Giorgio and Gabriel and see the prisoner doesn't get off the island.'

Salah scurried away holding his bloodied cheek. Drishya scoured the floor where floury footsteps led down the passageway. She swept past her mentor and followed the footprints as they diminished, but her keen eye saw enough traces of flour to lead them back towards the Hall of Mirrors.

Jameson had some difficulty finding an escape route. It was like a maze at a fairground. He leapt from behind the wooden panels and into the room of light beyond. The narrow passageway, he guessed, was just wide enough for a wheelchair. Probably designed as an escape exit for the man he now knew as Cambino. Jameson stepped between overlapping panels and into the room flooded with light. He hurried to the centre of the hall mesmerised a moment. Standing in the centre of the room he pirouetted like a dancer gaping at his reflection in hundreds of mirrors. He knew he was in trouble. He knew he had to move fast. But he burst out laughing. His comment at the breakfast table flashed back ...

I don't know how you get up in the morning and look yourself in the mirror!

Now he understood their mirth. Jameson noted everything in this mirrored chamber was centralised; mainly the Louis XIV Boulle writing desk with its bronze decorations ...

Awful taste.

But standing proud to one side was the most magnificent life size statue. Jameson was in awe of its beauty. Undoubtedly Roman. The quality of the art was exquisite and Jameson was certain he recognised the face of an emperor, Hadrian maybe.

Sitting on the writing desk's leather top was the stereo console, a laptop, a dashboard of electronic buttons and security screens ...

Security screens!

Jameson saw movement. As he watched Drishya returned. She navigated the passageways back towards this weird room of mirrors. The woman appeared to be following something ...

Foot prints?

Jameson checked his shoes. Flour! But most of it had worn off. Immediately Jameson noted a security pad at eye level against a far wall. On inspection he realised the large arched Amiel floor mirror with its many mirrored panels was actually an exit. Clever. It had closed shut.

Locked.

Jameson studied the security panel. It was coded for four numbers ...

Four numbers.

It was a long shot ...

Four numbers.

How old is Cambino? 45? That makes him born 1972. Jameson tapped in the numbers. *1-9-7-2.* Nothing. *50 maybe? 1-9-6-7.* Still nothing. *Christ, 48 then ... 1-9-6-9 ...*

Nothing.

Jameson twisted about to the monitor screen. An overhead security camera captured an angry Drishya gliding along the passage he had used. Cambino was on her heels. They were moments away.

The year is 2017 right? Jameson screamed in silence.

2-0-1-7

Nothing.

2-0-1-8

Nothing.

Jameson rushed to the controls. He cast an eye over the dashboard ...

Everything was labelled in Italian.

He heard approaching steps from behind the mirrored panels where he had entered. In desperation Jameson crushed a palm onto the button panel. The lights blinked out but a soft blue emergency light bathed the room with a frail luminescence.

Drishya pounced into the hall of mirrors. She spun about positioning her feet in the defensive zenkutsu position and with one hand balled and one knife-edged ready to strike.

Cambino wheeled in after her. 'Where is he?'

Drishya said nothing. With cobra like prescision she scanned the darkend room. Only the silhouetted figure of Emperor Hadrian stared back coldly. She scowered the floor. There were no floury footprints.

'He may have found the exit at passage five.' Drishya hurried to the security pad next to the Amiel mirror exit. She punched in four numbers. The mirror unlocked but with the power needing a reset she had to manually slide the *door* open. Drishya stepped into the passage, checked into the blackness then turned to Cambino now at the console, his figure nothing but a dark shape. 'You coming?' she asked.

'I don't know what's happened here but I must reset the power first.'

Drishya hurried away.

Jameson waited scarcely breathing and thanked his good fortune that his physique was not dissimilar to that of Emperor Hadrian. Balancing on one leg, right arm in line with the statue he had positioned himself perfectly behind the marble statue. The dark helped. Satisfied Drishya was at a safe distance he stepped from behind his cover.

Cambino snapped his head up from his desk and froze. 'You! You did this.'

'Sorry about your gnocchi Johnny,' Jameson felt his confidence return. 'Or should that be Cambino?'

Cambino wheeled out from behind the desk and manoeuvered directly for Jameson but Jameson was too fast for the handicapped attacker and sidestepped easily. He slipped into the blackened passageway and manually rolled the door shut where Cambino's protests were nothing but faded curses.

Jameson stumbled on blindly. Blind through a widening passage passing several other doors. It was not long – ten metres – when he came to a metal fire stair. Jameson mounted the steps three at a time. He could smell fresh air.

Salty sea air.

He arrived at the crash bars of a typical fire exit and slammed hard against them. The door crashed open against a concrete wall where there was space, a passageway, for an average person to squeeze by ...

Only just.

But this was not typical of a fire stair.

The concrete wall continued as a narrow alleyway lit with a soft blue sensor light. It was tight. Jameson crabbed sideways for another five metres before his path was blocked by another wall. Jameson groaned. He heard shouts approaching. He placed hands on the wall blocking him. It was wood, not concrete ...

But a dead-end no less.

Drishya's footsteps tapped up the fire stair.

Jameson stepped back. Looked up. The narrow space was two and a half metres high by less than 400mm wide. Claustrophobia clouded his judgement when he noticed a faint pencil thin rim of light bordering the wooden end panel. It had to be a door. Jameson threw his shoulder hard against it. It gave way and a soft daylight engulfed him. The moment he was through the door closed behind him on a powerful hydraulic arm.

Jameson stood stunned. His feet rooted to the spot, eyes darting about. He was standing in a kitchen ...

An old dilapidated kitchen abandoned decades ago and trashed by vandals. It looked industrial. An institutional kitchen. A hospital maybe ...

Military?

Or Asylum?

Jameson gaped at a grubby pale blue wall covered to head height with decaying yellow tiles. The extractor hood frame hung precariously. Stoves pushed on their sides. Trees invaded through windows. Macabre graffiti on walls and shattered crockery scattered the floor like the artefact field of a sea-wrecked ocean liner.

Jameson twisted about.

The wooden panel had closed. Vanished.

He was locked out.

But the siren Drishya approached beyond.

There was no trace of where he had made his exit. Jameson's brain clouded. It didn't make sense. A second earlier he was in the modern sanitary confines of some acentric antiquity thieves' secret bungalow and now this.

Mirrors, mutes, seductress killers, high tech surveillance ...'

There was no time to think ...

Jameson heard a scratching sound, like a rat in the eaves. Then the panel started to open. Jameson swivelled a full circle.

'Christ!'

Jameson looked for an escape ...

He ran towards a smashed window overgrown with foliage as ...

Drishya exploded into the kitchen.

Jameson didn't look back.

He dived through the window somersaulting into an overgrown courtyard dragging vines and branches after him. He leapt to his feet. Untangling his leafy shackles Jameson ran wild along an enclosed porch. Shuttered windows one side. Concrete wall the other. Underfoot he was barely aware of the detritus of crumbling ruins. The long porch-way ended. Jameson burst into the open ...

He wheeled about.

Gasping for breath.

Ruins. Ruins everywhere. Jesus! It reminded him of the abandoned asylum Willow Court back in Tasmania. Jameson snapped his head skywards,where a chapel steeple sneered down at him. It seemed to scowl from behind a forest of trees. *A hospital chapel ... or is it a penitentiary?*

'Where the hell am I?'

Approaching with the stealth and speed of a panther Drishya's advance was heralded by her crunching steps on broken glass.

Jameson scoured the forest.

A pathway!

He didn't hesitate. Jameson bolted for cover.

'Jameson!'

He heard his name as he burst into the open.

'You can't leave here.' Drishya's words streamed after him. 'We don't want to hurt you. You can become a rich man if you join us …
'

Daylight dimmed under the cover of the forest. Trees and vines joined overhead to form an evergreen burrow. Careful to cover his tracks he stepped into the thicket of bushes pushing through the leafy vegetation towards where he was certain he saw the glimmer of water.

Twigs snapped, dead leaves crackled. He was being followed. Jameson dropped to his knees behind thick wild shrubbery and waited. Seconds later he caught a glimpse of Drishya's orange shawl gliding along the path between the trees. He waited. When he was certain she had passed by he continued on to the water's edge.

Water. Sea air.

'No' he screamed silently. 'It *is* an island. It has to be. Christ, where am I?' Across the water Jameson saw buildings, another island or the mainland? He couldn't tell. But one thing was for certain, it was too far to swim. The overgrown bushland reached to the waterfront where a stonewall dropped two metres into the water. The storm wall followed the shoreline for several hundred metres in both directions with a ten-degree list towards the water caused by shifting land behind it. Jameson followed the wall, trudging through vegetation for fifty metres when it hit him.

'Venice!'

In the distance, some kilometres away Saint Mark's tower stood out like a beacon. Jameson had visited Venice with his parents. He loved Venice and had read much about the ancient city and had pored over photos since he was a kid. 'Venice,' he said softly. 'I knew it. I bloody well knew it.'

'Jameson!' Drishya's voice was near. Too damned near.

Jameson backtracked to where he first made his exit from the woods. There was nowhere to hide. He climbed down a breach in the crumbling stonewall. Jameson lowered himself into the water, thankful that his feet touched rocks at knee height. Hugging the wall he crept through the water, concealed, but if anyone were to approach from the opposite side he would be found.

'Jam-es-son.' The bitch was singing out his name. Singing! She was directly overhead, pushing through the thicket on the wall above. Crumbling fragments of stonewall fell about Jameson and he pushed back hard against the wall. 'We know you are here ... Jam-es-son, come out come out wherever you are ...'

The moment he was confident the woman had passed, Jameson climbed back up the eighty-degree slope of the wall . Inching along on his stomach Jameson crawled to a rusting abandoned boiler, a massive cylindrical iron drum riveted together in the early 20th century. And ...

Closing his mind to unwelcome creatures, he climbed inside.

They met on the woodland path. Salah's face said it all. Words were not necessary. Giorgio the launch skipper and all round handyman ran along beside him.

'Nothing?' Drishya stated the obvious. 'It can't be that difficult. He can't get off the island. You two split up.' Drishya signed to Salah to circle the shoreline. 'Giorgio, are you armed?'

'Si signora.'

'Then you check the asylum, the hospital and admin' buildings.'

'The asylum signora?' The man flinched.

'Yes, the asylum. Why are you scared?'

'I ... I ... you know wha ... '

'Look Giorgio, man up. What you saw in that building last week was all in your mind ... now go.'

'But ...'

'I said go. Move it.'

Giorgio sulked off. What he had seen in the asylum in broad daylight had frightened the hell out of him. He was well aware of the special effects wired into the buildings by the film expert from Las Angeles some years ago but this ...

This was not one of those effects.

Cambino Cardinale's eyes danced from monitor to monitor. He switched cameras frantically looking for their escaped prisoner. This was bad. Very bad and the only outcome could be eliminating the Australian before he found a way to escape the island. Besides, he was certain Vataea was where the chef had said it was. He had nothing to lose.

Drishya glided into the Hall of Mirrors a raging beauty followed by flowing silk and anger. She stood with Cambino at the desk of monitors. 'How-could-this-happen? How?'

'We must move the barge tonight.'

'Yes Cambino.'

The two had already determined that the Vataea collection was far too hot to handle at the moment. The collection would have to be hidden for a few years while things cooled off. Vataea was hot property and if they were to be caught with what they had ... well, it would be twenty year's prison. Twenty years Drishya could not afford. And to make things even more awkward the Swiss were not helping anymore. There had been far too much bad press lately.

But, Cambino told himself, *he could still lead a personal quest to locate the lance, from his island, and he suspected it would mean eliminating those fools Ricco Ricci and Silvano Marchetti.*

'It is a good thing we did not unload it last night. I will contact Dahna, the cargo ship *Alexa Cadiz* sails for Abu Dhabi day after tomorrow. We'll just make it.'

'What of the disguise?'

'I have already spoken to Dahna. She has arranged to have the Vataea pieces smuggled out of Italy for Mumbai, where the items will go underground for a year or so.'

'That's what I like about you Cambino, you are an organised man who does not let the grass grow under his feet.'

'Yes. But I fear I do not have the year or so to spare. As you know I am making preparations for you to take over Drishya. You have been like a daughter to me. I have no one. The empire will be yours. But I'll not go without a fight and priority number one ....'

'Get the barge away from here ... yes Cambino, I know.'

As if on cue a fierce pain attacked Man of Mirrors abdomen and Cambino coughed more blood. Drishya felt sentiment threatening her tough façade. She could only console the man with a gentle hand on his shoulder ...

And then left him to his memories.

• • •

Clare scratched about in *Olga's* galley. It was after six in the evening and she was starved. They were all hungry. They had anchored off the southern tip of Lido two kilometres away where they kept vigil. Nothing. But Di Stefano knew it was only a matter of time. They would wait for the cover of darkness.

'A tin of mackerel,' Claire cried out. 'From Canada! Jesus Luigi. Don't you even have some Italian sardines?'

'Sorry, but I not expect passengers today.' The skipper with the dreadlocks – whom Claire confided to Elspeth looked like he had combed his hair with a honey-dipper – scratched his scalp and frowned. It was cocktail hour for Christ's sake. Out came the grappa.

'Not expecting passengers ... huh! Not expecting passengers today or any day by the look of this lot,' Claire grunted into the galley cupboard.

'Here Bella,' Vincenzo handed Claire a packet of sweet biscuits.

'So what's the plan?' Elspeth asked Di Stefano who had just checked in with Antonio in Naples. Jameson's mobile was dead, either switched off, dead battery or destroyed. But all signal tower triangulations had pinpointed Poveglia Island.

'The plan? We will wait until dark and explore the island once more. If there are underground cellars or bungalows being used we should sense either light, motors or maybe we are lucky with cookeen smells.'

'Dark,' Elspeth checked the time on her mobile. 'What time's that?'

'Maybe seven.'

Behind them the sun was descending towards the distant Alps. Elspeth looked out at Poveglia Island. Under normal circumstances the church spire and ruins amongst the forest on the waterfront would have been a Kodak moment basking in a honeyed sunset glow.

But not today.

'Jameson,' she sighed to herself. 'Soon it will be dark.'

• • • • •

Ricco Ricci felt the last of the warm rays of the sun caress his face. Seconds later the magic minute passed, and the sun was lost behind the Alps.

Twilight had arrived.

He and Marchetti had docked off the northern side of Poveglia Island where the sand dunes were more cremated human remains than sand. Domenico was at the helm of their hired vintage motorboat, an early 1990s ex-water taxi with polished varnish bow and shiny chrome fittings. To all intents and purposes they were exactly that. A water taxi.

Ricci slipped into his wetsuit. He would snorkel dive along the shoreline and swim the canal to explore where the barge had disappeared the night before. Marchetti knew Ricci was more than qualified for the operation. The man was ex-commando and in particular a Special Forces Frogman. Ricci gave Marchetti the thumbs up and silently dropped off the stern ...

And sank into the inky water.

CHAPTER SIXTEEN

Jameson peeled the brambles from his shirt and inspected the damage. He had several tiny cuts for his effort. An hour earlier he had crawled from the rusted boiler on the shoreline and crept on his belly back through the woodland and towards the ruined buildings.

He was near Venice. He knew that much. And he was on an island with no obvious sign of escape. *But what was this island?* Several times one of the two searchers passed close by. Too close by. Jameson had managed to elude recapture, but for how long? The most eerie thing though, was the unexplainable feeling he was being watched. Were they simply playing games with him or was there some other malign menace on the island.

Jameson crawled through the window of the first building he came to. A laundry by the look of it. Lots of plumbing, huge galvanised troughs for rinsing. Another bus-sized boiler and crumbling wall tiles. Vandals had done their work here too, along with graffiti artists ...

Huh! Artists ... I don't think so.

Jameson looked at the demonic monotone coloured life size figures painted on one wall. They reminded him of the expressionist painting, *Scream,* by Edvard Munch.

No ...

These were more sinister, with cartoon bubbles containing inscriptions in an alien language. Nail like spikes protruded from their heads and one carried a club. They starred back at him with menacing wide-open angry mouths.

Jameson found a closed door at one end of the laundry. The door was jammed shut but he managed to force it open, scraping on the floorboards where tree roots had grown beneath it. Beyond was a large foyer with a tall two-storey high ceiling. At the far end, the stairs had completely collapsed. Only the iron balustrade survived, being slowly strangled by ivy as it curved up past a stair window. The sun was setting fast and Jameson felt a chill in the air where normally he would have thought the afternoons summer heat would have lingered.

What is this place?

Without warning a figure appeared at the window. A shadowy figure silhouetted by the setting sun. Jameson stepped backwards into the doorway, his eyes glued to the figure that did not seem worldly. Jameson knew the window to be three metres from the ground so how on earth had anyone managed to ...

Hover!

The figure elevated slowly. It was almost like it wanted to be observed.

Then it vanished.

'There!' Cambino shouted spittle at the security screen. 'Got him. He's in the laundry wing ... go ... go quickly.'

Drishya said nothing. She threw her silk shawl over her shoulder, checked her two-way radio, snatched her Berretta pistol from off the desk and left for the laundry.

'Signor,' Gabriel in the secret dock enclosure asked Man of Mirrors over the intercom. 'Shall I resume the search or take the barge to the rendezvous?'

'Take the barge. Go. Make the rendezvous and return to Poveglia as quickly as you can. We have unfinished business here.'

Turning fear into anger Jameson went searching for the old kitchen where he at least knew there was an entrance back into the underground. He walked the perimeter of the woodland when he stumbled on the canal. Immediately Jameson felt a rumbling underfoot. The ground started to shift.

Surely not another earthquake.

Suddenly Jameson right foot fell into a crevice. Waving his arms frantically he caught his balance and jumped off the moving embankment and onto stable land. It was then that he realised the land was opening up to reveal a concealed dock. Jameson hit the ground burying himself amongst bracken and dead wood. As he watched, the bow of a barge appeared, slowly at first, motoring out of the dock and into the narrow canal. Jameson recognised one of the men who had been searching for him, steering the flat-bottomed craft into position. The barge looked fully loaded, her gunwale close to the waterline. Once the barge was free an open launch followed. Salah was at the helm and Jameson guessed it was the craft that brought him to the island. Then, with a throaty roar from the engine followed by a churn of muddied water the barge headed out onto Venice Lagoon. And the launch followed.

Instantly the embankment started its re-positioning swivel. Jameson rushed along the canal side. Without hesitation, he dropped onto a steel plate ledge; not unlike the horizontal swinging bridge plates at the docks at home in Hobart. Suddenly Jameson realised his mistake. If he wasn't quick enough he would be crushed. The plates ground one over the other as the hidden dock sealed itself off from the outside world. Jameson had no choice. He sucked in a sharp breath and dived into the water. Kicking furiously he swam under the swinging counter-balance. His dive was clumsy and steep. Jameson hit the mud bottom at three metres. He kicked off to head for the surface within in the secret dock. But he was not alone ...

Immediately something clamped his leg holding him under ...

• | • | • | •

Luigi polished off the grappa. Half a bottle! And why not? That crazy red headed Australian girl called Claire was the only one who would join him, and even she only had two shots. He sat on the wheelhouse step and rolled himself a cigarette with his elbows resting on his legs looking contemplative. The man was certainly a character; athletic and unpredictable Claire guessed as she watched Vincenzo talking to his cousin quietly. As Di Stefano had banned any lights the two men were dark shapes in the approaching night.

'It's time,' Di Stefano said to Abandonato.

'I'll get my pocket torch,' Elspeth said.

'No Bella,' Di Stefano said. 'No. Just Dino and myself. This could be dangerous.'

'You're not going without me.' Elspeth huffed. 'End of story.'

'And me,' Claire said.

'And me,' Vincenzo's arm shot up.

'Wait a minute,' the policeman said. 'Thees was not the plan. Just me and my colleague Dino.'

'Listen dude,' Claire spoke with fiery grappa in her empty belly. 'Cop or not, you can't stop us from searching for our friend.'

Di Stefano sighed. He looked at Abandonato who shrugged in the darkness. 'All right then,' he said defeated. 'But you all do as I say, alright?'

'Forget *Constanza*,' skipper Luigi Villani said with a slight slur. 'Her motor, she too noisy. I take *Olga* around to rear of the island, away from buildings, where there is secondi island, okay. Then you go ashore there in much darkness.'

·   ·   ·   ·

Jameson twisted and turned underwater. Shark? Giant eel? Was he tangled in rope? Machinery ...

But he quickly realised it was a man's hand clamped onto his ankle. He kicked back but the grip was like a vice. Jameson needed air. Fighting panic he curled back on his attacker. The water was dark and cloudy with freshly churned mud. But hints of light filtered down from the interior dock. Jameson heard the giant door grind to a halt. He lashed out with his untethered foot. Whoever had hold of him was strong ...

But then he saw a blurred face. A mask. A snorkel.

Jameson snatched the mask ...

Wrenching it from his attacker's face.

Immediately a flurry of bubbles escaped. The man shouted underwater. Jameson threw a wild punch connecting with the attacker's nose. The assailant lost his grip.

Jameson kicked off towards the light.

He broke the surface greedily gulping air. Jameson was two metres from a seawall. He saw a steel ladder and swam hard, mounting the ladder as the water surface exploded next to him ...

The attacker rose from the water coughing hard. His hand snatched the back of Jameson trousers. But Jameson had a good hold on the ladder. He turned to face his attacker and recognised Ricci.

'You!'

Ricci tugged at Jameson's belt, like a rogue crocodile trying to drag his prey back into the water. Jameson twisted his body. He raised his foot once more ...

And ploughed the heel of his boot into the assailant's face.

Ricci cried out in pain.

He dropped back into the swirling water. Jameson clambered free, hurriedly taking in his surrounds. He was in a vaulted steel and concrete chamber ... an underground dock.

Very impressive.

Twenty metres by fifteen.

The only light came from an emergency exit light. Instantly Ricci broke the surface gulping down great lungfuls of air ...

Then Jameson saw the man was armed ...

Ricci rose from the water, one arm extended, Glock 17 ex-British Armed Forces pistol in hand. He had lost his mask. His eyes were red raw and his face fierce with rage.

Jameson raced for the fire stair, wrenching the door open the moment Ricci squeezed off two shots. Jameson felt the slugs tug at the doors fabric as it quickly closed behind him ...

And he hurried into the unknown.

• • • • •

'We'll start back at the asylum,' Di Stefano whispered along the line.

'Asylum!' Elspeth muttered doubtfully. 'Really?'

'Yes. I feel that building holds our answer.'

'You're the boss dude,' Claire said softly as they ventured further into the undergrowth. She twisted about to Elspeth as they bent below low branches. 'Garlic you reckon?' Claire said.

'What?'

Claire's head swivelled every which way at the sinister shadowy ruins appearing ahead, her imagination in overdrive after Elspeth's experience earlier. 'You said you smelt garlic before ... '

'Yes,' Elspeth sighed. 'And baking fish.'

'But this ghost thing Beth. You said you saw a ghost.'

'Jesus Claire, I don't know what I saw. Lets just find Jameson.'

'Yeh but garlic Beth ... doesn't garlic scare away ghosts?'

'That's vampires.'

'Jesus. Vampires!'

'And ghosts too I suppose ... don't worry about it.'

'But I am worried about it.'

'Keep quiet you two,' Di Stefano led the way pushing through the overgrown foreshore following the shoreline towards the main hospital and asylum. 'Keep your eyes open and heads down and most important, keep quiet.'

Instantly what sounded like muffled gunshots came from behind them. 'Did you hear that?' Di Stefano said quietly, urgently holding up a hand.

'Gunfire,' Abandonato concurred.

Di Stefano. 'Maybe.'

Vincenzo. 'Sounded like it came from the direction of the canal.'

'S-shots?' Claire stammered. 'Gunshots?'

'Si. What else?'

Claire wide eyed. 'You said nothing about gunshots.'

'Go back to the boat,' Di Stefano hissed at her.

'Bullshit.'

'Then please keep quiet.'

Abandonato took his service pistol from its shoulder holster. 'I'll double back,' he suggested.

'Si.' Di Stefano turned to Vincenzo in the fading light. 'Vincenzo.'

'Si signor.'

'Go with Dino.'

'Si.'

'Dude,' Claire said quietly to Vincenzo. 'Be careful huh.'

'Yes Claire.' Vincenzo whispered, touching Claire's cheek before he and Abandonato dissolved back into the shadows.

'You like him huh?' Elspeth said quietly as they moved on in Di Stefano's footsteps.

'Yeh. He's kinda cute.'

• • • • •

Marchetti turned his ear to the bleak landmark that was Poveglia Island, now a dark shape in the middle of the lagoon where he moored some distance away after dusk. Twenty minutes after Ricci swam ashore a fishing trawler landed passengers only one hundred metres distant. The trawler had not seen Marchetti anchored parallel and hugging the shoreline in the low water taxi. But what made Marchetti suspicious was they maintained a total blackout.

'Do you think they are Uomo di Specchi's men?' Domenico asked Marchetti.

'How should I know?'

'They could be ghost hunters,' Domenico said. Visitors to the island were rare, most being supernatural enthusiasts.

But suddenly something else spooked Marchetti. 'Did you hear that?' he asked Domenico.

'Si. It sounded like gunshots.'

'Merda.' Marchetti checked his IMI Desert Eagle and pocketed two spare clips along with a pencil torch. 'Get me closer to shore. I have to check.'

•   •   •   •   •   •

'I can't see him, over.' Drishya whispered to Cambino on her two way. 'The laundry is deserted.' Drishya could see the foyer door from the main laundry, forced open over the years by renegade tree roots. She stepped through, crushing shards of glass underfoot and cursing the noise she made. Night had arrived with its inevitable gloom and only the slightest illumination filtered through the upper stair window. The quarter moon was yet to present itself. Although she carried a flashlight she daren't use it for fear of losing her element of surprise. Drishya heard soft footsteps. She pressed her back stiffly to the wall ... and listened.

'Cambino,' she whispered again into the mike. 'Do you hear me? I cannot see him.'

'Drishya.' Drishya jumped. Cambino's voice was loud through the radio. She tweaked the volume as low as possible and whispered back. 'Can you see him? Is he above the laundry. I hear footsteps.'

'No he's not.'

'He's *not* above the laundry?'

'No.'

'But I hear ... '

'He can't have got too far.'

The gloomy foyer here was becoming a little overwhelming and Drishya had this foreboding of company in the hidden black corners near the collapsed staircase. The door next to her creaked as if in a breeze. But there *was* no breeze.

'Drish-ya.'

Drishya felt the hairs on the nape of her neck bristle. The voice called to her from the blackness ...

'Drish-ya.' It was barely a whisper but she knew she was not alone. 'Chef. Is that you?' There was trepidation in her voice. 'Jameson Rowley?' But Drishya doubted their prisoner would hang about and play games with her. Her breathing grew laboured.

'Drish-ya.'

'Dam you!' Drishya flicked on the torch sweeping the blackness with welcome light. But her hand was unsteady. Shadows danced. Shapes shifted casting unnerving patterns across the walls, along the floor ...

And leaping towards her.

'Drishya!' Cambino's voice was urgent, shrill. 'Drishya can you hear me?'

'Yes.'

'Where are you?'

'Foyer off the Laundry. Have you been fooling with me.'

'What?'

'Fooling about with your effects.'

'No. Why?'

'This place gives me the creeps.'

'Drishya, I am certain I heard gunshots ...'

'Gunshots ... where?'

'It sounded in the direction of the loading bay.'

'Loading bay. The barge has left, right?'

'Yes.'

'I'm on my way.'

Drishya panned the flashlight about the ruined foyer where she imagined demonic shapes lurking. 'Bah! Damned island.' Drishya took a deep breath, crashed back through the laundry and out into the welcome open.

· · · · · ·

Di Stefano, Elspeth and Claire stepped from the gathering darkness and filed into the Asylum; a chilling black space filled with bad vibes and evil memories. The air was still and the night eerily quiet. Somewhere across the water a church bell rang out. Or *was* it from across the water. Suddenly they were not certain.

Claire. 'That sounds close dude.'

'Si. It sound like eet ees the chapel here on the island.'

'Christ,' Elspeth shook her head. 'We can't be alone.'

'I agree.'

'This is not cool,' Claire said under her breath using the blue wash from her mobile screen to guide her every step. She took hold of Elspeth's arm. 'Where'd you see that ghost anyhow?'

'I said I didn't know what I saw Claire.'

'Yeh but ... I know but ... where were you though?'

Di Stefano stood in the centre of the ward amongst a pile of rusted iron bed frames thrown in a heap. Claire panned her light illuminating graffiti on the wall directly behind him. *La morte per i trasgressori.* 'Morte,' Claire read aloud. 'Means death don't it?'

'Si.' Di Stefano and Elspeth followed Claire's eye. The polizia pursed his lips.

'What's the rest say then?' Claire asked.

'It say, *death to the transgressor.*'

'Brilliant.'

Di Stefano followed his torch beam into the nooks and crannies, stroking his chin, thinking. He had no time for ghost stories, although he privately conceded the place was creepy. But the veteran Tombaroli Carabiniere had a powerful nose for intuition when it came to criminal behaviour ...

And all here was not what it appeared.

•   •   •

Drishya inspected the canal near to the loading bay. She swung her flashlight over the surface. Everything looked in order. Directly across the narrow canal the plague pit mounds of human ash reflected somberly the light of the quarter moon. Switching off the light she focussed across the lagoon towards Venice. Her trained eye soon spotted the blue stern lights of the barge headed to Dock 18 for the emergency rendezvous with the trucking service that would transfer the Vataea treasures to Trieste. Giorgio appeared to have almost completed the short journey. That at least, was one positive.

Once certain she was alone, Drishya stepped into the decaying ruin of what was once an ablution block. She slipped between crumbling walls and punched in code numbers on a hidden panel. A wall shifted on an automatic arm and seconds later she descended from decay into the modern steel and aluminium fire stair leading to the loading bay ...

And froze.

Leading away from the subterranean dock were two sets of wet footprints.

• • • • •

Marchetti forged a path through the thicket of trees hiding his boat from view at the north-east banks of Poveglia's adjoining island – *more like sand hills* the man thought as he unwittingly scrambled over the cremated chalky remains of thousands of plague victims. Once beyond the copse of trees he was more exposed. He crouched low, waiting a moment to survey the area. The night was tranquil with only a quarter moon, but Marchetti liked it that way. He turned his head slightly, listening ...

When a brief mist swirled before him only metres away. Marchetti blinked his good eye. He could have sworn the mist took the shape of a man ... a man wearing a hooded cape that dropped fully to the ground. On his head he wore a hat like a boater. Marchetti rubbed his eye. It was only mist ...

Wasn't it?

Instantly the vague shape drifted beside him once more. Fleetingly. Marchetti snapped his head about but the damned vision disappeared as fast as it had appeared.

He sucked a lungful of air feeling his heart quicken.

The shape appeared to have the face of a bird ... a black crow with a long beak ... or was it the morbid mask of the 16th century plague doctors so popular at Halloween parties these days.

Ridiculous he reprimanded himself. It was only mist. But the night was clear. The air motionless. Marchetti felt a chill shiver through his body and hurried silently across a narrow wooden bridge to the main island.

Instantly footsteps crackled dry twigs nearby. Marchetti dropped from sight lowering himself off the canal bank where he hid under the bridge. Seconds later Marchetti recognised Drishya's feline body. She moved through the night like a hungry wild cat where the sounds of gunfire had drawn her to the canal. As he watched, Drishya stopped at the canal edge shining a flashlight about her. The light then extinguished. It appeared the woman was looking out across the lagoon. She moved off, in amongst trees. Her darkened shape as slim as the tree trunks hiding her.

Silently, and with a measure of experienced guile, Marchetti anticipated her direction. He quietly dashed through the thicket to what he discovered was an old ablution block. He slipped silently inside taking refuge behind a shower bay wall, dissolving into the gloom ... and waited.

Less than thirty seconds later Drishya's stepped inside the building. Marchetti held his breath ...

Drishya stopped less than two metres away. Fearing to breathe Marchetti stole a glimpse of the woman through a slim gap. He watched her open the rusted steel door of what looked to be an old fuse box. Inside was a modern coded panel. Drishya hit the panel with her flashlight. With his one trained eye Marchetti had a clear view. Drishya punched four numbers and Marchetti smiled at the genius of it all when a wall shifted enough for her to step through ...

And closed once more behind her.

He waited a full minute. Checked his *Desert Eagle*. And he too punched in the numbers.

Di Stefano led Elspeth and Claire through a maze of wards. "Merda!" He said quietly. The wards and passageways seemed different from the afternoon's exploration and the entire island was beginning to unnerve him.

'Don't tell me we're lost,' Claire hissed.

'Lost? On this island?' Di Stefano forced an anxious chuckle and the torchlight below his chin accentuated dark shadows on his face, making him look like a pantomime villain. He tried to laugh off the matter. 'But to tell you true Bella, I think we *are* lost.'

'Christ.'

'Watch your step.' The polizia stepped around missing floorboards where a careless slip between joists could break a leg. A door appeared. It led to another passageway. Here windows to one side opened to a rising quarter moon offering the barest illumination on the purplish walls. Many of the shuttered windows were dressed with hanging curtains; now thin rags of decay. Outside the night air was still yet the curtains managed to shift slightly towards them in passing.

'Shit. That is creepy,' Claire swallowed hard. 'I've gotta get outside ... dude.'

'I'm trying Bella.'

'What are you looking for specifically?' Elspeth whispered to Di Stefano desperate to take her mind off her surroundings. 'Maybe we can help.'

'I look for, how you say ... ah... tell tale signs. Electric light possibly. There are underground cellars here, old bungalow maybe ...'

'Or dungeons dude,' Claire swallowed hard.

'Si dungeons. I just know this. We must find an entrance.'

At the end of the passage ...

A locked door.

Elspeth noticed a large keyhole. 'Now what?'

'Go back the way we came?'

Di Stefano's torch shone back down the passageway they had traversed. 'Mamma Mia!'

'Christ no!'

'Where are the windows?'

Instantly the three felt a chilling sense of doom.

'The windows have disappeared!'

'No!'

'Impossibile, si.'

'Shit Renato,' Claire panicked. 'I've gotta get out of here. Now!'

'I agree.' Di Stefano turned back to the door. He tried the handle once more. Locked. He bent down and placed an eye over the keyhole ...

Focussed ...

A figure flashed by on the other side ...

Di Stefano leapt away from the door.

'What is it?'

He said nothing. Freeing his torch hand he ground his teeth and raised his boot slamming it into the door.

Once ... twice ...

The wood splintered at the jam and the door flew open. Di Stefano signalled for the two women to stand behind him and stepped over the threshold. Beyond the space was total blackness. He wheeled about chasing torch shadows only to create more dancing figures. He kicked the open door again bouncing it off the wall. There was nothing behind it. He twisted about thrusting light into all corners. Nothing. There was nowhere for anyone to hide ...

Somewhere a door slammed.

'Jesus Christ what was that?'

Claire. 'Oh man, this place *is* haunted ...'

'I do not believe in these things,' the polizia grew angry. His head darted about. He lit every corner. The room was a dead end ...

Again, a banging door.

Di Stefano re-entered the passageway. 'Merda! Come out you bas-tard,' he shouted into the gloom. This time they watched as the door at the far end slammed, squeaked open and slammed shut only to once more creak open. Di Stefano thrust the torch beam along the passage.

'Oh shit!' Claire grabbed the polizia's arm. 'Is that really happening?'

'Si,' Di Stefano yelled at the door – defiant. 'Yes eet is. And it is a door out of here.' Dodging missing floorboards he raced forward. The door remained open. Di Stefano closed the gap in seconds ...

Slam!

The door closed so violently it almost swiped him off his feet. 'Merda!' he screamed at the door and gripped the handle twisting it angrily.

'Locked!'

•   •   •   •   •

'Huh!' Cambino laughed anxiously out loud to himself. 'So, you don't believe in ghosts! Well what do you make of that?' He squinted at the image of the man with the torch and the two women in an asylum corridor. The disappearing windows had worked a treat and the slamming door was brilliant but although his hidden camera resolution was high the rooms were so dark the reception was grainy.

But this, this *haunting*, was exactly the reason he had spent so much money on the special effects. The expert from Los Angeles had done well. Exterior sound effects and obscure malevolent figures drifting through the woods had proved a wonderful deterrent to the rare superstitious day-tripper to the island. And any nutty ghost hunter who had dared enter the building was usually scared witless by one of his hologram manifestations. But today's intruders were searching for his prisoner who was now loose on the island.

Nothing was going to plan.

Cambino, Man of Mirrors, looked at his recurring image in the antique mirrors surrounding him. He felt he had aged considerably the past few days. The sickness had worsened. Sitting at his antique desk in the middle of the room he stared off into eternity as one mirror-image reflected the other ...

Eternity he forced a smile. Immortality. The Lance of Destiny clouded his thoughts. Yes! He must have it at all costs.

I don't want to die, he screamed silently.

Not yet.

He smiled at the wisdom of securing most of his cash in Swiss banks. And thanked the gods he had had the foresight to send Georgio to the industrial docks with the barge of Vataea treasures. Once secured as arranged, Georgio would return in the launch and Cambino and his trusted subordinates would escape ...

Plan B ... Fast launch to Trieste. Rendezvous with the Vataea collection and cross-country to Hungary where Cambino had a safe house in Budapest.

Cambino was not concerned about the few antiquities remaining in the conservation laboratory on the island. They would simply be collateral damage when he detonated the five tonnes of RDX chemical high explosives planted around the buildings and underground bunkers. With his own mortality in question Poveglia Island was little to sacrifice in comparison to the holy relic now possibly within his grasp.

And this trouble-making chef from Australia? Yes! He could be destroyed along with the island ...

Shifting figures on the monitor caught Cambino's eye. The two women and the man with the torch, possibly polizia, were about to become victims once more.

'You can all die on this island, damn you!' Cambino spat at the screen. 'But for now, I will have some fun.' Cambino dragged his computer mouse across the screen. He double clicked the suitable icon and the dead-end room in the asylum suddenly exposed a loose panel to the intruders. He watched the three figures step through into another corridor and picked up the radio.

'Drishya,' he said softly. 'Where are you?'

'Loading dock,' her sultry voice came back in a whisper. 'We have two intruders inside.'

'You mean downstairs in the bunker?'

'Yes. There are footsteps here. Wet. Two sets.'

'God no. And I can see three others snooping about in the asylum also.'

'What do you want me to do?'

'Eliminate the two inside first.'

'Yes Cambino.'

Jameson pushed along the underground corridor lit by soft light from battery operated sensor lights on sixty-second timers. He had no idea which direction to go but knew he had a madman in a wetsuit armed with a pistol following. By running an open hand along the passageway walls Jameson found two side doors. Both were locked with coded panels. Desperately he looked for an exit. Suddenly he turned a corner into familiarity.

The *generatore* room.

It was still unlocked. Behind him he heard the approaching squelch of wet rubber on the polished cement floor. Jameson slipped into the generator room silently closing the door behind him. At the same moment the frogman rounded the corner, wary, hugging the passageway wall ...

Pistol ready at arm's length.

In the generator room two massive 20 KVA Deutz generators chugged softly on their rubber and spring mounts. The laminated steel casings were two metres by 1800 mm high. Designed for minimal sound the diesel-fuelled generators were fed from a 20,000 litre fuel tank disguised as an early 20th century rusting boiler up at ground level. Exhaust was expelled in an even more ingenius method. A hollow synthetic tree trunk transferred the exhaust into the woods where it dissipated amongst the foliage. Secured to the wall between the generators was a transfer box with dozens of wires snaking away along PVC conduit to power the underground bunkers.

Inside Jameson had triggered another sensor light on its timer and now noted that the generator room door could not be locked from the inside.

Jameson was trapped.

Looking about unsuccessfully for a weapon he tried to slip behind one of the generators and was questioning his decision when the door opened.

'Well isn't this cosy.' Ricci pointed the snub nose Glok directly at Jameson's head. 'What are you doing wandering around like you own the place?'

Jameson said nothing. He was trapped with nowhere to run. Immediately he had an idea. 'You know this place is haunted?'

'Ah! You don't believe in ghost stories, do you?' Put your hands where I can see them.' Jameson stepped out slowly from behind the generator. 'Now tell me,' Ricci said. 'Which way to this Man of Mirrors?'

'Man of Mirrors?' Jameson uttered buying time.

'Yes. You know who I'm talking about. Where is he?'

The automatic timer on the corridor light switched off and Ricci stepped further into the generator room, with his shoulder against the open door. 'Well?'

Jameson remained silent. He put his hands into the air.

Ricci grinned. 'That is more like it.'

Immediately the corridor sensor light triggered once more and Drishya appeared.

'Drishya,' Jameson cried out 'Just in time.'

Ricci spun on his heels.

Drishya fired her Barretta. Two sharp shots. But Ricci had jerked his head right. Jameson dropped to the floor the instant the bullets shattered the wire transfer box. The box exploded in a shower of sparks and flames escaped from behind its door as the room fell into darkness. Ricci fired back squeezing off two shots at Drishya. Both missed. Drishya's fired again this time hitting her mark. The first shot smashed into Ricci's shoulder and the second plugged through his eye socket. In the light of the electrical flames Jameson saw Ricci's body crash against the door. His weight slammed it closed in Drishya's face, blocking it as his body crumbled to the floor ...

Dead.

Ricci's pistol chattered across the floor to Jameson's feet. Jameson scooped up the weapon as Drishya threw her weight against the door. But Ricci's dead weight barricaded it. Jameson tore off his shirt, soaked from his swim, and doused the flaming power box. Acrid smoke billowed along the ceiling and the room was swamped in darkness once more.

The door inched open. Drishya's slender body silhouetted against the corridor's emergency floor lights slowly flickering to life. The silhouette stepped into the room.

'Not another step,' Jameson said coldly. 'I'm armed.' In truth, he didn't have a clue what to do. The door opened enough for the silhouette to step inside and dissolve into the blackness. Jameson fired a warning shot. The bullet ricocheted about the metal walls. He dropped to his knees and prepared to fire again when Drishya fired over his head. The light from her muzzle flash lit the room and now *she* had Jameson in *her* sights ...

Click!

Nothing. The Barretta's six-bullet magazine was empty.

Jameson was fuelled with relief. 'Step into the corridor where I can see you,' he shouted. The silhouette reappeared. Drishya's slinky body once again came into view. 'I said the corridor.' A sudden movement blurred Jameson's vision. He heard soft steps and the door close. Jameson floundered in the smoky darkness, grappling at the scarf Drishya had thrown over his head. Furious with himself Jameson stumbled into the corridor ...

But the siren had slipped away.

Cambino's heart skipped a beat. Anxiously he watched all monitors shut down and the mirror room was thrown into darkness once more. Immediately emergency battery operated sensor lights offered enough illumination to see his surroundings, but that was about all. 'Drishya,' he said quietly over the two-way radio. 'Where are you? What's happened? ... Drishya?'

Nothing.

Abandonato heard muffled pops. 'Did you hear that?' he asked Vincenzo in their native tongue.

Vincenzo. 'Yes, you think it was gunshots?'

'Sounded like gunshots. And it sounded like it came from ... in the woods maybe.'

They had heard gunshots all right, the sound escaping from air vents hidden in the ground foliage near the woods.

The two men backtracked from the canal where they had earlier found no sign of anything untoward.

'Now what?' Vincenzo asked the polizia.

'We better find the others.'

'I think that first building is the old hospital. Maybe we should start there first.'

Jameson was starting to see the big picture. This operation was far larger than he could possibly have imagined. Looting the odd tomb was one thing but this was state of the art, international antiquity thievery on the grandest scale. The underground system was a touch of genius and now that he had discovered the clandestine loading dock he knew how the island was serviced. He also had no illusions that that wild woman Drishya had gone for help and to reload. And now that he knew too much he was a dead man ...

Or was he? They want the location of Vataea. He told himself. *But they already had it ... pretty much. Jesus now what?*

Jameson's mind clouded.

The emergency backup generator had automatically sparked up, and floor lights like those of an aircraft, lit the passageways. Jameson backtracked towards the exit. Suddenly a shaft of torchlight splashed the corridor walls ahead. Someone was approaching. Jameson touched a door on his right. It opened. The power failure must have unlocked it. He slipped inside holding the door ajar a fraction for fear of locking himself in, and waited. Seconds later a figure passed by ...

Jameson peered through a pencil thin crack.

Marchetti!

Jameson saw enough of the figure to recognise one of his kidnappers from Naples. His heart sank. He was up against more than he suspected. Jameson's self-survival instincts kicked in. Marchetti *must* have arrived by boat. If he could find it he had a chance to get off this crazy island. Jameson hurried silently along the corridor following the floor lights when he saw his own wet footprints.

Eureka!

He followed his footsteps back to the loading dock. Here a steel fire stair led to the surface. At the top of the stair Jameson crushed against a panic bar on the door and burst into what looked like a decrepit dormitory shower block.

'Ricci!' Marchetti's eye followed the slumped arm splayed across the passageway floor and into the generator room. He choked a cough when he saw his colleague sprawled unnaturally, with his face on the cement floor and in a puddle of thick blood. Blood, oily black in the eerie soft blue light. Marchetti felt the man's carotid artery in the neck but there was no point. He knew his partner was dead. Marchetti took a handful of hair and turned the man's head about. He gagged. The right eye was a black orifice of oozing blood. He had heard gunshots and thought Ricci had shot Drishya. This was totally unexpected. Ricci was an ex- commando for Christ's sake. How could this happen.

Marchetti swallowed hard.

Then a plan started taking shape. A plan without his partner ...

A plan of greed.

* * * * *

Drishya was angry with herself. Infuriated. She was a martial arts master. Surely, she could have disarmed Jameson. Was she losing her nerve, she questioned her actions. *He had a gun pointed at me ... right?*

Bah!

Reload woman and sort this out once and for all.

'If that cheap tombaroli was here,' Cambino scowled. 'Then it means his accomplice is here somewhere. What's his name again?'

'Marchetti.'

'Marchetti. That's it. What on earth is going on. We have the tombaroli and the polizia carabiniere maybe, along with the Australians. It's time Drishya,' Man of Mirrors slouched painfully in his wheelchair. He was surrounded by an angelic amber glow from the mirror room emergency lights reflecting the gilt from the antique frames. 'Georgio should be returning soon. The moment he arrives we will leave.'

Drishya exchanged a look of anger and frustration. She knew their time on the island had finally come. They had after all enjoyed five years of anonymity at this location and they always knew this day would come. And although Cambino never complained, she knew he was dying. Cambino sat his precious laptop on his knee.

'With the monitors down we will have to wait for the launch at the loading bay. Go see that the emergency generator is ready to open the dock. I will program *Beelzebub for Operation Poltergiest.*'

Beelzebub.

Drishya's nerves bristled at the very name. Beelzebub the demon from the Christian scriptures. The devil. Satan. One of the seven princes of hell. Drishya allowed a wry smile at the name Cambino had affectionately given to the elaborate explosive setup wired to destroy the island and all its secrets. It was also the password for the detonation procedure. Cambino tapped the laptop lid with rhythmic fingers.

'It's safest for you to wait here,' Drishya told her mentor. 'I will return for you the moment Georgio returns.'

Drishya used her mobile to call Georgio. 'Georgio. Where are you now?'

'The barge has been successfully unloaded and Salah and I are on our way back in the launch.'

'ETA?'

'Fifteen minutes.'

'Good. Then as soon as you return it will be *Operation Poltergeist*.'

'Poltergeist?' Georgio's voice was hesitant.

'Si. Poltergeist. You know the drill. Now hurry.' Drishya turned to Cambino. 'Time for a change. I think it wise, you have made the correct decision.' She checked a fresh clip of bullets when she noticed the spare Beretta in the desk draw. 'Here,' she said checking it was loaded. 'Keep this ready.' Cambino nodded and sat the small handgun on his knee.

'I'll return shortly,' Drishya turned for the exit. 'But first I will rid the island of vermin.'

Abandonato and Vincenzo followed the sound of the other shots. At least they thought they were gunshots. Clearing broken glass and splintered wood from around a shattered window, they entered a hospital ward through the opening where vegetation almost blocked their entry.

Abandonato swept his torchlight the length of the ward and shivered. It had a cold melancholy about it. Almost malevolent he thought. Words were not needed. Vincenzo's wide alert eyes caught those of the polizia's. Both men were uncomfortable. Abandonato panned the light along the dark green wood panelled walls where a narrow sill ran its full length. Here and there personal items remained; decaying where they had been abandoned in 1968. Vincenzo lifted a small brass framed photo from the sill and gazed into the sad eyes of a dark-skinned woman starring back at him. A loved one? He felt a chill and reverently replaced it.

'Lead on,' he said to Abandonato.

The polizia was reluctant. Returning back through the window and into fresh air looked far more inviting. 'Lead on?' he questioned Vincenzo.

'Well you're the one holding the torch,' Vincenzo said. And he wanted to add; *and you're the one with the badge and the gun.*

Abandonato swept the beam across the floor mapping a path ahead through the detritus. 'Where the hell do you think the others are,' he said, finally heading to the far end of the ward with Vincenzo close behind.

'Your boss was talking about the asylum.'

'That's the next building, right?'

'It must be.'

At the far end they passed into a foyer and followed snaking vines up a stair to the first floor. Here another passageway waited with shuttered windows on one side. The merest of moonlight accentuated cracks in the shutters otherwise the only light was Abandonato's torch. Without warning the torch dimmed. The polizia stopped dead.

Vincenzo. 'Jesus what was that? Batteries?'

'Batteries are new.' Abandonato's voice lacked conviction. 'Keep moving. Let's find the others.'

The two shuffled with short steps to the end of the corridor. The beam picked up a sign over the door but it was unreadable.

Abandonato twisted the handle. The door opened. He brushed the room with light ...

A chalk white face starred back fixedly. Blank lifeless eyes and what appeared to have a shaved head. 'Mamma Mia!' To their immediate right a white porcelain phrenology head glared at them, its *shaved* head sectioned off in numbers inked in black glaze.

Vincenzo looked beyond the head. 'It's an operating theatre,' He muttered. The operating table stood in its original position in the centre of the room, otherwise the room was strewn with leather belts, chain, broken chloroform bottles, forceps and other and medical equipment.

A loud bang from the corridor had them jump.

'Merda! What was that?'

The men returned to the passageway to catch a light through the shutters. It appeared to be from the ground a floor below.

'It must be your boss?' Vincenzo cried out. He threw open the shutter and the light vanished. 'Jesus!' Vincenzo jumped backwards.

'What is it?'

'There's someone ... something down there. I saw it before the light went out. It was looking straight up at me.'

Abandonato rushed to the window. 'There's no one there.'

Vincenzo cautiously reapproached the window. Nothing. 'You saw the light,' he told Abandonato doubting his own sanity. 'You did ... didn't you?'

'Si.' The polizia's eyes darted about searching the blackness below. 'It must be Di Stefano.'

'I am telling you it was not your boss.'

'Then who? What did he look like?'

'He? I-I ... don't know what it was ...' the blood had drained from Vincenzo's face. He was as white as chalk.

'What? What do you mean it?'

'It looked more ... more animal ... and it didn't have a face.'

•   •   •   •   •

Claire and Elspeth kept close to Di Stefano as they negotiated darkness and fear through one dormitory after another. Claire tugged at the back of Di Stefano's shirt so tightly he feared she would pull it from his back.

'Bella ... my clothes per favore. You undress me if you not careful.'

'Sorry ... I'm just not crazy about being here.'

'Me to. But we must find your friend, okay?'

'Okay.'

Passing lavatories that would have offered little if any privacy in their day Elspeth could only imagine the deprivation. Male and female wards were distinguished only by one male and one female medical superintendent's office. The three intruders completed what appeared to be a full circle of the building. They stepped into the main entrance foyer; the same entrance they had found barricaded on the outside earlier in the day. The foyer was wide with a grand staircase gently sweeping in a half spiral up to the floor above, showcasing elaborate turned wooden bannisters. There appeared to be windows on the landing above but any moonlight was masked by long black drapes in various degrees of disrepair.

'Man, this reminds me of the haunted house ride in Disney Land,' Claire said.

Di Stefano encouraged the lighter conversation. 'You have been there, yes?'

'Yeh dude. My parents took me when I was twelve. You know I read on line that the staff at Disney regularly catch people spreading remains in the haunted house.'

'Remains?'

'Yeh. Cremated love ones.'

Elspeth. 'Ah gross.'

'I think it would be kinda cool,' Claire said. 'What the ... '

Di Stefano saw the sudden horror on Claire's face and twisted about. Elspeth's mouth sprang open in a silent scream. At the top of the sweeping staircase an apparition appeared.

'You-are-kiddin'-me,' Claire gasped in a rasping whisper. If they had any doubts before, this manifestation dispelled them. The phantom hovered over the treads, half hidden by the banisters. Appearing as a vague mist, the ghost was that of a woman. It appeared she was hanging by her neck. Her arms hung loose at her side and as the three watched in horrified shock the body revolved slowly to face them. Now they saw the eyes were black orbs and the jaw was more like the mandible of a skeleton behind a thin black funerary veil.

'Claire was frozen to the spot. 'I ... I ... are you seeing what I'm seeing?'

'Si Bella,' Di Stefano agreed; more in awe than shock. He shone the torch directly at the spectre. 'But look closer yes.'

'It's just starring at us,' Elspeth said wide eyed, also unable to move. Di Stefano said nothing and started up the stairs.

'Jesus dude, what are you doing?'

The polizia trained his torchlight on the apparition, which seemed undisturbed by the mortal's approach. At first his steps were guarded but the further he advanced the more confident his pace.

'Are you mad,' Elspeth cried out. Claire remained riveted to the floor when instantly the policeman burst into a hysterical laugh. He tore at the nearest drape and as the girls watched on terrified, he swung the torch like a club. There followed a loud shattering of glass. The ghost vanished and shards of glass scattered over the banister and fell at Claire and Elspeth's feet.

'What the hell ... '

'I tell you true, beautiful ladies,' Di Stefano yelled triumphantly down the stairs. 'I no believe in thees theengs you call ghosts.'

'What just happened?' Elspeth asked skipping up the stairs two at a time.

Claire was right behind her. 'You are one crazy mother Renato.'

'Hologram yes?' the polizia held a diamond shaped piece of glass and turned it back and forth slowly. The skeletal mandible morphed into the handsome jaw of a young woman. 'But what I want to know ees ... who would do such theengs. I ask myself this question and I'm thinking someone who does not encourage visitors, yes.'

'This is bullshit!' Claire yanked back the drape to expose the clear Perspex frame fastened to a mechanical arm that supported the hologram on its elongated film plate. Di Stefano washed the upper wall with bright light.

'There. Eet was illuminated by a laser light.'

Elspeth recognised the diode laser pointer from her university lecture days. This one had had the lens widened considerably. They watched the torch beam as Di Stefano bounced it off the walls and around the main entrance below. 'There.' He jiggled the light to draw their attention to anomalies at floor level on the skirting boards.

'Trip sensors. These are for trespassers who enter.' Intruders manifested the ghost themselves. Had they known the power failure had kept the hanging lady ghost in position rather than hinging her back out of sight behind the drape. The laser itself was powered by its own battery and the 'ghost' had been in situ since Drishya accidentally destroyed the generator cable box. Elspeth stepped up onto the upper landing and reached out running her fingers through a cobweb. She pulled a few strands towards her. 'Look, it's synthetic.'

'No!'

'Feel it.'

'Jesus you're right. This *is* a bit like Disney World.'

'Si,' Di Stefano nodded. 'Disney World run by kidnappers and criminals. We must search the grounds. There must be sometheen hidden beneath us.'

•   •   •

Marchetti had no trouble finding Cambino in his room of mirrors. Animated voices along the passageway led him to the eccentric's sanctum and when Drishya made her exit he hid in a side chamber. She passed right by him and he smiled with relief.

It was all too easy.

Cambino watched multiple images of the infiltrator as he attempted to surprise him. The mirrors, these magnificent antiques that he would soon be forced to destroy, had many a purpose.

'You pathetic fool,' he told the expected Marchetti over his shoulder. 'You don't know half of it.' The Man of Mirrors sat poised with his finger shaking anxiously; hovering over the console of coded keys wired to the explosive charges that would destroy Poveglia Island and everyone with it.

'So you are the Man of Mirrors. The enigma. The ghost people say. Who are *you* calling me a fool?'

'I called you a pathetic fool. Are you deaf as well as stupid.'

Marchetti noted the laptop. He saw the menace in the Man of Mirrors reflection. 'What are you doing?' Marchetti watched the threatening finger anxiously. He sensed danger. His good eye itched. He rubbed it carefully, with tender care, for the thought of losing his one eye and going blind was his paramount fear. 'Well?'

'You and your small-time operation,' the Man of Mirrors ignored the question. 'You come here to my island to threaten me. *ME!*'

Marchetti was unnerved by the mirrors. Shapes appeared and vanished in his peripheral vision. 'So this is why they call you "Man of Mirrors".' Marchetti tried to strategically position himself with his back to a wall but with all the mirrors it was an impossible task. 'What is it with all these mirrors anyhow?' he said angrily, agitated and waving his pistol at his own reflection.

'You ignoramus,' Man of Mirrors spat. 'You couldn't possibly contemplate the history these mirrors have witnessed, the people of power they have reflected; Napoleon, King Louis the Fourteenth, Marie Antoinette ... '

'Bah,' Marchetti scoffed waving the pistol at the nearest frame. 'What makes you think that?'

'Because some of these mirrors are from Versailles, fool.' Cambino scowled at the pathetic tombaroli with his ambitions to take what wasn't his ... to simply take at gunpoint what he had spent decades building. And what did he have to lose. His cancer in his bowel had returned ...

It had never gone. He had enjoyed a period of remission but now the recurrence was back with a vengeance.

He was going to die shortly anyhow. 'Oh, I see the doubt in your eye,' the Man-of-Mirrors was starting to enjoy toying with the lesser human being. 'I had copies of four of Versailles' prominent mirrors made in complete secrecy. Cost me a small fortune. And when restoration was being done several years ago I made a discreet exchange. No one ever knew. So, fool, I am certain the Sun King, Louis, the Fourteenth for one, would have preened himself in one or more of these mirrors.'

'Fool?' Marchetti shook his head with agitated contempt. 'In case you haven't noticed I'm the one with the gun.'

But something was making him very nervous.

. . . . .

Jameson slipped silently through what he imagined was a 1960s shower block. The open cubicles bespoke a lack of privacy. The ceiling-high shower roses allowed the inmates no control over their ablutions. It was a depressing and distressing place. The entire island was unsettling. He stepped out into the night and took in several deep breaths, when suddenly a torch beam sliced through the branches. Someone was approaching through the trees.

Drishya?

Jameson hurried to the edge of the canal. But at the same instant he heard a launch enter the canal opening from the lagoon. Instantly the light in the forest went out and a far more powerful spotlight flooded the canal. Jameson swung under the cover of the bridge ...

The moment the spotlight lit the canal like daylight.

If the light in the woodland was Drishya, Jameson wondered, why then did it extinguish so suddenly.

Marchetti?
But I left him in the bunker.

•   •   •   •   •

'Move your hands away from that keyboard,' Marchetti waved the IMI Desert Eagle at the Man of Mirrors' back. Directly behind his heart. Marchetti had positioned himself with his back to the mirrored wall so as to be in a defensive position if Drishya returned unexpected. But the Man of Mirrors appeared restless in his wheelchair.

'Did you hear me cripple? Put your hands where I can see them.'

Cripple! Cambino boiled with anger.

Cripple!

He kept his eyes on Marchetti, starring at his reflection in an 18th century boudoir mirror with naked women carved into the elaborate frame.

'You're too late,' the Man-of-Mirrors said after a considerable pause.

'Too late for what?'

'This island is wired to detonate. There is enough explosive buried here to take out all of Saint Mark's Square.'

'What are you talking about?'

'What? You deaf as well as a fool. I said, this-island-is-wired-to-detonate.'

'How?'

'The sequence has been activated,' The Man-of-Mirrors lied. 'We are all going to be destroyed with it.'

Marchetti looked decisively nervous. 'You lie. Why would you do such a thing? You would die too.'

'I'm dying anyway. Cancer. I have nothing to lose.'

Marchetti fidgeted biting his bottom lip. 'No. I don't buy it,' he finally decided.

'Suit yourself.' The Man-of-Mirrors managed a wry smile. 'Besides, I've sent your little collection on its way. You probably saw the barge leave.'

Marchetti's good eye twitched. Indeed, from where he waited for Ricci – with the hire boat on the north of the island – he had noticed the stern lights of a barge heading for Venice. But many barges ply the waters of the lagoon. Marchetti put on an audacious face. 'Do you think that bothers me? There is plenty more where that lot came from.'

'So you *have* found Vataea.'

'Of course,' Marchetti answered smugly. The Man-of-Mirrors was going nowhere so why shouldn't Marchetti boast. Marchetti had been wanting to crow about Vataea for some time.

Now the Man-of-Mirrors was on the defensive. 'So if you have found Vataea what do you want with me?'

'I want your operation signor Uomo di Specchi. I'm sick of being the wholesaler. I want your contacts, all of them.'

Cambino's attention was drawn to his mobile. It silently vibrated. It was a text from Drishya. *The launch has arrived. I'm on my way.*

'But there is plenty for everyone,' he said in a soft voice, finally calm. 'Vataea is an entire town, like Pompeii or Herculaneum, not some tomb in Tuscany ... there is plenty for everyone and you know that.' The Man-of-Mirrors was trying to buy time.

'Maybe. But I want the lot. I've been delivery boy too long.'

'The Lance of Destiny,' the Man-of-mirrors said suddenly in an attempt to distract the man.

'Lance of Destiny?'

'Yes. Have you heard of it?' He now raised his voice in the hope that it would warn Drishya on her return.

Marchetti thought to humour the antiquities dealer. If he had to play the game to get what he wanted, so be it. 'It's some holy relic isn't it?'

'*Some* Holy relic! It is the bronze spear head of the Roman centurion called Longinus who used it to slice open the prophet Jesus to ensure he was dead while on the cross.'

'So?'

The Man-of-Mirrors spun his wheelchair about so as to face Marchetti. Marchetti waved the gun; a loose threat but the cripple seemed harmless enough. The Man-of-Mirrors felt the Barretta between his thighs where he had allowed it to slip from sight when Marchetti first intruded. Now all he needed to do was to distract the man long enough to draw and shoot. He had often rehearsed this scenario and was an able marksman.

One bullet would be all it should take.

'The Lance of Destiny is buried at Vataea,' the Man-of-Mirrors looked Marchetti in his cold dark eye.

'What? How would you know that?' Marchetti said with disbelief.

'It is written about on ancient scrolls found in the library at Herculaneum.'

'And don't tell me,' Marchetti said sneering. 'There's a map pointing directly to it.'

'Yes. There is actually.'

Humour the man Marchetti thought. 'So what would this … ah … Lance of Destiny be worth?'

'Worth! Worth!' The Man-of-Mirrors said in disgust. 'The Lance of destiny has no value. It's priceless.'

'Everything has a price,' Marchetti spat with arrogance.

'It is but a rusted artefact. It is not gold. It is not imbedded with jewels. But that is the only artefact I desire from Vataea. You can have all the rest. You find me the Lance of Destiny and I will bow out of the business and introduce you to all my contacts.'

'You lie.'

'I am dying Marchetti.' And in this the Man-of-Mirrors was telling the truth. 'The Lance of Destiny is my only hope. It has healing powers to cure the true believer. It will cure my cancer.'

This was totally unexpected and Marchetti shifted his feet uncomfortably. The antiquity dealer looked ill he conceded. The story was so bizarre it could be true. The Man-of-Mirrors read Marchetti like a book. Marchetti shuffled about, clearly in thought. Marchetti wet his lips and looked purposefully about the mirrored room. 'What guarantee do I have that ... '

The Man-of-Mirrors aimed and fired. He may have crippled legs but his mind and aim were fast. But Marchetti caught the move in a dozen mirrors. He jerked his head the moment the Barretta exploded. Cambino's bullet shattered a mirror behind his target ...

The instant Marchetti squeezed off two shots.

The first bullet slammed into the chest of the Man-of-Mirrors. The hit at close range spun him about. The Man-of-Mirrors didn't hesitate. His finger hit the keyboard on his laptop. He punched in the four-digit code ...

The second bullet whispered by his ear ...

An alarm wailed ...

The Man-of-Mirrors fired another shot but his aim was wide. Marchetti fired back drilling a hole in the Man-of-Mirrors forehead bursting open his skull and spraying brains across the mirrored room. The Man of Mirrors died instantly ...

But the alarm wailed.

•   •   •   •   •

In the meagre beam of Di Stefano's torchlight Elspeth crept up to a second drape. It shifted as if in a breeze although the summer's night was still and balmy. *More trick effects* she thought to herself and ripped the drape away from the wall. 'Huh!' she grinned. A latex corpse on a pulley system grinned back. But at that very moment a siren penetrated the silence of night like a pin puncturing a balloon.

'What the hell!' Elspeth jumped back away from the corpse. Her grin vanished.

Claire stood watching, numb, her mouth wide open. 'What have you done?'

'I've done nothing.'

'You set off an alarm,' Claire screamed over the din.

'How?'

'Quiet!' Di Stefano yelled. He hurried to a broken window and listened. 'It's an alarm.'

Claire. 'No shit Sherlock.'

'Seriously. The whole island's alarmed.'

'Jameson,' Elspeth cried out. 'Where is he? Has this got something to do with him?'

'I don't know but we better get outside.' They followed Di Stefano, hurrying down the stairs to the main entrance. 'Here,' he handed Elspeth the torch. 'Hold this.' Instantly the polizia threw his shoulder into the main door.

'It's barricaded on the outside dude,' Claire reminded the man.

'I know. Find something to ram it with.'

Excessive force proved unnecessary. The rotting barricade was decades old and on the third blow one of the doors creaked open on a protesting hinge. They rushed out into the open ...

'Jesus!'

Abandonato and Vincenzo appeared from nowhere out of the night. 'I've had enough scares for one night,' Elspeth cried out over the alarm.

'What is that noise?' Abandonato yelled. 'Sounds like a fire alarm, yes?'

'Elspeth triggered something,' Claire shouted at Vincenzo.

'So loud it'll wake the dead.' Vincenzo said without thought.

'Funny aren't you?' Elspeth told him.

'Oh, I didn't mean ...'

'We must get back to the *Olga* and re-plan our strategy,' Di Stefano interrupted. 'Lay low. See who turns up, yes.'

'See who turns up?'

'Yes. See what happens.' The alarm was an overpowering wail, a penetrating signal that could surely be heard in Venice. 'This alarm has a purpose and eet might be a warning. Come.' The polizia negotiated the perimeter of the asylum and hospital buildings pushing off through the trees. Elspeth, Claire and Vincenzo rushed after them.

Drishya thought the worst. She hurried back though the maze of passageways ...

'Cambino!'

No answer.

'Cambino,' she cried again.

Drishya burst into the Hall of Mirrors. She was a trained assassin. She had killed men. Seen many a brutal death. But nothing prepared her for the sight of her mentor sprawled across the floor ...

He had tipped from his wheelchair ... his head opened like a melon. With the deafening alarm blaring its warning Drishya searched the mirror room. *Ricci was dead so it had to be Marchetti.*

Or was it that damned chef, Jameson? He had a gun!

The emergency power weakened. The vague blue light faltered. Drishya's eyes danced from mirror to mirror. She pirouetted about glancing at her own multiple images. But she was alone ...

Her heart felt empty.

Drishya took a last look at Cambino. No Lance of Destiny would help him now. The alarm wailed its warning. She thought of self-preservation. Then, above everything, she felt a surge to seek revenge.

Operation Poltergeist had commenced.

There was nothing she could do. Her time here was finished. Lifting Cambino's silk coat from the coat hook she covered his head. 'Arrivederci padre,' she farewelled the father she never had. 'I will continue our good work. I will avenge your murderer.'

And Drishya slipped away to find his killer.

Di Stefano, Abandonato, Elspeth, Claire and Vincenzo raced along the forest path when ...

Without warning ...

A powerful light swept the canal waterway probing through the trees like the searchlight from a prison tower.

'Down!' Di Stefano dived to the ground. He waved his hand behind him signalling for everyone to lay still. Elspeth was best positioned to catch a glimpse through the trees. A launch approached along the canal. She tapped Di Stefano's arm. 'It's a boat,' she mouthed.

Georgio manning the launch was nervous. *Operation Poltergeist* was a reality. Hidden amongst the trees the others watched as the launch skipper talked excitedly on his mobile. Another man – with an Arab appearance – swung a spotlight probing the cover of the trees. The beam passed overhead and the others took the opportunity to see what was happening. Immediately a woman appeared, seemingly from below ground level. She was tall and slender and the light pierced through her silken cape showing her body.

'Ah,' Di Stefano announced. 'At last the rats are coming up for air.'

Jameson guessed immediately what the alert signal heralded; the detonation of Poveglia Island. He burst back into the open the moment the launch passed him by.

The launch. Yes!

This would be his ticket off the island. He ran through the thicket following the canal but stopped dead in his tracks ...

The powerful spotlight swept back from the launch. He body rolled into long grass where he had been centimetres outside the beam's menacing periphery. Seconds later he dared raise his head ...

Drishya!

She appeared from the loading bay. She signalled the launch. Jameson had a sudden thought. He would be left deserted on this damned island if he didn't make his move ...

Now ...

Di Stefano checked his pistol. Abandonato did likewise. Both men crawled back to the forest path.

'What's happening?' Elspeth mimed to the polizia over the continuing racket. Di Stefano signalled for the others to stay put. The two men resumed crouching positions and started towards the woman near the launch when ...

A bare top man with a six-pack and attitude came hurtling out of long grass to their east.

'Jameson,' Elspeth screamed out. But Jameson heard nothing but the wailing alarm.

'Stop right there,' Jameson cried out to Drishya. He rushed forward oscillating Ricci's pistol between her and the launch.

'Ah. So there you are,' Drishya said coldly, her eyes darting about like a hungry lizard. 'You are a dead man. And for killing *John* I am going to enjoy killing you.'

'Killing John? What are you talking about?'

Drishya made to move forward ...

When several things happened at once ...

Di Stefano stepped into the open. Abandonato followed and both men trained their weapons on the woman.

'Stop right there,' they shouted.

Salah swung the launch spotlight directly into the polizia's eyes. They threw up an arm to shield themselves only to give Drishya the precious seconds she needed. Drishya twisted her torso, clenched her fists into a boxing position, planted her left foot firmly on the ground and kicked out with her right.

Jameson hadn't a chance.

Drishya's foot deflected off his shoulder. Jameson fell backwards, he lost his grip on the pistol and it bounced into the water. Drishya ran to the launch leaping onto the bow. Georgio opened the throttles of the two 150 horsepower motors. The two Bravo stern drives churned the mud of the shallow canal. The bow rose fifteen degrees propelling them forward and Drishya rolled over the windscreen dropping into the cockpit like a stuntwoman in a Bond movie. Both polizia rushed into the open as Drishya pulled her Barretta from its thigh holster squeezing off two shots. But with all the movement the bullets flew harmlessly. Di Stefano dropped onto one knee, raised his pistol, aimed and emptied his magazine. Abandonato did likewise. They watched their bullets pepper the frothing water at the stern of the escaping launch.

Several hit their mark.

But the escapees were spared. Jameson bounced back to his feet rubbing his shoulder. He was lucky it wasn't dislocated. He watched as the launch continued on, speeding through the canal escaping into the lagoon when ...

Elspeth appeared from the darkness of the trees. 'Jameson!'

'Elspeth!'

She rushed into his arms. 'Oh god I've been so worried. I thought I'd lost you ... where's your shirt?'

'Long story.' Jameson saw the others step into the moonlight. 'Claire! Vincenzo! You're all here.'

'Christ dude,' Claire threw her arms about Jameson. 'I missed you you crazy bastard.'

Vincenzo stepped up for a man hug. 'Si amico. I thought the bastards, they kill you.'

'How?' Jameson was shaking his head. 'I mean how on earth did you get here?'

'Long story.'

Di Stefano stepped forward. 'Nice to find you at last signor Rowley,' he yelled over the sirens. 'I am polizia, Renato Di Stefano and thees ees my colleague Dino Abandonato. But what ees thees thing, thees alarm?'

'Do you have a boat?' Jameson said urgently. 'The islands about to blow.'

Di Stefano frowned. 'Blow?'

'Explode!'

'Explode! Mamma Mia! Si. We have boat.' Unexpectedly a figure was seen streaking across the plague pits. A man. And a man in a hurry. Di Stefano swung his torch beam momentarily catching him. 'Who ees that?'

Jameson recognised Marchetti's solid build immediately. 'That's my kidnapper. The truck driver. Looter!' Jameson screamed out.

'Jesus Jam,' Elspeth yelled over the commotion as Marchetti disappeared behind the trees masking his hire boat. 'Who else is on this damned island?'

'Look!' Claire pointed to Drishya in the escaping launch. It had slowed considerably and there appeared to be panic on board. 'You musta hit something dude. Nice shootin' Tex.'

'Quickly we must get back to our boat,' Di Stefano hurried across the canal bridge. Twenty seconds later the six arrived at the shoreline. *Olga's* tender, *Constanza*, bobbed on a gentle swell.

'Is that it?' Jameson almost laughed. 'Is that our boat?'

'No we have a fishing boat out there somewhere.' Elspeth squinted out across the dark water and swallowed hard. 'I hope.'

Abandonato was first on board the tender. He sat heavily at the tiller. He kicked over the outboard motor. It coughed at the task ahead but started immediately.

CHAPTER SEVENTEEN

The first sign that the island was indeed about to explode was a shower of sparks raining down the chapel spire followed by a muffled rumble.

'Oh god! Did you see that?'

'Si.'

'Are we going to make it?'

'I hope so.'

The alarms went quiet …

And an eerie silence drowned the lagoon.

Just the straining whine of the stressed outboard.

Immediately a serious of charges, apparently deep underground, detonated in blinding flashes. The ground rose in massive mushrooms of loose earth reminding Jameson of Wold War 1 battlefield newsreel footage. Dirt and debris blasted hundreds of metres into the air. Thunder accompanied the succession of explosions.

It *was* a battlefield.

Almost immediately material, man-made and organic, dropped into the lagoon all about them.

'Can't we go any faster?' Elspeth asked. Claire crossed her fingers – on both hands. But tenacious Abandonato at the tiller ignored their pleas. His face tortured, jiggling the tiller in an attempt to dodge missiles. They would be lucky if they weren't swamped.

Skipper Luigi Villani appeared on *Olgas's* port side. 'Gesu Cristo!' he yelled from the darkness. 'What's happening?'

'Get the engine running,' Di Stefano cried out across the water.

'Si, si.'

They still had fifty metres to travel.

'Weigh anchor,' Di Stefano yelled as debris showered the small tender. Luigi unlatched the guardrail gate. He swung it open. He rushed to the wheelhouse. Instantly the next sequence of explosions ripped through the largest buildings, the asylum and hospital. Flames burst through the roofs chasing smoke and dust. Then, gaping in horrified silence, they saw the buildings implode on themselves. This was followed by secondary incendiary detonations clearly designed to create a maelstrom and destroy evidence of the looters hideout.

Suddenly a two-metre wave, a tsunami of displaced water created by chunks of land dropping into the lagoon, rolled out of the night, it's frothing white water crest reflecting the fires. It charged towards the dangerously low in the water craft.

'Is that what I think it is?' Claire bawled out.

'Hang on!' Vincenzo cried.

They gripped the gunwale.

Abandonato looked over his shoulder the moment the tender lifted on the wave. For a brief second they rode the crest. For a brief second there was hope they would surf over it. But the wall of water simply lifted them like a toy in a bath, twisting them broadside and slammed them into *Olga's* hull. The wooden dinghy shattered and everyone was tipped into the lagoon.

Olga fared better.

The wave rolled under her keel, bobbing her recklessly before settling once more. Luigi hurried back to the guardrail throwing life buoys overboard as Jameson bobbed to the surface first.

'Everyone alright?'

With no one injured Jameson managed to find humour as he trod water. 'Barrie Duggan my boating mate once told me, *if you're going out on the water you should always be prepared to get wet.*'

'Well isn't that the truth.' Elspeth was first to climb the portside ladder looking like a drowned rat and along with Luigi she helped the others on board.

'Look,' Claire pointed further out into the lagoon. Drishya's launch was stationery. 'It's that boat you shot at.'

'Are we going to make it?' Drishya asked Georgio of their launch, crippled from gunfire. Georgio inspected the damage with a flashlight as they were forced to slow down.

'There are at least three bullet holes beneath the water line which have penetrated the fibreglass hull. You will have to bail as I drive.' Water was pouring into the stern creating extra weight and lifting the bow even further. Drishya signed instructions to deaf Salah who fished about in the launch saloon looking for suitable containers for bailing water.

'Head for Piazza San Marco,' she instructed Georgio who returned a worried scowl. 'Surely we will make Venice.'

'I hope so.'

Suddenly the sparks raining down the chapel spire caught their attention. Like fireworks in the night. Immediately the explosions started. Drishya watched the destruction with mixed emotions. She had lost her mentor, close friend and benefactor. But for now there were more pressing issues.

•   •   •

At that same moment Marchetti had clambered on board his hire boat. 'Go, go, go,' he spat at Domenico. With the alarms blaring Domenico already had the motor idling.

'What about Ricci?' he asked.

'He didn't make it! Now go.'

Domenico knew better than to ask questions. He untethered the rope secured to a tree branch and rolled the throttle forward.

'The islands wired with explosives,' Marchetti said urgently. 'Get into deep water … now.'

But what the ex-water taxi enjoyed in aesthetics it lacked in grunt. The cruise across had been leisurely; but escaping was not going to be so easy.

'Who's that?' Domenico pointed out a stationery launch lit with a flashlight three hundred metres off their starboard bow.

'Huh!' Marchetti shouted. 'It's her. Man of Mirrors bitch. And I think I know where the barge went.'

'The barge?'

'Yes the barge with our delivery. It was never unloaded and it's been moved. Now get away from here and her. Fast.' At that same instant fragmented sparks, like welding or grinding sparks, on the silhouetted chapel spire, captured the men's attention. 'The islands going to explode,' Marchetti almost squealed in a panic. 'Hurry for god's sake.'

'There's the kidnapper!' Jameson tripped along the starboard gangway squinting into the night. Marchetti was escaping. Within seconds they could only see the white water wake reflecting moonlight. Marchetti was sailing blind without lights.

Drishya had seen him too. 'It's Marchetti,' she glowered. The pain in her heart had turned to cold revenge. 'Follow him.'

'Then I can only suggest you bail fast,' Georgio said with reservation, aiming the listing launch at Marchetti's dark shape.

'That crazy woman is chasing the first boat.' Abandonato observed.

Di Stefano. 'It appears that way.'

At eighteen knots Luigi Villani prayed the chase would be short. *Olga* was an old girl and her horses were ready for pasture. The two forty-five-year-old twenty-five horsepower diesel engines groaned and smoked. Luigi looked at the grappa bottle. It suddenly dawned on him that he had finished it. He blinked a dozen times and focussed. At least he *tried* to focus. Both launches seemed to have difficulty going faster than *Olga.* But then he realised. Up ahead a flotilla of flashing blue lights raced towards them.

The explosion.

It seemed every available emergency craft in Venice was headed to Poveglia Island, now a blazing inferno. *What will happen to the ghosts,* Luigi asked himself; and re-checked the grappa bottle ...

Hmm ... empty.

• • •

Marchetti watched the approaching Carabineri, Vigilli del fuoco and Emergenza Sanitaria craft rushing towards the island. Blue lights flashing in a sea of urgency.

'Turn our lights on,' he ordered Domenico. 'Or we will look suspicious and attract unwanted attention.'

He looked over his shoulder. They had several hundred metres on Drishya. 'And you better slow to the speed limit, we are in a shipping lane.' Poveglia Island was shrinking but the flames grew. 'Bah!' he thought. So much sadness there it is best it ended this way.

Then the outline of another vessel silhouetted against the distant flames. A fishing boat. Marchetti fished through Ricco Ricci's backpack and took out his binoculars. Slowly the *Olga's* image sharpened through the lens. *They're following* he told himself. *Now what?*

'Will I order the skipper to intercept them,' Abandonato nodded to the approaching emergency craft.

'Are you joking,' Di Stefano had the determination of a bull terrier. 'There's our quarry Dino,' his brow furrowed, he ground his teeth stabbing a finger at the escaping launches ahead. No one, especially the supercilious Venetian police department were going to steal his thunder. Not now he was so close. 'Let them deal with the damned fire,' Di Stefano shouted with a manic grin.

Jameson had a thousand questions. He paced *Olga's* deck starring in amazement at the emergency vessels now passing parallel two hundred metres off to starboard.

'I thought I'd lost you,' Elspeth threw her arms around Jameson pulling their bodies firmly together.

'How on earth did you find me?' he asked.

'Di Stefano. Naples police. We traced you with GPS on your mobile.'

'Jesus! Of course. But ... '

'So,' Elspeth cut in. 'Who is this woman anyway?'

'She-devil in disguise,' Jameson answered. 'A piece of work if I've ever met one.'

'Oh ... so where *is* your shirt?'

'I used it to put out an electrical fire after that woman shot at me ... now that you ask.'

'She shot at you ... '

Claire appeared with one grubby towel. 'We have to share.' She threw it over Elspeth's shoulder. 'And here.' Claire had also found an unwashed denim shirt for Jameson. 'Pity to cover those pecks though,' Claire giggled flapping her eyebrows.

Abandonato joined Di Stefano and Luigi in the wheelhouse. 'They head straight for Piazza San Marco Square maybe. Is good place to jump off and mix with crowd, si.'

Di Stefano agreed. He turned to Luigi. 'Can't you go any faster?'

'Not really,' Luigi grinned with grappa fuelled enthusiasm. 'But I know a short cut.' As Luigi suspected, the racing launches veered east at Giudecca Island and sped through the channel between Giudecca and the Island of Saint Giorgio Maggiore. Luigi ignored their manoeuvre and headed for Rio della Croce, a narrow canal running the two hundred or so metres directly through Giudecca Island, south to north.

Olga nosed dead ahead at full throttle.

'Aren't you going to slow down?' Di Stefano was transfixed on the canal opening. Luigi had managed to push *Olga* to eighteen knots and he wasn't about to throttle down now.

'You tell me go faster!'

'Yes ... but ... '

On the approach, the canal mouth looked reasonably wide ...
Reasonably!

But it rapidly narrowed with dozens of private pleasure-craft moored along the northern bank. Jameson, Elspeth, Claire and Vincenzo assembled at the bow.

'Christ we're going a bit fast aren't we?' Claire held the rail grinning like a kid on a coaster ride. Vincenzo was a little more reserved. Luigi entered the canal pushing a bow wave ahead of them. To their right, magnificent parkland, on their left a convent. Runabouts and pleasure craft bobbed wildly at their moorings as *Olga* ploughed through Rio della Croce without a care in the world.

'Jesus Villani ... careful,' Di Stefano cautioned the mad fisherman. Boat owners gathered on the parallel pedestrian promenade screaming abuse while craft after craft washed onto each other in *Olga's* wake.

Luigi focussed ahead the best he could. *That* grappa sneaked up on him in waves. Two hundred metres further was the open lagoon and then the entrance to Venice's Grand Canal. Venice night-lights beckoned with the domed roof of the magnificent church Santa Maria della Salute prominent. Di Stefano was the first to warn Luigi of the pedestrian bridge at the far end of the canal.

'We fit underneath, no problem,' Luigi maintained full throttle and determination. 'Short cut, si?' But as the bridge approached it appeared the clearance might be a little tight.

'Ah ... Luigi ... ' Vincenzo joined Abandonato in the wheelhouse. 'We won't fit under the bridge.'

'Nonsense. I do thees before.'

The bridge approached at a frightening speed. More voices screamed warnings along the promenade. Instantly bystanders on the bridge scrambled either side.

'Luigi!' The men in the wheelhouse yelled.

'I do thees before. No worries.'

The fly bridge snapped away like balsa wood making one hell of a racket but not as much noise as the wheelhouse roof, which splintered like kindling in a mechanical woodchopper. Everyone threw their hands about their heads and hit the deck. Besides losing the upper superstructure Olga made it under the bridge and back into the lagoon. Claire, Elspeth and Jameson on the bow looked back towards the stern.

The fishing boat looked like a fighter jet had strafed it.

As they watched four heads popped up from behind the shredded wheelhouse.

'You've been through there before, have you?' Di Stefano muttered sarcastically.

'Well, maybe it was another bridge,' Luigi belched a fug of grappa, gaping about wild-eyed for his escaping adversaries only a hundred metres away. 'Huh!' he shouted. 'There! I tell you true yes.' And Luigi pointed out the launches, one behind the other. 'Short cut.'

Drishya couldn't believe what she had just seen ...

Sheer determination.

She did a double take. The superstructure was missing but it was definitely the same fishing boat she thought they had lost. And it was now closing in on them.

'You think its polizia?' Georgio called out while Drishya and Salah bailed water from the damaged launch.

'Yes. I am certain.'

Marchetti weaved between gondolas aiming for the first canal through Venice, Rio de S Moise, creating disturbing waves and infuriating both the gondoliers and their passengers.

Drishya followed.

Luigi nosed *Olga* towards them.

Di Stefano gripped the mutilated wheelhouse dash ...

His knuckles white.

'Luigi! No ... '

Luigi's eyes danced with excitement. 'Ees another short cut.'

To the right of the canal, diners under red umbrellas looked up from their plates at the Ristorante de Pisis. Two speeding launches was one thing but a fishing boat looking like it had been through a shredder ...

And all travelling at four times the five-knot limit.

There was a chorus of gasps at the bow. Claire waved back at gaping faces while Jameson and Elspeth hid theirs in their hands.

'I don't believe this is happening,' Elspeth said through clenched teeth.

'Look El, Venice's Statue of Liberty,' Claire pointed to a Statue of Liberty, a similar landmark to New York's, if a little smaller, on the canal waterfront. Within seconds they were deep into the waterway at a point of no return.

More shouts. Screams and curses.

Either side the buildings of Venice rose directly from the canal waters, the ultimate in water frontage. They were close.

Too close.

Shuttered windows opened at the commotion. Heads peered down at them in total astonishment. More yelling. More abuse. Abandonato buried his face in his hands. Surely this wasn't happening.

Then gunshots ...

Their report echoing tenfold off the nearby walls and over water. Drishya's second bullet shattered Marchetti's windscreen. Domenico at the wheel turned hard to port where the canal widened momentarily and became Rio de l'Barcaroli. Another footbridge loomed.

'Cristo!' Di Stefano prayed all bridges were uniform in height. If not ...

'Short cut okay,' Luigi roared with nervous laughter. Heads ducked at the last second. They barely clipped beneath the stonework.

More gunshots.

Stray bullets crumbled stonework ... ricocheting and narrowly missing pedestrians.

Di Stefano drew his own handgun. 'We must stop them before a bystander gets killed.'

On the pedestrian promenades the evening crowds of tourists and locals scrambled in chaotic panic. Jameson saw at least four people elbowed into the polluted waters of the canal. Passing gondoliers struggled to stay afloat with bow waves threatening to tip them into the canal. There was nothing they could do but hang on for the ride. *Olga* scraped under three more bridges before the canal changed once more to Rio de S Luca and rejoined the Grand Canal that for a millennium had snaked its way through the water city.

Marchetti escaped the confines of the narrow canal at eighteen knots. He was panicked, fearing for his life. Drishya was relentless. A rearing cobra. She emptied her clip and reloaded the Barretta. Domenico at the helm wheeled their hire boat hard to starboard only to T-bone a gondola. The weight of the launch easily breaking the shiny black-lacquered craft in two. The gondolier surfaced the moment Drishya followed in Marchetti's wake, his curses swallowed by the canal as he dived beneath the surface a second time.

Olga wasn't far behind.

Here the Grand Canal was at least a hundred metres wide. But this is Venice's main thoroughfare. The canal was packed with craft cruising in both directions. River night cruises, water taxis, public ferryboats, gondolas, pleasure craft and Venetians coming and going as Venetians do.

'Awesome!' Claire yelled over the cacophony of yelling, whining motors, horns, music and city din. She leant over the bow rail waving for craft to move out of their path. They passed under the Rialto Bridge with its Renaissance arches as crowds gathered to watch the mayhem. Cameras flashed. Anger mingled with laughter. There was little time for Jameson, Elspeth and Claire to appreciate the view of one of the world's most beautiful cities.

Drishya lost all sense of discretion. She stopped bailing and took careful aim … Squeezing off three shots.

On the *Olga* they sounded like pops; but the screams from witnesses closer by as Domenico's head exploded in a red mist were real.

'Jesus!' Jameson yelled. 'She shot him.'

Domenico slumped.

Dead.

His lifeless body slumped across the wheel. The launch turned sharp to port ...

Directly into the path of a passenger ferry.

They heard a tremendous crashing sound as the fibreglass and mahogany launch fragmented under the steel hull of the ferry.

They didn't stand a chance.

Marchetti let out a painful scream before his body was dragged below the surface to be effectively keel hauled the ferry's full length and shredded by propellers at the stern where he was spat out like bilge waste.

Di Stefano aimed his double-barrel semi-automatic handgun at Drishya but she was too distant and there were too many people. Too many chances of something going horribly wrong. He lowered his weapon hoping for a closer shot.

'This is crazy dude,' Claire ran along the starboard gunwale watching the outcome of a gondola precariously struggling to stay afloat. The faces of Japanese tourists taught with fear. With all polizia heading out to Poveglia Island – now burning like a giant beacon on the lagoon – the madness on the canals went unchallenged.

'She's getting away,' Jameson shouted as they passed under the contemporary arched Constitution Bridge. 'The bitch'll escape.'

'Soon the Grand Canal, she finish,' Luigi shouted. 'The bast-ards ... they will be back in the lagoon. We will have to ... '

A loud explosion below deck killed the conversation ...

Black smoke spiralled from *Olga's* engine room. Instantly they heard a second loud bang. *Olga* lost all power, the bow dipped and a wave washed up the stern.

'What was that?' Di Stefano looked like he had been hit with a bullet.

'The engine,' Luigi groaned. 'She broken.'

'Runaway engine,' Abandonato knew his diesel engines. Vincenzo. 'Runaway?'

'These engines are over forty years old,' Abandonato said shaking his head at the tired old tub. 'We have pushed them too hard. If engines are worn gases blow past the sides of the pistons into the crankcase. They draw extra fuel creating higher and higher RPM. Engine go faster and faster until they explode. It is probably a seizure from lack of oil also.'

'That's all very well Dino,' Elspeth said. 'But what do we do about it.'

'Engine kaput, si.'

'Si.'

'Now what?'

'Now what?' Luigi's bloodshot eyes glared at the polizia as he scratched at his dreadlocks, incredulous at the question. 'We go nowhere. That ees now what.'

'We can't just sit here,' Jameson grew agitated. 'She's getting away.' As they all watched sDrishya's crippled launch slipped amongst the hundreds of other craft escaping into the lagoon.

Di Stefano was already busy waving to water taxis but the skippers were cautious with him waving a handgun. Eventually, by waving his polizia badge, he caught one skipper's attention.

'We've lost them,' Vincenzo said as the water taxi slapped up against Olga's hull. All gaped off into the night where darkness swallowed the fugitives.

'Yes. But I know where she's going,' Elspeth said quietly, also staring off into the inky blackness beyond.

• • • •

Chapter eighteen

Leaving the night lights of ancient Venice behind them the water taxi scootered across the Canale Industriale to the industrial wharves north. Here Elspeth instructed the skipper to allow them disembark discreetly three hundred metres from the disused cement factory. Then, as a tight knot in the dark, they crept forward to where Elspeth had spied on procedures the night before.

Nothing.

No lights. No activity.

Elspeth had a sinking feeling. 'I could have sworn she would end up back here ... I mean this is the direction she was headed. Right? And this is where I saw her last night ... her and those thugs.'

'You were here last night?' Jameson said taken aback.

Elspeth. 'Long story.'

'Jesus Beth ... '

'Tell you later.'

'Yeh ... well,' Jameson scratched the back of his head. 'I saw a barge leave the island earlier and head in this direction,' Jameson said. 'I'm assuming it was the same one that was here last night. But I was blindfolded then.'

'Look!' Claire stabbed a finger towards the dark shapes of four great cylindrical grain silos a few hundred metres further north on the abandoned wharves. 'I just saw a light.'

'A light. I see it,' Di Stefano watched on.

Abandonato. 'A torch maybe.'

Vincenzo. 'Now that ees suspicious, ees it not?'

Jameson recognised the Moroccan cook Salah in the dark. Salah used the torch sparingly, lighting the path for the skipper climbing up onto the dock from the sinking launch.

'Wait here,' Jameson told the others. 'I'll go and investigate.'

'I'm coming with you,' Di Stefano insisted.

Elspeth, Claire, Abandonato and Vincenzo melted back into the shadows and watched the two men creep forward.

Jameson saw Drishya first. He silently pointed out her slender shape barely visible in the darkness. She looked like she was waiting for someone, standing beneath the grain chute of a thirty-metre-high concrete silo. She paced up and down looking impatient. Angry.

Without warning her mobile screen lit up. She took the call giving Di Stefano a brief moment to admire her stunning face before stepping further into the shadows.

'Now what?' Jameson muttered.

One minute later a tanker-truck approached at speed. It passed the cement factory, its air brakes hissing impatiently as it cornered onto the straight parallel with the water and …

Raced towards the silos.

Jameson and Di Stefano melted into the night as the truck passed them by. Immediately roller doors of a warehouse next to the furthest silo opened. The tanker entered a softly lit area within and the doors rolled closed.

'*Giulia Grano*,' Di Stefano read the inscription on the tanker. 'What's a grain truck doing here at thees time?'

'Let's get closer and see,' Jameson led the way forward, hugging a two-storey office building. The two men hid behind a skip now only twenty metres from the roller door. 'Everyone appears to be inside.' Jameson was about to walk into the open when Di Stefano roughly jerked him back by the arm. Instantly Jameson saw the torchlight but at the same second he dislodged an empty paint can from the overloaded skip. It landed heavily clunking noisily on the wharf. Di Stefano and Jameson froze. The can rolled briefly creating a hollow din prolonging their tension. They waited.

Nothing.

Then Jameson remembered Salah. He was the one with the torch. 'He's deaf,' Jameson said louder than he intended adding to the polizia's anxiety.

'Deaf?'

'Yes.'

Moments later Salah entered the warehouse through a side door. 'Look,' Jameson pointed to a window next to the door. The two crept forward.

'Now that ees some-theen,' Di Stefano was stunned. Illuminated with the light from a single fluorescent tube hanging from the high ceiling they saw the grain tanker, parked in the middle of the warehouse. But what was so amazing was the top half of the tanker was hinged on one side and opened like the lid on a bar-b-q. Huge hydraulic pistons opened and closed the lid of the grain truck at the flick of a switch.

'Genius,' Di Stefano whispered. 'Look at thees peoples will you. Genius.' As the two watched, a forklift and a of block and tackle were being used to carefully lower the Vataea hoard into the grain tanker.

'Once they've loaded the antiquities they will fill the tanker with grain. Brilliant.' Jameson was also impressed.

'Si. Brilliant. But now we make the arrest.'

'Ah ... ' Jameson was about to say. 'Ah, but we are outnumbered and they are armed.' When Di Stefano slammed his shoulder into the side door and crashed the party.

'Hands where I can see them,' he screamed out in Italian and fired a warning shot into the warehouse roof.

Jameson stood in the open doorway, gobsmacked. Immediately the warning shot summoned Abandonato who charged out of hiding, pistol drawn.

'Hands in the air, hands in the air,' Di Stefano oscillated his pistol from the truck driver to Salah to Georgio on the forklift and then to Drishya. Drishya's eyes shifted from Georgio to the polizia. Suddenly Georgio hit the ground, rolling under the truck. He pulled a Glok from an ankle holster. Di Stefano threw his back to the wall and fired ...

Georgio screamed in pain as the bullet buried in his hip.

Drishya saw her chance.

She pulled her Barretta free and managed two covering shots to see her out the exit. But Di Stefano was fast. He fired once as she escaped hitting her in the back of the knee. Drishya cried out from the pain but ...

She managed to disappear into the night.

'Watch them,' Di Stefano shouted to Abandonato as he leapt through the door. Jameson saw Drishya escape. He raced around the outside of the warehouse to cut her off as two more gunshots rang out. Jameson heard a painful yell. Di Stefano had been shot in the hand but Georgio paid for his action with his life as Abandonato's single shot hit the man in the jaw. He died instantly.

Outside Drishya was limping, badly wounded. She crossed to the silos unnoticed. Jameson found Elspeth, Vincenzo and Claire rushing to the warehouse. 'She's out here somewhere,' Jameson said in a loud whisper.

'Who?' Elspeth asked. 'That woman?'

'Yes. But I'm certain she's wounded. And she's armed. Get to the warehouse.'

'What about you?'

Jameson ignored the question and hurried off in search of Drishya. Vincenzo looked at Elspeth and Claire. 'What will we do?'

'Do?' Elspeth hissed. 'Spread out, we'll find this bitch ourselves.'

'Si,' Vincenzo felt his manhood challenged. 'Si, spread out.' The three stole away into the dark.

Jameson circled the warehouse.

At the exit he saw evidence of Drishya's wound. Blood spots. He followed the trail. She must be badly wounded he thought. The sporadic drips, like black dots in the soft moonlight, led him to the silos. Jameson heard a noise. More a subtle echo. The sound of a foot on metal.

He looked up.

Badly wounded, Drishya's attempt to hide in the silo proved a poor decision. Silently Jameson watched her climb the external bucket elevator used to hoist the grain up and into the silo. But her usual leopard like movements were crippled by her wound. Drishya had no idea she had been spotted when she disappeared from sight. Jameson waited a moment ...

And then started climbing the elevator.

'What the hell are you doing?' Elspeth urgent hushed voice called out to Jameson from the shadows. Immediately Elspeth was re-joined by Claire and Vincenzo. Ten metres up Jameson turned and waved for the others to keep quiet. He pointed to the top of the silo. 'Get the police,' he ordered quietly.

'Jameson! What are you ... '

But Jameson waved angrily. Hissing. 'Quiet.'

Jameson climbed over the elevator head and the first thing that struck him was the view. It was breathtaking and not one the average tourist saw. The lights of Venice to the south and the distant flames of Poveglia to the west.

There was no sign of Drishya.

Jameson crawled across the closed lid of the garner. He clambered awkwardly down the side to the roof level of the main silo. Here, a conveyor belt would transport a movable tripper from the elevator where the grain would be tipped into the silo. There seemed nowhere to hide, so where was she? Aware of a sheer thirty-metre drop onto the concrete wharf below Jameson was suddenly questioning his heroics ...

When he heard the squeal of rusted steel hinges.

There was another level directly underfoot. The access hatch was open. Jameson descended into pitch darkness.

Immediately the enclosure was illuminated with the torch light from a mobile. The concentrated circular beam shone directly into his face.

'So it *is* you,' Drishya said. She stood three metres away and Jameson could clearly see the small black gun barrel pointing at his chest. This woman, he knew, would not hesitate to kill. Jameson's mind scrambled in a vain attempt to distract her until help arrived.

'You're wounded,' he said rather lamely, as if he cared. Drishya's face, Jameson could now see, was pale from the loss of blood.

'What would you care?' She said.

Jameson took one step forward. 'You need help.'

'Get back.'

'Look I want to help you.'

'Help me! Huh,' Drishya jeered. She looked about. She was trapped. Behind her was nothing but grain; a silo full of Italy's finest destined to be turned into fettuccine, spaghetti or ravioli. She felt her own warm blood trickle about her ankle.

She felt weak, her eyes heavy.

'Drop the gun,' Abandonato's voice said calmly from the pitch-darkness outside Drishya's torch beam. She jerked back to full consciousness, trying to throw light in the voice's direction.

'I-said-drop-the-gun.'

With nothing to lose Drishya answered with a shot into the darkness. Jameson felt the bullet sing by his face. He heard the ricochet as Abandonato fired back. Jameson dived for the floor. Drishya fired again blindly, leaping painfully onto the grain to cross to an external stair exit.

But the grain surface was unstable.

Beneath it a large air pocket collapsed creating an instant suction above. Drishya's body was immediately drawn into a vacuum ...

Like quicksand.

She didn't stand a chance.

'Help me!' she screamed out. Jameson crawled to edge of the silo. He stretched out his hand. But the grain was draining like the sand of an hourglass and Jameson knew there were thirty metres of cereal beneath them. For the briefest of moments the tips of their fingers touched. But the siren was beyond salvation. For the briefest of moments their eyes locked before Drishya's terrified face disappeared in a silent scream under the collapsing grain.

CHAPTER EIGHTEEN

The next morning.

'Are you thinking about that Indian woman?' Elspeth asked Jameson who had been more than vague over breakfast at their Hotel Antiche rooftop terrace restaurant. Jameson nodded. The view over Venice's Grand Canal was a tonic after the last few days. 'Anyone would think there was something between you two.' Elspeth knocked the top off a boiled egg and the golden yolk oozed over the shell.

'It's just the way she died Beth. The look in her eyes. Suffocation. I nearly had her but ... ' his voice trailed away.

'She was a killer Jam,' Elspeth answered. 'She could have killed you.'

'I wonder how you're mate Renato Di Stefano is faring,' was Jameson's answer to Elspeth's comment. 'The handsome polizia. He certainly took one for the team.'

'Abandonato said he'll be fine,' Elspeth said dryly. 'The bullet went through flesh only. He was lucky ... '

'You call that luck?'

'Anyway, the main thing is he got what he wanted. He broke the tombaroli racket.'

'Here you are,' Claire, bubbling with life, found Jameson and Elspeth on the roof. Vincenzo followed. Both wore faces of total contentment. They had shared a twin room, the only room available, found by Abandonato at the eleventh hour last night, literally.

Jameson could imagine the room now, two single beds pushed together with bedclothes discarded in haste. He dissolved the image.

'So,' Jameson started with renewed verve steering the conversation from seductive killers to Vataea. 'The Lance of Destiny huh.'

'The what?' Claire sat and stole a bread roll from their breakfast basket.

Jameson made a sign for Vincenzo to take a seat also. 'Abandonato told us last night that the antiquity thief, the big fella himself known as Man of Mirrors for reasons I will tell you later, was really after the Holy Lance or the Spear of Destiny as it is also known.'

'So what is the Lance of Destiny?'

Vincenzo sat. 'It was the spear used to cut Jesus when he was on cross, yes.'

Claire forked a slice of prosciutto from Elspeth's plate and crammed it into the bread roll. 'Are you for real?'

'Yes Claire. The lance, eet belong to a centurion called Longinus. Eet was kept in a synagogue in Jerusalem but was looted during the Roman-Jewish war. Recent scientific methods of reading burnt scrolls excavated from the Herculaneum library revealed information that confirms the lance is hidden in the home of a retired centurion called Cethegus.'

'Who lived in Vataea,' Elspeth acknowledged.

'Si.'

'Yes. And it is supposed to have healing powers,' Jameson said. 'This Man of Mirrors had terminal cancer.'

'This lance,' Claire was clearly fascinated. 'When did all this happen anyway?'

Vincenzo. '66AD.'

'Thirteen years before Vesuvius blew her top.'

'Si.'

'Apparently this holy lance is mentioned in the bible,' Jameson said. 'Not that I've ever read the bible ... '

'Gospel of John,' Elspeth offered.

'Si. Thees ees correct. Cethegus, you see, was centurion in the wars. He was ... how you say ... custodian of the spear and was ordered to take it with him back to his homeland and hide eet. But you know thees things don't you,' Vincenzo asked Jameson.

'Wait a minute,' Jameson had that look of intense concentration. 'Cethegus ... Cethegus you say ... '

'Si.'

Jameson leant down fossicking through his backpack finally taking out the carefully wrapped pieces of the terracotta lamp Mario had broken.

'Good thing Elspeth took care of your backpack, eh,' Claire said eyeing the cheese.

Jameson held the pieces of lamp together. It had been a clean break and would repair successfully. Instantly Jameson had the grin of a man recently offered immortality. He displayed it for all to see. Along one side of the lamp the name Cethegus could clearly be read.

'You-are-kidding-me,' Elspeth jaw dropped open. 'Why didn't we pick up on that before?'

'Cethegus,' Jameson said with renewed reverence. 'Cethegus ... I knew I had read it somewhere ... but on this very lamp.'

'That ees incredible. I agree. Really incredible. But eet has no archaeological value,' Vincenzo groaned. 'Thees thieves, thees tombaroli, looters, they take from the ground with no reference ...'

'Provenance,' Elspeth said.

'Si. Provenance. Stronzo. So we know this lamp, eet belong to Cethegus who hide the lance in his home. But where is his home?'

'Vataea of course.'

Elspeth noted the face of avarice displayed by Claire. 'Before you get too excited Claire, the Naples Archaeological Museum are all over it already.'

'Literally all over it,' Jameson said. 'The site is heavily guarded already and we are told archaeologists are taking up residence as we speak.'

The waiter hovered. He nodded warmly to Claire and Vincenzo. 'I'm *ravished*,' Claire said. 'I'm having the full buffet thanks.'

The waiter looked at Vincenzo who had noticed the forty-five Euro tariff on the menu and swallowed hard. 'You'll go the buffet too wont ya Vin?' Claire insisted.

He nodded sheepishly.

'And I'll tell you what,' Claire placed a hand on the waiter's arm. 'Bring the wine list.'

The waiter, who's grasp on English was minimal, shrugged.

'Lista dei vini,' Vincenzo told him.

'Ah si.'

The waiter walked off and Claire turned to Jameson. 'I'm washing brecky down with bubbles. It's your shout dude.'

'What!'

'Well last time you made me shout breakfast because you reckoned you saved my arse. But since we saved your arse yesterday, it's your shout.'

• • • • •

Chapter twenty

Melanoma Cottage. Storm Bay. Tasmania.

It was one of those unpredictable Tasmanian days. One of the reasons Tasmanians really cherish where they live and would not move to Australia for all the tea in China, as Barrie Duggan liked to say. Jameson and his builder mate Barrie stood on Jameson's balcony watching the weather change before them. A nor-westerly blew across the River Derwent creating white-caps on the water while misting the balcony in a fine spray. The sun had taken shelter behind assembling clouds so it seemed a good downpour was also a certainty.

'It might blow over Jam,' Barrie said, necking his second stubbie and studying the weather with a boatman's eye.

Ah yes, a typical Tasmanian day, unpredictable.

Jameson had spent the past half hour giving Barrie *the guts* on his holiday and Barrie listened like the listener he was.

'Well all I can say is, Jesus Jam, ya lucky to be alive. And it all started with that Ity bloke's auction. Christ. And here's me planning to tell you all about how good those lead light windows I bought at the auction look in the bay window at my New Town reno.' Barrie took one last draw at his hand rolled cigarette pinched between forefinger and thumb, flicked the butt towards the water and blew the offending smoke out his nostrils. It was time to go inside, where Elspeth and Barrie's wife Lou waited for lunch and exchanged travel stories over a glass of Janz.

'So,' Barrie went on. 'This Ity, Italian bloke Victor ... '

'Victor Renzo.'

'Yeh. He was a bit dodgy eh?'

'Yes Baz. It turns out he went back to Vataea some time after the war. There were a few involved. All locals. But sometime in the early 1950s the three other guys involved were all killed in a mysterious car crash.'

'Oh?'

'Their car went off the cliff road near Positana and crashed into the sea. This left Victor the sole survivor and only person who knew of Vataea. He continued his illegal digging but the authorities were onto him so he changed his name and migrated to Australia bringing with him his expertise and knowledge of Roman artefacts.'

'And he started forging stuff.'

'That's it.'

Barrie ran an eye over the Vataea terracotta lamp sitting on the bookshelf, and faithfully re-joined with super glue, much to Elspeth the conservationist's disgust. Barrie daren't touch it.

'What's next then?' Barrie said.

'Eh?'

'Well you said the museum in Naples are giving you guys the credit for discovering ... '

'Rediscovering Baz ... '

'Yeh, rediscovering, this old town. What's next on ya plate, you adventurous bastard?'

'Funny you should ask Baz.' Jameson finished his Boag's Premium and looked at Barrie's empty stubbie. 'Glass of red?' he asked his mate. 'Those slow cooked beef cheeks and pink eye mash are begging us to sit at the table.'

'Yeh mate. Open that shiraz I bought.'

Jameson fetched the bottle and unscrewed the cap.

'Well then?' Barrie persisted. 'What's next?'

Jameson poured four glasses of Marion's Vineyard 2012 Shiraz. 'Remember that coin and that pottery shard we found last week,' he said waiting for his guests to sit. Barrie shot his wife a side-glance. She didn't know about the fit he had had in the wheelhouse, for he simply hadn't told her. 'How could I forget?'

'Well I've been thinking,' Jameson said. 'It must have come from a wreck. And a wreck from the 17th century in the Derwent estuary beggars belief.'

'And the shark?' Elspeth asked.

'That was a rare sighting Beth. Do you think it just hangs around the Iron Pot?'

'There's only one way to find out,' Barrie grinned, warming to the glass of shiraz in his hand ...

'Cheers!'

'Salute.'

Habit des Medecins, et autres personnes
qui visitent les Pestiferes, Il est de
maroquin de levant, le masque a les yeux
de cristal, et un long nez rempli de parfums

EPILOGUE

Melanoma Cottage. Sunday. Three months later.

It was a magnificent afternoon in Tasmania and nowhere did the sun shine warmer or could the blue sky be bluer than Storm Bay in the island's south. The throaty Pacific gulls mewled overhead in never-ending circles; their greedy eyes fixed on Jameson and his mate Stu as the lads necked a few Boag's Premiums while lazily fishing off the rocks below Melanoma Cottage. The River Derwent's flathead were running. Eight fish already flapped crazily in the bottom of a plastic bucket. It would be bar-b-qued *flatties* tonight and the two restaurant cooks bounced recipe ideas off each other.

'I reckon we should wrap 'em in baking paper with tarragon and lemon,' Stu suggested as he stood to cast his fly into the water. Jameson watched Stu stand unsteadily on the slippery rocks, his movements clumsy after the beers.

'Easy mate or you'll fall in the drink,' Jameson laughed. Stu cast his line ...

'Jesus!'

The line curled about as Stu swung his arm but his throw was awkward and the hook pierced Jameson's board shorts with the barb burying its point in Jameson's thigh.

'Oh Christ!' Jameson screamed out, pain shooting up his side.

'What!'

'Don't pull it ... Jesus ... you've hooked me for Christ's sake ... '

Elspeth stepped onto the balcony. 'Jam ... ' She waved his mobile. 'Jam ... you've got a call from Italy ... it's important ... ' Elspeth watched the two men a moment. They were pre-occupied. She hurried down the embankment and onto the shoreline rocks. 'Jameson!'

'Jesus Stu!' Jameson was desperately trying to pull the barb free.

'Jameson!' Elspeth hissed loudly. Urgently.

'What?'

'You've got a call ...'

'Not now for Christ's sake,' Jameson yelled out. 'Jesus Stu ya clumsy prick ...'

"Jameson.' Elspeth waved her hands about to keep him quiet. 'Jameson. It's a call from Italy ... '

Stu's attempt to loosen the needle like hook only made matters worse.

'Argh. Fuck! Leave it ya stupid prick ... '

'Jameson!' Elspeth snapped through grit teeth. 'It's the Vatican!'

'Shit! The what?'

'The Vatican ... it's the pope!' Elspeth whispered, holding Jameson's mobile at arms length, her face twisted with horror.

'The ... the po ... pope?' Jameson eyes were red from the sea air and beer. 'The pope ... as in *THE* pope.'

Elspeth wanted to bury her head in the sand. 'Sorry to keep you waiting your holiness, here's Jameson Rowley.' Elspeth thrust the mobile into Jameson reluctant hand. The fishhook was now drawing blood and the look on Jameson's face one of excruciating pain.

'H ... hello. Jameson speaking.'

'James-son, hello.'

'H ... hello.'

'James-son ... I am the honorary Prelate of the Roman Catholic Church and the private secretary of Pope Francis. My name is Alfred Xuereb,' the Maltese born secretary spoke in good but strong accented English. Jameson stood frozen, his eyes watering with pain and struggling for words. 'The Holy See, Pope Francis, wished that I call you and thank you in person. Pope Francis you see, does not speak English.'

'Th ... thank me?'

'Yes Jameson. I will be brief. The Holy Lance also known as the Lance of Destiny has been discovered ... '

'The lance? ... Discovered? ... Y ... you found it?' Jameson's words were strained with agony and he snatched short sharp breaths.

This wasn't really happening ... surely!

'Your discovery of Vataea combined with the information gleaned from the Herculaneum scrolls finally lead archaeologists to the lance ...'

'You found the house of Cethegus?'

'Yes, my son,' the man of god said, proud to be the messenger of such great news. 'And now it is going through the conservation process before being interred in Saint Peters Cathedral. But Pope Francis insists it will be on public display and that a small plaque will honour you and your friends for its discovery.'

Beads of sweat poured off Jameson brow. He felt he was going to faint. 'I ... I ... I don't know what to say ... I'm ... ah ... '

'Say nothing my son.'

A short silence followed while Jameson heard voices in the background. Other people were in the room with his holiness. Jameson was desperate to say thank you and terminate the call when the secretary finally said. 'Now Jameson, as I said the Holy See, Pope Francis, does not speak English but he insists on giving you a personal blessing over the phone. Do you mind James-son.'

'M ... mind. Do I mind. Pope Francis? Ah ... ' *Jesus Christ are you kidding me?* 'No sir, your eminence. I'm most grateful.'

The eighty-one-year-old man of god, the Bishop of Rome, the sovereign of Vatican City and the holy Pope of the Roman Catholic Church spoke softly to Jameson through his mobile.

'Buon pomeriggo signore Rowley,' Pope Francis started before launching into a private blessing. Jameson was gobsmacked. He can't remember what he said in return but experienced a divine revelation, a celestial moment of euphoria before crumbling in agony after Stu made his final attempt at extraction, ripping his skin in the process ...

'Jesus!'

WRITER'S NOTE

I grew up with a passion for archaeology and history in general. I wanted to be an archaeologist well before Indiana Jones made the profession popular. But gazing, daydreaming of the past out the classroom window was never going to see me enter university. It didn't. I became a chef instead. With the same romantic notion.

Vataea never existed.

Whilst Pompeii, the most famous of Vesuvius' victims, and Herculaneum are well documented, who knows what is buried under the foothills of one of the world's most active volcanos. So why shouldn't a lost community surface from the rich soil of Campania.

The Lance of Destiny or the Holy Spear or Lance of Longinus as it is sometimes referred to does exist ...

Apparently.

But at least four institutions claim to own it, the most prominent being the Vatican where it is preserved beneath the dome of Saint Peter's Basilica.

Antiquity theft and tomb robbing in Italy today is a major problem. In all fairness it is a major problem worldwide.

ABOUT THE AUTHOR

After decades in the hospitality industry and the best part of forty years since opening the Drunken Admiral Seafood Restaurant, Craig hung up the apron to leave family at the helm and indulge in his other passion, writing fiction.

Craig was born in Hobart, Australia, and has traveled extensively giving him the experiences and escapades he so enjoys putting into print. This includes working as a chef for a restaurant owned by Sydney underbelly figures in the early 70s and cooking in Darwin when cyclone Tracy destroyed the city. Life has been busy and interesting to say the least. In the 90s, Craig independently shot two feature films, a murder mystery set in Southern Tasmania which aired on television and a splatter comedy still available online. He wrote, produced and directed both.

Having led a 'normal' life of work and duty Craig Godfrey decided to follow his real passion of writing fiction. And with Tasmania's fascinating past he has plenty to write about. Using Tasmania's history as a blank canvas, Craig loves nothing more than to weave adventure, mystery and mayhem involving colorful characters from all walks of life. He has written 36 previous titles.

NOTE FROM THE AUTHOR

Word-of-mouth is crucial for any author to succeed. If you enjoyed *Poveglia Island*, please leave a review online—anywhere you are able. Even if it's just a sentence or two. It would make all the difference and would be very much appreciated.

Thanks!

Craig Godfrey

We hope you enjoyed reading this title from:

BLACK ROSE
writing™

www.blackrosewriting.com

Subscribe to our mailing list – *The Rosevine* – and receive **FREE** books, daily deals, and stay current with news about upcoming releases and our hottest authors.
Scan the QR code below to sign up.

Already a subscriber? Please accept a sincere thank you for being a fan of Black Rose Writing authors.

View other Black Rose Writing titles at www.blackrosewriting.com/books and use promo code **PRINT** to receive a **20% discount** when purchasing.

www.ingramcontent.com/pod-product-compliance
Lightning Source LLC
Chambersburg PA
CBHW010512100726
47903CB00009B/2713